IT'S ALL Relative

A NOVEL BY

S.C. Stephens

First Edition: 2010
Second Edition: February 2016
Library of Congress Cataloging-in-Publication Data
It's All Relative – 1st ed
ISBN-13: 978-1523698905 | ISBN-10: 152369890X

This one is for the Fictionpress fans.
Thank you for your endless support!

One Night

There was a nip in the air. Of course, for October in Colorado, it wasn't unusual to feel a nip in the air. Dampness clung to the cold, and the few brave and bundled bodies rushing along the sidewalk stepped into bars and restaurants in some vain attempt to delay their inevitable exposure to the frigid environment. It didn't rain a lot in Denver, but the weather had been making up for that fact over the past three days. Thick, dark clouds swallowed up what little of the stars would have been seen against the glare of the city. Whenever the moon peeked through the swath of rain-filled blackness across the sky, it was a pale, thin sliver, offering no comfort and little light. The pallid glow of streetlamps and the harsh buzzing of neon business signs—some open, most closed—only made the night feel emptier. Cool wind whipped through the streets, whistling up lonely alleys, and swirling clusters of bright red and orange leaves along the edges of the road.

All in all, it was not a good night to be out and about. And as Jessie soon discovered, when she stepped into a deep, bone-chilling puddle, it was an exceptionally bad night for her to be out. Letting out a surprised squeal, she immediately hopped on one leg and shook out her sodden shoe. Water dripped from the open toe of her high heel, and she let out a long, *Why does the world hate me?* sigh. Her soaked, freezing foot was only the latest example of her string of bad luck.

Jessica Marie, as her family insisted on calling her, was suffering from a severe case of heartbreak. Her boyfriend of the last eighteen months had ended things with her a few weeks ago...after Jessie had launched a heavy glass vase at his head. Jessie wasn't normally a violent person, but after getting off work early and catching him in a compromising position with his neighbor, she'd had no choice but to use his skull as target practice. She'd wanted to surprise him at his duplex, but the surprise had been all on her. The asshole had even gone so far as to claim he'd only been consoling the woman over the loss of her cat, but friendly, innocent comfort did *not* include naked bodies, a rumpled bed, and the words, "Yes, fuck me harder!"

He'd shattered her heart just as completely as she'd shattered her favorite vase, but as the painful ache of loss had started to fade, red-hot rage had swept into its place. Now she couldn't stand the thought of that two-timing prick. Jessie missed the obliterated vase more than she missed him. But a hurt was still a hurt, and the betrayal and rejection still stung. Much like her foot.

Trying to resume the blood flow to her chilly extremity, Jessie hopped up and down. "This is a bad idea. Let's just go home and watch a chick flick." The two friends beside her could barely contain their laughter at her misfortune, and Jessie gave them each a steely glare. *Keep it up and I'll make sure I'm not the only one leaving wet footprints on the pavement.*

Her friend, Harmony, flashed a bright smile; her blue eyes sparkled with playfulness and humor. "No way, Jess. You need a little fun." Jessie and Harmony had been friends for as long as Jessie could remember. As a little girl, Jessie had always been envious of her flaming red hair, adorable freckles, and super-long legs. At the time, she'd felt her own curly brown hair was too plain, her short, stubby legs too ordinary. She'd wanted to be unique, like Harm. But then puberty had hit, and Jessie had shot up and filled out, and she'd finally come to accept and love her body; although, she did still wish for Harmony's fiery hair.

With an annoyed grunt, Jessie grabbed Harmony's arm and pulled her forward. Hopefully moving her foot would halt the tingling sensation slowly creeping up her leg. As if to mock her, Jessie's shoe squeaked when she started walking. "I have plenty of fun, Harm. This is cold and wet and...not fun."

Jessie's other friend, April, laughed at her comment. April came from a conservative Japanese family, the heritage evident in her beautiful ebony hair and deep olive skin. She didn't share her family's penchant for modesty, though, which was clear from her revealing club outfit. April's mother never would have let her leave the house wearing a backless top and tight leather pants; from the back, she looked topless.

The Asian beauty ran a hand through her perfectly straight hair. "This will be a lot more fun once we get a few shots in you. Promise." She gave Jessie a charming smile and batted her eyelashes; small raindrops collected on the long, black tips.

Jessie let out a dramatic groan as April grabbed her arm, and, with Harmony's help, pulled her toward the club up the street—right in the heart of downtown Denver. Jessie couldn't help but feel for the handful of beggars and homeless people they passed as she was hustled through the cold. She tried to imagine the horrible turn that had taken them down such a dark path, and wondered if any of them would recover from it. Their tragic stories made her wet heel seem like good luck, and, as she approached the door to the club, she hoped the poor souls found some way to stay warm in this mess.

Ignoring the roped line of people waiting to enter the club, April led them straight to the heavy, closed door vibrating from the force of the thunderous music behind it. She curled her fingers in a seductive wave at the muscled man barring the entrance. He smiled as he swept her into a bear hug. April came to this particular club a lot, and had secured herself a permanent spot on the VIP list. The man opened the door to the club, and the force of the sudden, uncontained music made Jessie back up a step.

Adjusting her short, black dress, she followed April and Harmony to the girl collecting money and stamping hands. With an excited squeal, April hugged the blonde. After exchanging a few pleasantries, the woman quickly stamped everyone's hands, then waved them through to the interior of the club. Jessie was grateful for the heat the instant she stepped inside the club. Seconds after removing their coats, and checking them, some men April knew spotter her, and she was promptly whisked away to the dance floor.

Harmony glanced at April shaking her ass with a group of attractive guys, then turned to Jessie and nodded toward the far end of the packed room, where the bar was situated. The music thumped through Jessie's chest as she navigated the crowd, making her ears buzz. Bodies jostled against her, warm and sweaty. Jessie didn't particularly enjoy the sticky contact, but she knew she'd be warm and sweaty soon too.

Harmony led her to a fifteen-foot bar that traveled the length of the back of the room, the dark wood chipped and damaged from years of drunken abuse. Putting her elbows on top of the sticky surface, Harmony expertly emphasized her cleavage in her tight red top. The male bartender instantly noticed, his eyes drifting to her chest and staying there, as he cocked his head to hear her shout her drink order.

Nodding, he got to work pouring them shots of a dark liquid, covered with a light creamy liquor. Jessie smiled as Harmony turned to her. "Bottoms up!" she yelled, handing Jessie one. The two girls clinked their glasses and tilted them back. The sweet yet potent drink burned all the way down Jessie's throat. Shaking her head and laughing, she stopped feeling bad about her wet foot, her asshole ex-boyfriend, and the state of the downtrodden strangers outside. Resting against the bar with Harmony, Jessie showed off her no-less-impressive amplitude. The bartender grinned at seeing two racks on display for him and poured another round of drinks.

Three rounds later, the girls finally went to find April on the dance floor. They found their gregarious friend in a swarm of beautiful boys, each one trying to get a hand on her slim body. She expertly slinked between three or four, placing her hands all over them, but somehow managing to stop them from groping her. It was an impressive feat to watch, and Jessie laughed at the sight.

Giggling in delight, April squealed at seeing her two friends. With arms on each other for support, and to keep back the eager boys, the girls danced together effortlessly. As the alcohol burned through Jessie's body, her moves loosened, her dress rode a little higher. A couple of guys nearby took advantage of that, resting their fingers on her toned legs. Enjoying the feel of a man's attention, she let them. She even laughed when one forward guy wrapped an arm around her waist and pulled her hips back into his. She allowed herself to grind with the older man, but immediately broke away from his grasp when it became obvious that he was enjoying it a little *too* much.

Grabbing April and Harmony's hands, she pulled them over to the bar for another round. The man looked highly disappointed, but Jessie could only laugh at his dismay. He was really too old to be at a club purely for the fun of it, and Jessie was sure he spent his weekends trolling, looking for young, easy hookups. He even completed the player look with a paisley dress shirt, opened about three buttons too far, and a gaudy gold chain poking through his chest hair. Approaching the dark, stained bar, Jessie wished him luck, but she had no intention of being an easy score.

The next several hours went by in much the same way—the girls found a group of guys to dance with, then left them to grab more shots at the bar. The bartender started offering his suggestions on what they should drink, and pretty soon they had moved past the sweet, creamy liquors to the hard stuff. Several guys, hoping to speed up the inebriation of three attractive girls, bought them even more drinks. Each man was obliged with a swift kiss to the cheek and an intimate turn on the dance floor, but not much more than that.

Jessie was pleasantly buzzed, laughing with her friends at the bar, when she felt a set of eyes on her—different than the eyes she'd felt all night. Twisting to search for the source of the heat, she instantly spotted a guy at a nearby table. He was standing by himself, sipping on a beer and staring at her. Jessie couldn't help but return his focused gaze. Even if she'd been completely sober, he would have gotten her attention. From their proximity, he looked tall and athletic, the cut line of muscle clearly visible on his arm as he tilted back his bottle. While his body seemed nice enough, that wasn't really what had captured Jessie's attention. It was more his face.

An intriguing blend of ethnicities fused the man's genetic code, but Jessie's muddled brain couldn't quite place what they were—an appealing mix of Caucasian, Latin, Asian, or maybe even Puerto Rican? His skin was that beautiful mulatto color that always looked deeply tanned, regardless of the season. But even that wasn't what had Jessie still staring at him. It was the eyes. He had the most stunning pair of bright blue eyes. She wanted to be closer, so she could see for sure, but she was positive it would be like staring at a tropical ocean. In her carefree state, she suddenly wanted to be swimming in those eyes.

Almost as if he'd finally realized they'd been staring at each other for a while, the man blinked and looked down at his table, like he'd just been caught doing something wrong. Jessie knew she had a certain attractiveness to her. Her mother had graced her with the aforementioned cleavage and a trim waist to emphasize it, and her father had given her his dark brown hair with matching chocolate eyes. Harmony and April hadn't let her leave the house tonight until she'd shucked off her I've-just-been-dumped sweats, and she'd spent a good hour giving herself sexy smoky eyes, painting her lips the perfect shade of red, and taming her naturally curly hair into thick ringlets. The alcohol flowing freely through her veins made her think she looked particularly amazing.

She bit her lip as the beautiful boy kept his eyes downcast; a small, adorable smile curved his mouth. Jessie couldn't be sure, but he didn't seem to be waiting for anyone. Maybe still feeling her eyes on him, he lifted his gaze back to her position at the bar. As Jessie was still staring at him, he quickly returned his vision to the table, but his smile grew a little larger.

Laughing that the most attractive guy in the club was actually being shy with her, Jessie twisted around to order them a couple drinks. April and Harmony looked at her expectantly, but furrowed their brows in question when she only purchased two of her favorite drink—rum and vodka with a splash of orange juice. Seeing their confusion, Jessie nodded her head at the man. "He looks lonely. I'm gonna go cheer him up."

Her friends laughed and immediately—and not subtly—checked him out. April nodded her approval. Harmony raised an eyebrow and waved at him. Jessie swung her head back around, hoping her friends hadn't scared him off, but he was still there, shaking his head and laughing as he stared at his table again.

Throwing her friends a warning glare, Jessie started stumbling her way over to him. Ignoring a few slurred greetings as she waded around a couple groups of men, she approached his table with what she thought was a sexy swagger. Immediately, she got her foot stuck in a crack. Luckily it wasn't enough to twist her ankle, but it did jar her step, and she stumbled and started to fall.

Strong arms wrapped around her waist, steadying her, as she squealed in surprise. Jessie was now completely pressed against a hard, flat stomach, and a lean, muscular chest. But his body barely registered as she stared into the most incredible set of sea-green eyes she'd ever seen. They were even more amazing than she'd hoped they would be, and she was reminded of travel brochures used to promote faraway island getaways. He was just…spectacular.

"Are you okay?" he asked over the heavy beat of the music.

As Jessie struggled to pull her eyes from his, her languid mind suddenly remembered the awkward situation she'd gotten herself in. She laughed, the alcohol in her system covering her embarrassment. "Yeah, I'm just not having a good shoe day." She lifted her foot; the insole was mostly dry by now, but still a little squeaky, she was sure.

Not understanding, the man only smiled as he gently released her from his arms. Jessie found that she missed the contact, and stepped into his side, closer than she generally stood to complete strangers. He didn't back off, though, just continued to sweep those amazing eyes over her face. Even in her drunken haze, it pleased her that he was focusing his gaze more above her neck than below it.

She handed him a drink, or what was left of it, since some had splashed onto the floor during her scuffle. She raised her own as he tentatively took the glass. "Drink with me?" she asked, in a way that really didn't sound like a question.

Smiling, he raised his glass to hers. "Cheers."

They touched glasses, and Jessie watched as he closed those marvelous eyes and tilted back the drink. As she watched him, she wondered how those full lips, pressing so softly against the glass, would feel pressed against her mouth, her neck…her breasts. A little surprised at the immediate sexual attraction she felt for this unnamed man, Jessie shook her head and downed what was left of her drink.

When he was finished with his half-full drink, the man gently set his empty glass on the table and politely told her, "Thank you." Jessie flushed at his simple words as she set her own empty glass next to his. Amazing how two small syllables were doing so much more for her than an entire night of grinding had done.

With a captivating smile, he examined her heated cheeks, then stuck out his hand, right at hip level. As Jessie's hips were nearly pressed into his side, she had to back up a step. "My name's Kai."

Jessie grinned at the excuse to grab his hand. She didn't shake it, so much as clench it and press it against her belly. His mouth popped open at the unexpected contact. Jessie instantly loved the warmth she felt radiating from him; just his fingers against her was enough to cause a tingle of excitement to flash over her skin. "Kai...with the beautiful eyes," she drunkenly murmured. "Hi...I'm Jessie."

Still smiling, he leaned an elbow onto the waist high table. The move brought his head just a bit closer to hers. She bit her lip. "Thank you for the drink, Jessie." The way he said her name made a chill run down her spine. She kind of wanted to hear him moan it.

Surprising herself, she asked, "Are you here alone?"

He glanced down at the table, seemingly shy again, then peeked up at her. "I am...just got into town actually. I don't really know anybody yet."

The fact that the beautiful man in front of her was unattached made Jessie's lips twist into a playful smile. "Well, would you like to get to know me?" A small section of her slow brain was shocked that she'd just asked him that. She generally wasn't that forward...but there was just something about him.

In a gesture that she found exceedingly cute, he looked down again. Then, raising his eyes, he unwaveringly held her gaze. "I think I'd like that."

Smiling and stroking his fingers still resting against her stomach, she glanced at the empty glass she'd brought him, the nearly empty bottle of beer he'd been drinking before her arrival, and decided that she needed to get this shy guy up to her level of carefree. Taking a step back, she pulled his arm so he would follow her. "Come on, we need to get you caught up."

He smiled and willingly allowed her to lead him. Jessie carefully avoided the section of the bar where her friends were watching her every move. She didn't need them interfering and scaring off the guy. At the other end of the long bar, a girl was tending to the customers. Jessie walked up to her with her newfound friend's arm firmly around her waist. Sidling up behind her, the beautiful boy kept a slight, respectful distance between their bodies. Wanting to feel that hard body along the length of her, Jessie leaned back until they touched. His free hand trailed down her bare arm, and she shivered, even in the heat of the club. God, he felt amazing.

Jessie shouted an order at the straining-to-hear bartender, and stepped back with the boy once she was handed a couple of shots of Jameson. After thanking her, he closed his eyes and tilted the drink back. Jessie smiled as she watched him gulp his drink, and again pictured those wondrous lips all over her body. Her pain and heartache was so far buried under alcohol and tropical eyes that it was like it had never happened. Harmony and April were right; this was exactly what she needed.

Her companion winced as the strong liquid burned through him. Jessie had been drinking hard stuff from the get-go, so it didn't even faze her now, but apparently he hadn't gotten there yet. She spent the next several minutes *getting* him there. When his smile was loose and easy, and his hands casually slipped over her body, Jessie decided to move their foreplay to the dance floor. There, his fingers all over her would be very natural.

With his absorbing eyes glued to her face, Jessie strategically placed one leg between his. Draping her arms around his shoulders, she pulled him flush against her. Running his hands down her back, he pulled her hips into his body, and they began to seamlessly move together. Jessie couldn't help but notice that being with him felt more natural than any of the boys she'd danced with earlier. As their hips briefly touched while they swayed together, Jessie was reminded of far more intimate actions—actions that she hadn't done in a while. Her sloppy mind could easily picture doing all sorts of intimate acts with this man.

As other gyrating bodies danced around them, Jessie let herself get lost in his captivating eyes. Running her hands through his dark hair, she brought her face closer to his. He stared down at her, his lips partly open as he softly breathed. Jessie pulled her eyes from that intense gaze, to stare down at those lips—so full, so perfect. She was near enough to feel his light breath against her skin, and she was drunk enough to take it a step further. Letting her earlier fantasy of kissing him fuel her, Jessie shifted their heads until their lips connected.

It was brief, a bare brushing of soft lips against soft lips. Except for the sudden flare of burning heat in her body, it could have been an accident. His hand clenched her hip. Her hand tightened in his hair. This wasn't something Jessie usually did—making out on a dance floor with a guy whose name she couldn't even remember—but she had been denied a physical encounter with a man for a while now. And, April *had* promised her that tonight would be fun. And she was really drunk, and he was really sexy. She didn't want to be good, didn't want to play it safe.

Jessie noted his eyes fractionally closing as they continued slowly moving against each other. They weren't keeping time with the fast, thumping music anymore, but making a beat of their own, perfectly in sync to the rhythm of their bodies. Jessie gasped after the brief contact, and felt the anticipation of another kiss rip through her, igniting her. Her body instantly responded, the fire quickly building to an invigorating boil. She hoped her new friend was feeling it too. Unlike the sleazy older man she'd danced with earlier, she wouldn't mind feeling some of *his* hardness grazing her thigh.

When his eyes reopened, Jessie could see the heat of desire in them. Maybe she couldn't feel his body yet, but she knew he was, at the very least, interested in her. She smiled and brought her lips to his again—tentative, soft, and teasing. Her dance partner didn't let her leave it at teasing for long though. As she ran her lips over his, he shifted his head and fully enclosed her mouth. The electricity was immediate. One of his hands left her hip to grab her cheek, holding her securely to him, and his soft lips encouraged hers to part as the tip of his tongue slipped inside. Jessie moaned into his mouth as she heavily leaned against him, closing every gap between their already smashed together bodies.

Lightly tugging on a handful of his hair, Jessie shifted his mouth so she could feel all of his tongue sliding against hers. She felt the rumble in his chest as he groaned in approval. She hoped that if he hadn't wanted her before, he did now. When his hand slinked over her backside, bringing her leg slightly up his hip, she could feel his need for her pressing into her body.

Suddenly eager, she ran her other hand up his shirt and considered ripping it off him. Whoever this man was, he appealed to her, and she clearly appealed to him. Jessie wasn't one to jump right into a physical relationship, but her fuzzy mind and torn heart just wanted to feel good. And his erection pressing just above her pubic bone felt really good.

Forgetting her earlier idea of not being easy, forgetting that her two best friends were witnessing her very public make out session with a stranger, she broke away from his mouth and ran her lips to his ear. Over the loud music, she panted, "You live close by?" She really hoped he said yes; a long cab ride would probably douse her buzz and change her mind, and her body was screaming for this. She didn't want to change her mind.

With a movement that had nothing to do with dancing, he pulled her hips into his. In her ear he said back, just as breathily, "Yes. A couple blocks up the street."

When he returned his mouth to her lips, the hand on her cheek slipped to her breast. If they didn't change locations soon, Jessie was never going to be able to show her face in this club again; though, this was April's scene more than hers. She pulled back from him, and his tongue lightly flicked against her lip as they separated. Hissing in a quick breath, she ran a finger down those amazing lips. "Take me there." Again, she was shocked at her own forwardness, but she was too drunk to care.

His mouth dropped open at her words, and Jessie took the opportunity to playfully suck on his bottom lip. As he let out an erotic noise that she wished she could hear better, his eyes fluttered closed. When he reopened them, he crashed his lips back down to hers. Their bodies grinding almost uncontrollably now, she heard him mutter, "Yes, God yes."

Lifting her mouth to his ear again, she said over the music, "I'll meet you outside in five." Then she sucked on his earlobe. He shuddered, and his thumb on her breast swept across her nipple, sending ripples of desire down her body. Not wanting to let him go, she rested her head against his as she pushed their bodies away from each other. With how badly she wanted him right now, staying on this dance floor any longer was not a good idea. Giving him one last kiss, she brushed past him. Needing to feel it, she ran her hands down the front of his jeans as she left. He did *not* disappoint her.

Without a thought of anything else but dissolving into his arms, Jessie headed straight for the exit. She was suddenly halted by a curious redhead blocking her path. "Going somewhere, Jess?"

Not wanting a conversation at the moment, Jessie tried walking around her concerned friend. But she soon found her bare arms tightly enclosed in Harmony's surprisingly strong fingers. "No, seriously, where do you think you're going?" Her light blue eyes narrowed as she looked over Jessie's face; could Harmony tell by looking at her that she was having trouble focusing? Jessie wanted to be on her way, but she knew that if the tables were turned, there was no way she'd let her friend leave alone. Girls got killed that way.

But then again, Jessie wasn't leaving alone. Giggling, she leaned in to give her friend the good news. "I'm going home with the hot guy."

Harmony looked over her shoulder, like she was looking for whom Jessie was talking about. Frowning, like she wasn't seeing him, she firmly stated, "I don't think so." Bringing her eyes back to Jessie, she shook her head. "That's a bad idea."

"What's a bad idea?"

Jessie was assaulted from behind by a set of arms slipping around her waist and a head of dark hair nestling over her shoulder. Jessie could smell the booze coming off April and knew that her friend was feeling as little pain as she was. Laughing, she snuggled into April's embrace while Harmony answered April's question.

"She thinks she's going off with some guy she just met."

April brightened and twisted Jessie around; her expression was a mixture of pride and shock. "Oh, your first one-night stand." She placed a hand over her heart and beamed at Jessie like an overjoyed parent. "I'm so proud."

Jessie giggled again while Harmony sighed. "April, she shouldn't—"

Not needing a voice of reason at the moment, Jessie cut off Harmony's objection with one of her own. Slurring a little, she stated, "I'll be fine. We're just going a few blocks up the street." She lifted the small sparkly bag draped across her body. "I have my phone in my purse. You can track me." They'd downloaded an app for their phones that tracked each other's locations, mainly for the fun of teasing each other when someone popped up in an odd place, say, the sex shop downtown. As a precaution, they always turned the feature on whenever they went out together, just in case they got separated.

Harmony still looked unconvinced as she crossed her arms over her chest, but April thought Jessie's solution was perfect. She clapped her on the back. "Great, have fun! You need it after your last loser."

Harmony seemed torn on what to do, and Jessie took that moment of indecision as her chance to get away. "Have a good night. I'll call you later." With that, she gave Harmony a sloppy kiss on the cheek.

While trying to weasel away from them, Jessie's arm was suddenly grabbed by April. "Wait! Here…" She reached into the pocket of her tight pants and pulled out a silver packet. A smile blossomed on her face as she folded Jessie's fingers around it. "Fun is great, but safe fun is even better."

Confused, Jessie opened her hand. Seeing a ribbed-for-her-pleasure condom packet in her palm, she looked up at April. She'd had that in her pocket? April shrugged, smiled, and left to rejoin her group of flirty boys on the dance floor.

Harmony watched her leave, then looked back at Jessie with stern eyes; even her spattering of friendly freckles seemed to say *Listen and obey*. "Call me. Soon." Clutching her prophylactic tight, Jessie grinned and nodded. As she scooted away, Harmony called out, "Within the hour, Jess! If I don't hear from you by then, I'm calling your dad!"

Jessie cringed. Getting her coat from the coat check girl, she stuffed the condom inside her bag and made sure her phone was turned on. Even sloppy-drunk, she was still sort of cautious.

As she put on her coat, the bottom still slightly damp from her incident earlier, uncertainty hit, and she began to wonder if going off with a stranger was a bad idea. But then she stepped out into the frigid air…and saw him.

He was standing with his back to her, his hands stuffed in the pockets of his jeans and his shoulders bunched up like he was extremely cold, even in his thick, dark jacket. Leaning on one hip, he looked out over the street, watching the cars and people. His faded jeans perfectly highlighted his backside, and desire instantly trumped every other emotion in Jessie's head. As if he felt her approaching, her date turned, and those sea-green eyes locked onto hers. She knew right then, only good things were going to happen tonight. Really, really good things.

He smiled when he saw her, relief over her showing clear on his face. She walked up to him, as seductively as her drunken steps allowed, and tossed her arms around his neck. Their lips reunited, cold from the outside weather, but warming with their hot breath and needy, frantic movements. His hand slipped inside her trench coat while hers ran though his hair. She groaned when his palm cupped her bottom. *If only their clothes weren't in the way.*

"Where?" she asked, her voice low and seductive. His response was a rough grunt as he started pulling her up the street.

It was the longest couple of blocks that Jessie had ever walked with someone. It didn't help their progress any that they often stopped to lean against walls or railings, or in some cases, shop windows. And it didn't help that every time he pressed against her, he seemed to be even harder, even more ready for her. And God, was she ready for him too.

Just as she was considering pushing him into an alley and having her way with him right there, he pulled her toward a flight of steps leading up to an apartment building. He fumbled in his jacket for his keys, his mouth still firmly locked on hers. Somehow he managed to open the entryway door and step inside. They walked into a nearby elevator, and Jessie immediately began taking off his jacket. As the metal contraption lifted them into the air, he pressed her against the back wall and nuzzled her neck.

His jacket in one hand, he pulled her out of the elevator when it dinged open. As she leaned against him, rubbing the front of his jeans, he tried to unlock his door without closing his eyes. Grunting in frustration, he nearly broke the door in his eagerness to open it. Jessie gasped when he roughly pulled her through it, and then groaned when he immediately closed the door and pushed her back against it.

After her coat was ripped off, Jessie unslung her bag and tossed it somewhere into the apartment. His hands moved over her body, clenching and unclenching the fabric of her dress like he wanted to tear it off her as well. Eyes and voice needy, he exhaled, "God, I want you."

Alcohol, anticipation, excitement, and a surge of lust rushed through her. "I want you too." Bringing her fingers to the waistband of his jeans, she muttered to herself, "God, I hope you're packing. I don't need another Jeremy."

He only had time to murmur, "I...um...", before she had his jeans unzipped and her hand inside his underwear. Much to her relief, he was hard, thick, and delightfully sized. "Oh, thank God," she breathed. Her philandering ex-boyfriend had frequently been none of those things.

He laughed deep in his throat, then attacked her mouth. Pulling her away from the door, he flicked on a light switch and led her deeper into the apartment. Mouths still connected, they walked through what looked like a small kitchen area into a room that Jessie assumed was the living room. She didn't really know, and she didn't really care. When they stopped moving, Jessie removed his shirt. Tossing it on the shaggy carpet, she eyed his wonderfully colored skin. Much to her surprise and delight, there was an intriguing black tattoo coming over his shoulder and swirling down to his collarbone. Jessie traced the dark design, then placed a soft kiss at the ending point of one of the swirls. He made a pleased noise in the back of his throat as he began to unzip her dress. The rest of his chest was as fit as his arms, and Jessie lightly ran her fingernails down the firm muscles, making him shudder. Once he was done with the deceptively long zipper of her dress, Jessie shrugged it off her shoulders, and let it fall to a heap at her feet.

Pausing, he took a moment to enjoy the sight of her scantily clad body; her lacy black bra and underwear matched the heels she was still wearing. After his thorough inspection, he popped off his shoes and quickly pushed down his jeans. Jessie bit her lip as she breathlessly watched him. She felt like every inch of her was burning with need, and she was going to explode soon if he didn't satisfy the ache. When he was just in black boxer-briefs, he reached out and pulled her forward. She stumbled into his body and then crashed into his lips. Catching her off-guard, he suddenly shifted and twisted her around. With a cry of surprise ready on her lips, Jessie lost her balance and they began to fall. Just as she braced herself for impact on the hard floor, they landed on a soft, springy mattress.

Looking around, Jessie noted that his apartment was a studio—everything but the bathroom was enclosed in one giant room—and they were safely resting on a mattress in the middle of the far wall. Just a mattress. No headboard, no box spring, no bed frame to raise it off the ground. The rest of the large room was an assortment of opened and closed boxes; he really had just gotten into town. Just as she thought to comment, he settled himself between her thighs, and finally pressed that wonderfully full manhood against her. She wouldn't have cared if they were screwing on the floor after that.

The feeling of him being so close to where she needed him had her squirming in anticipation; the scant fabric of their underwear barely separated their needy flesh. With a throaty groan, he moved his hips against her as rhythmically as he had in the club. His soft mouth placed languid kisses down her jawline, then her throat. While Jessie gulped down air, his marvelously soft lips traveled down to her bra. He kissed her once, through the fabric, then gently moved the lace aside. Her nipple peaked as her breast was exposed to the cooler air, and Jessie moaned in delight when his hot mouth closed around it. His tongue swirled around the nipple, his teeth lightly tugging, and she arched against him as she writhed in torturous bliss. *Yes, more.*

Tucking her hands behind herself, she popped open her bra; it took a couple of tries with her numb fingers. When the material was loose, he paused to rip it off her, then turned his attention to her other breast. Moaning, "Yes," she clutched his head to her.

With a satisfied groan, he left her breast and started heading south. She arched her back and pushed his head down, wanting what he was suggesting; just the thought made her feel like she was about to climax. Her drunk mind spoke her body's wishes. "Yes, do it…I want you to taste me."

He paused with his lips against her belly, his hands clenching her hips. "Damn, that's hot," he muttered into her soft flesh.

Not feeling the embarrassment she might have felt sober, she pushed his head again, urging him to keep going. With a soft curse, he harshly ripped off her underwear. He kissed her calves as he pulled the material off her, but he left the heels on. Jessie loved that. Breathing heavily, his beautiful eyes full of wanton lust, he watched as she squirmed on the mattress. Wanting him to continue touching her, she ran her hands down her front, squeezing the breasts he'd placed so much attention on earlier. *Do it…*

His eyes flared with passion, then he settled himself between her thighs. As she dug her heel into his leg, he ran his tongue up her core. Jessie cried out as waves of bliss washed over her. Before closing her eyes and succumbing to the euphoria, she noticed that the tattoo around his collarbone curved up and over his shoulder, ending in a tribal design that extended all the way down his shoulder blade. *God, that's hot.*

That marvelous tongue in that beautiful boy's mouth brought her right to the edge of releasing, as he sucked, stroked and teased her into near oblivion. Pushing him away before she toppled over the edge, Jessie aggressively shoved him all the way to his back. His breath heavy, he let her take control without complaint. Starting at his neck, she gave his body the exact same attention he'd just given her. When her lips were firmly wrapped around his glorious manhood, he cried out and clutched her hair.

She brought him to the edge of releasing. When he was rocking against her and moaning in a rhythm she recognized, she removed her mouth and pulled back. She took a second to enjoy the firm body lying before her; his head was tilted back as he recovered his breath, and his marvelous eyes were firmly closed. Just as he was opening them to look at her, Jessie crawled onto his lap and pushed herself down on top of him. A surprised gasp left his lips, but it quickly shifted into an erotic sound of satisfaction. Jessie closed her eyes as a similar noise escaped her. The feel of all that length and width inside her was unlike anything she'd ever felt before. Even drunk, she appreciated it.

Their hips moved together automatically, slowly at first, then steadily increased to a fierce rhythm full of drive and purpose. Jessie leaned back on his thighs, exposing as much of her body to him as she could. His fingers reached up to explore her; one hand cupped her breast, while the other slid down to where they were connected. As he drove into her, his thumb rubbed small circles against her core. The erotic sounds releasing from Jessie were uncontrollable. She knew she was close; she could feel the pressure building to a glorious breaking point with every stroke. She shifted her hips, to feel more of him against her, and instantly cried out as she was suddenly struck by a deep, intense climax. She rode out the sensation with tiny groans of pleasure; it was the most powerful, satisfying orgasm she'd ever had. Ten times more than Jeremy had ever given her. She felt like her entire body was trembling.

As she came down, he sat up under her, grabbed her thighs, and pushed her up and over. With a grunt and a couple of readjustments, he had her back to the mattress. Resting on top of her, he drove into her again with a needy groan. Wanting him to experience the joy she'd just had, Jessie met him thrust for thrust, and even though she was drunk on alcohol and an amazing orgasm, she enjoyed the sensation of their joined bodies rocking apart and coming together.

As he panted heavily in her ear, Jessie trailed her fingers through his dark hair. The pleasure slowly started building again, and as Jessie wondered if she could orgasm twice, she let her head roll off the edge of the mattress. From her vantage point, she could see their tangled, naked bodies reflected back to her in a television set nearby. She watched their bodies move together, watched his face as he approached his climax. It was an incredibly erotic sight, and she felt her body quickly responding. Yes, she could come twice.

Like he knew he was being watched, his eyes drifting to hers in the TV. "Are you watching us?" he murmured, his voice tight. She groaned and smiled, and he dropped his head to her shoulder. "Jesus, that's hot."

Jessie continued her voyeurism, feeling and watching the way his body shifted as he drove into her. It was mesmerizing and overwhelming, and she couldn't take much more; she was close again. So very, very close. Needing just a little push to get her over the edge, she moved her hips harder under his. He groaned against her shoulder, his hand on her waist encouraging her vigor, then he sucked in a quick breath. "God, I'm close." His voice was tight as he added, "Yes...I'm ...yes..."

He let it trail off, and Jessie grabbed his head, bringing his eyes back to hers. "Say it," she panted, again shocked at her own aggressiveness. Hard alcohol did surprising things to her.

He opened his mouth, and his beautiful face broke into a look that men only got when they were about to release. On most, it wasn't that appealing. On him...it was breathtaking. "Oh God...I'm coming..." Then he let out a series of low groans as his hips slowed over hers.

Feeling him, hearing him, the eroticism of the moment hit her all at once, igniting her climax, and she started coming for a second time. Clutching each other, they rode out their joint orgasms together, and as he released inside her, Jessie's slow mind suddenly remembered the one tiny little thing she'd forgotten in the heat of the moment...the condom tucked away in her purse. Oops.

One Morning

K ai was still enjoying the last lingering remnants of his outstanding release when Jessie's phone started ring- ing. It took a moment for Kai to register what the odd, musical sound was and where it was coming from. Real- ly, it took his slow mind a minute to register anything other than — *that was the best orgasm I've ever had.* As he panted on her shoulder, he felt her shift beneath him, like she was uncom- fortable.

Not wanting to crush her, he pulled out and shifted to her side. Jessie ran her hands through her dark brown hair, her chocolate eyes closing. Kai had been mesmerized by those eyes in the club. He'd never seen eyes that dark that had also been that alive. They'd trapped him almost instantly, even be- fore all the booze she'd poured down his willing throat. Com- bined with the way she moved and the aggressive way she talked, and he was hers, she could have done anything she wanted to him. He smiled as he considered that, in a way, she had.

He ran a finger through a ringlet of her dark hair, loving the way it wrapped around him, possessing him. Her satisfied eyes shifted to him, running down his body before flicking back up to his face. "God, that was…"

She trailed off as she finally heard her phone ringing. Adorably scrunching her face into an expression of concern and annoyance, she started looking for the source of the sound. "Shit," she exclaimed, as she searched around his mattress. Her lean, toned body twisted in intriguing ways as she started rummaging through their clump of clothes, desperately trying to find the culprit. With an almost frantic look in her blurry eyes, she sat up and stared at him. "What time is it?"

Sitting up, Kai wondered why time was an issue. He wasn't kicking her out or anything. "I have no idea. Why?" Thinking she might just be looking for an excuse to leave, he added, "I know I don't have much, but you can stay."

Shaking her head, she slipped on her underwear and attempted to put on her bra. She had a little trouble enclosing those wonderfully full breasts in the fabric though. Kai brushed some of her hair over her shoulder, so he could help her with the clasp on the back. Since she seemed to be in a hurry, he resisted the urge to kiss the top of her shoulder when he was done. Jessie gave him a grateful smile for the help, but firmly shook her head again. "She's gonna kill me if I don't—" She cut off as her phone stopped ringing. "Shit!" she exclaimed again.

Kai grabbed her dress for her as she ran a hand through her hair. Concern filled him as he watched her; she looked a little panicked now. "What? Who is going to kill you?"

Grabbing the dress, Jessie staggered to her feet as she slipped it over her head. Pulling on his underwear, Kai stood beside her; he felt himself swaying a little as well. His head swam as he tried to focus on her face. She was quickly becoming more and more frustrated as she looked around his boxes for the purse she'd flung into his apartment earlier. "Harmony. She's going to kill me if she can't get ahold of me."

Kai came around the other side of the mattress. On the way, he noticed a small shiny bag poking between his box of books and an open box of dishes. Careful to not fall over, he bent down and picked it up. Walking around to where Jessie was now digging through a box of clothes, he handed her the purse. Wildly searching through the box, she didn't notice what he was giving her. "Here," he said quietly, wondering if she would take off the minute she had it. Not hearing him, Jessie started muttering that this Harmony person was going to call her father, and then S.W.A.T. would be knocking down the door. Furrowing his brow and hoping she was exaggerating, Kai tapped her shoulder with the bag to get her attention. "Jessie, here."

Finally noticing him, Jessie paused and glanced his way. Looking relieved, she straightened as she grabbed the bag. "Oh, thank you, um…yeah, thank you." Biting her lip, she opened the purse and pulled out her phone. Kai noticed a small packet drop to his floor, but he ignored it as he began to wonder if Jessie even remembered his name.

With his vision starting to spin, Kai sat down on his bed, then laid back. He'd overdone it at the bar, and he was beginning to pay the price for it; his pleasant buzz was taking an unpleasant turn. Jessie pressed a couple buttons on her phone, then started stumbling back and forth, like she was pacing. Kai ran both hands back through his hair, and focused on taking deep breaths—in through his nose and out though his mouth. Maybe her leaving right now was an excellent idea. He didn't want to ruin the memory of their night together by throwing up in front of her.

As Kai tried to calmly breathe through the discomfort churning in his stomach, he listened to Jessie connect with her friend on the phone, "Hey. No, I'm fine. I couldn't find the phone. Yes, I'm dressed." She sounded a little agitated at that, and Kai peeked up at her. Her beautiful lips were set in an adorable pout as she leaned back with a hand on her hip. Kai smiled, but then his vision of her started to twist, and he shut his eyes. That made everything start to spin, so he opened his eyes to stare at one spot on his ceiling.

"You're in front of the building? Okay, okay...God. I'm coming down," he heard her say.

She disconnected the phone, and Kai risked shifting his gaze to look at her. Stumbling on her feet, she stuffed the phone back in her purse. "I have to go...my friends are here." She frowned, like she really did want to stay, and then her eyes slowly raked over Kai's body. Even drunk, tired, and on the verge of vomiting, Kai reacted to her inspection; he could feel himself begin to harden, and wished her friends weren't here and he felt better, so they could do all of that again.

Not noticing his growing arousal, Jessie sighed and attempted to lean down to kiss him. She ended up falling over his body instead. Still trying to not be sick, Kai laughed with her as he carefully helped her regain her balance. Jessie paused, hovered over him. Her long ringlets curtained their faces for a moment, blocking out everything but them. She let out a wistful sigh; the faint scent of alcohol on her breath worried his stomach, but ignited his body. Cupping his cheek, she whispered, "I had a great time." Then she leaned down and placed those full lips on his again.

Desire, passion, and need trumped the queasy sensation in his gut, and more than anything, Kai wanted her to stay. He knew she couldn't though. Angling his head to feel more of her mouth on him, he deepened the kiss. He wanted to savor this; he wanted to remember this. His hands dug into her curls, holding her head to him for a moment. She let him explore her, feel her, but eventually, she pulled away. Expression reluctant, she murmured, "I have to go," just as Kai heard a car honking on the street. Also hesitant, he released her. Suddenly exhausted, he nodded as his eyes fluttered closed.

With another conflicted sigh, she gave him one last lingering kiss. Then her lips retreated, and Kai heard her grab her coat from the kitchen and open the door. "Bye," he whispered, before he lost the war against sleep.

As he started to fade away, he heard her say, "Goodbye," in return and close the door behind herself. It was only then that he realized they hadn't swapped numbers. He didn't know her last name, didn't know where she worked, didn't know much about her at all. He had no way to contact her, and goodbye was the last thing he'd ever hear her say.

Kai slept fitfully, tumbling in and out of consciousness as he dreamt of the encounter over and over. He would have dreamt about it all night and well into the morning, but long before an acceptable hour, his phone started ringing. His cell was set to an annoyingly loud, shrill tone, and right as his hand flopped over to find the damn thing, he vowed to change the setting.

Cursing that he couldn't find his phone, he also vowed to get his place in order soon. He'd moved in a couple of days ago, and had only meant to go out last night to explore his new city. Not knowing many people here, he'd set out in the hopes of finding someone his age to hang out with. He had certainly never expected what had happened. One-night stands were *not* his thing. He liked steady dates that eased into sexual relationships. But that girl... Something about her had appealed to every single part of him. Plus he'd been a little tipsy to begin with, and when she'd started supplying drinks, well, everything had sort of amplified after that.

Sitting up, he squinted in the bright lights of his still-lit studio. Bringing a hand to his throbbing head, he grunted in pain; his annoyingly loud phone was not helping anything. Wishing he could ignore it, he pushed himself to his feet; he wobbled a bit before he gained his equilibrium. Seeing his jacket near the door, he sighed and staggered over to it. Grabbing the thick material with half-numb fingers, he shoved his hand into the pocket and gratefully silenced his phone by answering it.

"Yeah," he mumbled, his forehead pounding. He'd definitely overdone it last night. On several different levels.

A too-bright voice answered his slurred greeting. "Oh, hi, honey. It's Mom."

Kai contained a sigh. His mom always announced that it was she who was calling, like somehow, after twenty-three years, he wouldn't recognize her voice. "Hi, Mom." Looking over his shoulder, he glanced at the time on the microwave. Just as he'd suspected, it was hardly a decent hour for her to be calling. "You do realize I'm four hours later than you, right?"

His mother gasped as she realized the time. "Oh, shoot. Sorry, honey. Sometimes I forget just how far away Colorado really is from Hawaii... I hate you being so far away."

Kai stifled another sigh. He loved his mother, but it was entirely too early for this, and his head was killing him. Returning to his mattress, he yawned as he sat down. "Why are you still awake? It must be past midnight there?"

She let out a dreary exhale. "I just couldn't sleep. I've been worrying about you. Are you all right? Is it nice there? Have you met anyone yet?"

Wondering how to answer her, Kai stared up at his ceiling. His hand traveled over his bare chest to scratch a phantom itch, and he finally let that sigh escape. He couldn't tell his mom about his one-night stand, and he was pretty sure that wasn't what she meant about meeting someone anyway. "It's fine, I'm fine. But I've only been here a few days, Mom. I haven't even had a chance to see Grandma yet." He yawned into the phone again. "I was going to do that tomorrow...or, today, I guess."

His mother sighed into the phone again, and he could easily picture her on their back porch, worrying about him as she stared out at the dark Pacific Ocean. He thought he could even hear the waves pounding in the background. It gave him a surprising twinge of homesickness. "Right, I'm getting ahead of myself. I just miss you. When do you start work?"

Lying back on his messy sheets, Kai wished he could fast forward this conversation and his headache; both were paining him at the moment. "Monday, Mom."

"Right...of course." She paused for a long time, and Kai thought to sneak in a, "Talk to you tomorrow," so he could attempt to get back to sleep, but she beat him to it with, "Have you met your boss yet?" Her voice came out tentative, like she was unsure if she wanted to ask him that.

Kai frowned at hearing the odd tone. His new boss was his parents' friend — or maybe just an acquaintance. Kai wasn't entirely sure what their relationship was with the man, other than they'd all worked together once, back in Hawaii. It was how Kai had gotten a job here, all the way in snowy Colorado. "No...I've only talked to him on the phone. I guess I'll meet him Monday too."

Another long pause from his mom. "Oh, right. Well, I suppose I should let you get back to sleep. I love you, Kai. I'll try not to call so early next time."

He grinned into the phone. "I love you too, Mom. And thank you." Kai ended the call and tossed his phone to the floor. Still praying for his head to stop throbbing, he shut his eyes and let exhaustion pull him back into his dreams about the beautiful, sensual girl he'd probably never see again.

He was awoken several hours later by a bright shaft of sunlight striking him in the eyes. Although it had to be close to noon now, Kai's body was sluggish as he sat up and ran a hand through his dark hair. He couldn't entirely blame the lethargy on his overindulgence last night. While recovering from the alcohol was definitely making him feel like he was moving in slow motion, it was more adjusting to the different time zone that was throwing him off. His body still wasn't used to it, and while the clock on the microwave confirmed that it was nearly twelve-thirty, his body was trying to tell him that no, it was only eight-thirty. He hoped that he could finally convince his body to play along with Mountain Time by Monday morning.

Standing, he shuffled to the bathroom and stuck his head under the faucet to relieve his thirst; his throat felt like it had been scoured with a Brillo pad. Rifling through a box on the counter, he found a bottle of aspirin on the very bottom and took four of them. His head was still throbbing, and although the room had thankfully stopped spinning and his stomach had settled, he needed a little extra help to get through this hangover.

Kai decided to take a quick shower. As the warm water cascaded down his back, he again experienced a painful surge of homesickness. In the past, whenever he had overdone it at some party on the beach with his friends, he would just dive into the ocean to perk up his spirits. There was nothing quite like the mix of muggy air, warm water, and pounding waves to make you forget the throbbing, thirst-inducing torture of waking up from a drunken night of debauchery.

Wrapped in a towel after his shower, Kai's thoughts again shifted to the mysterious woman he'd slept with last night. Thinking about his evening with her was almost like watching a movie about someone else—it just wasn't like Kai at all to bring a strange woman home, toss her onto his bed, and drive into her like both of their lives had depended on it. But while it hadn't been a typical night, he had to smile as he rummaged for some clothes in a box beside his bed. Whatever it had been …had been amazing.

Shivering a bit in the coolness of his apartment, Kai threw on some jeans and a couple of long-sleeved shirts. Then he shuffled the three steps it took to get to his kitchen. Since he hadn't gone shopping yet, and didn't have a whole lot of food in his cupboards, he made his standard meal: a bowl of cereal. He had every intention of getting the stuff he needed today and putting his place together…once his body stopped kicking him in the ass.

Leaning against the counter, eating his breakfast, Kai looked around at all of the numerous opened and unopened boxes. Most of his things didn't have anywhere else to go besides the box they were in, since he didn't have much in the way of furniture, not even a bed frame for his mattress. Thinking of everything he still needed to get was a little overwhelming. Shaking his head as he finished his meal, he decided that he would deal with the apartment later. First, he needed to visit the only person he knew in this city, his grandmother.

Feeling that he should probably call her before he just showed up at her door, Kai trudged through his mess to once again find his cell phone. As he retrieved it, he couldn't help but stare at the television screen. He could see his bed reflected back to him, and the memory of Jessie watching them have sex flooded through him. Her face as she'd stared at their bodies moving so intimately had been one of the hottest things he'd ever seen. And her smile when he'd started getting close … Goddamn. Kai was sure that the mental snapshot of that moment was going to stay with him for a long time, and he again kicked himself for not getting her number. He definitely wouldn't mind seeing her again.

Kai sat on his mattress again and rubbed his temple while he searched for his grandmother's number. His head was feeling better, thanks to the miracle of modern medicine, but he still felt rundown. The phone rang forever, and on the sixth or seventh ring, Kai started to get worried. He'd called his grandmother often when he'd started making plans to come out here, and she never let it go past three rings.

His grandmother was a pretty tough woman. She'd had nine kids in half as many years. She'd home schooled them all and sent all of them off to really good colleges. She was big on family bonds and managed to stay in touch with every member of her dispersed, expanded family. She'd even visited Kai in Hawaii every year, right up until the time his parents had gotten divorced. After that, she'd stopped coming around, but she'd never stopped being a part of Kai's life. She called him throughout the year, sent him cards and handmade gifts on holidays and his birthday, and even baked him cookies. While it had been years since he'd actually seen the woman, Kai had never stopped feeling that special bond with her.

When her phone switched over to an answering machine, Kai started pacing his small room. After ten minutes, he decided to call back. She could have been in the bathroom or maybe outside, tending to her greenhouse. Kai's grandfather had died several years ago, and with most of her children spread across the globe, his grandmother been living alone at her house for a long time. Kai knew she was self sufficient, but she wasn't getting any younger either. She was well into her eighties, and people that age could get hurt pretty easily.

When she didn't answer the phone on his second attempt to get ahold of her, Kai felt that a drop-in wouldn't be uncalled for. Making sure he had his wallet and keys, he grabbed his jacket from the floor of the kitchen and locked up his apartment.

He found his street bike right in the spot he'd left it in his building's underground parking. He hadn't had a whole lot of cash when he'd moved here, but a finding a cheap motorcycle had been a top priority. Slipping on the helmet that he kept on the handlebar, he settled himself over the bike. He'd discovered the ad for a used 2005 Suzuki GSX-R1000 while searching for an apartment. Kai had secured and paid for the bike while still in Hawaii, knowing that he could probably fix anything that might be wrong with it. He'd been around bikes his entire life, and had spent several summers fixing them up with his dad.

As he started the engine, he thought he'd gotten pretty lucky—it ran like a dream. But as he sloshed through the wet streets of downtown Denver, he started questioning his decision about owning a motorcycle in the freezing Mile High City. He was a bike guy, though. It was bright blue and unbelievably fast. Maybe one day Kai would save up and get a Jeep too, so he could be a little more insulated from the icy chill, but for right now, he could get by with just this.

Flying down the wet streets, the bottom of his jeans getting soaked along the way, he drove to where his grandmother had told him her house was located. It should have taken him fifteen minutes, but not knowing the city very well, it ended up taking him well over half an hour. Finally finding the place, he shut off the bike, propped his helmet on the handlebar, and walked up to the modest, white, one-story dwelling.

Empty flower boxes were in the windows and an empty bird feeder was perched right in front of a large bay window. Kai peeked through the window as he approached the house, but all the lights inside were off, and it was pretty dark. That was odd to Kai, since his dad had told him that Grandma didn't leave her house much anymore. His father had even considered putting her in a home, but Kai had convinced him that he would check in on her as often as he could while he was living here. Kai understood the importance of independence. And besides, from what he knew about her, his grandmother would never agree to move to a home anyway.

Just as he brought his hand up to knock on the front door, he heard someone say, "Are you looking for Millie, son?"

Turning, Kai saw a wrinkled old lady peeking her head out the front door of the house next to his grandmother's. "Um, excuse me?" he asked politely, his head still feeling a little slow.

The old woman stepped out of her home and shuffled onto her porch. Clutching a fuzzy blue robe around her body, she tilted her head at Kai. "Millie Harper. That's her house, but she's not there. Are you looking for her?"

Kai turned to the neighbor and dropped his hand from where he still had it raised to knock. "Uh, yeah. Do you know where she is?"

The old woman beamed, like she was bursting at the seams to finally be able to tell someone everything she knew. "Oh, it s been a busy morning. Ambulances, fire trucks. Very exciting!"

Kai's eyes widened, and he took a step toward the woman. If his grandmother had had a heart attack while he'd been sleeping off a hangover, he didn't think he would ever forgive himself for not taking a few minutes out of his day to come out and see her. "Is she okay?" he called out.

The woman frowned at seeing the shock on his face. "Yeah, she'll be all right, son. Don't fret. She fell, broke her hip."

Kai puffed out a quick breath as relief flooded through him. Immediately, concern rushed in to replace it. "Is she at the hospital then?" He looked around the neighborhood in despair. He could barely remember where his apartment was from here, let alone a hospital he'd never been to.

The woman coughed loudly, her small body racking with the movement. Concerned now for a different reason, Kai wondered if maybe he'd have to rush this curious little old lady to the hospital too. After a moment, her spasm passed. "Yeah, they drove her away. She's probably already been patched up."

Closing his eyes, Kai hoped everything had gone okay. When he reopened them, he looked around the streets again. "Um, I'm new here. Can you tell me where the hospital is?"

The old lady smiled. "Sure. How do you know Millie, boy?"

Kai walked across the lawns between the small houses. Coming up to the woman on her porch, he softly said, "She's my grandmother."

With a sympathetic smile, the woman put a gnarled hand on his arm when he was finally in front of her. "I'm sure she'll be fine, son."

Kai nodded in appreciation, and then listened carefully as she went over the confusing directions.

Twenty minutes later, he was approaching the hospital where his grandmother had been taken. The massive building loomed before him as he shut off his bike and pulled off his helmet. The woman's directions had been almost impossible to follow, relying more on landmarks than actual road signs, but eventually he'd deciphered where "the house with the purple door" and "the yard with the 'beware of dog' sign" were, and made it here. Slipping his helmet over the handle bar, Kai headed toward the entrance to the hospital; nervous energy was coursing through his veins.

After convincing the nurse at the front desk that he was family, he was given his grandmother's room number. Walking through the antiseptic-smelling halls, he considered if he should call his father or not. He wouldn't call his mom, since there was no love between his grandmother and her, but his dad would definitely want to know she was hurt; however, he could call him after he'd talked to her and found out how badly she'd been injured. He lightly knocked on door number 210.

A musical voice answered him. "Come in."

Kai smiled at hearing the perkiness in her voice; she sounded fine. His grandmother visibly brightened when he walked into the room. Upon seeing him, her frail hands came up to cover her mouth, and tears started forming in her warm brown eyes. "Kai, oh honey, you're here."

Kai shook his head as he sat on the edge of the bed. "Don't cry, Gran." Leaning over, he gave her a quick, careful hug. He didn't want to jostle her too much. "Are you all right? Are you in pain?"

She shook her head resting against the pillow as he pulled away. "I'm fine, honey." Then she lightly smacked his chest. "Why didn't you call me the moment you got into town? I would have picked you up from the airport, made you a big meal, and then helped you put away all the boxes that are probably littering some tiny little apartment."

He laughed as he studied the tiny woman; she looked so frail lying in that big bed, but she really wasn't. "That's why I didn't call, Gran. I wanted to get settled myself." His smile was warm and affectionate as he held her paper-thin hand. Although he wished they weren't reuniting in a place like this, it was nice to see her face-to-face again.

His grandmother didn't really look much like Kai, but that was to be expected. His mother was native Hawaiian, born and bred, and he'd inherited a lot of her exotic Polynesian looks. His skin was a deep golden brown, his features almost slightly Asian, with the exception that his eyes were a shade of bluish-green that he'd been told his entire life was remarkably beautiful. His eyes were the only thing that really set Kai apart from his mother. The woman before him now reminded Kai of his father—fair skin, dark eyes, and before it had turned silver with age, warm brown hair.

Patting his hand, his grandmother smiled. "Well, I'm glad you're here now."

Kai started to reply that he felt the same way when someone stepped through the open door. Hoping it was a doctor, so he could find out just how badly his grandmother was hurt, Kai automatically looked up. When his eyes locked onto the person standing there, shock froze him solid. He didn't think anything could have surprised him more than seeing her striding into his grandmother's hospital room.

Jessie. What the hell was she doing here?

She looked more put together than when he'd last seen her, early this morning. Her dark curly hair, loose around her shoulders before, was now pulled back into a cute ponytail that exposed the curve of her neck. Her chest, emphasized earlier in that short, sexy dress, was now covered in a light gray sweater that clung to every curve. And low on her hips—hips that he'd been grasping in ecstasy just a handful of hours ago—was a pair of perfectly faded blue jeans. He held his breath as he took in the oddity of seeing her in the same room as his healing grandmother. Maybe she worked here? Although, she certainly wasn't dressed like a nurse.

41

Jessie didn't notice him at first; her gaze was only focused on the old woman lying on the bed. "They only had apple and orange juice, I couldn't find any cranberry." She stopped talking about the juices she was holding when she finally spotted Kai sitting on the bed. Her mouth dropped just as far open, and her dark eyes widened to an almost comical level. Kai wanted to talk to her, wanted to ask her what she was doing here, but found he couldn't speak through his own shock.

As they wordlessly stared at each other, Kai's grandmother broke the sudden silence. "Oh good, I'm glad you're back, dear. Look who showed up!"

Jessie's face clouded over with what looked like anger, and Kai found himself instinctually retreating from her glare. She stepped up to the edge of the bed. "Are you following me?" she asked, her voice both heated and concerned.

Her feisty reaction loosened the hold on Kai's tongue. "Following you? You're the one following me. How did you know I would be here?"

She blinked in confusion. "What the hell are you talking about? I didn't know you would be here. And why the hell are you here?"

Kai's grandmother spoke up, "Little Miss, you watch your mouth. That is no way to talk to people." Her gray brows bunched as she looked between Kai and Jessie. "Have you two already met?" she asked.

Jessie's face flushed as she set the juices on the nightstand. "No, not really."

Kai scoffed at her comment, but didn't elaborate on his objection after receiving a scathing glare from Jessie. Not really? What they'd done had kind of been a little more than the average getting to know you. However Jessie knew his grandmother, though, she obviously didn't want to share intimate details of their night together with her, any more than he wanted to share those facts with her. There were just some things his grandmother didn't need to know.

Gran grinned as she simultaneously squeezed his hand and patted Jessie's arm. "Well, I'm glad you're getting a chance to officially meet then. You two should get along pretty well, since you're about the same age."

Confused, Kai looked over at Jessie and indicated his grandmother with a nod of his head. "How do you know her?" he asked. His eyes, locked on hers, gauged her reaction carefully.

Jessie stared into his eyes for a long moment, like she'd gotten lost in them. He shifted his head to return her attention to his question, and looking a little embarrassed, she shook her head and straightened to her full height; the movement subtly highlighted her chest, and Kai found himself a little lost too. He couldn't help but remember his lips on that chest.

Her words, punctuated by the acerbic tone of her voice, returned his attention to her face. "Me? I'm sure I've known her a lot longer than you. How do *you* know her?"

Kai raised a disbelieving eyebrow. "You've known her longer? I highly doubt that."

Gran laughed, then patted them again. Smiling at Jessie, her eyes oddly warm and loving, his grandmother said, "Technically, he's right, dear."

They both looked over at her. The curiosity was nearly killing Kai at this point. Was she a family friend? Maybe that nosey neighbor's granddaughter? Maybe she'd found his grandmother and had called the ambulance? His chest

warmed at the thought of Jessie being his grandmother's sav-
ior, and a smile graced his lips.

His grandmother shifted her eyes back to Kai. Nodding
her head at Jessie, she warmly told him, "Jessica Marie was
born two months after you, Kai."

Kai felt his face draining of blood as he slowly turned to
stare at Jessie. *Jessica Marie.* He knew that name. But that
couldn't seriously be the woman he was staring at. Jessie, the
person he'd just had incredible sex with last night, could *not*
be Jessica Marie. No, she had to be someone else, anyone else,
other than... Kai's stomach rose as he gaped at her. No, she
couldn't be...

Jessie stared back at him, frowning. She hadn't made the
connection yet, or else she wouldn't still look confused. Kai
put a firm hand on his stomach, suddenly afraid he has going
to heave whatever alcohol was still in there. "Jessica Marie?
Oh God," he muttered. "Oh...God..."

He watched Jessie twist her face in irritation. She clearly
didn't like that he knew something she didn't. But with what
he knew, he was positive she would prefer ignorance. As his
throat tightened and his stomach twisted, he knew that he
would certainly prefer to go back to ten minutes ago, when his
one-night stand had been a pleasant memory.

Not having heard his low mutters, his grandmother
smiled brightly at Jessie, like nothing at all was wrong with
this picture. "Jessica, my dear, this is the boy I told you was
coming up, to live here with us in Denver." She turned her
bright smile to him. "And all the way from Hawaii too."

Jessie still looked confused, like she had no idea what the
old woman was talking about. She wouldn't stay confused for
very long. Feeling ill and still about to be sick, Kai lifted his

eyes to hers, right as his grandmother finished with her intro-
ductions. "This is Kai Harper, dear…your cousin."

3

What's in a Name?

J essie couldn't breathe, couldn't move. She was positive that the instant she did, the very second she physically reacted, what she'd just heard would slam into her like a wrecking ball, knocking her to the ground. So long as she just stood still, she'd be fine…just fine.

Except everything wasn't fine. She'd slept with…

Unwilling to let her thoughts complete that sentence, Jessie kept her gaze glued on Kai. He seemed ill, like he'd accepted the truth and it sickened him. Jessie couldn't believe it. She refused to. Someone had made a mistake. A horrible, horrible mistake.

A machine humming in the room was the only sound, but even that was too much. Jessie shook her head, and the movement caused the floodgates of pain and remorse to begin to crack open. She took a step back, in retreat. "No, no that's not possible."

Jessie's grandmother was clearly confused by her reaction, but Kai flinched as if her words had stung him.

"I know you haven't seen him much...or maybe ever, but he *is* your cousin," her grandmother stated. "My oldest son, Nate, is his father." Hearing it said so plainly, so surely, sent a knot of disgust racing up Jessie's throat. She clamped her hands over her mouth to hold it in. *No...*

Jessie's eyes watered as she looked from her grandmother to Kai. How could this have happened? Kai hung his head, like he was wondering the same thing. Jessie heard her grandmother ask her if she was feeling all right, and she violently shook her head. No, she wasn't all right. She might never be all right again. She felt like she was going to be sick or start sobbing. Maybe both. But she couldn't do it here; her grandmother wouldn't understand...and she didn't want her to. Ever.

Like he could read her mind, Kai stood and said, "We need to speak outside for a moment, Grandma. We'll be back in a minute, okay?" He smiled, but like Jessie, he looked ill. The words he'd just said echoed in Jessie's head as she watched him lean down and place a kiss on the old woman's cheek. *Grandma. She's his grandma. She's* my *grandma.*

As horror filled her to the breaking point, Jessie began murmuring, "Oh my God, oh my God, oh my God..." She was about to lose it, about to have a complete and total meltdown in front of her grandmother. Who would then ask why, and wouldn't let go until she knew the truth. Oh God...

Kai grabbed her elbow, told her, "Not here," then pulled her out the open door. Sadly, his touch sent a flicker of excitement through her, until she remembered why it shouldn't. With a wave of nausea, she shoved the feeling aside. Once they were a ways down the hall, out of their grandmother's earshot, Kai released her arm. Jessie immediately hunched over. Resting her hands on her thighs, she inhaled and exhaled deep breaths through her nose. She was going to be sick, her stomach was going to come right up her throat and spill onto the floor. She'd just had the most amazing sex she'd ever experienced...with her cousin—her incredibly hot cousin, who was staring down the hallway of the hospital, looking just as sick as she.

Thinking back over her reaction to the news in her grandmother's room, Jessie couldn't help but wonder if the older woman suspected something. How could Jessie ever explain the truth to her if she did somehow find out? God, she couldn't even explain it to herself.

Looking up at Kai, she managed to squeak out, "We're... related?"

Kai's face contorted in an expression of disgust and confusion that Jessie understood all too well. "It would seem so..." His hand clamped over his stomach and Jessie was certain he felt the same illness she did. How could they not have known they were related? True, she'd never met Kai before, but she'd seen pictures and she'd heard of him often enough. Grandma had several children, and each one of them had had numerous children. Except for Uncle Nate. He and his wife had struggled to conceive, and had only had one child before their marriage ended. Kai.

As Jessie straightened, her fingers clutched the light fabric of her sweater. She watched Kai's eyes flash down her body, then immediately dart away; his face paled. Crossing her arms, Jessie tried to hide as much of her curves as she could. While she'd enjoyed his attention before, she definitely didn't want him looking at her that way now. Honestly, she wasn't sure how she wanted him to look at her. Putting the cousin

48

aspect aside for the moment…as difficult as that was…Jessie hadn't been expecting to see him today. Really, she'd thought she'd probably never see him again. She'd accidentally run out of there without giving him her number.

When Jessie had been dragged away from his place this morning, it had been frustrating; she'd wanted to stay longer. But she knew Harmony was just concerned for her safety. And Harmony would have called her father, too, if she'd felt the need. Jessie hadn't wanted that sort of trouble on her hands, so she'd grudgingly left his side.

Once home with her friends, she'd successfully avoided any of their questions by faking that she'd passed out. She'd even slept on the couch to sell her act. Jessie just hadn't wanted to talk about him yet. And truthfully, she hadn't had a whole lot to say. He'd been amazing, and their connection had been intense, but she hadn't known anything about him; she hadn't even remembered his name, a fact that still embarrassed her. But Jessie had never been that drunk before, and she hoped she was never that drunk again.

After her thunderous hangover had subsided, Jessie had gone out to visit her grandma, the same as she did most Saturday mornings. When she'd arrived, she'd been greeted by a swarm of rescue vehicles and chaos. Grams had fallen while getting the mail, and her kind neighbor had called in help for her. Jessie had kicked herself the entire drive out to the hospital that she hadn't been there. If she hadn't been so slow that morning, she wouldn't have been an hour late, and her grams wouldn't have gotten hurt.

Jessie had done all that she could to make her grandmother comfortable at the hospital; luckily, she'd only fractured her hip, and not broken it. Coming back into the room and seeing her fling from the previous night causally sitting with her grandmother had freaked her out. She was so sure he'd been stalking her. She'd heard of that happening with girls. Guys got obsessed and couldn't let go. But the truth of who he was and why he'd been cuddling with a frail old woman was so much worse...

Watching Kai now, seeing the conflict swirling through his beautiful face, Jessie could still feel a trace of residual attraction. She couldn't help it. He had perfect skin, a charming smile, amazing hair, and a sculpted physique. And then there were his eyes...so remarkable that she couldn't even look at them anymore.

As if sensing her thoughts, Kai suddenly muttered, "I need a drink."

Plagued by memories, Jessie frowned at him. "Isn't that what got us into this mess in the first place?"

He ran a hand through his hair as he looked her over. "Do you want to go for a walk?"

Jessie nodded automatically, even though she wasn't sure if that was what she wanted or not. A part of her wanted to go back to her grandmother's room and hide under the blankets with her, like she used to when she was five. Another part of her still wanted to hide under the covers with Kai. She immediately hated that part of herself.

He started walking, not looking to see if she was following. Shaking her head, she hurried to catch up. Once she did, he glanced her way. "I can't believe this. I just can't believe this..." His hand touched his stomach again.

Jessie let out a shaky breath as his eyes flicked over her face. "I can't either. I mean...what are the odds that we would...?" As they walked down the hall, nurses and patients scooting around them, Jessie truly debated that question. Of all the cities, of all the clubs, of all the nights she'd let herself go, she'd run into her cousin…who, until recently, had lived his entire life on an island she'd never even been to. Crazy. Irritated at the universe, she glared at him. "Why didn't you recognize me? You knew I lived here?"

As they walked through a set of double doors into the main artery of the hospital, Kai's expression turned incredulous. "I haven't seen a picture of you in years. And the last one I did see, I think you were twelve." He flung his hand out at her body. "You certainly didn't look like this." His eyes lingered on her hips for a moment, before quickly pulling away.

Jessie flushed and tried to shield herself as they walked down to the first floor. "Well, you could have recognized my name. I did give it to you."

He stopped walking. "You're joking, right?" She was about to speak when he added, "They all call you Jessica Marie. You introduced yourself as Jessie. How was I supposed to make *that* leap?"

Putting her hands on her hips, Jessie watched Kai's face as he struggled to keep his gaze above her neck. Irritated at his very good point, she took a step toward him. "You're the one who came here, a city where you knew I lived. You should have been looking out for me."

With a tight jaw, he cocked his head and said, "I wasn't expecting you to throw yourself at me." Her eyes widened and as her mouth dropped open, she considered storming off. His next comment firmly ground her though. "Besides, Gran had nine kids, and they all had a crap load of kids. Do you have any idea how many cousins I have?"

Annoyed again at his good point, Jessie snapped, "Yes! I get the yearly Christmas letter too!"

Kai cringed, but recovered quickly. When he spoke again, irritation was thick in his voice too. "Why didn't you recognize *my* name? How many Kais have you heard of around here?"

Jessie's hands dropped to her side as she sputtered on something intelligent to say. He made a very good argument. Several of them. But she had thought he was still thousands of miles away. She hadn't expected him to show up at April's favorite club, looking all hot and lonely. Plus, she'd sort of forgotten his name…right after he'd said it.

Seeing that she was at a loss for words, Kai smirked. "You didn't remember my name, did you?" Stepping back, Jessie tried to look defiant and offended. He saw right through it, and with amusement in his eyes, he crossed his arms over his chest. The movement reminded Jessie of his tattoo; horribly enough, she wanted to see it again. "Admit it. Immediately after you commented on my eyes, you forgot my name, didn't you?"

Jessie really hated how that sounded. She was generally very good with names, but she'd had quite a few drinks at that point in the evening, and barely remembered. Although she thought she faintly recalled the stupid rhyme he was referring to. "I was a little…out of sorts."

His crooked grin turned disturbingly sexy. "*You* were wasted."

Her hands returned to her hips. "And you were supposed to be on a tiny island in the middle of nowhere, not in my backyard." She let out a defeated sigh. "Yes, I didn't remember your name. But Grams didn't know exactly when you were coming, and I wasn't expecting to come across you at a club in my city."

He only stared at her with his eyebrow still cocked. How damn attractive that was made Jessie inwardly swoon, even as her stomach churned. With a groan, she grudgingly added, "Yes, I was wasted, okay. I've been having a bad streak lately." A bad streak that had somehow shifted into an *atrocious* streak.

Relaxing his arms, Kai started walking down the hallway again. Stopping at a vending machine, he plopped in some quarters, and they watched in silence as the machine spit out some black liquid that vaguely resembled coffee. When it shut off, Kai handed her the cup and put in some more quarters. Jessie found her eyes straying to his hips, and her mind flashed back to memories she really shouldn't be revisiting. When he turned to face her, Jessie was still staring at his hips. She flushed and swiftly raised her eyes to his. Being caught staring at her cousin's privates was not helping the situation any.

Giving her a sympathetic expression, Kai indicated a door leading to an outdoor courtyard. Jessie turned, grateful for the excuse to stop looking at him for a moment. She inhaled a deep breath as she stepped into the refreshing, cool air. Gray, heavy clouds trudged across the sky, but it was wasn't pouring yet. The benches spaced along the pathway were wet with small puddles of rain from last night's storm. It had been absolutely dumping when she'd left Kai's apartment. The entire ride home she'd wished she was still at his place, wrapped in his sheets with his warm body next to hers. Now, as he stood beside her, his arm brushing against hers, she was torn between still wanting that scenario, and being revolted by it.

With his head down, Kai nodded over to a bench quaintly nestled under a tall tree. Its leaves having long ago fallen to the ground, the bare branches stretched up into the sky like skeletal fingers. The hospital had placed the bench at the very edge of the cracked concrete, and the berm directly behind it was bursting with clumps of green shrubbery. Jessie imagined that in the spring, it was probably beautiful out here. Maybe that helped ease the mind of frazzled family members, waiting on the outcome of their loved ones' surgeries. She wished it had the same effect on her current condition; her mind was spinning in endless circles.

Kai wiped the droplets off the bench with his free hand, the extra water dripping from his skin. He sat on the edge and brushed the residual moisture on his thigh before motioning for her to sit beside him. She exhaled softly as she sat; their hips just touched on the small seat.

Kai flicked a glance at her then took a sip of his drink. Jessie did the same. As the warm coffee soothed her throat, the feeling of horror in her stomach started to shift into something tragic. She could like this man. A lot. Her night with him had been amazing. But, even if they were the exact perfect match, and last night had been some fated meeting to bring them together, it couldn't happen. They were related. They shared the same gene pool. Being with him in that way was wrong, taboo. Her friends would be disgusted. Her family would disown her...and him. They'd lose everyone. And she wasn't sure, but there were probably laws somewhere, preventing and punishing the very thing that they'd done last night. Marriage was certainly out. As were children. That thought made her stomach roil again. God, no, their genes were too similar to ever risk children.

She sputtered on the sip of coffee she'd just taken, and her hand flew to her aching gut. She'd suddenly remembered the forgotten condom in her purse last night. While she was still on the pill and pregnancy wasn't an issue, it brought that *This is too gross to be true* feeling right back to her.

Kai stopped drinking and stared at her as she choked on her awful vending machine coffee. "What?" he whispered.

With tears of frustration and revulsion in her eyes, she immediately told him, "A part of you is still inside me." Embarrassment hit her after she said it, but it *was* what was churning her stomach at the moment. He had released inside of her. A part of her cousin was currently swimming through her body. Oh God…

Kai's face turned so pale, Jessie thought he might be light-headed. Closing his marvelous eyes, he inhaled a long breath. "Jesus…" Without opening his eyes, he whispered, "Could you get pregnant?"

She shook her head, but he couldn't see it, since his eyes were still shut. So he would know they were okay in that sense, she verbally added, "No, I take the pill, but it's still grossing me out."

Kai finally peeked his eyes opened and looked at her. "I'm so sorry. I don't usually… Things like last night aren't common for me. But, we didn't know, Jessie. We didn't know."

With a heavy exhale, Jessie let her hand drop to her lap. "Things like that don't happen to me either. I just… You were so…" She swallowed and shook her head. "This is so messed up."

Looking pensive, Kai ran his thumb around the edge of his coffee cup. Jessie tried to block out the knowledge of the other places that thumb had been recently. Staring down at the thick, blackness inside his cup, he again said, "We didn't know."

They sat in silence for a few moments, and then he lifted his gaze. "You know, it's not all that crazy." He shrugged at seeing Jessie's confused expression. "In some cultures, cousins are arranged to be married. Didn't Jerry Lee Lewis marry his cousin?"

She wrinkled her nose. "We have the *same* last name. Sorry, that doesn't make me feel any better. And Jerry Lee Lewis? Ew."

Kai laughed, just once, and then released another melancholy breath. "I'm just trying to make this not seem so..."

"Awful," Jessie whispered.

He shook his head, his eyes trailing over her face. "Yeah, awful."

They finished their bland cups of coffee, and then Jessie started picking at her cup. Not sure what to feel right now, she alternated between disgust, sadness, desire, and curiosity. Feeling that the last emotion was the one she could entertain the most at the moment, she looked over to see Kai also tearing apart his cup. Their similar habit made her smile. "So... Hawaii? I hear it's nice."

"Yeah, it can be," he said with a smile.

Jessie shook her head, trying not to notice the charm in his boyish grin. "I can't imagine why you'd come to Colorado. If I lived in paradise, I'd never leave."

His smile widened as he leaned back on the bench. "Well, once you've gone through a couple rainy seasons, you get a different opinion of island life." He shrugged. "I guess you just get used to the beauty, once you've lived in it your whole life.

Jessie bit her lip, and for just a second she let herself think that she would never get used to *his* island beauty. Shaking her head to clear the troubling thought, she said, "Well, I've always wanted to go there." She laughed. "I used to try and get my parents to visit yours every summer when I was younger. I wanted to learn how to surf so badly. I used to practice on the lawn."

Kai laughed, but abruptly stopped when what she'd said sunk in. Parents. Family. Cousins. Jessie would have given anything to visit Kai as a kid, and that made everything they'd done last night seem that much weirder. Jessie cleared her throat. Would every topic be awkward? "Well, I hope you're not too disappointed, living here."

Kai stared at her in silence for a few seconds. When he spoke again, his voice was soft and full of meaning. "So far, it's been pretty incredible." He reached up and tucked a loose curl behind her ear. A lump formed in Jessie's throat, and her eyes began to glisten as the back of his knuckle lingered on her cheek. Why did she have to be related to him?

Dropping his hand from her skin, Kai returned his gaze to his coffee. Surprisingly, Jessie instantly missed the contact. Voice soft, he told her, "Maybe it's because I grew up on a beach, but I've always wanted to ski." He looked up at her, and Jessie had to blink several times to clear her eyes. "Maybe you could teach me?"

She wasn't sure how she would be able to handle spending that much intimate time with him, but she nodded anyway. They were family, and it was the least she could do for him. "Yeah, of course." Another moment of silence passed between them, but there was a comfortable companionship in the silence this time. If they weren't who they were, their personalities would have been very well matched; they probably would have made an amazing couple. But as fate would have it, they *were* who they were, and any companionship between them had to be purely platonic.

Grumbling in her head over how unfair the universe was, Jessie crumpled the empty cup in her hand. "What do we do now, Kai?"

He reached over for her ruined cup. "We go see how our grandmother is doing. I continue getting my place together, and getting ready for my new job. And you...you go back to your life." He gave her a serious look. "And we forget this ever happened, and never tell *anyone* about it."

Jessie's eyes misted again. He made it sound so easy, but she knew it wasn't. "Yeah...no one." There was no one she could tell anyway. Or no one she *wanted* to tell at any rate.

Kai's gaze flicked over her face as he nodded. His eyes locked on hers, and he leaned in slightly. Jessie leaned in as well. Without even thinking about it, they had considerably closed the distance between their faces, and Jessie found herself lost in the perfect ocean of his eyes. Kai leaned in just a fraction more, and her lips parted as her breath increased; her heart started pounding. Even knowing what she did, her body still reacted to him. Biting her lip, she struggled to remember that he was family, and this was wrong. Very, very wrong. Kai paused, and his eyes narrowed, like he was struggling to remember that too.

This was going to be harder than they thought.

Expression intent, Kai shifted his movement and gave her a light peck on the cheek. Even still, Jessie found herself closing her eyes at the tender touch; she only reopened them when he pulled away. He quickly shifted to stare at the cracks in the worn concrete at their feet. He seemed just as dazed as she. Jessie hated that the only guy she'd ever been able to so physically effect was a blood relative. Figured.

Kai exhaled slowly, then stood up and glanced back at her still sitting on the bench. "We should get back to Gran. I told my dad I'd keep an eye on her." His face suddenly turned guilty, like he felt that he'd failed in his duty since she'd gotten hurt. Jessie smiled as she stood with him; he seemed to have the same sense of responsibility for their grandmother that she did.

He watched her rise, then they headed back into the hospital together. A comfortable silence fell around them as they made their way to the second floor. Jessie watched his back as she followed a step behind. Images of his broad shoulders flooded her head, and she had to shift her gaze to his shoes to redirect her thoughts. Remembering what he'd said about getting his place together, Jessie recalled the piles and piles of boxes she'd seen in his tiny apartment. Then she remembered him sweetly telling her that she could stay if she wanted, right as she'd been hurrying to leave.

A soft, wistful noise escaped her at the memory, and Kai turned his gaze her way; concern darkened his beautiful face. "What?" he cautiously asked. By his wary expression, he clearly thought she was going to break down at any moment. He also seemed unsure about what he would do if she did. His nervousness made her laugh, and as they approached the stairs to the second floor, his cute look shifted to a disgruntled one. "What?" he asked again, less cautiously.

Jessie shook her head, her curly ponytail swishing back and forth. "Nothing, you're just...nothing." Knowing she couldn't call her cousin adorable, not under these circumstances, she sighed and let it go. Kai just looked confused by her answer, so she softly explained with, "I was just thinking about what a mess your place was. Do you want some help arranging it?"

He frowned at her summation of his home, but then he smiled. Studying the ground for a moment, he murmured, "Yeah, not the coolest spread to bring a girl back to." Flinching, he looked up at her; he seemed worried about how she would respond to a clear reference to their steamy encounter.

Jessie paused on the steps. Kai took one more, then stopped and looked back at her. A small sigh escaped him as their eyes locked. Jessie knew that they could easily destroy any connection they had, familial or otherwise, if they let this guilt they felt consume them. Even though her stomach was still clenching with horror, she decided that he was right when he'd said that they hadn't known, and they couldn't be faulted for knowledge they hadn't had. Not knowing any other way to dissolve the building tension, and wanting that comfortable feeling to return, Jessie decided to try some lighthearted humor. Giving him a crooked smile, she coyly said, "Well, it worked. You got me."

While Kai gaped at her, shocked, Jessie smiled and walked past him up the stairs. Her heart was hammering as she listened for his reaction. Then she heard him chuckle and mutter, "Well, all right then." Smiling, she looked down in relief. He was going to try and not let this weirdness enter their relationship either. Good.

Once they both got to the top step, they were smiling at each other. Now that Jessie was looking for it, she thought she could spot some similarity to her in the bridge of his nose, the fullness of his lips. It was fleeting though, and she really could have been seeing something simply because she was told to see it; like a shape in the clouds, because someone let you know it was there. In all honesty, his looks were unlike anything she'd ever seen before. A beautiful blending of genetics that made him his own person, inside and outside.

When they got back to their grandmother's room, she was staring at the ceiling, seemingly lost in thought. Jessie hoped she wasn't thinking about her odd, dramatic exit. She really should have handled that better, but finding out she'd slept with a relative wasn't exactly something that happened to her every day. There was no way she could have possibly been prepared for that shock.

Gram's contemplative expression changed when she finally noticed that Kai and Jessie had reentered the room. She gave them both bright smiles as she patted the bed. "You two all right?"

Kai sat on the edge of the mattress while Jessie sat in a nearby chair. Gently folding his fingers over the old woman's hand, he warmly said, "We're fine, Gran. But how are you? Are you feeling okay? Do you need anything?"

Their grandmother laughed as she patted his hand. "I'm fine, dear. They're taking good care of me here. I'll think they'll keep me for a few days, just to watch over me." She grunted in annoyance and rolled her eyes. "It's completely unnecessary. I could hop on a horse if I needed to. I could swing dance, if I had a good partner." She raised a suggestive eyebrow at Kai, clearly asking him if he'd consider it.

He laughed at her implied request, and the sound was warm, light, and full of love. "Maybe when you're better, Gran." Jessie could easily see him putting up with that possible humiliation for Grams. It was a sweet thought, and a painful one too; she remembered all too well what it was like to dance with him.

Jessie let out a soft laugh, but it quickly turned into a wistful sigh. Her grandmother gave her an odd glance, and Jessie immediately pushed away that regret, and replaced it with another one. Placing her hand on Grams's arm, she softly said, "I'm so sorry I was late this morning."

Kai looked equally remorseful. "Yeah, and I'm sorry I didn't visit sooner. I was running a little slow this morning." He looked at Jessie. Her stomach clenched, but she gave him a soft smile. *They could get through this.*

Grams studied the two of them for a moment, then shook her head. "I appreciate the sentiment, but I'm a grown woman. I don't need the two of you fretting over me, like I'm some invalid. I slipped. Happens every day. Probably happens to the two of you on occasion." Jessie had to bite her lip at that. *If she only knew.* But no, she couldn't ever know. No one could. While Jessie schooled her features, her grandmother pursed her thin lips and told them, "I don't mind you both coming to visit me, but I can take care of myself."

With a shake of his head, Kai gave her a warm smile, then leaned forward and kissed her head. "All right, Gran."

The display of affection made Jessie softly sigh. He was charming, caring, thoughtful, and hot. It really wasn't fair. But few things were, and dwelling on what she couldn't have wouldn't help her. Returning her attention to her grandmother, Jessie smiled and said, "Okay, Grams. What *can* we do for you then?"

Grams eyed the two of them oddly for a moment, and Jessie thought she saw some hidden knowledge in the woman's warm brown eyes. It was gone before she could be sure though. Lips twisting into a smile, she patted Jessie's hand and told her, "Jessica Marie, my dear, why don't you and Kai go through my place and get rid of that old furniture for me. I was going to have the church come take it, but as Kai probably needs some things, maybe he could take it for me?"

Kai immediately started shaking his head. "Oh, Gran, no, you don't have to —"

Her grandmother cut him off with a swift shake of her head. "Nonsense. You must need something. Do you even have a bed yet?"

Kai's tan face lost a little color as his eyes locked onto Jessie's. *Oh God...did he ever.* Jessie worked hard to keep the multitude of emotions battering her from showing on her face. It was difficult. One simple question had bombarded her with an image of Kai that she shouldn't have — that she couldn't have. She needed to erase that night; she needed to forget. But how?

A deathly quiet fell over the room. Jessie was afraid to breathe, lest she say or do the wrong thing. Luckily, Grams took their silence as an admission that Kai needed help. Turning her attention to Jessie, she matter-of-factly stated, "Clean out the spare bedroom. I have no need for anything in there right now."

Jessie nodded. "Okay, Grandma." Anything to get out of here, to get away from the memories plaguing her.

Kai glanced down before looking over at Jessie. His face was still pale, but he managed a small smile. "I guess I could use your help after all."

4

So Wrong, Yet So Right

After making sure she truly was going to be fine, Kai and Jessie left their grandmother and headed outside. When Jessie spotted Kai's motorcycle, she gave him an amused smile. "You're not going to be able to move much with that," she stated.

Knowing she was right, Kai frowned. "Yeah...I really hadn't expected to be moving furniture anytime soon."

Jessie laughed, and Kai found that he really loved the sound. "Well, good thing for you I have a truck. I'll follow you home, then we'll go to Grandma's."

Kai nodded in agreement and hopped on his bike. He felt a little guilty for taking Gran's stuff, but he knew her well enough to know that if he didn't take it, she'd just show up on his doorstep with some burly men she'd hired to haul it for her. At least this way, he was saving her the expense of hiring movers.

Jessie walked over to her truck parked a few spaces away, then they drove back to his place. After Kai pulled into the garage, he shut off his bike and hooked his helmet over the handlebars. Jessie pulled up next to him in her little Ford Ranger. He would have expected her to pick a girly color, turquoise or purple or something, but it was solid black.

She was biting her lip as she watched him swing his leg over the seat. Kai wondered what she was thinking about. If she still felt ill about the whole thing. He did. Sort of. He was trying to let that nauseous feeling go; it wasn't their fault. But when he thought about the intimate moment they'd shared, it did gross him out some. It also turned him on a little. It had been the most amazing sexual experience he'd ever had. A part of him wanted to have it again, even knowing what he knew. But that couldn't happen, and he was going to have to accept that.

With a quick sigh, Kai walked around to the passenger's side of Jessie's truck and got in. As she drove away, he rubbed his hands together, warming them with the hot air blowing from the heater.

Cocking an eyebrow at him, Jessie asked, "Is it cold here to you?"

Looking over at her, Kai smiled. "Well, I'm wearing two shirts under this jacket and wool socks." Grinning wider, he laughed. "I even considered doubling up the underwear."

Jessie flushed as she glanced at his jeans, and Kai instantly thought that maybe he shouldn't say anything that could be perceived as suggestive. That might hamper their conversations quite a bit, since almost everything could be made suggestive. Like his clueless Grandma asking him if he had a bed yet. Jesus.

Jessie's dark eyes darted to his ankles before returning to the road; the bottom of his pants were still wet from the water splashing on them as he'd driven around town. Definitely not helping him warm up. "So...you bought a bike?" she asked, a tight smile on her lips.

Kai smiled as studied her. He liked her sober, playful personality just as much as her drunken aggressiveness. "I know, kind of dumb, but, I heard it only rains 300 days out of the year here, so I thought my odds were pretty good. So far, it's dumped on me every day. Guess my odds are shit." Laughing, he looked out the window. "But really, the weather doesn't matter. I'm a bike guy." Amused at his own comment, he wondered what he would do when the roads got slick. He'd never driven on snow before. He'd have to invest in some studded tires...and a snowsuit.

Jessie chuckled. "Well, at least you look hot on it." She immediately stopped laughing and looked over at him. He shook his head. Looked like they would both have to work on not saying suggestive things.

"Um...thanks." He smiled, then sighed. *Would they ever be able to forget?* They drove the rest of the way in silence.

Jessie backed into Gran's driveway once they got to her house. Stepping out of the truck, Kai noticed the helpful old lady next door peeking through her window. He thought there probably wasn't much that happened in the neighborhood that the woman didn't know about.

Following Jessie inside, Kai smiled as he took in his grandmother's home. It was warm and welcoming, painted in a cheery yellow with pictures and mementoes of family taking up almost every available space. Kai noticed a few pictures of himself, from when he was much younger. He remembered Gran taking those pictures, remembered the bright woman behind the lens, snapping away at everything, like she could store her memories away in each click. Seeing the green foliage of home in the background brought on a twang of homesickness, and he thought maybe his grandmother was on to something.

As Jessie turned to walk down a short hallway, he noticed a multitude of her pictures throughout the home. Having lived here with Gran for so long, she'd been around a lot more, and that was evident in the sheer volume of photographs. Kai saw bits of Jessie's entire life splashed along bookcases, mantels, and end tables. Proms, birthdays, ski trips…it was all around the room for him to see. A brutal reminder of the chasm between them.

Closing his eyes to block out the sudden rush of sadness, Kai twisted to follow Jessie down the hallway. He walked into the room where he could hear her shifting things around, and was instantly struck with a stale, musty odor. Gran was right; she rarely used this room.

Jessie had grabbed a box from somewhere and was placing photos inside it. Glancing up at him, she pointed across the hall. "There are some boxes in Grams's room. Let's pack up her stuff so we can move the furniture."

Nodding, Kai looked around at all the mementoes, knickknacks, and tchotchkes. This room was sort of a shrine to collectibles, each one with their own small doily. Cleaning it out was going to take some time. Kai found a box, then rejoined Jessie. She was carefully placing several horse figurines into the box, on top of the photos. Noticing that one of the pictures was of his dad, Kai knelt down beside Jessie and shook his head. "This is so weird. You're placing ponies on top of my dad's head. That is something I would not have imagined happening yesterday."

Jessie paused in her packing and glanced up at him. He couldn't quite read the emotion on her face. Finally, she glanced down at the box she was packing and murmured, "Uncle Nate is your dad. That's still so weird…"

He tilted his head as he stared at her. Weird was an understatement. "Yeah, Nate is my dad…"

Shaking her head, Jessie sighed and resumed her packing. "Seeing pictures of him, hearing you talk about him, it just makes all of this that much more…real." She glanced at him as he started packing objects into his box.

Kai sighed in agreement with her. Yes, it was all getting horrifyingly real.

They worked in silence for a while, organizing the surprisingly packed room, then Jessie cleared her throat. "So, what part of Hawaii are you from?" She glanced his way. "I don't remember."

Kai was frowning as he placed a photo of a blonde relative he didn't know into the box. One of the downsides of being so far away was that he hadn't met very many members of his family. He had never imagined that would be a problem until last night. Not letting his recurring sadness enter into his voice, he answered Jessie, "Kukuihaele." He bit the inside of his cheek to keep himself from smiling as she processed the odd-sounding name. Well, odd for someone who wasn't used to Hawaiian names. There were several that were odder.

She scrunched her brow as she stared at him, her dark eyes curious and confused. It was pretty adorable on her, and his repressed smile broke free. "Kuk…u…huh?"

A laugh escaped with his smile, and he shook his head as he stuffed a fragile doll into the box; it looked to be about a hundred years old. "Kukuihaele. It's on the big island. It's pretty remote, not quite as touristy as some places in Hawaii." With a smile, Jessie nodded and resumed packing. Feeling a need to let her know something more personal about him, he softly continued, "My mom's home is near the beach. I used to play in the surf all day and fall asleep every night to the sounds of waves crashing. My dad's place is farther inland, and when I stayed with him, we used to go horseback riding every night. We'd stay out until we could barely make out the trails, but the horses knew them so well, I was never afraid."

His mind took him back to both locations, and he let himself get lost in the fond memories. When the past faded back to the present, Kai looked over at Jessie. She was sitting back on her heels, watching him. Her lips were curved into a soft smile, and he had the overwhelming urge to lean over and touch those lips again. Remembering the feel of them firmly wrapped around him made the smile instantly fall from his face. He needed to let last night go. It was wrong to think about it.

Clearing his mind, Kai started harshly shoving objects into the box. He heard Jessie sigh as she continued her own packing. "Anyway, there's an estuarine research reserve nearby where my parents both work. It's what got me into studying the environment."

Standing up to put her full box in a corner, Jessie made a surprised noise. "Oh, I didn't know that's what you did."

Smiling, Kai closed up his own full box. "Yeah, I wouldn't go so far as to call myself an environmentalist, but I do have a certain respect for where we live, and would like to find a way so that we could all be on Earth…without choking the life out of it." He gave her a crooked grin, and Jessie laughed. Such a beautiful sound.

Standing, Kai handed her the box. She placed it on top of hers, and he couldn't help but note that they lined up perfectly. Just like they might...in another life. Hands on her hips, Jessie gave him a friendly grin. "So, instead of staying to study a tropical island, you chose to study...Colorado?"

Her never-ending disbelief that he would leave what she considered paradise made him laugh. Shaking his head, he said, "The Earth is the Earth, no matter where you go." She responded by rolling her eyes. Shrugging, he added, "My parents focus more on protecting the coastal areas, but I wanted a broader approach. My father understood that and got me a job here, with a friend of his who used to work with him." Kai pointed to the mountain ranges. "He runs a small research team near the base of The Rockies."

Jessie's grin was contagious. "In the mountains?" Kai nodded, confused by her obvious glee. With a playful wink, she told him, "You better get to work on those ski lessons, water boy."

Kai laughed as they both went to get more boxes. That might not be a bad idea, so long as she was the instructor. But no, that probably *was* a bad idea.

Not too much later, they had all of Gran's treasures neatly boxed in a corner. With only her bare furniture left, they began hauling things out to Jessie's truck. The more time he spent with her, the fonder Kai became of his cousin. They had a similar sense of humor and easygoing personalities. It gave Kai a wistful ache to know that if things were different, she would be such an easy girl for him to date. Jessie didn't complain, didn't gab on and on about herself, didn't make fun of the fact that he obviously didn't have much in the way of possessions, and she laughed at all his stupid jokes. Yeah, if only that one pesky little fact of being related could be removed, he would ask her out on a proper date in a heartbeat.

Kai kept his head down as he warmed his hands over her heater on the ride home. Wishful thinking wasn't going to get him anywhere. He needed to stop thinking about her as an option. She wasn't.

"You okay?" she quietly asked.

Peeking over at Jessie, he saw her worrying her lip. Smiling for her benefit, he whispered, "I'm great, Jessie. Thank you for helping me today."

Her face relaxing, she smiled and placed a hand over his. The contact instantly sent a shock through him, and not just because her hand was so much warmer than his. She apparently felt the spark too, because she immediately pulled her hand away. Keeping her eyes intently focused on the road, she said, "No problem, Kai. It's the least I could do…for family."

When they got back to his place, Kai watched Jessie let out a long exhale as her eyes swept the room. He supposed she was remembering the last time she was here. It seemed a little shocking to him that it had only been several hours ago; it felt like a lifetime ago. Throwing his keys on the counter, Kai ran a hand through his hair. "I suppose we should move my crap out of the way."

Jessie let out a nervous laugh as she followed him into the main room. He heard her roughly swallow when she saw the mattress in the middle of the wall. Lifting it up, Kai shoved it against the wall; he didn't want the reminder either. It blew his mind that just this morning he had been pleasantly reminiscing about his recent activities on that bed.

Clearing his throat, Kai turned back to Jessie and apologized. He wasn't sure why he was apologizing to her, but he felt the need to do it. Jessie nodded, her beautiful face still pale. They started moving his boxes in front of where his mattress was propped against the wall, both hiding it, and making room for his new furniture. Halfway through the process, he heard Jessie gasp. He quickly shifted his eyes to her, wondering what she might have found. She was kneeling on the floor, putting some clothes into a box. She looked close to passing out; her lips were nearly white.

Concerned, he squatted beside her. "Jessie?" His fingers came up to touch her cheek, and he tried to ignore how nice her skin felt. Her eyes began to water, but she wouldn't look at him. He tucked a loose curl behind her ear. "Jessie?" he tried again.

"I'm gonna be sick," she muttered. Kai worried that she really would be sick by the look on her face. Confused, he tried to pull her gaze from whatever she was staring at. When that didn't work, he started searching for what had her so enthralled. That was when he felt the bile rising up his throat. There was a condom packet on the floor, right in front of the TV. It was unopened. A perfectly sealed, purple and silver wrapped reminder of everything that had happened between them. The memories relentlessly flooded his head, and like it was happening again, he remembered driving into her over and over, remembered telling her he was going to come, right before the euphoric explosion took him over. His stomach tilted just as surely as desire swept through him.

"Throw it out," Jessie whispered.

Kai immediately released her face and grabbed the obtrusive thing. He vaguely remembered something falling out of Jessie's purse when she was getting her phone. She must have had some with her. Maybe she'd planned on screwing someone last night, and he'd fit all of her requirements. It made him feel a little odd that what had happened between them might not have been the result of an unbelievable attraction that had led to something bigger. Maybe what had happened, she'd planned from that very first glance.

Tossing the packet in the garbage under the kitchen sink, he twisted to look back at her, still kneeling on the floor. No, she'd said she wasn't like that, and he believed her. Besides, he preferred to think that what they'd shared was rare, that it had been fate pulling them together. Then again, what they'd shared was so wrong he shouldn't even want to think about it at all. If that was fate, then he didn't want it meddling in his life again.

Coming back into the main room, he squatted by her side. Out of instinct, he started to reach for her, but then he stopped himself. Jessie let out a soft exhale as she looked his way; her eyes were less wet now, and she looked a little embarrassed. "Sorry. I'm trying to be okay with this, but that was a little…" She shrugged and then let out another nervous laugh.

He sat down on the floor by her feet. "I know. I'm trying too." He gave her an encouraging grin. "It will get easier." Kai hoped that was true.

Jessie nodded, her eyes locking onto his. It took a lot of willpower, but Kai squelched the rising desire he had to feel those lips again, to touch her face again. A wistful noise escaped her, and he wondered if Jessie was having just as difficult a time. If it weren't for how much the thought twisted his stomach with disgust, he would ignore the fact that they shared a last name, lay the mattress back onto the floor, and take her one more time.

With a visible effort, he stood and extended a hand to her. Jessie accepted it and let him pull her up to standing. They ended up being closer than he'd intended, their bodies brushing together. Kai didn't pull away though, and continued to stand with his chest against hers, his flatness a sharp contrast to her fullness. As he clutched her hand tight, he suspected that for the first time all day, they were the same temperature. He knew he felt hot all over as he stared down at her. Wondering how to shut off the desire he still felt for her, even now, when it was mixed with guilt, revulsion, and self-loathing, his lips parted in anticipation. They couldn't do this; it was wrong on so many levels, but as his body started reacting to her nearness, he knew that at least on *one* level, he could do this.

He lowered his forehead to hers, and she gasped, her mouth opening as well. His other hand wrapped around her hip, pulling her closer to him. Kai couldn't believe he was seriously contemplating this, after everything he'd learned, after all the times his stomach had churned while thinking about it. Even though he knew it was disgusting, his body was willing to overlook that fact because goddamn…he wanted her.

Jessie raised her chin, bringing their lips dangerously close, and he thought she might be willing to overlook it too. His hand on her hip lowered to cup her backside; their free hands, still joined, tightened. Kai sucked in a quick breath, not sure what to do, not sure which part of his body to listen to. Jessie ran her hand up his chest to his neck, and made a noise that was both lustful and conflicted.

Kai was torn. She was so beautiful, so wonderful, and felt so incredible in his arms. Without realizing what he was doing it, he shifted his lips, just a fraction, until they minutely brushed hers. Closing his eyes, he exhaled a deep breath. The brief contact flooded him with remnants of last night—her taste, her passion. He wanted to taste her again; he wanted to push her away. While his body and mind shifted him in opposite directions, his head began to pound. This was so wrong, but it felt so right.

At the brief kiss, Jessie's breaths quickened, and she shifted in his arms. Her hips firmly pressed against his, and he could feel the blood rushing down as his body hardened. If that piece of him took over, it would almost make things easier…until after. Then they would be faced with the awful fact that they had known the truth, and done it anyway. At least with the first time they could claim ignorance. If they allowed it to happen a second time…well, they wouldn't have any excuse left to defend themselves.

Jessie's hips bumped against him in a restless pattern as she squirmed in his arms, just as torn as he was. Kai wondered if she was aware of how much the swiveling was turning him on; she would be aware in a moment, if she didn't stop. Just as her lips were coming back to his for more, Kai found a well of resolve inside him, and released her hand so he could grab onto her hips and still them. "Stop, Jessie," he whispered, immensely proud of himself for being able to utter those words.

They worked like a blast of cold water on Jessie. She immediately pulled away from him, breaking their intimate contact. "Oh, God," she muttered, running her fingers through her curls. "I can't, we can't…this is so wrong, Kai."

Her breaths grew sporadic; she looked on the verge of losing it. Kai stepped forward and put a hand on her arm. "I know. It's okay, I know."

Giving him an apologetic smile, she withdrew from his touch. With a similar smile of his own, Kai gave her space. "We're going to have to be more careful." He let out a weary exhale. Much more careful. "I'm sorry, Jessie, you just, you don't feel like family. The idea grosses me out, but not... I still want...I still want you."

Looking at the floor, Kai felt horrible and guilty for admitting that. Jessie sighed as she moved even farther away from him. "I know...I want you too." Glad that at least they were in the same awful boat, Kai peeked up at her. She shrugged when they made eye contact. "But even if we don't feel like it, we *are* family, and this can't happen."

He nodded. "I know."

"So what do we do?" she asked with a shake of her head.

Kai clenched his fingers into fists as he resisted the urge to walk over and tuck a stray lock of hair behind her ear. "We try not to get too close to each other. At least, until this feeling ...passes." It had to pass. Jessie nodded, and the chocolate depths of her eyes glassed over. Kai hated seeing her turmoil; it was so similar to his own. All he wanted was to get closer to her. Wanting to ease her pain, and his own, he cracked a small smile. "But, can I get your help with the furniture first?"

Jessie laughed, causing a tear to release and drip down her cheek. With a small smile of her own, she nodded. "Yeah, of course."

They made quick work emptying Jessie's truck. With several of the larger pieces of Gran's stuff, they had to bypass the elevator and use the stairs. When they got a dresser wedged in a corner, they both laughed pretty hard, and Kai jokingly told her that he was at her mercy. Growing quiet, Jessie gave him an odd look full of longing and pain. Kai had to remind himself for the millionth time that she wasn't some beautiful girl he could flirt with whenever the mood struck him. She was so much more, and so much less.

After a couple hours of sweaty work, they finally moved in all the furniture: two dressers, a nightstand with a lamp, a large bookcase, and a frame and headboard for his mattress. Considering the size of Jessie's truck, it was amazing that they'd been able to fit everything in only one trip. Looking over at Jessie as she blew a loose curl off her shiny forehead, Kai smiled. It was easy to fit things into place with her. Too easy.

When all the furniture was arranged, they lowered his mattress onto the frame and replaced the sheets. The same sheets they'd had sex on. After they were finished, they both stared at the spot that had changed everything in their relationship. An awkward tension began to build, and Kai found himself whispering, "Who is Jeremy?"

Jessie flinched, and Kai felt heat rush into his face. He really hadn't meant to ask her that, but curiosity had driven it out before he could stop himself. She'd mentioned something about a man named Jeremy, right before she'd shoved her hand down his pants. She'd been comparing his size to that guy. At the time, she'd seemed pleased with what she'd found.

Color stained Jessie's cheeks as embarrassment flashed through her. Walking over to one of Kai's boxes, she opened it and started pulling out his clothes. She was going to stay and help him put his stuff away? While he was grateful for that, since he really wasn't looking forward to doing it, he was pretty surprised, too, especially after what he'd just asked her.

Jessie let out a long exhale as she folded some crumpled T-shirts and placed them in a dresser drawer. Not looking at Kai, she answered, "He was my last boyfriend, who found it very difficult to keep it in his pants." She glanced over at him as he blinked in surprise. "I caught him with another woman once, and that was enough for me." Her gaze washed over the front of Kai's jeans, and her face colored even more. "I think he was just insecure," she muttered, a devilish smile twisting her lips for a second.

Kai laughed, then sighed. She was comparing her ex to him...this was all so weird. Reaching into a box, Kai started putting away some of his books. Jessie shook her head as she watched him. "God, I can't believe I said that to you last night." Looking horribly embarrassed, she stopped unpacking his clothes and stared at him. "I'm generally not that..."

She bit her lip as she let her thought trail off. Kai smiled as he remembered. "Aggressive?"

Jessie groaned and let her head fall back. Then her hands came up to cover her face. She looked mortified. Kai wanted to reassure her, let her know that she had no reason to be embarrassed about her actions. Everything else aside, the physical part of their night had been amazing. Quietly, he told her, "I've never had anyone be like that with me. It was amazing, you were amazing." Deciding to be perfectly honest with her, he admitted, "It was the best sex I've ever had."

She slowly lowered her hands; her face reflected his own sadness and revulsion. "That makes me feel wonderful...and horrible." Kai gave her a sad smile. He knew just what she meant. Shaking her head again, she stuck her hand back into his box of clothes. "This is so messed up, Kai."

Returning to his box of books, he muttered, "I know."

After another hour or so, they had emptied all of Kai's boxes. Jessie laughed at several of his private things. A mug he'd made in art class one year—it had an obvious lean to one side. A photo of a group of his friends tossing him into the ocean. A Tiki statue with a gigantic schlong. One of his friends had found it in an adult shop, and had thought it would bring Kai good luck in the girl department. Kai wasn't sure if it had or not.

Jessie smiled to herself as she flipped through one of the photo albums his mom had made for him. She stopped on a picture of him and his friends standing shirtless on the beach. Her finger languidly traced the swirling pattern of Kai's tattoo peeking up over his collar bone. As he came over to sit beside her on the bed, his chest ached with the memory of her soft lips touching his tattoo last night. "Does it mean something?" she asked, her finger pointing to the black ink in the picture.

Kai smiled and shook his head. "Not really. They're just tribal markings. A group of us decided to get them after graduating from high school." He pointed to his friends in the pictures, to the various spots on their bodies where they'd each gotten the swirling, slashing tattoos.

Jessie glanced at the tattooed arms and legs in the photo, and her gaze drifted to Kai's shoulder. She bit her lip, and he could tell that she wanted to see it again. Not thinking about why he shouldn't show her, he lifted his layers of shirts up enough so that she could see the bulk of it along his back, along the blade. Jessie's mouth popped open as her finger came out to touch the dark design. Her index finger traced a swirl, and her nail teasingly grazed his skin. The heat of the contact instantly shot through him. Realizing how close they were getting and where they were sitting, Kai stood and let his shirts drop down into place.

Flushing, Jessie looked away. Not getting too close was going to be a lot harder than Kai would have ever imagined. Smiling reassuringly at her, he casually asked, "Hungry?"

Shutting the book, Jessie nodded. "Yeah, starving. There's this great pizza place nearby. I'll call." She stood up and headed to the kitchen for her phone in her purse.

Running a hand through his hair, Kai glanced up at the ceiling and prayed for the strength to get through this. He was about to reply to Jessie's suggestion when she shot back, "Hawaiian, right?" When he dropped his gaze to hers, he spotted a playful grin on her face. Seeing it relaxed him. *Yes, they could do this.*

Teasing her back, he said, "No, Haole don't make it right. Pepperoni is fine."

Jessie twisted her lips and rolled her eyes as she made the call. Kai dug into his wallet for some cash and handed it to her when she was finished ordering their dinner. Jessie shook her head and tried giving it back to him, but Kai refused to take it. "You've done so much for me today, it's the least I can do." With a calm smile on his face, he hoped she would let him do this for her. Try to repay her kindness in some small way.

Jessie gave him an expression that clearly said it wasn't necessary, but she did stuff the bill into her jeans. Happy that she'd accepted, Kai leaned back against the counter. Jessie copied him on another counter and they passed the time with small talk, mainly Jessie filling him in on all the attractions Denver had to offer. She teased him good-naturedly on his island heritage, but by the way her eyes drank him in, Kai could tell that his looks appealed to her. Of course, he'd already known that. Pushing that fact out of his head, he focused instead on the soothing sound of her voice.

5

It Will Get Easier

Jessica Marie woke up Sunday morning with less of a head-ache than yesterday but a throbbing skull, nonetheless. She was having quite a weekend. She'd met a man, an attractive man. She'd gone home with him and let herself be someone she really wasn't. She'd fulfilled a fantasy, a fantasy that was supposed to help heal her bruised heart. It wasn't supposed to give her heart a different sort of ache. The man was not sup-posed to be her cousin.

Letting out an irritated sigh, Jessie shoved aside her mountain of covers and hopped out of bed. She immediately slipped her feet into a pair of fuzzy slippers. The entire house had wooden floors, and they were especially chilly early in the morning. Jessie could hear the sound of cartoons and laughter coming from the living room when she opened her bedroom door; her roommates were awake. She'd managed to go an entire day without them grilling her about her hookup. She'd been reluctant to share details about that night before, but now… Jessie had no idea what she should tell her friends.

Hearing them softly talking with each other, Jessie darted into the bathroom so she could buy herself some time with a refreshing shower.

Wondering what to tell her roommates, she thought about the man in question. Kai Harper. The boy bearing the same last name. Groaning, Jessie tried not to dwell on that fact. Hanging out with him yesterday had been enjoyable. Kai was interesting, funny, smart, and outrageously handsome. He was the kind of guy she could see herself with for a while, maybe even long term. But that wasn't an option for them. At all. Not only was the thought disturbing, it would be impossible to explain their relationship at family reunions. That thought made her groan again.

Rinsing off the last, lingering bubbles, she reminisced about their dinner together. They'd sat on the floor in front of his bed, the pizza box spread between them. As they'd talked and ate, they'd each occasionally glanced at the bed, remembering. It was going to take some time for the memory of that eventful evening to leave their brains. Kai had admitted that she was the best sex he'd ever had, and while she hadn't said it back to him, she'd been thinking the exact same thing. An incredible night like that wasn't the sort of thing she could just suddenly forget, even if she wished she could.

Stepping out of the shower, Jessie started piecing together her day. She wanted to check on Grams again, make sure she didn't need any help with anything yet and she wasn't in too much pain. After that, she wanted to go get some groceries for Kai. Rummaging through his kitchen for something to drink last night, she'd instantly noticed that all he had was an almost empty carton of milk in the fridge. When Jessie had given him a quizzical look, he'd apologized, saying he hadn't gotten around to shopping for food yet. Jessie wasn't sure, but she thought he was probably filling himself up on junk food. Boys had a tendency to do that, especially boys left to their own devices.

She wanted to help him. Aside from the fact that she actually liked Kai, he was family, and that was what family did: helped each other. Plus, a small nagging part of her brain really wanted to see him again. She tried to ignore that part as she got dressed.

Finally feeling more put together to face her inquisitive friends, she walked out into the living room. April was sitting on the couch sideways, her feet up on the cushions, her hands around her knees. She was engrossed in her conversation with Harmony, sitting on the opposite end of the couch and didn't notice Jessie. Harmony did. She looked over when she spotted her. Having lost her audience, April finally noticed Jessie, as well.

"Oh, she surfaces. Feeling better?" April winked, and Jessie knew she wasn't talking about her hangover being gone.

Ignoring the churning in her gut, she gave April as bright of a smile as she could. "Much better, thanks."

April laughed. "No problem. You needed it." Harmony frowned but didn't comment. She looked as if she still didn't approve of letting Jessie escape with Kai, and now, knowing what she did, Jessie wished Harmony had fought harder to stop her from leaving. If only their embarrassment was a heated kiss on the dancefloor. April jumped around to lean over the back of the couch. "So…how was he?" She wriggled her eyebrows suggestively and Jessie suppressed a groan. *And it starts.*

"I...don't really remember." Jessie shrugged as she walked around the couch and into the living room.

She plopped down in a chair under a bay window. It looked out over the city and had a pretty spectacular view of the mountains. Her dad had secured this place for her after he'd gotten transferred to Washington D.C. He'd wanted to make sure Jessie lived in a decent area of town before he left, and he was even paying her rent for a year. Just in case, he had said. It wasn't necessary, Jessie had a job, but she was the only girl in a family full of boys, so her father was a little overprotective. And since he had a prestigious, well-paying job for the government, thanks to his recent promotion, he also had enough extra income to do things like that for her. He wouldn't be happy if he ever found out how careless she had been the other night.

April's incredulous snort returned Jessie's attention to her. She was staring at Jessie like she'd grown two heads. "Your first one night stand, and you don't remember? How lame." She raised a questioning eyebrow. "Are you messing with me?"

Jessie shrugged. "I'm sorry, I was really wasted. I don't think we even did anything." Hoping her cheeks didn't betray her lie, she glared at April. "You guys called too fast."

April leaned over and smacked Harmony. "See, I told you they needed more time."

Harmony gave Jessie an appraising onceover, but then shook her head. "We were just looking out for you, Jessie. Going off with strange guys, even hot ones, is not a good idea."

Jessie gave her concerned friend a warm smile. "I know." *God...how she knew that now.*

April swung her head back around to look at Harmony. "Was he hot? I don't remember...he was the blonde one, right?"

Jessie bit her cheek to not smile. If they didn't remember Kai, it would make introducing him to them later so much easier. Harmony met April's gaze as she answered her. "No, he had dark hair." Jessie suppressed a sigh. Harmony might have started out the night drinking, but she'd eventually stopped so she could drive them home. Jessie hoped she'd still been buzzing when she'd first spotted Kai, then her memory might still be fuzzy. Tilting her head at Jessie, Harmony asked, "He was Latin, right?

Jessie quickly nodded. *Yes, please believe that.* Kai vaguely looked Latin enough that, seen from a distance, it was plausible. "Yeah, his name was Spanish. Something like..." She racked her brain for something good, something sexy. Unfortunately, only one name popped up, and she immediately spat it out. "Ricardo."

April started uncontrollably giggling. "Seriously? I'm sorry I missed hot Ricardo, your almost Latin lover."

Shaking her head at the woman, Jessie stood to leave the room; she'd given them enough tidbits for now. As she was walking away, April said, "I made out with a Javier once." Harmony laughed at her comment while Jessie meandered into the kitchen. Going slowly was difficult; she really wanted to run. As she walked she heard April add, "Yeah, that whole myth about them being amazing lovers — not true." Harmony laughed harder at that, and Jessie, finally out of their view, leaned over the kitchen counter and took some deep breaths.

Had she successfully thrown them off Kai's trail? She was sure April wouldn't remember him; hot guys were a dime a dozen to her, but Harmony…well, she hoped the fake name and ethnicity kept her from connecting anything. Even so, Kai was going to have to stay away from Jessie's place for a while. At least until the details of that night faded from her friends' minds. She wished they would fade from hers already. What she wouldn't give for that night to be blacked out.

Gathering herself, Jessie grabbed a protein bar and a yogurt smoothie from the fridge. Since she couldn't appear anti-social to her friends, for fear someone would ask her what was wrong, she headed back to the living room to eat her meal. As she ate, her eyes drifted over the knickknacks in the room: photos of her family, a framed print of the Rockies, a cluster of candles. Everything in her house was tidy and organized. It screamed — *Three girls live here!*

As she listened to April and Harmony discussing the various men April had slept with, Jessie noticed something she hadn't before; she had a lot of stuff. Idly looking around, she decided to box up some extra things and give them to Kai. He might like having a few candles, maybe the woodsier scents that she kept in her closet. And he might like the picture of Seven Falls that she'd tucked away in the bathroom. The famous waterfall might remind him of home. Jessie was softly smiling to herself as she ate, thinking about which things she could give him.

"You *so* did sleep with that guy!" April suddenly exclaimed.

Jessie snapped out of her reverie to see both girls staring at her. "What?" she cautiously asked.

Harmony raised an eyebrow at her. "We've been talking to you. Where have you been?"

Jessie felt her cheeks heat as she opened and closed her mouth, searching for an answer. April snorted. "You did sleep with Ricardo." She giggled incessantly. "I knew it! You totally had that freshly-fucked glow when we picked you up."

Jessie gasped and chucked a pillow at her friend. She completely missed, and April doubled over with laughter. Jessie stuttered again, then shook her head. "Grams got hurt yesterday," she ended up sputtering.

April immediately stopped laughing. "Oh, God. Is she okay?"

Jessie inwardly smiled, happy to distract them. For their benefit, she let out a troubled sigh. "She fractured her hip. She's going to be in the hospital for a couple of days. I was just thinking about what to bring her, to cheer her up." This diverted all of the girls' attention away from "Ricardo," and they spent the rest of her breakfast thinking of things to do for the sweet woman.

An hour later, Jessie was arriving at the hospital to visit her grandmother. She knocked on her door and opened it when she heard her cheery greeting. Grams was chatting with a nurse when Jessie stepped into the room. They were shooting the breeze so easily that anyone observing them would probably think they'd been the best of friends for years. But knowing Grams, she'd probably just met the woman.

Mid-chuckle, her grandmother looked over as Jessie approached her bed. Smiling at the nurse, she brightly said, "Oh, Susan, this is her, this is my granddaughter, Jessica Marie."

Jessie smiled at the woman and raised her hand in a wave. "Hello."

Susan smiled at her. She was around the age of Jessie's mom, but short, blonde, and round as could be. "Millie, what a beautiful family you have. Between her and the boy, you're very lucky."

Grams raised an eyebrow at Susan. "You just wait until you actually see Kai. He's quite a looker. Do you have any single girls?"

Jessie instantly wanted to protest, but she couldn't find a reasonable excuse. Luckily for her, Susan shook her head. "Nope, all boys." She glanced over at Jessie. "Are you single, dear?"

Jessie's eyes widened at the implication. "I...uh..."

Susan laughed as she patted her on the shoulder. "I'm just teasing, dear, don't panic. I'll check on you in a little bit, Millie. You let me know if you need anything."

Looking around Jessie, Grams cheerily said goodbye to her nurse. Jessie watched the woman leave, then turned her attention back to her grandmother. She patted the edge of her bed, and Jessie sat beside her. Putting an arm over her grandmother's frail shoulders, Jessie noticed some new magazines, a warm blanket, and a bag full of knitting needles and yarn. "Did someone bring you some stuff, Grams?"

Grams looked at the new additions to her room and smiled. Glancing at a bouquet of daisies in the window, her aged eyes glowed with pride. "Kai. He came in late last night." She returned her gaze to Jessie, and Jessie tried not to seem too surprised by her comment. Kai must have come to the hospital after she'd gone home, and that had been pretty late. Grams watched Jessie's face, then patted her knee. "He said he couldn't sleep, still adjusting to the time zones." She nodded at the door. "He charmed his way past the nurses, tried to leave me gifts while I slept, but I woke up, caught him red-handed."

Grams laughed, and Jessie found herself shaking her head and smiling, as a warm feeling settled in her chest. "That was sweet of him," she quietly said.

Grams patted her knee again. "Yes, it was. He's a good boy. You'll see that, the more time you spend with him." Her grandmother gave her an odd look as she studied Jessie. "He told me you got everything moved into his place." Careful to not show any of her turmoil, Jessie nodded. Being in his place had been hard, especially at first.

Her grandmother's expression shifted to concern. "Is he okay there? Does he have enough? Does he have any food?"

It amused Jessie that even though Grams was the one laid up in a hospital bed, she was still trying to take care of others. Noticing how her grandmother's thoughts were so in line with her own made her smile. Maybe the desire to help was genetic. "He's fine, Grams."

She didn't look convinced as she relaxed into Jessie's side. Her face overly serious for the situation, she clasped Jessie's hand and gave her a hard stare. "We need to look out for him. We're all he has here."

Jessie swallowed the sudden lump in her throat. Praying her eyes didn't water, she nodded at Grams and then rested her head against the older woman's. "You just worry about you, Grams. I got Kai," she whispered. Just saying the words made her heart constrict painfully. They were true though. No matter what, she would take care of Kai.

Her grandmother let out a relieved breath as she squeezed her knee in approval. "Good, dear. He needs you." The words made a surge of delight run through Jessie. She liked the idea of Kai needing her. Liked it far too much.

After making sure Grams didn't need anything else, Jessie gave her a kiss goodbye and left the room. As she walked back to her truck, she flicked a couple of tears off her cheeks. Really, she needed to let this go. Sure, Kai was amazing, funny, attractive, and exceedingly sweet, but he was first and foremost her cousin. And not even a distant cousin. He was her *first* cousin.

Climbing into her truck, she drove to a grocery store. Despite the internal conflict, she was determined to fulfill her promise to take care of Kai. She started loading up a cart full of foods that she thought he might like. It was tricky, since she didn't really know him. Not in that way at least. About halfway through the store, she gave up trying to guess what might interest him, and just bought foods that she loved. If she couldn't guess his tastes, then she could at least introduce him to her favorites.

Pushing the squeaky cart past the produce section, she came across some fresh pineapples. Immediately reminded of him, she plopped one into the cart. When she had a full load, she headed to the checkout line. As she watched the cashier ringing up her groceries, Jessie hoped Kai wasn't offended by her bringing him bags of food. Well, if he was, she would just tell him that she hadn't had a choice; he had no food, and he couldn't carry that much on his motorcycle. She didn't want to see him starve to death. Silly boy. Who moves to Colorado in October and buys a bike? He was going to freeze his ass off when the weather changed in the next couple months. While he was right, and it usually was sunny and dry here, it also got pretty damn cold. Below freezing cold. Much chillier than the tropical boy was used to, she was sure. Jessie absentmindedly smiled as the cashier talked her ear off. He was a bike guy. Ridiculous man.

A half hour later, Jessie was knocking on the ridiculous man's door. Well, really she was lightly kicking it with her toe. Her arms were lined all the way from her hands to her elbows with bags that were quickly cutting off the circulation to her fingers. Hoping Kai was home, she kicked a little harder. After another few seconds, the door finally opened. When he pulled it back enough that she fully saw him, Jessie instantly forgot about her numb limbs.

Apparently, he'd just gotten out of the shower. He had jeans on, but they weren't buttoned yet, and he was rubbing his hair dry with a towel. He didn't have a shirt on yet, either. Jessie's eyes immediately snapped to his chest, mesmerized. She couldn't stop staring at the tattoo peeking up over his shoulder.

Kai stopped rubbing his hair. "Jessie? What are you doing here?"

The surprise in his voice returned Jessie's awareness back to the situation, or more accurately, the lack of feeling in her fingers. Peeking up at his enchanting sea-green eyes, she squeaked, "Help."

He finally seemed to notice that she was filled to the brim with grocery bags. "Oh, sorry."

Swinging the door wide open, he started grabbing things from her. Jessie sighed with relief when the pressure released, and the blood started circulating again. She hated making trips, and really hadn't thought that carrying that many bags would be so challenging. As Kai took the remainder of them, Jessie was a little surprised to find that she was breathing heavily. Kai set the bags on the counter, and Jessie studied his bare back as she shut the door. Leaning against the closed wood, she started imagining her fingers trailing over that intriguing black ink again. Funny, she'd never much cared for tattoos...until she'd seen his. Now she couldn't seem to get enough of it.

Kai twisted to look at her. "You bought all this, for me?" His expression shifted into one of adorable confusion. Jessie was too preoccupied with her fantasy to answer his question though, and his face turned quizzical. "Jessie?" he quietly said, taking a step toward her. Jessie's eyes flashed down to his open jeans, and straightening, she stared at the ceiling. She couldn't let herself think that way.

Deciding to try humor again, she told him, "Yeah, well, I noticed your fridge last night. It reminded me of when my dad used to travel all over the place when I was a kid." Her eyes tentatively lowered to his body. He'd buttoned his jeans and draped the towel over his shoulder, hiding himself from her. While she appreciated the gesture, she had to sigh at the loss. "Whenever I talked to him, he'd say he was having a five-star meal." Kai cocked an eyebrow at her, and she laughed. "That was our code for cereal." Kai grinned, and she smiled in return. Stepping toward him, she indicated the slew of bags. "I figured if you were anything like most men, you were probably living off Lucky Charms."

Kai gave her an adorable pout, then opened a cupboard next to the sink. In it, was a box of Lucky Charms. Shaking his head, he moved the box aside. Jessie laughed at what was hiding behind the box of cereal. "I also have a can of Spam," he said, his voice on the edge of laughter.

Jessie made a disgusted face. "Spam?"

Leaning against the counter, Kai folded his arms across his chest. "Don't knock it. I could make you a Spam sandwich that would have you turning your back on every other sandwich in the world."

He lifted the corner of just one lip at her. It was startlingly attractive, and Jessie had to exhale very slowly. *Damn.* "Well, I would have to see that to believe it."

His lips curved into a full grin. "Deal."

She helped him put the food away, and a small thrill of delight shot through her whenever he said he loved something. More than once he asked her how she knew exactly what he liked. It thrilled her, and it saddened her. They were so compatible. The very last thing he pulled out was the pineapple. His expression odd, he quietly said, "You bought me a pineapple?"

Jessie couldn't tell if he found her addition humorous or not. Maybe she'd crossed a line and offended him? "Um... yeah." Feeling foolish for her obviously ethnic choice, she flushed. "Sorry, kind of...cliché, isn't it?"

Setting it down, he put a hand over hers on the counter. His was warm from the shower, soft. "No, it's very nice." His eyes got a faraway look for a second. "Reminds me of home." Returning his eyes to hers, he smiled warmly again. "Thank you, Jessie. For everything."

He whispered that last part in a low, sultry voice, and Jessie found herself inching toward him. Not breaking eye contact, she placed a hand on his chest, just under the towel still draped over his shoulder. Jessie felt his muscles stiffen, watched his lips part. Hers did, too. She knew she shouldn't touch him like that—it was too intimate, too close—but she felt drawn to him; she couldn't stop herself. Her fingers

94

curled, lightly grazing his skin. She felt tears of frustration stinging her eyes as their gazes locked. She wanted to be close to him, and she couldn't. It was killing her.

Kai noticed her tears. One of his hands cupped her cheek, while the other removed her fingers from his chest. "It will get easier," he whispered. Seemingly torn, he stared at her for long seconds before finally giving her a light peck on the forehead. Jessie briefly closed her eyes, savoring the connection even as her stomach twisted. "I should finish getting dressed," he mumbled. And then he left her alone in the kitchen, staring at the spiky fruit on the counter. Stupid pineapple.

●━━━━━━━━━━━━━━━━━●

Needing a minute to pull himself together, Kai walked into the bathroom. He'd pushed her away when all he'd really wanted to do was grab her and lock those beautiful, perfect lips to his. He still wanted that, even though his stomach churned at the thought.

He couldn't believe her timing. In the shower, he'd just been wondering how he was going to get a full load of groceries home on his bike. He figured he'd have to make several trips to fill up his pantry, and he hated making trips. He probably would have settled on eating out a lot or buying only a couple of days' worth of meals at a time. Kind of an annoying way to live.

But Jessie had saved him from having to worry about it. And she'd managed to pick up a bunch of things he routinely craved. Sometimes it was like they were cut from the same cloth. Closing his eyes, Kai suddenly remembered that technically, they sort of were cut from the same cloth. He knew genetics didn't account for personality and tastes, but it was partly the reason why they were so similar. Too similar. Don't touch her similar. Don't walk back into that room and throw her down on the mattress similar.

Running some water, he splashed his face in an attempt to clear his thoughts. He needed to get a handle on this if they were going to be an important part of each other's lives. And they were going to be, he could already tell. Right or wrong, he wanted her around.

After his common sense returned, Kai wiped his face with the towel on his shoulder, and then hung the towel over the rack on the wall. The small room was still warm from his shower, and dampness clung to the air. Wanting to feel a little bit of mugginess, he'd cranked up the heat while he'd been in there. Running his hands down his bare arms, his skin soft and full of moisture, he walked back to his bedroom. He glanced at Jessie as he moved toward his dresser. Her eyes had drifted to his chest, but she quickly looked down at the floor.

Kai sighed in frustration. Normally, he enjoyed getting checked out by a girl, but right now it only complicated things. Especially when he couldn't stop staring at the tight, button-up shirt that she'd put on today. It was fitted in all the right places, and a dark chocolate color that perfectly matched her eyes. It looked amazing on her, especially paired with the long gray skirt and what he had to imagine were thigh-high boots. Well, that was what he preferred to imagine anyway.

Rummaging through his drawers, he sighed again. She looked too amazing. Maybe he should tell her to ugly herself up, if that was even possible. The thought made him laugh as he grabbed a deep blue sweater his mom had ordered online for him. She'd been positive that the temperature here would be twenty below, every day. But Kai was always a little cold, so thanking his overprotective mother, he slipped it on.

From the kitchen he heard Jessie say, "What's so funny?"

She was watching him smooth the sweater over his chest. It was tightly knit, soft, and looked like a long-sleeved T-shirt than a sweater, but it was keeping him warm enough that he didn't feel the need to double up. Remembering what had made him laugh, he smiled and shook his head. "Nothing."

Still eyeing his chest, Jessie gave him a sly grin. "We're going to have to buy you long johns when it actually does get cold around here."

Kai frowned; it was already cold. Shaking his head at her tease, he walked over to the kitchen. "The next time I go visit my parents, you should come with, and then we'll see who's more uncomfortable." He grinned at her, and for a second, it seemed like she'd stopped breathing. Not wanting to read too much into her body language, Kai turned away. It was best if he didn't think about it.

Grabbing the pineapple Jessie had brought over, Kai decided to share it with her. Pineapples were a traditional welcoming gift, meant to impact well wishes on the new arrival. He wasn't sure if Jessie had known that when she'd purchased it, but he was touched by the sentiment, regardless. And it really did remind him of home.

Leaning against the counter, Jessie gave him a playful smirk. "That's no challenge. I kick ass in a bikini."

Kai stopped his hand an inch from the cutting board on the counter and turned to stare at her. God, she probably looked amazing in a bikini. Jessie was giving him a grin that was slightly seductive. Combined with the curvy imagery in his head, he couldn't stop the sudden wave of desire. He had an overwhelming urge to cut the pineapple, run a piece along her lip, and suck the juices off. He wanted that more than anything. He closed his eyes to banish the alluring vision, and reason slowly returned to him. No. he couldn't do that, not with her.

He heard Jessie let out a soft grunt of annoyance. "Oh, um …damn it," she muttered.

He cracked an eye open to look at her. She seemed mortified, and he couldn't help but smile. Had she really not seen the sexiness in her statement and her face until just then? God help him if she was clueless about her effect on men. Or maybe just her effect on *him*. He shook his head. "I'm going to pretend you didn't just say that, cousin." He said the word teasingly, wanting to dissipate the tension that always seemed to build between them, but she raised an eyebrow at hearing it.

Her face warmed into a beautiful smile. "Right…cousin."

Her body was blocking the set of knives that he needed, but instead of just reaching around her, like he'd do with any other beautiful girl, he pointed at them. "May I?"

She glanced behind herself, then moved out of the way. "What are you doing?"

Grabbing a knife, he held it up to her. "I'm hungry, and I owe you big, again, so I thought I'd prove a point." Her features scrunched in confusion and he laughed at how adorable the expression was on her. Opening his cupboard, he grabbed the can of Spam. She immediately frowned and he laughed even harder. "Deal's a deal…cousin."

Kai found that the more he called her that term, the more distance he could put between them. Like an unflinching reminder. Jessie smiled at hearing him say it again; maybe she enjoyed having the verbal barrier there, too. Maybe she needed it as much as he did. A part of him wanted her to need it as much as him, and that made him feel horrible as he started slicing open the pineapple. A part of him actually wanted his cousin to want him as badly as he wanted her. Jessie had nailed it yesterday, when she'd said their situation was messed up. It definitely was.

While he instructed her on how to slice and fry up the Spam, he called her cousin about five more times. She followed his instructions with a laugh, mocking his deli choice the whole time. The smell of spiced, processed, ham-like meat soon filled his small home, making his mouth water. Grabbing some bread that she'd bought for him, he toasted some slices and prepared the mayonnaise, lettuce and tomato. Jessie had brought over everything he could have asked for and more.

After setting their finished sandwiches next to a pile of fresh pineapple, Kai handed her a plate. Then they walked to his bedroom, sat on the edge of his mattress, and began to eat their lunches. Kai smiled as he watched her take her first bite. She'd been grimacing as she did it, until the taste hit her. Then she smiled, and she made an almost erotic pleased noise in her throat. He tried to ignore the sensuality of the sound and laughed at her reaction. He knew she'd like it. Everyone did, once they gave it a chance.

Jessie was studying his bare walls as she ate her meal. He thought to ask her why, but he didn't; he was enjoying the silence of her company too much. Once they finished their meal, Kai grabbed her plate and took it the few steps to his kitchen. He started to set their dishes into the sink, vowing to clean up later. Ceramic plate in hand, he glanced back at Jessie still sitting on his bed, looking around his room. She was leaning back on her elbows now, and the comfortable position was emphasizing her curves. Her body strained against her shirt, one key button just about to pop open if she moved back any farther. Kai thought he could see a trace amount of snow white skin through the seams of the dark fabric. Suddenly remembering that creamy skin in all its fully naked glory, he dropped one of the plates into the sink.

Jessie's gaze snapped to his at hearing the loud clatter. As Kai turned back to the sink, cursing, she sat up on the bed with furrowed brows. The plate in the sink was now cleanly split in half. Great. Kai didn't know how to smoothly talk his way out of this one; he turned on the faucet simply to give himself something to do. He was pretty sure his cheeks were bright red. They felt on fire. *Stupid, stupid, stupid.*

Sometimes it was so easy and causal to be around her. Other times…it was the exact opposite. Kai hung his head as the situation suddenly overwhelmed him. Why her? Of all the girls that he'd ever slept with, which really wasn't all that many, why did she have to be the one who stirred his desires the most?

Kai leaned against the counter, his head still down as he watched the water swirl some of the smaller chips down the drain. A hand came up to rest on his back, and he closed his eyes and sighed. Why her?

He heard the water shut off, felt her fingers on his face, turning him to look at her. Kai opened his eyes to see her brows knotted in concern as she examined him. He felt wiped. He'd had to adjust so much coming here—the different time zone, the different climate, the different altitude, leaving all of

100

his friends and his close family behind—but adjusting to Jessie …that was harder than all of it.

Her hand rubbed small circles into his back as she stepped closer to him. "Kai," she whispered. The soft murmur of her voice sent a painful ache through him—awful, wonderful. Shaking her head, Jessie looked him squarely in the eye. "It will get easier, cousin."

Closing his eyes, he melted into her embrace. Yes, it had to.

6

Pinned in Place

Monday morning, Kai woke up before the alarm he'd set on his phone. That surprised him, since seven in the morning still felt more like three. And because he'd had trouble sleeping. He'd had trouble falling asleep, and he'd had trouble staying asleep. His dreams, when he'd slipped into slumber deep enough to have them, had all centered around a dark-haired, dark-eyed girl with amazing curves and an unbelievable smile. A girl he dreamed of kissing, but shouldn't have. He'd give anything to stop thinking about Jessie that way. How had one woman so completely turned his world upside down?

Standing and raking his fingers through his hair, he decided that a nice, long, hot shower would help. And he would not think about her body while he was in the shower, either.

When he was done showering, Kai considered dressing in every piece of clothing he owned. He would be up in the mountains today, and it was bound to be even colder there than in the city. Smiling as he rummaged through his grandmother's dresser drawers, he thought about Jessie's comment about long johns yesterday. That was actually a pretty good idea. Maybe he'd pick some up later.

Kai made a quick bowl of cereal after slipping on his multiple layers. When his stomach was full of the sugary substance that he'd lived on before Jessie's generous shopping trip, he took a moment to savor the feeling of being nice and toasty warm in his apartment. He was pretty sure he wouldn't feel that way for the rest of the day. Inhaling a deep breath, he grabbed his jacket and prepared for his first day as a research assistant at Kriley Research Center. Their base was located near Golden Gate Canyon State Park, about thirty miles outside the city.

Sliding onto his motorcycle, Kai shifted his thoughts to what was important right now: his new job. He wanted to make a good impression on his parents' friend and wanted to be an invaluable member of his team. Maybe if Kai played his cards right, he could take over when the man retired. From what Kai's father had told him, Mason Thomas specialized in entomology, and was making huge strides in discovering why certain honeybees were dying off for no apparent reason. While that seemed small to some people, Kai understood that it wasn't; every creature was connected to the earth, and what affected one species, no matter how small, eventually affected all of the rest. What happened to the lowliest animal could happen to those higher up.

Kai started his bike and began his journey out of town. Thinking about his father and his new job brought Kai's mind around to his mother. She had called him again last night, thankfully not as late—or early—as the last time. She'd again asked about his job, and he'd again reminded her that he hadn't started yet. There'd been a really long pause after he'd said that, and then she'd apologized for not remembering. Kai wasn't sure why she was bringing up his job so much. She did almost the exact same thing in Hawaii, just with a different sort of habitat than what he would be studying. Maybe she was just hoping that he would hate it here and come home.

As Kai approached the majestic mountains, the cool wind whipping his jeans as he sped along, he thought his mother might be in for a disappointment. He could learn to love it here, once he got used to the colder temperature. The snow-capped monoliths were a thing of beauty, and even though it was approaching winter, colorful flora dotted the lower portions of the mountains. The Aspens, ranging from bright yellow to deep red, washed the hills in a sea of glorious color. Kai couldn't remember the last time he'd seen something quite so beautiful. Well, maybe last night, when Jessie had smiled while saying goodnight.

Frowning under his helmet, Kai recommitted himself to not thinking about his cousin like that. Unfortunately, he had a feeling he'd be reminding himself to not think about her in that way for a very long time. He purposefully tried to think about anything other than the way Jessie had laughed last night, or the way she'd run a hand back through her curls, or how she'd shown her never-ending concern for him by asking if he needed anything else before she left. Failing miserably at pushing her out of his head, Kai eventually made it to the outskirts of the state park.

Winding his bike up a steep hill, Kai noted that the base of the mountain was still thankfully clear of snow. He slowed his bike as he came upon a series of plain, gray buildings. The researchers inside were clearly more concerned with the wildlife around them than aesthetics; the buildings were low, squat rectangles that stood out in harsh contrast to the spectacular nature bursting around them. Kai smiled as he turned his bike off and removed his helmet. A thick green forest butted up against the back of the buildings, and he could easily picture himself spending countless hours in them, tracking migration patterns, studying the local plant life, and maybe even helping to capture and tag some of the animals.

Just as he was swinging his leg over the Honda, he heard a voice calling, "Hey, you the new guy?"

Kai propped his helmet on his bike and turned to see a guy around his age approaching. The man had a shaggy head of medium-brown hair and the beginnings of a very nice Grizzly Adams type beard. He also looked like he hadn't showered in about two weeks. With the wide smile on his face as he stepped up to Kai, it was obvious that he was happy to see him.

As Kai nodded and told him that he was indeed the new person, the man's smile turned exuberant. He extended his hand. "Oh, good. Fresh meat. We've been running a little lean. Everyone will be so excited that you're finally here." He eyed Kai up and down after they finished with their handshake. "Especially Missy." He laughed, and his eyes were suddenly mischievous. "She'll be ecstatic that you're here."

Kai tried not to read too much into that and gave the man a polite smile. "My name's Kai Harper."

He nodded, like he knew that. "Right, yeah, I'm Louis. That's Louis with an 's'. I don't do that weird, my name ends in an 's', so change it to an 'e' and call me Louie, thing."

Kai bit his cheek. The smart-aleck in him wanted to im-mediately call the man Louie, but he didn't know him well enough to mock him, yet. Kai had the distinct feeling that Jessie would have mocked him anyway. The thought made him smile.

Louis extended a hand to the largest of the gray buildings. "Your new habitat will be here." Giving Kai a wry look over his shoulder as Kai followed him, he added, "We'll get you a team shirt, so you match the herd, and a GPS unit, so we can track your movements in the wild."

Louis smirked at his own joke, and Kai lightly shook his head. Researcher humor. His dad used to do that when he was younger. Chronicling the life of a five year old human child like he was Dian Fossey and Kai was a gorilla in the mist.

Looking down at Louis, Kai noted the teal polo he wore with the name of the center in the upper left corner. Louis paired it with khaki slacks, slightly muddy around the knee area, and a black belt that looked like some type of superhero utility belt. Gadgets and gizmos hung off it in various places: a cell phone, a satellite phone, the aforementioned GPS unit, hopefully containing a detailed map of the mountains on it, and hanging off one hip, what appeared to be a tranquilizer gun. Kai didn't think it was necessary to carry a tranq gun around at all times, attached to the hip like Han Solo or something, but he figured Louis enjoyed feeling like some Indiana Jones type explorer.

They walked through the double doors of the building, and Kai was hit with the smell of purified, recycled air. It reminded him of a lab, and he instantly felt at home. Growing up with parents who were big on environmental science, Kai had a healthy respect for developing theories and either proving or disproving them. While most kids' only real science experience was making baking soda volcanoes, Kai had assisted his mom and dad in an actual lab. When he was ten, he'd even helped his dad carbon date some fossilized palm fronds. It kind of made baking soda volcanoes seem a little…mild.

As Kai's eyes swept over an informal gathering area, where a couple men were sipping some coffee, and a blonde woman was eating a bagel, he spotted someone intently studying him, like he was a newfound species or something. She had frizzy hair and a face full of freckles, and was lifting and lowering her glasses, like she couldn't believe what she was seeing. Confused, Kai looked around, but there was no one else; she was definitely staring at him.

As Louis proceeded to explain to him what the various rooms were — dining hall, bathrooms, spare bedrooms, labs, library, offices, etc. — the woman hopped up from her chair and walked over to them. Her amazed look still firmly on her face, she shook her head as she approached Louis.

"And what did you find, Louis?"

Pausing mid-sentence, Louis looked over at her, then back at Kai; that mischievous gleam was in his eyes again. "New guy," he told her.

Her mouth dropped as her eyes dragged over Kai's body, and Kai started feeling a little violated. Being admired was one thing, having all of his manhood analyzed and broken down into specific attributes, quite another. Hoping to break the ogling, he stuck his hand out. "Kai Harper," he politely said.

Her eyes were still sweeping over him, and her grin was gigantic as she grasped his hand. "Wow, you are beautiful," she matter-of-factly told him.

Kai felt heat flood his cheeks as Louis started laughing. The woman didn't look embarrassed in the least as she continued shaking his hand. She looked like she'd merely stated an observational fact.

"Um...well, thank you?" Kai mumbled.

She shook her head. "No, I'm serious. You are, by far, the most attractive researcher we've ever had here. I look forward to working with you every day." Kai wanted to pull his hand back, but she still had it tight. Stepping forward, she seductively intoned, "Name's Missy. Missy Jones."

Kai flicked a glance at Louis, who was still laughing at Kai's obvious discomfort. Shrugging, he told him, "See, I told you she'd like you."

Missy pulled on Kai's hand and started absconding with him down a hallway. Louis waved goodbye, still chuckling in amusement. Kai frowned at the sudden change of events, then turned to watch where this short, wiry woman was leading him. She was wearing the same teal polo shirt and khaki slacks as Louis, and her belt had just as many gadgets, although, she wasn't wearing a tranq gun. With a suggestive smile on her face, she opened a door and beckoned for him to follow her into a room.

As she prattled on about the comings and goings of life at the research center, Kai started to wonder just what she planned on doing with him. Flicking on a light, she closed the door behind them. They seemed to be in what looked like a storage room. Confused, Kai scrunched his brows. Why had she brought him to a closet? Missy pointed over to a tall cupboard, and Kai let out a sigh of relief. He didn't need another awkward moment with a woman; he had enough of those with Jessie.

Aside from the closet built in the wall, there were wire racks forming aisle ways in the large room. On the shelves were various computer parts, extra lab equipment, and a box labeled "lost and found". Kai could just see the tip of a bright pink feather boa in that box. Shaking his head, he returned his attention to Missy as she opened the cupboard. Rambling about the various men who had either worked here before or worked here now, she rummaged through a box.

In the middle of a story about an ex-coworker who used to smell like Pine Sol, she paused and asked Kai, "You're a medium, right?" Before Kai could answer her, she pulled her hand out of the box and thrust a teal polo at his face. Blinking in surprise, Kai grabbed it before it fell. Missy began scrutinizing his pants, and he twisted a bit, not exactly liking where her gaze was fixated. "Thirty, right?"

He again thought to answer her, but she reached into another box and pulled out some slacks before he could. Kai was a little impressed that she'd sized him up so accurately as he grabbed his pants.

"Um, thanks." Kai had never worked at a lab that required uniforms before. The place where his parents worked was pretty relaxed about what the employees wore. At least he wouldn't have to worry about what to wear every day, although, he would definitely be adding layers to his short-sleeved polo. "Where can I...?" He looked around, hoping she'd get the hint.

Missy smiled brightly. "Oh, just change right there. We're all family here." She started searching for more items, and with a raised eyebrow, Kai resumed scanning the room. He really didn't want to change in front of her; he had a feeling she'd enjoy that too much. When she looked back and saw that he hadn't stripped yet, she frowned, then nodded her head to the side. "There's a bathroom in the corner." She shook her head, disappointed.

Kai walked over to the bathroom in disbelief. If their roles were reversed, and he'd just done that to her, he was pretty sure he'd be sued. Double standards. They worked both ways, which, he supposed balanced out the double standard, making everything fair and even again. The marvel of the universe.

Eyeing himself in the mirror once he was changed, he noticed that the teal shirt brought out the green in his blue-green eyes. They looked even more surreal now. Looking at the closed bathroom door, he hoped the effect didn't make Missy's interest in him worse; she was probably already picturing him naked. For a split-second, Kai wondered if Jessie would like this color on him. Pushing that thought aside and shaking his head to clear his wandering mind, he grabbed his regular clothes and opened the door.

Missy was staring at the door when he stepped through, and her pale eyes were narrowed intently, like she'd been trying to see through it. Lifting her gaze to his face, she didn't seem even remotely bothered that she'd been caught. She fanned her face when she noticed his eyes, and Kai sighed. She definitely found the color appealing, and was even more intrigued by him. Kai was beginning to think that Missy might make his days here pretty long.

She gave him a broad smile that showed almost all of her teeth; her expression, plus her frazzled hair made her seem wild and untamed, much like the wilderness around them. "Holy crap, you are one attractive man." Stepping right up to him, she casually asked, "You want to take me out?" Again, she didn't look embarrassed in the slightest for being so forward.

While Kai pondered how to politely get out of this, Missy moved even closer, her hands reaching out for him. Backing away, he quickly told her, "I wish I could, but...I don't date coworkers." Frowning, she dropped her hands. Kai bit back a smile as he tried to look remorseful. "Sorry, personal rule."

Missy eyed him up and down, then exaggerated a loud sigh. "Oh, too bad." Brightening, she bumped Kai's hip with hers. "Well, if you ever have an itch that needs...scratching, I'm your girl. No dating involved," she added with a wink.

As Kai wondered what the hell he was supposed to say to that, Missy spun and turned away from him. Pausing at the exit, she looked back over her shoulder and said, "And, just so you know, I do...everything." Her gaze flicked down to his pants, then she grinned and left the room.

"Jesus," Kai muttered to himself. So far, Colorado had been very welcoming to him. Odd. Yes, he'd had his share of admirers in Hawaii, but nothing to this extent. Maybe his looks were just unique here. Back home, every third person looked similar to him. Well, maybe in coloring. He'd always been told that his eyes were unique.

Straightening, Kai raised his chin and adjusted his shoulders. He was a man, and he could deal with these forward women. Besides, he had no intention of taking Missy up on her outlandish offer. He was here to work, and that was it. But as he exited the room, he *was* a little curious what "everything" meant.

Thankfully, Missy was nowhere in sight when he stepped out of the supply room. Having left his regular clothes on a shelf in there, he adjusted the belt and equipment that Missy had left out for him. Feeling like a full-fledged member of the team, he looked around for his new boss, Mason Thomas. Not seeing anyone in the empty hallway, he made his way to the back, where Louis had indicated the labs were.

Right in front of a set of hermetically sealed double doors was a row of hooks with crisp white lab coats hanging off them. Kai slipped on a coat before entering the clean room. When the doors hissed open, Kai stepped in and took a look around the stark, white room. There were several cages holding small forest animals; most of them were waiting to have their health checked and recorded by a busy researcher before being released. Sizes, sexes, general health and diet samples, were all things they would be tracking. Keeping an eye on the welfare of the smaller creatures, gave the scientists an idea on the welfare of the larger creatures, right on up to humans.

Seeing stations set up for running those tests, along with various others, Kai spotted an older man standing by a honeycomb of bees encased in glass. It was getting close to the bees hibernation cycle, but Kai figured some swarms would still be active until the first frost. The bees outside in the hives were fumigated with smoke when researchers needed to study them. It didn't hurt the bees, but drove them into a feeding frenzy. While preoccupied with eating, in preparation to flee from the approaching fire, the bees were mellower, less protective of their hives, and easier to capture.

The older man was bent over a table where he had a few bees pinned down. Not wanting to startle the man while he was obviously deep in thought, Kai stepped behind him and softly cleared his throat.

Straightening, the man twisted to face him, and Kai was the one startled. The older man appeared to be in his mid-fifties, his dark hair streaked with gray along the sides. He had the healthy tan of someone who spent a lot of time outside, his face lined and lived-in, and he was around Kai's height and build. But none of those things had surprised Kai. It was the man's eyes. Kai had never met anyone with eyes anywhere near his shade before. Most blue eyes that he'd seen were either a pale, sky blue, or fell into the blue-gray category. Kai's were more blue-green, like a tropical ocean. The man meeting his gaze now, had eyes the exact same shade as Kai's.

Gathering himself, Kai glanced down at the man's name embroidered on his lab coat. Mason Thomas. Just the person he needed to see. Extending his hand, he politely said, "Hello, sir, I'm Kai Harper, we spoke on the phone."

Kai could have sworn the man paled, and his eyes definitely widened in surprise. His jaw even fell open before quickly snapping shut. It took him a solid ten seconds to finally accept Kai's extended hand, and in that time, the mood in the room shifted. Kai couldn't help the feeling that Mason was apprehensive to meet him. And reluctant. Like he'd rather be doing anything other than shaking Kai's hand. Kai wasn't sure why Mason would feel that way about him. He used to work with his parents ages ago. Maybe he was just suffering from a sudden case of nostalgia.

Kai smiled as they shook hands, and Mason finally gave him a stiff smile. "Right...Kai. We're...glad you could join us here."

Kai's response was exuberant. He'd been looking forward to this for a while. "I'm grateful for the offer, this is an amazing place you have here, sir."

As they separated, the older man's gaze drifted over Kai's body, before snapping back to his face. Kai couldn't be sure, but he thought that he still seemed a little pale. "Thank you. Please, call me Mason. Aside from the outfits, we're not formal here."

Kai laughed as he lightly tugged on his polo. "Yeah, this is a little different than I'm used to."

With a warm smile, Mason indicated behind him. "We're so close to the state park, we sometimes get tourists or hikers here." He shrugged. "I found it was easier for everyone, if we looked more official." He leaned into Kai, and conspiratorially whispered, "It helps keep the civilians at bay."

Kai laughed again, and Mason's expression turned oddly appraising. With a harsh swallow, he turned back to his bees. Kai shifted uncomfortably. Was he doing something wrong? "What can I assist you with, sir?" Mason looked back at him and Kai quickly amended with, "Mason."

Mason's brows knitted, and he slowly shook his head. With a clearly forced smile, he pointed to the honeycomb wedge enclosed in glass on the tray beside him. "I'm done with this batch. You could return them and bring me another?" He pointed to a set of sealed double doors at the back of the room. "Those lead outside. The apiary is straight out back, a few hundred feet from the farthest building."

Happy for something to do to help his new boss, Kai smiled as he grabbed the tray. "Yes, sir...Mason."

Kai walked away from Mason, but he felt the heat of the man's eyes following him the entire time he left the room. He wasn't sure what he was doing to cause such strange reactions, but he hoped it had more to do with him being a new addition to an already established team, and that it wasn't something about Kai personally. But Mason didn't needed to worry about Kai fitting in, if that was what his concern was.

Kai was sure he'd eventually blend in; he was pretty good with people.

As the second set of double doors hissed closed behind him, Kai hoped he could impress his boss with his first task. He'd never wrangled bees before. Containing a small frown, Kai hoped he didn't get stung.

Falling Fast

Jessie rubbed a sore spot in her back while she opened the door to her place. She'd had a long day and had been dreaming about a bubble bath for the last twenty minutes. The irony of Jessie's muscles being sore wasn't lost on her; she was a masseuse and alleviated kinks for a living. Jessie preferred to think of her work as physical therapy and was based out of an esthetician's office and not a spa. She was thinking about expanding her talents into acupuncture one day, or maybe concentrating solely on sports therapy. She still wasn't sure what course she wanted to steer her life.

Setting her purse on the kitchen table, Jessie noticed some of the things she'd thought to bring Kai yesterday. Smiling to herself, she wondered how his first day at his new job had gone. She still wasn't entirely sure what he did for a living, but he'd seemed excited to do it.

Forgetting all thoughts of a relaxing soak to ease the ache in her back, Jessie headed to the laundry room to grab the large box that the girls used as a dump area for laundry left behind in the dryer.

Walking into the living room with it, she squinted her eye, tilted her head, and tried to picture her things through Kai's eyes. What might he like to see in his home? Picking out the more masculine things she owned, Jessie began filling the box. First, she found the candles in her closet. Then she went through some of her picture frames. Removing her photos first, especially the one of her when she was twelve with mile-high hair and god-awful braces, she tucked them into the box. Finding a couple of black throw pillows in a corner, victims of April's last temper tantrum, she stuffed those in as well. In the bathroom, she picked out a few decent towels, since she knew his weren't very plush. On a whim, she included a six inch figurine of a camel that her dad had brought home for her once. The thing was atrocious and gaudy, but it always made her smile for some reason. She loved the thought of it making Kai smile.

Just as she was closing the top of the box, Jessie heard the front door open. April walked into the room, chatting on her cell phone. Jessie could tell by the high-pitched timbre of her friend's voice that she was talking to a boy. As Jessie took one last sweep of her home, mentally searching all of her rooms for anything she might have missed, April sank onto the couch and plopped her feet up on the coffee table. Noticing some old magazine under the table, Jessie squatted down and grabbed a couple. Kai might like something to read on the nights he stayed up late, unable to sleep.

Jessie reopened the box to smash some gossip magazines inside. Tossing her phone on the couch, April tilted her head and asked, "What 'cha doing?"

Thinking about showing up on Kai's door with a box full of goodies made Jessie smile. She didn't know if he would be home yet, but she could always leave it in front of his apartment door if he wasn't. Then she frowned. Would he think it was weird that she was giving him a box of what, she supposed, he could consider crap? Most guys weren't into dressing up their place, not as much as girls at any rate. And Jessie didn't own anything garish for his bachelor pad — no beer signs or nudey magazines — although Kai didn't strike her as the type of guy who was really into either of those things.

Her smile returning, she answered April. "I'm going through some of my extra stuff. My cousin just got into town, so I thought I'd share the wealth." She laughed, once again hoping that Kai saw value in the trinkets she was offering him.

April set her feet on the floor and leaned forward over her knees. "Oh, cousin? Are we taking her out this weekend?" She wriggled her hips on the couch in a movement that Jessie was sure meant dancing.

Jessie smirked at her eager-for-adventure friend. "He. My cousin in town is a guy." A very attractive guy who Jessie knew all too well, in some ways at least. She bit the inside of her cheeks to hold back another frown. She really shouldn't think about that anymore.

Successfully hiding her thoughts from April, she watched as her friend's face lit up; she was truly excited now. "Oooh, a guy...is he hot?" She raised her eyebrows alluringly.

Jessie sighed. He gave new meaning to the word. To April, she shrugged. "He's family...I don't know."

Frowning, April stood up and smoothed the loose cardigan she wore over a long, modest skirt. April worked as a receptionist in a medical office. Her daily appearance was prisingly reserved, considering her provocative persona. April's parents highly approved of work-April. "Only (way to know for sure. I'm coming with you."

She pointed to the box, and Jessie bit her lip. She real didn't want to introduce Kai to April right now. For one, sh wasn't sure if April would remember Kai or not. Secondly April was attractive and seductive, two things that usually got a man's attention. And once April saw Kai...she'd go straight for him, especially since Jessie had just written him off as nothing more than family. Jessie knew she couldn't hold up Kai's love life, since they really were nothing more than family, but, she didn't want to speed it along either. She wanted him to herself for a bit.

"Um, actually, he's not home from work yet. I'm dropping and dashing." She really wasn't sure if he'd be home or not, but she wasn't about to let April know that. Guilt washed through Jessie as she realized just how many lies she'd told her friends lately.

Accepting her answer, April shrugged and started walking toward the hallway, most likely to strip off her moderate clothes and replace them with something much more formfitting. "All right, but I want to meet this hottie soon." Twisting her head to look back at Jessie, she gave her a brilliant smile. "Invite him up this weekend for...dinner." Her grin turned mischievous, and Jessie knew exactly what she meant by dinner.

Jessie frowned as her friend disappeared into her room. Keeping April away from Kai might not be easy, or even possible. She sighed. It also didn't matter. Jessie couldn't have anything with Kai but friendship. Best to let him move on quickly and she supposed that him being with her roommate would be better than him being with some random stranger. At least if Kai was with April, she would have an excuse to see him often.

Hating her train of thought, Jessie picked up the box. She hated the queasiness in her stomach whenever she had intimate thoughts about Kai, hated the fact that she was still attracted to him, and hated the horrible feeling in her heart at the thought of him helping April remove all of her modest clothing.

With those troubling, conflicting emotions tumbling in her mind, Jessie shoved the box into her truck and drove to Kai's apartment. Twenty minutes later she was in the parking garage below his place, staring at his bike in the next stall. With his helmet slung causally over one of the handlebars, it was obvious that he was home. It made Jessie smile that he was here, and she forgot her queasy thoughts as a surge of butterflies flitted through her. She would get to see him. Wrong as it was, for now, he was only hers.

Grabbing the awkwardly large box, Jessie shuffled over to the elevator, and pressed the third floor button. She leaned back against the wall as the cage started to rise. The lifting movement mixed with her butterflies and increased her anxiety. She swallowed three times to calm herself. Really, she'd seen him every day since the club. She should be used to the anticipation by now.

The doors dinged open, and she headed to his apartment. Once again, her arms were too full to knock, so she kicked a greeting with her toe. She heard a muffled, irritated reply, followed by what sounded like low curses. Worrying her lip, she started wondering if maybe she shouldn't be bugging him again. He was going to think his cousin was stalking him if she kept this up. Just as she decided to set down the box and leave without bothering him, the door swung open. Jessie's gaze locked with Kai's, and she halted her movement. And her breath. She just couldn't get used to the absorbing color of his eyes. She couldn't look away.

He tilted his head as he regarded her standing there. "Jessie?"

He sounded a little peeved, and Jessie was sure he wasn't happy to see her...yet again. Shaking her head to jolt herself out of the trance created by the color of his eyes, she sputtered, "I'm sorry, you're busy. I can come back later." Her cheeks felt red-hot, and she suddenly wished she could hide the massive box she was holding behind her back. Guys didn't care about this kind of stuff. He was going to think she was an idiot, and maybe she was.

Kai's face softened, like he just now realized that he seemed grumpy. Shaking his head, he reached out to touch her arm. With pleading eyes, he said, "No, I'm glad you're here. Please help me." His face scrunched into an adorable expression of helplessness.

Confused, Jessie cocked her head as she studied him. It was only then that she noticed he was half-naked. Dressed only in jeans, he was scratching his bare chest, just below the black ink of the tattoo swirling over his collar bone. Her eyes widened fractionally at the sight of him, and she thought she should leave for an entirely different reason. But...he was family, and he'd asked for help. She couldn't leave now. Nodding, Jessie followed him into his studio.

Giving her a bewildered expression, Kai gingerly took the box from her once she was inside. "What's this?" He lifted the box a little, indicating it. Jessie's eyes strayed to his flexed biceps when he did. *Damn.*

Clearing her throat, Jessie helped him set it on the floor in front of his bed. *The* bed. "Uh, just some crap I had lying around." Looking at all his bare walls, Jessie began envisioning where she could put everything. "Just a little something to make your home a bit...homier."

When she returned her eyes to his, Kai was staring at her; he seemed stunned. Finding his voice, he whispered, "You didn't have to...you've already done too much...I can't..." He bit his lip, still scratching his body, and Jessie smiled at his overwhelmed face. Finally, he shrugged and said, "Thank you, Jessie."

She felt warm in places that her cousin really shouldn't be warming her. Looking away, she muttered, "Well, don't get too excited. It's just some candles, art, knick-knacks...nothing to write home about." She peeked up to see him softly smiling at her. He was also still partially nude. It was so distracting; it hitched her breath.

Trying for casualness, she touched his chest with her fingertips. His skin was cool...and inviting. "For someone who's always cold here, you sure are shirtless a lot." She started to laugh, but it came out in a nervous titter, so she stopped.

Instead of laughing with her, he sighed and dropped onto his bed. "Stupid bees," she thought she heard him mutter.

Sitting down next to him, the huge box at their feet, she started twirling a curly lock of hair around her finger, mainly to stop herself from trailing them down his chest. "What?" she asked, still distracted by the shape of him.

Kai glanced back at her, and his expression froze, like something she was doing was equally distracting to him. They stared at each other in silence for a second, and Jessie swore that if she leaned in to kiss him, he'd lean in too. She let the fantasy fill her for the briefest moment, until the accompanying horror flooded over the top of it. They couldn't.

Looking away, Kai seemed to snap out of it, too. "Uh…" Frowning, he scratched his shoulder blade. "I got stung today …stupid bees."

He seemed so sullen about the incident that Jessie couldn't keep from laughing. Kai snapped his eyes to her; his weren't amused. Smoothing her face, Jessie finally stopped her giggle. Kai smiled at her restraint and reached behind her. The move brought his bare chest in contact with her arm. He was colder than she was, and a shiver went through her entire body, but she was certain his temperature had nothing to do with that. Her eyes half-closed, her breath increased. They shouldn't.

Finding whatever he was looking for on his messy bed, Kai started to straighten. When he noticed her face, he paused. His body was still leaning against her arm, and his head was directly in front of hers. His tropical eyes flashed over her face, taking in the desire that she knew was apparent in her features, clear in her fast breath. His gaze flicked down to her mouth, and his tongue darted out to briefly wet his bottom lip. Grotesqueness filled Jessie, but it was squashed by the rising need for him to press those lips to hers. They couldn't. They shouldn't. But…if he did…she would, too.

Kai leaned in, and Jessie leaned forward. When she was certain it was happening, that they were going to willingly cross that line, Kai suddenly flinched and pulled back. Irritation on his face, he ran a hand over his shoulder to rub a spot on his back. Taking long, slow breaths, Jessie moved away. No …they couldn't.

As Kai's face twisted in discomfort, he lifted a jar of what appeared to be a natural salve for stings, bites, and burns. His expression miserable, he pleaded for her help. "Please?"

Grateful to have something to do other than fantasize about kissing him, Jessie took the jar of ointment. As he twisted around to show her his back, Jessie's eyes ran over the tattoo across his shoulder blade. It curled and spiraled in a delightful way, and it took everything inside her to not trace the lines. Focusing elsewhere, she finally noticed the angry red welts upon his skin. Several of them. Jessie laughed again as she unscrewed the cap. "What happened to you? You walk into a swarm of killer bees?"

Kai hung his head with a sigh as she rubbed a nasty bump on his back. He flinched then groaned in relief. "No…honey bees."

Jessie laughed harder, and he looked over his shoulder and glared at her. Biting back her giggles, she applied some healing cream to the spots that he hadn't been able to reach. Smiling, Kai shook his head. "My boss is studying why the bees are dying, and I was helping him." He shrugged. "Apparently, I suck at it, and the bees let me know…repeatedly."

Enjoying the feel of his skin under her fingertips, Jessie finished up with all the angry areas that she could see. "Oh," she quietly stated as she studied the pleasing contrast in their skin tones. "Well, at least you're not allergic." She twisted her lip as she thought about that. She wasn't allergic either. Was that a genetic thing? She wasn't sure. Sighing, she added, "Maybe you won't have to do that again for a while."

Kai grinned as he looked back at her. "Next time, I won't try to be so macho...and I'll put on the damn suit." He shook his head. "I just didn't realize how offensive bees found me. Now I sort of hope all the little bastards die."

Jessie giggled and then let out another wistful sigh. She didn't find him offensive at all. Since a good deal of the cream was still on her fingers, she started to work out the kinks in his shoulders; he *had* had a long day. With a groan, Kai relaxed in her hands. Even though the professional side of her immediately kicked in, the satisfied noise he'd just made gave her a small thrill.

He let out another one just like it. "God, Jessie...you're amazing. You should do this for a living."

Pausing, Jessie laughed. "I do, Kai."

He looked back at her with a grin. "Really?" She nodded, and he closed his eyes. "Well, good, you're amazing at it."

Her hands drifted down his back, trailing along his spine and working outwards. "You should come by my work sometime. This would be so much better if I had some oil, and you were lying down." He held his breath, and a different sort of massage immediately flew through Jessie's mind. Her fingers low on his back, she sucked on her lip and tried not to engage the fantasy spinning through her head. She couldn't entirely push it out, though.

Kai slowly twisted his head to look at her. Face serious, he quietly said, "I think I'd like that."

She had no idea if he was talking about seeing her at work, or if he was sharing her fantasy; since the image had popped into her head, she had to assume it had popped into his, as well. And when his eyes flicked to her lips, she was certain it had. Jessie watched his face, watched the desire and conflict building. She knew her expression matched his. She also knew letting this feeling run away with them was wrong and stupid and would lead to nowhere good. Giving him one last squeeze, Jessie removed her hands from his skin. "All done."

His eyes lingered down her body, igniting it. They slowly drifted back to her face, and he gave her a warm smile. "Thank you, Jessie."

She flushed and nodded. Then she shucked off her shoes, brought her legs up onto his bed, and crossed them—anything to put some distance between them. Even with all their vows for space, they seemed to subconsciously drift toward each other.

With a deep, cleansing inhale, Kai grabbed the jar and lathered some spots on his chest before closing it up. Jessie sort of wished that she could have helped him with the front too, but it was for the best that she hadn't. Besides, he could handle that part himself. As he slipped his shirt back on, hiding all that glorious skin from her, Jessie sighed. Such a shame. Needing to think of something else, she spouted the first thought that came to her head. "My roommates really want to meet you."

He looked over at her as he smoothed out his long-sleeved shirt. "Oh?"

Trying to stop herself from reliving the feeling of his skin under her hands, Jessie nodded. "Yeah, they are very curious about my just-in-town cousin." She didn't mention just how curious April was; she didn't want to think about that again.

Kai studied her for a second, then turned his attention to the box at their feet. "Were they the ones checking me out at the club?"

Jessie tensed. She'd forgotten that he'd seen that. Of course, a lot of that night was still a little hazy, and, unfortunately, a lot of that night was perfectly clear. Glancing at their reflection in the TV, she swallowed. Jessie saw Kai look up at her in the set, then twist to look at their reflection, too. By the pained expression on his face, she knew that he was remembering, as well.

Clearing her throat, she turned away. "Yeah, um, I don't think they remember much about you, though." She tossed him a smile. "April thought you were blonde. Harmony thinks you're Latin."

Shaking his head, he leaned down to open the box. "Well, if they won't remember that it was me that night...I don't see why we can't all meet."

The awed look on his face as he picked out and examined the things that she'd brought over for him made her smile. She hoped he was right, and her roommates didn't piece together their secret. She didn't want them to ever know that she'd slept with a family member. Thinking of it that way returned that horrible nausea to her stomach, and she scooted away from him a little bit. Sometimes it felt so right with him; sometimes it felt really wrong.

She watched Kai chuckle as he pulled the camel out of the box and set it on his nightstand. He seemed as amused by it as she was, and that delighted her. Digging through the box, he picked out various items and set them around himself, occasionally shaking his head; he smiled the entire time. Jessie tried to not notice how amazing his lips looked when they were curved up in a small grin. She also tried to not notice how nice his back looked, as he stretched and flexed while he moved and twisted. She tried to not notice, but it was difficult. He was just very attractive.

Kai pulled out a picture and his smile dropped as he examined it. Curious, Jessie shifted her attention to look at it, too. It was a picture of a red-rocked river that Jessie had bought from a local nature photographer. The photo had been taken so closely, and captured so expertly, that the water streaming past the crimson rocks appeared to still be moving. The photograph seemed alive. It was a breathtaking piece, probably Jessie's favorite.

Kai's finger drifted over the glass in the large frame, barely touching it. After another silent moment, he softly said, "This is great. Are you sure you want to get rid of it?"

He was clearly touched by her gift, and Jessie smiled seeing the uncertain appreciation in his eyes. "Yes, I want you to have it."

He tilted his head and stared at her, like he was completely taken aback that she would willingly part with something so beautiful. Jessie loved that he seemed to like the piece as much as she did. Watching him drink her in, she had the odd thought that the photographer should take a picture of Kai's eyes. Truly, that would be his most stunning work, because nothing on this earth could be as beautiful as Kai's eyes. She swallowed under his intense gaze.

Still looking dazed, he told her, "Thank you, Jessie."

His hand lifting from the frame, started to reach out for her. Jessie was sure he was going to cup her cheek or run a hand through her hair. The anticipation of the tender contact made her heart begin to beat faster, but then Kai dropped his hand to his knee instead. Jessie's heart stubbornly sank.

Smiling as he put the picture back in the box, Kai motioned to the kitchen. "Hungry? I could make us some soup."

It amused Jessie that he wanted something warm in his stomach. She nodded. "Sure, sounds great."

Standing, Kai gave her a brilliant grin before heading to the kitchen. Jessie sighed as she watched his backside walking away from her. Seriously, she needed to shut off whatever part of her was still attracted to him. Kai was *not* an option. It would be better for her if she went back to her two-timing ex-boyfriend.

Kai prepared a couple of cans of soup; he was still smiling over her box of goodies. While he was busy, Jessie put his new things away. He glanced over at her when he noticed what she was doing, but he didn't say anything, didn't ask her to stop. She finished putting everything away in the spaces she had envisioned for them just as dinner was done. As she was smiling to herself at how much homier his place seemed, and how perfectly suited to him the decor was, Kai approached her with a bowl of soup in each hand, and a plate of grilled cheese sandwiches balanced on his arm.

He motioned to the bed she'd straightened for him. Slightly blushing at the intimate memory she still recalled whenever she looked at the damn thing, Jessie sat down and rested her back against his new headboard. He sat next to her, handed her a bowl, and placed the plate of sandwiches between them. Grabbing a sandwich, Jessie gave him a crooked grin. "We should really find you a table."

Kai returned her smile as he grabbed a sandwich. "I like eating in bed."

She grinned at the comment and felt her cheeks heating again. Kai cleared his throat, like he was trying to clear the sudden tension, and then they began eating their meal. They sat in a comfortable silence for a while, then Kai turned on the TV. He found a sitcom for them to watch, one where the family's problems seemed even more complex than their own. They couldn't help but laugh at the absurdity.

After the light meal, Jessie snapped up Kai's dishes and washed them for him. It was the least she could do, since he'd made dinner. Kai protested at first, but the longer he sat in the bed, the more tired he appeared to get. After thanking her, he settled back into his pillows and closed his eyes. Jessie peeked at him while she cleaned up, wondering if he was falling asleep.

Once everything was washed and put away, she walked back over to him and started taking off his shoes. He cracked his eyes open and grinned at her. "You're too good to me," he whispered.

She smiled as she took off his other shoe. "No, I'm just anal. You shouldn't have shoes on the bed." He laughed at her comment and sat up. Ignoring the memory of her wearing heels in his bed while they'd done…stuff, Jessie sat next to him again.

Kai looked over at her, then let out a tired sigh and rested his head on her shoulder. Feeling like he was suffering from exhaustion, Jessie scooted down the headboard to rest her head against his pillows, bringing him with her. He twisted into her body, and she brought her arm around him, so he was nestled in the hollow of her shoulder.

Sighing contentedly, he moved his hand to rest it on her stomach. "Is this okay?" he whispered.

She nodded and pressed her lips into his hair. "Yeah." Jessie wasn't sure if it was technically okay or not, but it felt so warm and safe, she didn't care.

He sighed again. "Good, you feel nice."

He'd barely murmured the words, and Jessie pulled back to examine his drawn face. Running her fingers through his hair, she asked, "Are you all right?"

Opening his eyes to look at her, Kai let out a weary exhale. "I don't know if it's because of all the stings, or because I got up so early today, but I feel wiped, and a little sick." He frowned, obviously not wanting to be ill.

Jessie frowned too as concern filled her. "Well, you could be suffering from a little altitude sickness? You're used to living much closer to sea level. I'm sure you'll feel better in a couple of days."

Nodding, he closed his eyes again. Jessie gently squeezed him as she listened to his even breath. Just when she was sure he was sound asleep, he whispered, "Thank you, Jessie, for everything." His voice came out thick with exhaustion.

Smiling, Jessie rested her cheek against his head. "It's not a problem, Kai. We're family, that's what family does." Her admission made her frown. Maybe how they were resting wasn't appropriate. Maybe she should leave.

Kai's hand on her stomach shifted to her hip. He gently squeezed, holding her to him, almost like he knew she was considering leaving. Jessie heard him mumble thank you again, and she pressed her lips to his hair again as a tender ache tore her heart apart. Closing her eyes, Jessie cursed her lack of willpower. Hadn't she vowed earlier to keep some space between them? Since he was tightly cuddled into her side, it was evident that neither one of them could maintain distance for long. Jessie wasn't sure what that meant for their future.

Eventually, his grip loosened, and his breathing slowed. Pulling back, Jessie peered down at him. "Kai?" She moved farther away when he didn't respond. "Kai, are you asleep?"

Watching his face, Jessie waited for him to answer her. He didn't. Carefully sliding her arm out from under him, she settled him on his pillows and adjusted the covers around him, so he wouldn't get chilly as he slept. After tucking a stray foot under the blankets, she stared down at him. His face was completely relaxed, his full lips slightly parted as he took long, low breaths.

Even asleep, she could see the exhaustion in his face, the circles under his eyes. He'd adjusted to a lot of changes coming here, and it was wearing him down. Furrowing her brow, Jessie hoped she wasn't one of the troubling things he was acclimating to. At least the physical changes would get easier on him. His body was just going to punish him for it first. Thinking about his multiple bee stings made her smile again. Poor guy. Not the greatest thing to have happen on his first day.

Her heart swelled with warmth as she looked down on him. Slowly leaning over, she placed her lips to his forehead. Kai exhaled and muttered something that sounded like her name. Jessie pulled back and peered down at him intently. His eyes were still closed, his face still peaceful in slumber.

Smiling, she ran the back of her finger down his cheek. "Goodnight, Kai," she whispered.

His lips twitched, like he was smiling in a dream. Jessie wondered if he was thinking about her, then hated herself for wanting him to be thinking of her. He shouldn't be as tortured as she was. Well, she shouldn't *want* him to be as tortured as she was, at any rate. What he felt for her, besides gratitude and maybe some residual attraction, Jessie wasn't sure. But she was beginning to understand what she felt for him more and more with every second they spent together, and it terrified her.

Leaning down close to his face, she whispered in a shaking voice, "I think I'm falling for you."

Her heart hammering in her chest, she lightly pressed her lips to his. She pulled them away instantly, but not before she felt him minutely respond, his lips softly moving against hers. But she must have been imagining that. He was asleep. He probably wouldn't kiss her back right now, not with how tired he'd been.

Putting her fingers to her suddenly hot lips, she swallowed the painful lump in her throat. He shouldn't ever kiss her back, just like she shouldn't ever kiss him. Cursing all the feelings that she couldn't seem to shut off, Jessie stood and grabbed her things. Then, shutting off the lights, she closed his door and left him alone in his slumber.

Someone to Love

Kai woke up the next morning from a disturbing, but pleasant, dream. Pleasant, because he'd been dreaming about Jessie. Disturbing, because he'd been dreaming about doing very inappropriate things with her. In his dream, she'd told him that she was falling for him, and then she'd tenderly kissed him. As he lay awake in his bed, his eyes straining to make out any coherent shape in his dark room, he still felt the thrill those words had given him.

He wearily ran a hand down his face. What he wouldn't give to hear her actually say those words to him. But no. That was a really horrible thing for him to want. Jessie shouldn't be dragged down into his confusion. It would be best for her to find a way past the attraction that he could sometimes feel from her, and only see him as family.

He was struggling with doing the same.

Kai had been isolated from his extended family for so long, that the only person who actually felt like family to him was his grandmother. Everyone else, all of the miscellaneous cousins, uncles and aunts, were nothing more to him than a long list of names on the annual family letter that Gran put together every year, but DNA didn't lie, and Jessie and Kai couldn't share that kind of future.

Sighing, he sat up and rubbed his eyes. Grabbing his cell phone off the nightstand beside his bed, he glanced at the time. He'd given into sleep much too soon, and now he'd woken up well before work. He would probably be exhausted by the end of the night again. Oh well. At least his body was shifting in the right direction, and Kai was sure that, given another couple of days, a week at the most, he would be in line with the people here.

Yawning, Kai noticed he'd missed a call from his mom. She was probably curious how his first day had gone. It was too early in her time zone to call her back. He would just have to call her after work. As he rubbed the sore, healing spots on his back, he wondered what he'd tell her. He didn't have very many positive things about his first day that he could share. The strange Louis, the horny Missy, the damn bees, and his oddly distant boss.

Frowning as his thoughts turned to Mason Thomas, Kai got out of bed. For someone who was connected with his parents in some way, the man had sure been strange to him. As Kai had gone about his day, helping Mason with various projects, learning the ropes, the man had alternated between being curious, reluctant, kind, and standoffish. Kai had tried not to take it personally. It couldn't be because of him. Aside from silently suffering from multiple bee stings, Kai hadn't done anything wrong or inappropriate. He'd tried to be as friendly and helpful as he could, without seeming like an overeager suck-up. And he thought he'd pulled it off well, but his boss had still seemed uneasy around him.

Sighing as he shuffled to the bathroom, Kai shook his head. Maybe Mason was just trying to not show favoritism toward Kai to the rest of the team, since he was sort of a family friend. Yes, maybe he just didn't want to appear like he was doing Kai any special favors. Stepping into the shower, he turned the water on and twisted the knob to scalding hot. No, Mason was definitely not treating him like he was special. Kai hoped today would be smoother.

He also hoped the hot water didn't aggravate his tender spots. Quickly undressing, he gritted his teeth and stepped into the stream. He flinched as the hot water entered the slight pricks in his skin, then he sighed as the water relaxed him. The steamy shower was nearly as soothing as Jessie's miraculous fingers. Smiling, he remembered the wondrous feeling of her hands running over his skin. Scrubbing a bar of soap over his body, he closed his eyes and visualized her soft fingers trailing over him. It had felt amazing, and he swore, for a moment there...it had been so much more than just a massage. For a second, a single thought had entered both of their minds, he was sure. A thought that involved bare bodies, tangled limbs, slippery oils...and a spacious bed.

As his mind took over, and his fantasies took flight, Kai started pretending that his hands were hers. The act of cleaning himself forgotten, he started tracing the distinct lines of his muscles. His body instantly reacted; warmth, blood, and a growing ache in his groin. Biting his lip, he knew he should stop this, knew he shouldn't let himself think about her that way. Putting the soap back on the shelf, he rested his head against the shower wall. He'd gotten carried away, and his body was completely hard now, ready for a woman who wasn't even around. A woman he couldn't ever have again. Another sad sigh escaped him.

Ignoring the ache, Kai washed his hair. He kept his hands away from his waist and forcibly shifted his thoughts. His mind drifted to Jessie's generous box of decorations that she'd brought over yesterday. The stupid but charming camel, the waterfall photo that painfully stoked memories of home, a few candles to help mask the scent of "bachelor," and that one amazing picture of a red-rocked river. Kai liked that one the best. He had a special connection to water, and the photo impossibly and perfectly captured the flowing movement of a rushing stream. By the warm glow in Jessie's eyes, he'd known that the picture meant something to her, but she'd given it to him anyway. She was so sweet and so good to him. In two days, she'd seen everything that he'd been missing, and without asking, she'd stepped in and taken care of it for him. He was blown away by her.

Thinking of her warm heart and generous nature did nothing to drain the need surging through his body. By the time he was rinsing off, his situation below hadn't improved any. Looking down at himself, he shook his head and muttered, "You're not helping anything, you know. We can't have her."

Amused that he was actually having a conversation with his throbbing manhood, he smiled...and considered. He was alone. He could satisfy the ache that was only growing stronger the longer he thought about it. He could close his eyes and let himself believe he was with her, let himself believe they were nothing more than strangers, that he could have her, over and over again, as often as he wanted.

His hand drifted down, his fingers barely brushing the stiff shaft. His body twitched at the contact, and his breath increased. God, what was he doing? Not sure, but knowing he needed more, he slowly curled his fingers around the thick, hardness. A low groan escaped him as he ran his thumb over the sensitive tip. Yes, he could do this. He could satisfy his own needs, moaning her name as he came. It would be clean, neat, efficient, and no one would have to know that he was pleasuring himself to the image of his cousin.

Cursing internally, he removed his hand and shut off the water. No, he couldn't. While it was true, no one would know what he was doing but him...*he* would still know, and he'd feel slightly even more ill every time he looked at her. And besides, knowing him, he'd start doing it every morning. Then every evening. Then he'd be doing it all the goddamn time... and he wasn't sixteen anymore.

Once he was finished getting ready for the day, Kai decided to surprise his grandmother with a decent breakfast since he had the time. A part of him wished he could surprise Jessie with a nice breakfast, too, but he couldn't really show up at her house unannounced yet. Not with her having roommates. Especially roommates who had been checking him out on *that* night. They might have been a little tipsy, but they'd probably watched the two of them making out on the dance floor.

As Kai hopped on his Honda, a surge of disgust *and* desire cropped up. Jessie had been so damn hot that night. Aggressive, passionate, lustful. As he started the bike, he wondered if that was what being in a relationship with her would be like. She'd definitely been drunk the night they'd been together, but that intensity had to still be there, buried under the surface somewhere. Revving his engine, the warmth of the machine warming his thighs, Kai let himself wonder if he could stoke that desire in her while she was completely sober. His body started stiffening at the thought, and he cursed again. He seriously had to stop that; he could not walk around town with a never-ending hard-on because he was thinking about her. Squealing out of the garage, he let the feeling of flying across the pavement clear his mind.

As he headed to a bakery that he'd spotted on the way home yesterday, Kai shifted his thoughts to Jessie's roommates. He really hadn't been paying too much attention to them at the club—Jessie had absorbed all of his focus—but he seemed to recall there being two of them. One with dark hair, one with red hair…if he was remembering it correctly. He also knew they were protective of Jessie, since they'd hurriedly swept her out of his room almost immediately after they'd…

But Jessie swore they didn't remember what he looked like. And if they truly didn't then officially meeting them should be okay. Jessie seemed reluctant, though. She hadn't said it, but he got the feeling she would prefer it if Kai never met her roommates. Maybe she was just nervous, worried that they would piece things together once they saw him again. Or maybe Jessie was embarrassed to be seen with him.

Kai laughed into his helmet as he pulled into the parking lot of the bright and cheery shop. No, while he might affect Jessie in strange ways, he was pretty sure he didn't embarrass her. He frowned. Well, what they'd done probably embarrassed her. It embarrassed him too. People always preached about being careful about sleeping with strangers for pregnancy and STD reasons, but no one ever mentioned that the world was microscopic, and fate was one cruel bitch. No one had *ever* warned Kai that the hot girl shoving her hand down his pants and her tongue down his throat, might be a family member.

Twenty minutes later Kai was walking into the hospital. He'd called Gran yesterday at work, and she was getting out sometime today. Her fractured hip would need a lot of rest, but she looked good. All her tests were showing that she was healing well, so they were letting her go back to her life. Knowing his gran, she would be knee-deep in potting soil by the afternoon. Tough old broad.

The nurses gave him wide smiles as he entered. Ever thankful for the wonderful care his grandmother was receiving, Kai had brought a box of donuts for them. They gave him swift hugs and told him she was awake if he wanted to surprise her. After a kiss on the cheek by a sprightly nurse named Susan, who eyed him like she was mapping out his future in her head, Kai ducked into his grandmother's room.

She was propped up in her bed, reading glasses nearly falling off her nose as her gnarled hands clicked and clacked the knitting needles Kai had brought for her. Her aged hands flew over patterns they had obviously repeated so many times, she could probably do them in her sleep. The result of all the miraculous, repetitious movement was a blanket flowing down the side of her bed in a myriad of bright colors. A little amazed at how a seemingly chaotic series of events could result in something so beautiful, Kai smiled as he watched the progression.

The older woman beamed at him when she noticed his entrance. "Kai, dear, I'm so glad you came by."

Gran could be in a body cast, head to foot, pain in every limb and joint, and she'd still smile warmly and say she was glad to see him. Tough…yet sweet, old broad. "Good morning, Grandma."

She patted a spot beside her on the bed as she set down her needlework and glasses. "You seem tired, sweetheart. How are you holding up?"

Kai frowned. He thought he actually looked better today, having gotten a decent amount of sleep last night; even the slight sickness that Jessie had thought was related to the different altitude had lifted. Immediately switching to a smile, Kai leaned down and kissed the woman's head before sitting beside her. "I'm great, Gran, don't worry about me." He set a muffin down on her side table. It was blueberry, with some sort of crumble on the top; it smelled incredible. Grabbing her hand, he stroked her fingers with his thumb. "You just worry about you."

Gran dismissed his comment with a swish of her free hand. "Nonsense, nothing to worry about with me. But you …?" Her eyes gave him a penetrating, calculating examination, almost like she was looking for something specific in his expression. He tried to keep a relaxed, pleasant smile on his face. He didn't want her to see any of the turmoil that had been in his heart lately. "How are you doing…with everything?" she asked, her voice oddly sympathetic.

Kai smiled wider. "Like I said, I'm great. Jessie is taking care of me." A flush heated his cheeks after he said it, and he hoped Gran couldn't see it through his skin tone. He shouldn't react that way to Jessie's name, but there it was.

Gran didn't seem to catch his odd reaction. Instead she asked, "How was your first day at work? Do you…like it there?" Her eyes narrowed, and she suddenly seemed very anxious about his answer.

Kai wondered why at first, but then figured that, like his mother, Gran was merely hoping he was adjusting well to his new life, his new career. Frowning as he remembered his boss's odd reaction to him, Kai shrugged and said, "I think it went okay." He again altered his expression; he didn't want his grandmother worrying about him. "I think I'll like it there."

She studied his face for a moment more, sighed, then curved her lips into a small smile. She finally seemed to believe Kai was doing okay, and that made him feel better. He *was* doing okay, all things considered.

Patting his thigh, she told him, "That's good, dear. I wouldn't want your new job to be...unpleasant for you."

Kai absentmindedly scratched where a bee had stung his shoulder. "It's not..."

As Kai started reminiscing about his day, his grandmother brightened. She sat up higher on the bed, and Kai caught a flinch in her face as a twinge of pain went through her. She didn't comment on it, and Kai didn't have a chance to ask her about it, because her next question froze his tongue solid. "Did you meet my nurse, Susan? Lovely girl. I tried to set you up with one of her daughters."

Kai's eyes widened. The "girl" he'd met in the other room was named Susan. She'd made sure Kai knew it, as she'd excitedly taken a maple bar from him. The nurse had to be his mother's age, at least, but to Gran, he supposed that was still young. Wow. He hadn't even been here a week yet, and his grandmother was already trying to fix him up. This could be a problem if he didn't put a stop to it right away.

Finding his voice, he muttered, "I appreciate the thought, Gran, but I can find my own dates." True, his last one had ended up being related to him, but at least he'd found her himself.

Gran gave him a look that clearly said she did *not* believe he was capable of such a thing. "Well, no need to worry, she only had boys." She laughed in short, bubbled bursts. "I tried to throw them Jessica Marie's way, but she gave me the exact same look you just did."

Kai forced a smile, but he had to look away. He really didn't like the idea of Jessie going out with some random guy who Gran had set her up with. Then again, he didn't particularly like the thought of her going out with anyone. He frowned as he realized she would one day, and he'd have to come to terms with it.

Skin that felt paper-thin reached up to touch his face. Turning his head, he caught his grandmother giving him worried eyes. "You all right, honey?"

With a soft smile, he nodded. "Of course." Hating what he was about to say, he told her, "I was just wishing that I could be home with you today, to take care of you once you leave here." While he actually did feel that way, his thoughts had been nowhere near concern for her when she'd asked. Whether or not the sentiment was true, it felt like a lie, and he hated it. His frown returned.

His grandmother tried to forcefully turn his frown into a smile with her finger. "You just go to work and have a good day." Kai smirked at her gesture and she added, "And if it makes you feel any better, Jessica Marie is going to be with me for most of the day. She works the later shift on Tuesdays."

Kai's mood darkened when he realized he wouldn't be seeing his cousin tonight. How strange that he'd already gotten used to seeing her on a daily basis. And honestly, he'd been looking forward to an unexpected knock on his door this evening from her. Knowing that probably wouldn't happen bothered him. Maybe he should take her up on her offer of visiting her at work. Another massage sounded really nice.

Gran patted his thigh again. "Now, you don't fret over me. Jessica Marie is a fabulous caregiver. I swear, sometimes that girl frets more over my happiness than her own." She sighed. "At least she finally got smart and dumped that boy she was seeing."

Kai looked up from where he'd been studying the aged woman's hand in his own. Her skin seemed so frail and fragile in contrast to his. It was almost startling how different their hands looked, one on top of the other.

"Jeremy?" Kai couldn't hide the contempt in his voice when he said *that* name. He wasn't sure what had really happened between him and Jessie, but he knew that the man hadn't been faithful to her. That made him a lowlife in Kai's book. A very stupid lowlife. Jessie was amazing.

Seeming happy that Kai knew a bit about Jessie's past, Gran nodded. "Yeah, that one was a piece of work. I never did trust the hoodlum."

Kai grinned. Something about his grandmother not liking Jessie's ex made a swarm of happy butterflies lift Kai's belly. He looked down briefly as his brow bunched together. That was an odd feeling to have.

Confused, Kai made a show of checking the time. "Sorry, Gran, I should go." He gave her an apologetic smile, but really, he needed to leave, needed to get back on the road and clear his head. He was really looking forward to the long, peaceful drive to work now.

Nodding, his grandmother pulled his body toward her so she could kiss his cheek. "Of course, dear." After their long hug, she once again gave him an odd, appraising look. "Have a good day at work."

Kai stood up and gave her a breezy smile. "I will." Pointing at her with a stern finger, he added, "You take it easy when you get home. No tree climbing or anything."

She laughed at him, and he leaned down for another quick hug. "I'll wait at least a week for that, I promise."

Laughing, he shook his head. "You better." He indicated the oversized muffin he'd brought for her. "Make sure and eat your breakfast before the nurses steal it. I brought them donuts, but you never know." He gave her a teasing wink, and she promised that she would.

Kai walked into the hall, then glanced back at the door to see her smiling and shaking her head at him. He silently wished her well for the day, and then silently did the same for himself. Hopefully he could get through the day without being stung. Again.

9

An Invitation

Jessie was having a long week. After seeing Kai Monday night, life had kept her too busy to see him again for a few days. Well, life and taking care of Grams. Jessie found that she missed talking to him face to face. Missed it in a way that was a little disturbing to her.

Whenever she thought about the moment she'd told him she was falling for him, Jessie mentally cringed. God, what the hell had that been about? She couldn't fall for Kai. It wasn't allowed, wasn't acceptable, and definitely wasn't a path she could go down. Thank goodness Kai had been asleep and hadn't heard her. How mortifying if he had.

While getting dressed for her Friday morning shift at the clinic, Jessie thought about the past couple of days. Instead of visiting Kai, she had spent her free time with Grams. Helping her to recover went a long way in helping Jessie move on. Kind of. Grams had a way of bringing up Kai every five minutes. She hadn't appeared to be testing the waters or anything, but out of concern for her grandson, she mentioned him frequently.

She was always asking Jessie to check on him, to make sure he was getting along in the city okay. Finding out where everything was could be confusing to a new person. Jessie constantly assured Grams that she would take him sightseeing when she got some free time. She'd even told her that they might go exploring this weekend. Grams had loved the idea.

She also seemed to be in love with the idea of setting Kai up. Jessie hated whenever Grams asked her for advice or help in finding Kai a girl. He was fine being young, single, and free. He didn't need to be saddled with a relationship right now. Although, in a bit of a shocking revelation, Grams had hinted that she wasn't necessarily talking about a "relation-ship" for Kai; she'd even used the phrases "sow his oats" and "explore his options". Jessie still had a hard time believing the old woman was actually suggesting her grandchild should sleep around. Shouldn't all parental types be opposed to such a thing? At least on the surface?

Jessie felt heat rising in her cheeks as she pulled her hair into a curly French twist. She couldn't even think about Kai's love life without thinking of their intimate moment together. It haunted her sometimes, slipped into her mind at the most inopportune times. For that reason alone, it was a small relief to her that she hadn't seen him in a few days, regardless of how much she missed him. Kai had a way of looking at her, being close to her, or even just breathing on her that instantly shoved Jessie's thoughts into the "do not enter" zone. Space was good. Distance was good.

And hard.

Jessie was ready to see him again. Aching for it really. Once she was home for the day, she frequently found herself imagining that she was knocking on his door. She pictured how surprised he would be as he laughingly swept her into a hug. And of course, he was almost always shirtless in her fantasies. Jessie couldn't help it. He had a pleasing shape. Wrong as it was, she ached to see his body again, too.

Jessie did often wonder how he was getting along without her. Not that he needed her or anything, but she liked to think that he was missing her as much as she was missing him. What he was doing wasn't as much of a mystery. Jessie and Kai usually exchanged texts throughout the day or talked on the phone. He also called Grams a lot, and the old woman seemed to relay every single in-depth conversation they had back to Jessie. If Jessie were a different sort of person, she might have been a little jealous over how close Kai and Grams were. But she wasn't that type of girl. And really, it only reaffirmed why they had to stay away from each other. He was family — beloved family. There was just no way to get around that fact.

Gram's conversations about him usually centered around Kai's job, and she always seemed concerned when she brought up his work. Jessie couldn't be sure, but she felt like Grams was waiting for something bad to happen. Jessie had no idea what that might be. From all of Gram's stories, it was pretty clear that Kai was loving it there. He'd healed from the bee fiasco, and luckily hadn't had any other sting incidents, and was thoroughly getting into the plant and animal life of the Rocky Mountains. He'd even adjusted to the new time zone and wasn't suffering from as much exhaustion.

Jessie was happy to hear it. He'd seemed so tired when he'd fallen asleep in her arms, his own wrapped around her. Those warm, strong arms…

Sighing, Jessie gazed at herself in the mirror. A couple of untamed strands had fallen out of the clip securing her thick locks in place. Refusing to redo the style, Jessie tucked them behind her ear. She shouldn't think about cuddling with Kai, about him asking in a whisper if it was all right, then telling her that she felt good. Those words should not give her stomach a jolt of electricity. But they did.

Watching her deep brown eyes start to water, Jessie shook her head and turned on the faucet so she could splash her face with cold water. She shouldn't linger on that last kiss either; her lips pressing into his mouth, him responding ever so slightly. The softness, the heat, the light exhale along her skin … She needed to move on from the memory, and so did he. Maybe Grams was on to something. Maybe she should set him up with someone. Maybe she should set him up with April, since April still asked Jessie nightly if her mysterious cousin was making an appearance anytime soon.

Straightening, Jessie dried her face and started doing her makeup. Their tryst had only been a week ago. A week ago tonight. Was that long enough for her inebriated friends to forget his face? Jessie had no idea. Only one way to know for sure, she supposed.

Slipping on her shoes as she sat on her bed, Jessie glanced out her bedroom window. On her cement patio, under a shaded overhang, was a round table with two matching chairs. It was the wrought iron type that you might see outside a small Parisian café. Jessie stood up and walked over to the window to look at it closer. It was a tiny set that had seen better days.

The girls never really used it, as evidenced by the spider webs laced throughout the bars. Jessie occasionally went out back to read a book in the sun, but she generally sat in the more comfortable lounge chair when she did.

Remembering how Kai was eating his meals on his bed, or probably standing in the kitchen next to his sink, made Jessie smile. She recalled mentioning to him that he should get a table for his place. He'd made a joke at her comment, but he hadn't seemed opposed to it. It had been more like he'd felt Jessie was doing too much for him. That wasn't true, though. Really, besides buying him some more nutritious food, all she'd done was given him a bunch of odds and ends that she hadn't needed.

Her mind made up, Jessie headed out back through a slider in the living room. The patio set was pretty light, and Jessie got in through the house and into her truck with relative ease. She even wiped off the stray spider webs. As she closed the end of her truck, she realized that she now had a legitimate reason to knock on Kai's door again. She couldn't stop the grin that exploded onto her face, or the nervous butterflies that flew through her stomach at just the thought of seeing those ocean eyes again. Oh boy, she really needed to stop that reaction.

Moments later, Jessie was walking into the warm, cheery office where she worked. As she smiled hello to the receptionist, she took in the large space that was her current home away from home. Soft music was coming through the speakers inlaid in the ceiling, and every wall was painted a pleasing, butter-cream color. The accents were all done in various shades of green, resulting in a waiting room that was peaceful and relaxing. A dozen or so padded chairs lined the walls with several round tables sprinkled throughout, each holding several different types of magazines. One or two clients were already there, flipping through the pages, waiting to get their chemical peel or facial scrub from the esthetician, or maybe even waiting for a body rub from Jessie.

Getting ready for the day, Jessie tucked her purse into a drawer in her desk and hung her jacket on an awaiting coat rack in the corner. Her room was designed for ambiance with her massage table taking center stage. The plush, padded slab had a circle cut out of the top so a person could rest their head straight down, keeping their spine perfectly aligned for Jessie to work all the kinks out of overworked muscles.

The walls were a beautiful mauve color, showcasing an assortment of dewdrop photos. If you looked really closely, you could see images and reflections in each drop. They were astounding, but most people that came in here never really got to see them, as the room was kept pretty dark. Jessie switched on a softly glowing lamp, highlighting the various oils and creams she used without over-lighting the room. Then she lit a half-dozen scentless candles placed in clumps throughout the space. As she'd quickly discovered when she'd started working here, some of her clients couldn't handle heavy scents; it hadn't taken Jessie long to switch to odorless mood lighting.

Once the room was flickering with a peaceful glow, she turned her stereo on low, a stream of calming music quietly spilling out. Opening a bottle of lavender oil, she poured a small amount into a potpourri dish. The light scent filled the room with subtle tranquility.

Sitting on the edge of her table, she looked over at the clock on the wall. Her first client should be here soon. As the peace of her office flowed into her, Jessie warmed her hands for a day of action. Her thoughts drifted to Kai as she did. She pictured him spread out on the table she was sitting on, imagined his broad back, his lean body, his bare legs, and only a plush towel resting over his hips as her hands glided over his body. Then she imagined her hands slipping under that towel …

"Jessica, can you believe it's Friday again already? Where does the time go?"

Jessie was startled out of her inappropriate thoughts, and her heart was pounding as she glanced at the door. The older gentleman that she saw every Friday morning was standing there, smiling at her. Hopping off the table, Jessie calmed her heart and returned his smile. "Good morning, Mr. Tinley." Giving him a playful grin as she patted the table, Jessie prayed that she wasn't bright red. At least the dim lighting would hide it if she were. "The week may have gone by fast for you, but the time until I got to see you again, dragged on and on for me."

He laughed as he sat on the table and began undoing his shoes. "Careful now, Jessica. Flirt with me anymore, and I may just think I've got a shot with you."

Jessie laughed at the man old enough to be her grandpa. "I'll be back in a few minutes, Mr. Tinley."

He nodded and Jessie stepped out of the room to give him time to undress and lay on the table. Heading to a bathroom, Jessie quickly stepped inside and exhaled a long breath. Her brief fantasy of Kai had gotten her a little worked up. Even now, knowing Mr. Tinley was in there changing, she was picturing her cousin slinking off his clothes. And if Kai were here, she wouldn't have left the room.

The arousing thought made Jessie's stomach tighten uncomfortably. Stepping over to the faucet, she stared at herself in the mirror. "Stop it, Jessie. You can't be with him, so stop thinking of him like that," she whispered to herself. With her own irritated eyes glaring back at her, she sighed again and turned on the water. Wishing she could splash some on her face without completely ruining her makeup, she settled on feeling the rushing coolness filter through her fingers instead. After another long, cleansing moment, she headed back to Mr. Tinley.

Her brief self-scolding in the bathroom cleared her head a little, and for part of the day, she was able to tuck Kai away into a tiny, unused portion of her brain. But not for long. Eventually he came out, disrupting her work by churning her stomach and igniting her body. The first time he slipped out, she was massaging the shoulders of a man whose back was covered with wiry gray hairs. But Jessie didn't see the gray hairs. She rarely ever noticed her clients' oddities, more focused on the muscles beneath the skin, but today her mind completely evaporated the chalky whiteness glowing in the candlelight, and replaced it with the deep, sun kissed shade of Kai's skin.

And that was only the first time he disrupted her thoughts. She thought about him while working on a strained calf muscle, a bad case of plantar fasciitis, and a shoulder blade stress knot. She pictured her oiled hands running over his taut body as she rubbed down a figure that was not so toned. She visualized the swirl of his tattoo as she worked on a woman whose skin rivaled the depth of color in that dark ink. And between clients, she found herself staring out the window in the break room, hoping to see Kai pull up in that sporty bike of his.

No, as much as she tried, Jessie just couldn't seem to get Kai out of her head, and it made her feel awful. But wonderful.

With her thoughts drifting and her cousin filling up her brain, Jessie's day was a long one. She was grateful when it was over, and she was waving goodbye to the receptionist. Glancing at the patio table in the bed of her truck, she wondered if maybe she should wait to drop it off later; he was just affecting her more than usual today, and she wasn't sure what might happen if she were around him right now, especially if he was being affected by her absence, as well. But then again, while talking on the phone with Kai was soothing and refreshing, it wasn't enough to keep Jessie satisfied. She needed more. She needed to see him.

And maybe not seeing him for a while was the cause of her problems? Maybe he was something she needed to gradually pull away from, not quit cold turkey. Not that she ever intended to truly quit him. Kai was family, and family didn't abandon each other, even if being around one another was difficult at times. Her decision reaffirmed, Jessie climbed into her truck and set off to her cousin's place.

Jessie sighed in disappointment when she pulled into his underground parking garage. The spot reserved for his bike was empty. He wasn't home yet. Not sure whether she should leave the table in front of his door or not, Jessie climbed out of her truck and stared at the white lines outlining the space where his motorcycle should be. She'd really been hoping to see him.

As if fate wanted them to keep meeting up, Jessie heard the growl of his bike while she was staring at the white lines. Joy lifting her spirits, she twisted around to see his sleek form approaching on that smooth bike. He looked completely natural on it, like he'd been riding bikes his entire life. Effortlessly pulling into the spot she was standing beside, he set his feet on the ground as he shut the bike off. Pushing down the kickstand, he turned to look at her. Beneath the pitch-black helmet, Jessie had no idea if he was happy to see her or not. She was hoping he was. She was certainly happy to see him.

Sitting back on his bike, he popped his helmet off. The grin Jessie saw there was exactly the one she'd been hoping to see. "Hey there, cousin. What brings you to my neck of the woods?"

Jessie suppressed a cringe at hearing the familial term he'd placed between them. Usually she was grateful for the reminder, but after all the fantasies she'd had this afternoon… well, she sort of wanted to forget.

Mad at herself for actually wanting to forget they were related, Jessie smiled brightly at him. "I have a surprise for you …cousin."

Kai didn't react to her term either, only tilted his head at her statement as he swung his leg over his bike. After slinging his helmet over his handlebar, he walked up to Jessie. Standing directly in front of where she was leaning against her truck, he reached out for her hand. Loosely holding her fingers, he ran his thumb up and down the back of her hand. It was exquisite torture for Jessie, and she really hated how much she loved the slight caress.

Smiling warmly at her, Kai's sea-green eyes swept over her face. "You don't have to keep doing things for me, Jessie," he whispered her name, and Jessie's heart skipped a beat. No, the face-to-face absence had definitely not been a good idea. His presence was overwhelming her so much right now that she wanted to grab his neck and pull his mouth to hers. But …she couldn't, not with that cousin word still hovering in the air.

As she absorbed the tender look in his eyes, she finally noticed what he was wearing. It was some sort of uniform: khaki slacks and a bright teal polo with the research center name in the corner. The color of the shirt emphasized the color of his eyes, even in the fluorescent glow of the parking lot lighting. He was even more spectacular, and for a moment, Jessie was too awed to answer him.

She moved away from the truck and into his body. Kai didn't pull back, not even when she took a step forward and pressed the entire length of her body into his. He said nothing; he did nothing, other than part his lips as he started to breathe heavier. Clenching his hand, Jessie brought her other palm to his chest, resting it on the lean muscles she'd been picturing all day long.

She ran her fingers up to his shoulder, but he still didn't step away, still didn't react negatively to her nearness. In fact, his free hand drifted to her hip, pulling her into him. Feeling bolstered by his touch, Jessie moved her head closer to his. "I've missed you," she breathed, her lips just mere inches from his.

Kai's head lowered as his eyes half closed. "I missed you too, Jessie," he whispered. His breath over her face made her feel weak, allowed her to ignore every warning bell going off in her brain. She knew they were too close, she knew they were being too intimate, but his hand on her hip was sliding around to her backside, and she just couldn't care enough to stop him from touching her in that way. Honestly, he could touch her any way he wanted to right now.

Her fingers trailed up his neck to tangle in his dark hair. They moved toward each other simultaneously. The distance between their lips was slimming by the second, when suddenly a car zoomed around the corner, breaking the spell. The car had been going too fast for the tight turn, and slid out a little as it came toward them. Kai immediately grabbed Jessie and shoved her behind him.

The stupid sports car came within two inches of hitting the back of Jessie's truck, before the driver finally regained control and continued speeding away. Yelling an obscenity at the asshole, Jessie glared at the red tail lights until they disappeared. What was it about fast cars that made people think they were invincible?

When the jerk-hole was gone, Jessie finally noticed how Kai was pressing her into the concrete wall, protecting her. Clinging to his shoulders, her fingers dug into his thick jacket as adrenaline pumped through her. She'd been so sure that car had been about to hit them or their vehicles, and Kai had thrown himself in front of her. No one had ever done anything like that for Jessie before, and a surprising rush of warmth filled her.

Kai stepped forward and then slowly twisted to look back at her. Jessie wasn't sure if he was dazed by their near-kiss, the squealing vehicle that had almost smashed them, or the lingering feeling of protectiveness that was still hovering in the air. Either way, his breath was much quicker when he finally faced her again. Brows drawn together in concern, he searched her body. "Are you okay? Did I hurt you?"

It was only then that Jessie felt the slight ache in her shoulder from where he'd roughly shoved her into the wall. Not wanting him to feel guilt over shielding her, she smiled and shook her head. "No, I'm fine," she said, reaching out a hand for him.

Looking relieved, Kai took it. As he squeezed her fingers, he gave her a devilish grin. "I didn't realize you had such a dirty mouth." Jessie blushed; the words she'd yelled at that maniac driver hadn't been ladylike. Side effect of growing up with four brothers. Kai's grin widened when he noticed her flush. "That was kind of hot."

His smile immediately dropped, and he released her hand. Both looking torn, they stared at each other for a long, painful moment. They had nearly caved into the temptation to kiss each other — *really* kiss each other. Jessie was sure that if their lips had touched, it would have ignited the sexual tension between them, and they would have spent the night testing out the strength of Kai's new headboard…the headboard that belonged to the woman who was a grandmother to them both.

Swallowing the bile in her throat, Jessie broke the silence by indicating her truck. "I brought you a table," she muttered, not even sure if coming here was a good idea anymore.

At hearing her dejected tone, Kai's face fell, but then he brightened as he looked over at her truck. "You did?" He walked over to examine the table in the truck bed, then looked back at Jessie, stunned. "You actually went out and found me a table?" He seemed perplexed that she would take the time to do that.

She shrugged. "I had one…we weren't using it, so…"

Kai smiled at her as he shook his head. "You take care of everything, don't you?" There was such love and warmth in his sentence that Jessie felt it in every cell of her body. The way he talked to her, the way he looked at her, it made Jessie want to do everything that she could for him, even if some of the things she wanted to do were wrong. Very wrong.

He studied her face for a moment, then shifted his gaze to the ground. "Thank you, Jessie," he whispered, peeking up at her from the corner of his eye. Grinning, Jessie flushed with pleasure. God, she loved doing things for him.

Laughing a little as he moved to the back of the truck, Kai shook his head and said, "I should just get that printed on a t-shirt, since I seem to say it so much."

Jessie laughed as she followed him. "You're just being overly gracious. I really haven't done all that much."

As he pulled the table from the truck and set it on the ground, he gave her an incredulous expression. "You've done more than I ever could have…" He stopped and sighed, and a multitude of emotions passed over his face. Jessie wasn't sure what they all were, but she thought she saw pain there. And longing.

Clearing his throat and shaking his head, Kai grabbed the table while Jessie grabbed the chairs. "Come on, I'll make you something to eat. We'll have dinner on my new table. It's the least I can do."

With a wistful smile on her lips, Jessie followed him.

Kai unlocked his apartment and walked in with Jessie close behind him. He still couldn't believe she'd been waiting for him when he'd gotten home, and he hoped she hadn't been waiting long. Missy had held him up after work, begging for a ride on his bike. Politely refusing her, Kai had gotten out of there as quickly as he could by telling her that he was running late to meet someone. Little had he known that his lie was actually the truth.

And what a pleasant surprise that had been. Kai had been missing Jessie for a while. He hadn't seen her since Monday night, and all day long she'd been on his mind, infiltrating his every thought as he'd stared at slides in a microscope. Somehow, Jessie had a way of even making cellular decomposition sexy. And knowing he shouldn't think that way about her had kept Kai in turmoil for hours.

But upon seeing her, all that turmoil had lifted into joy. While he'd talked on the phone with her all week, Kai had missed seeing her. He'd missed her eyes, missed her smile, and missed the crinkle of her nose when she laughed. He'd missed...his cousin.

God, he hated that word. It was necessary to keep using it, although, sometimes Kai wondered if that word would ever truly be enough to keep them separated, to keep them from going down that disastrous road. But they had to keep trying to resist. As hard as it was, they had to try. Because willingly going down that path wasn't an option.

As Kai closed his door behind Jessie, he thought over their heated moment in the parking garage. As they set the table and chairs up in the small kitchen space, he considered the horrible fact that he'd *wanted* it to happen. Sickeningly enough, he'd wanted her lips on his just as firmly as her breasts had been pressed against him. He would have done anything in that moment to not be related to her, to not feel the gut-twisting guilt that often accompanied the desire. Things would be so much simpler if they didn't share the same blood, but some obstacles were insurmountable. Genes was one of them.

As Jessie sat at his new table, miming opening a menu and looking through the contents like a discerning food critic, Kai smiled at her. His heart was still pounding over the near-incident with that damn car in the parking garage, but given the same circumstances again, Kai would always try to keep her safe. Come to think of it, given all of the same incidences again tonight, none of his actions would probably change. Admitting that hurt his stomach. He shouldn't let them get too close. At least, not like that. It wasn't healthy for either of them.

Since he'd already treated Jessie to his out-of-this-world Spam sandwich, Kai decided to make the second dinner he could cook well: spaghetti. Jessie took in the amount he gave her with wide eyes, but said nothing. After placing their heaping plates down on the wrought iron table, Kai opened a bottle of red wine. He poured them each a glass, then sat down across from Jessie.

She thanked him with a warm smile, and Kai's entire body heated at the look on her face. Sipping on his wine, he was again amazed at her generosity. It was like she spent all day thinking of ways to make him happy and comfortable. Kai didn't think he actually took up that much space in her brain...but a small portion of him liked to think that he did. He forcefully tried to ignore that part of him.

They ate their messy meals in comfortable companion-ship, laughing whenever someone got a stray splash of sauce somewhere. When Jessie tenderly reached out and rubbed some off his chin, Kai momentarily wished that she had someone to nurture. Someone she could love and dote on with no awkward, guilty feelings. Someone worthy of her, much more so than that her asshole ex Jeremy had been. Jessie was so good to Kai...he just knew she would be amazing as a girl-friend. Someone else's girlfriend.

Kai felt his throat constricting, and it took him a few swal-lows to ease the ache. Eventually that would happen, and Jes-sie would find someone to love. Girls like her didn't stay sin-gle for long. Kai had no idea what he would do when her de-votion to him was suddenly diverted to another man. And just the thought of her being with someone else made a surprising rush of jealousy flash through him. He hated the non-existent man already.

"You all right?"

Kai looked up at hearing Jessie's concerned voice. Trying to look as carefree as he could, he brightly said, "Of course." Pointing to Jessie's half-eaten plate of spaghetti, he attempted to distract her from deciphering his mood by asking, "Is it okay?"

Jessie glanced at her plate and smiled. "It's wonderful. I haven't had spaghetti in forever."

Kai felt a little guilty that he hadn't made something more elaborate, even the sauce had been from a jar, but she seemed genuine with her answer. "Good...I'm glad."

As he went back to eating, Jessie paused with her wine glass to her lips. Kai studied her thoughtfully while he chewed his food. She seemed like she wanted to ask him

162

something. Wondering what she might possibly question him about made him a little nervous. If she brought up them, and what had almost happened downstairs...well, he wasn't sure what he could say about it. Nothing that he should probably say out loud. It was best if Jessie didn't know just how often he thought of her...how often he dreamt of her.

When she pulled the glass from her mouth, Kai froze; he was rigid with tension when her question finally escaped her lips. "Would you like to come to my place tomorrow night? Have dinner with me...and my roommates?" She added that last part after a momentary pause.

Relaxing, Kai swallowed his food and smiled. He'd been imagining much harder questions. "Sure, I'd love to see your place." He thought about that for a second while she smiled. "Would your roommates...? I mean...has it been long enough ...? Would they suspect that you and me...?" Kai let his voice trail off. He didn't know how to ask her if her roommates would figure out that he was Jessie's one night stand once they saw him. God, even thinking the question made him nauseated.

Knowing what he was vaguely referring to, Jessie immediately averted her eyes. "No, I don't...I don't think so." She looked back with a shrug. "If I introduce you as my cousin, the thought shouldn't even cross their minds. They'll just assume that you and I would never..." She bit her lip as her cheeks turned a beautiful shade of pink.

Nodding, Kai took a large gulp of his wine. It seemed reasonable enough to think that her friends wouldn't make that connection. Because who would suspect that, as family, they'd never met before that night? That, thanks to nicknames and lots of alcohol, they hadn't recognized each other in the club.

That they'd gone all the way without ever really finding out anything about the other. That they'd had mind-blowing sex without ever realizing that they shared the same last name.

No, who would ever be twisted enough to come up with that scenario?

10

Guess Who's Coming To Dinner?

K ai woke up Saturday morning feeling pretty good. And not just because he had finally adjusted to the time change and was up at a reasonable hour for a weekend morning. No, what had a smile plastered on his face when he opened his eyes, was the thought of going to Jessie's place later.

Standing and stretching, he threw on a T-shirt and shuffled to the kitchen to make some coffee and have some cereal at his new table. He smiled the entire time he ate his breakfast, enjoying the ease of sitting at a table, and the sentiment behind the gift. His cousin was such a generous person. As Kai finished his bowl, he idly wondered if there was anything he could give to her. Some small, reciprocal token of appreciation. Unfortunately, he really didn't have much yet. Maybe later, when he started getting some decent paychecks, he would get her something, or maybe take her out to a nice meal. Nothing too date-like though. Kai wouldn't want to make either of them uncomfortable.

His first week had gone by in a blur. Getting to and from his job was a longer commute than he was used to, but the freedom of riding a motorcycle was something he enjoyed, so he often looked forward to his rides. Although, he could already tell that he was going to have to wear something heavier over his work clothes when he rode. He was just getting too cold. Maybe he'd do a little shopping today.

The actual work part of work was going smoothly enough. Truly, doing the work was the easiest thing about his job. Cataloging, studying, analyzing...they were all tasks that he found intriguing. It was dealing with all of the various personalities at the research center that was the real challenge.

Louis seemed to think that he and Kai were best friends now, and while Kai liked the man, he wasn't sure if he liked being treated to the non-stop rendition of the *Tao of Louis*. He had an opinion on everything, and was none too shy about sharing it. He was also 100 percent certain that Kai had screwed Missy on that very first day in the backroom. He hadn't even hesitated to ask Kai for the details, and had only been surprised when Kai had refused to admit they'd done the deed. To Louis, it was just another fact catalogued in his brain. His sureness made Kai wonder if Missy was telling people that was what had happened.

As for Kai's actual relationship with Missy, well he probably had a decent case for sexual harassment on his hands. He wasn't about to take it that far—he could handle being hit on every day without formally complaining—but it was taxing at times. Kai hoped that after a while of his purposeful disinterest in her advances, she would stop. So far, she hadn't yet. If anything, she'd gotten a little bolder as they grew more comfortable around each other. Just yesterday, when she'd been bugging him about the bike, she'd also grabbed his ass.

Kai had politely, but firmly, asked her to not ever do that again. He was sure she would, though. Really, he wouldn't be surprised if she cupped his junk one day. He was seriously hoping that day didn't happen anytime soon.

Then there was his boss, Mason. After a full week he'd finally somewhat warmed to Kai. He seemed to truly appreciate Kai's work ethic and ability to multitask. He'd commended him on his analyses and often asked Kai to help him with projects he was working on, most of them involving those damn bees. Fortunately, Kai hadn't been stung again by the little bastards.

But even with all that, Kai got the feeling that Mason would prefer it if Kai weren't around. Like, for some unknowable reason, Kai upset him. Mason wasn't obvious about it when he spoke to Kai, but Kai was observant, and he noticed the tightness of Mason's eyes, the guarded way he smiled, and the small sigh that escaped his lips whenever Kai entered a room. Yes, Kai wasn't sure why, but he was positive that his boss didn't like him.

That bothered Kai. He really looked up to Mason, admired his mind and his goals. The work he was doing was important, noble even, and Kai had a great amount of respect for him. He wanted to turn the man's opinion around, get him to like and accept Kai as an important member of the team... he just wasn't sure how to do that. The only thing Kai could really do was keep his nose to the grindstone, keep doing his job to the best of his ability. Maybe, given enough time, whatever Kai had done to Mason would fade away, and they could be close colleagues.

Kai hoped so.

Just as he was feeling better from his mental pep talk, he heard a soft, lyrical ringing. He looked over at his nightstand, to where his cell phone was softly playing a song. Frowning, Kai picked it up. He'd lowered the volume of the ringer on his phone, but he was pretty sure he'd never changed the ring-tone to "Endless Love." Rolling his eyes, Kai wondered if Missy had somehow stolen his cell phone and messed with it. Great. He was positive her number was now in his contact list.

Glancing at the name on his display, Kai frowned even more. Answering the call, he held the phone to his ear. "Mom? Why are you up so early?"

His mother seemed surprise that he'd picked up. "Oh, hi, Kai. I wasn't sure if you'd be up this early on a Saturday. I was just going to leave a message."

Kai looked over to the clock on the microwave and let out a soft laugh. "It's not that early for me, Mom. It's after ten. But it is for you. Why are you up so early?" he asked again, relax-ing back against his headboard as he idly watched TV.

His mom hesitated. "Oh, I just…had a couple phone calls to make. I was a little anxious about making them, so I really wasn't sleeping well anyway."

Hearing the stress in his mom's voice concerned Kai. "Everything all right?"

She hesitated again, like she was debating whether or not to tell him something. He had no idea what she might want to say, and it worried him. "Of course, honey. Don't you worry about me. How are you doing? How's work going?"

Her oft-repeated question relaxed him. She had called him every day, and the one thing she always asked him about, was his work. "Since yesterday, Mom? It's fine." He laughed as he answered, amused by her curiosity.

Kai heard a sound from her that he could have sworn was a disappointed sigh, but all she said was, "That's good." Kai wanted to ask her again if everything was all right, but before he could, she said, "Well, I was just calling to let you know that I sent you a care package. You should get it any day."

Wondering what she'd sent him, Kai smiled as he rubbed his stomach. The women of his family were so incredibly thoughtful. Despite all of his current complications, he was a lucky guy. "Thanks, Mom. You didn't have to do that."

She scoffed at his response. "I'm your mother, honey. It's exactly what I have to do."

She laughed softly, and Kai shook his head. "Well, again, thank you."

Just as Kai was hoping his mother had sent him some of her world famous chocolate chip macadamia nut cookies, she asked him about a touchy subject. "So, you meet a girl yet?"

God, Kai hated that question. Curiosity about his love life was one of the unfortunate side effects that came along with having caring women in his life. If it were up to Gran and his mother, he'd be halfway down a wedding aisle by now, but with everything that was going on with Jessie—which was nothing really—Kai just hadn't had a moment to think about seeing someone else. It kind of hurt his heart to think about it.

Playing up his annoyance, Kai groaned in frustration. "Come on, Mom. Between you and Grandma, I swear, you'd think I was some desperate loser who couldn't get his own dates."

His mom was quiet for a moment after his statement. Then she asked, "Millie tries to set you up?"

Kai could hear the edge of irritation and concern in her voice, and he cringed. He shouldn't have mentioned his grandmother. She and his mom didn't exactly get along. There wasn't any real animosity on his mom's side, but there was definitely no love lost in the other direction. For some reason, Kai's grandma did *not* care for Kai's mother. At all. Kai had thought to ask her about it while he was here…but somehow he could never bring it up around her. It was too awkward, too personal. Kai had to think his mother was worried that his grandmother was trying to set him up with a girl who could be turned against his mother, but Kai didn't think his grandma would ever intentionally be that vindictive. And Kai would never date someone who couldn't form their own opinions.

"Don't worry, Mom. She hasn't sent any she-devils my way." His mom let out a soft laugh at his obvious joke and Kai smiled. "Besides, I'm too busy with work right now to worry about that stuff." Knowing his mom wouldn't take that as an excuse, since she did want grandchildren one day, he quickly added, "Maybe once I've settled in some more, I'll start… looking."

His mother sighed, and there was clear defeat in her exhale. "All right, Kai. Don't work too hard."

Kai smiled as he pictured his tired, worried mother. "I won't, Mom. Love you."

"Love you, too, Kai. I'll call again soon."

Knowing soon was probably tomorrow, Kai laughed. "All right, go rest. Take a nap or something." She assured him that she would, told him she loved him again, and hung up the phone.

Shaking his head at his anxiety-prone mother, Kai turned his thoughts to his father. He hadn't heard from him since he'd arrived here. Thinking it was odd that his dad hadn't called to check on him yet, Kai briefly wondered if he should give him a call, to make sure everything was okay. Plus, he still hadn't told his dad about Gran falling. Kai was sure he would want to know that his mom had gotten hurt. Glancing at the clock again, he set down his phone. It was too early to call. He'd do it later, when it was a more decent hour.

Later in the day, after Kai had finally gotten up to take a shower, he called his dad. Surprisingly, the conversation was brief and almost strained. Kai wasn't sure why it had felt awkward when he ended the call; he and his dad had always had a good relationship. They had similar personalities and common interests. Truly, they got along great, and Kai was a little mystified by the detachment he'd heard on the other end of the line. He'd also been surprised that his dad had already known about Gran's accident. He hadn't known all the specifics, and Kai had filled him in as best he could, but he hadn't been surprised to hear about it. Gran must have called her son at some point and told him herself.

As Kai wondered why everyone in his life seemed to be acting strangely, he got ready for his day. Maybe it was just the distance that was making everyone so odd. His parents were used to seeing him every day. His grandmother was used to not seeing him at all. Surely, they were all just reacting to the strangeness of their new situation. Kai knew he was.

Locking up his apartment, Kai headed down to his bike in the garage. He was going to do a little shopping before meeting up with Jessie, pick up those long johns she'd suggested, or something similar. And maybe he would find something to surprise her with while he was out. It was the least he could do, since she was always surprising him with nice things.

Kai smiled as he climbed onto his bike. He suddenly knew just what he could get her.

———————◆———————◆———————

Jessie was pacing, and anxious nerves were coursing through her body as she watched the clock on the living room wall get closer and closer to five o'clock. She had no idea why, but in a moment of weakness, she'd asked Kai to come over for dinner. It wasn't a good idea, but her roommates would have to meet him eventually. Her friends were just too much a part of her life for that not to happen. The girls frequently hung out together or stayed home together. Living with her best friends was a bit stifling at times, but the girls were close, and it would be really odd if Jessie kept keeping her newly-in-town cousin away.

She really didn't know if her friends would remember Kai or not, and just the thought of them discovering what she'd done with him had her stomach in a tangled snarl. God, they'd be sick if they knew. Jessie put both palms on her stomach as she walked around the spacious room. It still made her feel sick, and she'd had over a week to come to terms with the fact.

Her home was filled with the smell of a roast simmering away in her crockpot. Jessie hadn't known what to make Kai for dinner, but pot-roast had seemed like a good choice; it screamed comfort food to her. If Kai was feeling a little homesick, and he had to be on some level, then maybe the meal would remind him of his mom. Assuming she'd made the same meals for him that Jessie's mom had made for her, of course.

Jessie wasn't sure, since she hadn't ever heard much about Kai's mom. For some reason, no one in the family really talked about her. Jessie didn't know the details, but apparently, her divorce from Uncle Nate had been a nasty one. Kai still seemed to be close to both parents though, and his mom and dad still worked together, so some small level of respect must still be present between them. Jessie didn't want to ask Kai about his parents though. It felt too…intrusive.

Her stomach rumbled as she ran her hands through her ringlets. She'd spent longer than she cared to admit taming her hair into distinct, defined curls, instead of the wild, out of control mess it could easily fall into sometimes. She hoped Kai liked it. Sometimes she caught him staring at her hair; he usually smiled when he did. A wistful sigh escaped Jessie. She shouldn't care if a boy liked her hair. This wasn't a date. This was her cousin coming over for dinner, nothing more.

Just as she was about to check on the potatoes roasting in the oven, April sauntered into the room. Her long black hair was luxurious, shiny, and super-straight. Sometimes Jessie wished she had her friend's hair. Her kinky mess could be so frustrating at times.

"Hey," April stated, as she sat on the couch and crossed her ankles. She was wearing a miniskirt with black boots that almost went past her knees. The skin showing between her knee and the skirt's short hemline was lean and trim, and for a second, Jessie wished for her friend's slim figure. Jessie's curvier physique wouldn't have pulled off the look nearly as well.

Tucking a dark strand behind her ear, April looked over to the kitchen. "Can I help with anything?"

Jessie smiled and shook her head. "Harm beat you to it. She's already in there making a salad."

From the kitchen both girls heard, "A kick-ass salad!"

April laughed and rolled her eyes. Jessie thought again of checking on the potatoes, but April spoke before she could excuse herself. "You okay?"

Jessie threw on an unworried smile as she looked around to make sure everything was neat and tidy. It was. She'd spent all afternoon making sure of it. "Yep, I just want everything to be perfect for Kai." Not sure how that sounded, she added, "He's a long way from home, and I want to make sure he feels welcomed." Suddenly feeling lame, she shrugged.

April gave her a crooked grin. "Don't worry, I'll make sure he feels plenty welcomed."

Jessie frowned at her friend's suggestive comment. She really didn't want April entertaining him in *that* way, but she also didn't have a say in the matter. April was an adult, Kai was an adult...and both of them were single. Placing her hands on her hips in a teasing stance that was obviously not meant to be serious—although, in Jessie's mind, it completely was—she told April, "*You* stay away from him. He's family, not a plaything."

April smirked. "I'm just saying, if he's new in town, he might want some company." She smiled suggestively. "And I'm great company."

Jessie rolled her eyes as she tried to hold her irritation in check. It wasn't April's fault she was a flirt, and normally it didn't bother her. "Well, just tone it down then." She smacked her friend's boot. "You'll scare him straight back to Hawaii."

April laughed, then purred. "Mmmm, Hawaiian boy. Yum."

Giving up, Jessie made herself laugh as she walked into the kitchen to see her more reserved friend. Harmony was cutting vegetables at the counter; she smiled when Jessie entered. The deep color of her brilliant red hair contrasted nicely with the dark green of her blouse, making her look like the living embodiment of autumn. Cocking a fiery eyebrow, she tilted her head at Jessie. "You do look a little freaked. Everything okay?"

Jessie wanted to cringe, but she smiled instead. "Yep, just hoping I didn't burn the potatoes." Her heart was racing faster than normal when she popped open the oven. The heat wave hit her in the face, and she stepped away to let it escape.

"I'm sure they're fine, Jess. He'll probably appreciate the sentiment anyway. I mean, he probably hasn't had a home cooked meal in a while, right?" Harmony said, her hands flying over red and yellow bell peppers.

Jessie poked a knife into the potatoes and smiled when it easily went right through. Straightening, she closed the oven door and turned down the heat to warm. "Yeah, I think he'll love it."

Harmony gave Jessie an odd, appraising look, and Jessie realized she'd sighed in a way that sounded romantic. She had to imagine her face was also looking a little love-struck. Not liking that thought, she relaxed her features and went to the fridge. She needed to avoid looking like she was in love with Kai. Sure, she was attracted to him, but he was family. She could *love* him, but she couldn't love-love him or anything. That was just the ways things had to be. Whatever she'd felt when she'd stupidly told him she was falling for him, she had to put the brakes on it.

But she still mentally arranged him out of order, placing attraction before family, and she had no idea how to stop doing that. Annoyed, she looked around for some wine to have with dinner. Over her shoulder, she asked Harmony, "Do we have any of that chardonnay left?" Jessie could have sworn that she'd opened a bottle just a couple of nights ago.

The sound of chopping resumed as Harmony went back to her salad prep. "Nope. April had a guy over Wednesday night. They drank it all."

Jessie shut the door with a sigh. So much for that. She really should have known an open bottle wouldn't keep for long around here. From the living room she heard April yell, "Sorry!" Shaking her head, Jessie went about making some Crystal Light. At least she wasn't offering him Kool-Aid.

Just as Harmony was mixing her special blend of spices into a small bowl of mayonnaise—her super-secret salad recipe that she wouldn't share with anybody—the doorbell rang. Jessie nearly dropped the pitcher of juice she was putting in the fridge. Before she could get it all the way inside, she heard April exclaim, "I'll get it!"

Cursing, Jessie hurried her slow hands. In her haste, she banged the pitcher on the lip of a shelf and bright red liquid sloshed over the edge to splash on the floor; a couple of drops hit her sweater, but thankfully, she was wearing black.

"Damn it," she muttered, grabbing a towel from Harmony, who'd automatically reached for one. As she cleaned up the spill, and Harmony finished the salad, Jessie heard April's excited greeting to Kai; it was immediately followed by a flirtatious giggle. Jessie could just imagine April's thrill at seeing her cousin. He was…well, he was just about the most attractive man Jessie had ever seen.

Wanting to see him again herself, Jessie slopped up the mess and tossed the towel into the sink. She finished at the same time as Harmony, and they walked into the living room together, where Jessie could hear April chatting with Kai.

Jessie took in the sight of him with bated breath. Smiling politely at April, he was holding a canvas grocery bag in one hand; his other was casually shoved into his dark jacket. He was angled in such a way that his tattooed shoulder blade was facing Jessie. She felt hotter all over as she stared at the spot under his clothes where his ink was hidden away from the world. It gave her a rush to know that none of her friends were aware of it, that for now it was a secret only she was in on. Then April's hand flitted across his shoulder as she slinked her fingers over his body, in no way being discreet about checking him out. The obvious move made Jessie frown, and ice instantly doused her warmth. *She can't touch him like that.* Only, she could. She had no reason not to.

Harmony edged past Jessie as she approached Kai. While April probably wouldn't think about if she'd seen Kai before, Harmony might. Jessie anxiously watched her friend's face; her insides felt like a dam about to fail, like every last bit of control she possessed was about to burst. *Please don't let her recognize him.* But as she watched Harmony greet him, her face was only curious and her words were only polite. She didn't suspect anything.

Hearing Kai say his name out loud made Jessie's heart do strange things. This was too much, too intense. She was going to lose it while she waited for her roommates' memories to snap into place. Swallowing, she wondered if they'd notice if she started hyperventilating into a bag. But so far, nothing bad had happened. Harmony was smiling, April was smiling, even Kai was smiling. They were all enjoying a bit of small talk, Harmony and April asking Kai how he liked living here. Nothing about their stance or appearance looked horrified. Nobody was piecing together anything, and they would have by now if they were going to. She could relax. The moment was over.

Feeling better, Jessie finished walking into the room. Kai turned to face her as she did. He took a step toward her, like he was going to hug her, but then he stopped, like he suddenly thought he shouldn't. Jessie felt her body tremble with a mixture of anticipation and disappointment, but she only smiled at him. As always, those absorbing eyes stole her breath, and transported her to a place where only the two of them existed. For just a fraction of a moment, they were the only two people in the room, maybe the world.

"Hey," he softly said.

Jessie felt her skin begin to tingle as his eyes drifted over her face, and then very discretely, over her body. Suddenly remembering her friends, Jessie hoped she didn't look flushed, or flustered, or anything out of the ordinary. She also hoped Kai liked the way she looked. "Hey, glad you could make it," she calmly told him.

Like he realized he'd been examining her, Kai cleared his throat and shifted his gaze to her house. "This is a nice place. Much better than mine." Bringing his eyes back to her, he added, "Thank you for having me."

Harmony pointed to the bag in his fingers. "What's that?" she politely asked, stealing a quick glance at Jessie. Jessie cursed herself for not asking him that first. Seeing him just took a minute for her to get used to.

Kai grinned at Harmony as he reached into the bag. "Well, I wasn't sure what we were having." He pulled out a bottle of white wine and handed it to her, then reached back in and grabbed a bottle of red. "So I brought one of each."

Harmony smiled as she took them. "We were just saying we needed some." She raised an eyebrow at him and smiled. "You must be psychic."

Kai glanced down at the floor, embarrassed. It was adorable, and Jessie watched both of her roommates' smiles brighten. Shaking his dark head, Kai reached back into the bag. Peeking up at Jessie, he started to hand her a small bouquet of flowers, but as soon as April spotted them, she plucked them out of his hand.

"Oh, carnations, my favorite." April beamed as she smelled them.

Knowing that he'd meant the flowers for her, Jessie frowned. She couldn't exactly protest over April grabbing them, though. It would be better if he'd brought the flowers for the house. As April giggled, Kai shrugged. "Yeah, well, it was all they had at the store." He looked at Jessie after he said it, and there was a clear apology in his eyes.

Jessie shook her head and gave him an encouraging smile. It was for the best. He shouldn't be bringing her flowers. This wasn't a date.

April bounced on her toes, clearly delighted at Kai and his gifts. "I should put these in some water," she announced. Backing away from him, she pointed at the couch. "Make yourself at home, Kai."

He nodded at her, slipped his jacket off his shoulders, and slung it over the side of the couch. All three girls stopped and took a moment to appreciate the fit body that even multiple layers of clothing couldn't hide. Giggling as she watched him sit down, April grabbed Jessie's arm and dragged her into the kitchen with her. Lightly laughing at April, Harmony followed them.

Once in the kitchen, April turned on the water then twisted to Jessie. Her face was incredulous. In a low voice that Kai couldn't overhear, she said, "He *is* hot! Why didn't you tell me he was so hot?"

Jessie shrugged, and a trickle of something odd and awful ran up her spine. Jealousy or disgust, she wasn't sure. "He's family. I don't see him that way." Jessie could almost physically feel the lie in her words.

Harmony appeared to as well. "Yeah, sure, Jessie," she playfully said as she slipped the white wine in the fridge. Setting the bottle of red wine on the counter, she gave Jessie a knowing smile. "My older brother might be family too, but even *I'll* admit he's good-looking."

Feeling uncomfortable and trapped, Jessie reached up for a vase, just to give her hands something to do. "Fine," she muttered, filling the vase with the running water. "He's attractive."

April snorted as she unwrapped the flowers. "Attractive? He's downright edible." Smiling at thoughts that Jessie knew were lurid, April popped the carnations into the too-full vase. Water seeped out the sides, and Jessie sighed.

Well, she supposed her roommates being attracted to Kai was preferable to them knowing he was her one night stand. She'd suspected that April would be interested in him anyway. Shaking her head, Jessie set the flowers on the counter. Carnations were April's favorite, really? Jessie knew for a fact that was a lie. April was a classic rose girl. It was truly the only traditional thing about her. Jessie had often heard her tell men that every other flower out there was just the rose's sad, inferior cousin, and at the moment, Jessie empathized with the carnations.

Smiling at each other, Harmony and April started returning to Kai. Making a show of examining the roast, Jessie stayed where she was; she needed a minute to collect herself. Seconds after they disappeared, April poked her head around the corner. Giving Jessie a playful smile, she whispered, "I'm gonna ask Kai out. That okay with you?"

Jessie froze in place. She didn't want April dating Kai, but she had absolutely no good reason to tell her friend that it wasn't okay. She couldn't tell April that the idea of another woman being with Kai sickened her. She couldn't tell her that she wanted to be the only woman in his life. She couldn't tell her that picturing Kai's hands on April made her want to vomit. And Jessie definitely couldn't tell her that earlier this week, a few days after having an incredible one night stand with him, Jessie had told his sleeping body that she was falling for him. And against her earlier desire to somehow halt those feelings, Jessie was afraid it was too late; she'd already fallen.

Not able to say any of that, she smiled as realistically as she could. "Yeah, sure. I don't care." As an afterthought, she spit out, "He's family though, so you know…be nice." But not too nice. Oh God…how could she stand this?

April giggled and bounded out of the room. Jessie sighed and closed her eyes; they burned with unshed tears. She had to…it was for the best.

After giving herself several long moments to slowly count to ten, Jessie straightened, lifted her head up confidently, and strode back into the living room. Her step almost faltered when she came upon April sitting as close to Kai as she could, playing with a long strand of her dark hair as she openly flirted with him. For his part, Kai only seemed to be engaged in a friendly conversation with April, not ogling her, as she wanted him to.

Kai was sitting on the edge of the couch, with April practically on his hip, so Jessie sat on the smaller couch with Harmony. Jessie's friends politely asked Kai questions about his life and his family, and Jessie starting spacing out as she listened to the rise and fall of his voice. She studied the way his lips formed phrases, the way the edges of his mouth curved up, the way his teeth gleamed when he smiled. Jessie had a sudden vision of her tongue running along those teeth. So deeply lost in thoughts she tried to never have, she quickly found herself being swept away. She blatantly stared at him while he gestured with his hands as he told a story about work. Jessie instantly pictured those hands on her body. Biting her lip, Jessie felt her skin begin to tingle, felt her heart begin to quicken, and felt her breath begin to increase.

His tropical eyes—eyes that would rival the most fabulous oceans in all the world—flicked glances at her every now and again. When she bit her lip, they locked right onto the sensitive skin. He adjusted how he was sitting on the couch, and Jessie let herself imagine that he was reacting to her. Clearing his throat, he tore his gaze from her mouth to look over at Harmony, who'd just asked him a question.

Jessie saw him adjust his posture again, watched as he pulled his jeans down a bit, and she wondered if his clothes were getting tighter. She hoped so. Running a finger down the v-neck of her shirt, she pulled it over slightly to play with her bra strap. Harmony and April were too fascinated with Kai to notice what she was doing, but Kai's eyes immediately snapped to her; he stuttered on his sentence. Not knowing why she was doing it, Jessie let her fingers travel over the cup of her bra, swirl around her nipple. Kai completely stopped talking and ran a hand over his jaw. His eyes flashed up to hers, and Jessie could see the desire there, burning under the surface. She had to adjust how she was sitting now, as desire surged through her, too.

Then April set her hand on his thigh. Kai jumped as he turned to look at her, and a sudden flood of horror rushed through Jessie. Jesus, she'd actually been flirting with her cousin. No, more than flirting. Seducing. Her hand slapped over her mouth, just in case her stomach decided to heave. It was so wrong, on so many levels. Jessie saw Kai's face going through all the same conflicting emotions she was going through, as he half-listened to April talking about her job. Even though his skin hadn't changed color, Jessie thought he looked paler.

Jessie shot to her feet, drawing everyone's attention to her. "I'm gonna...open the wine for dinner." A drink, that was what Jessie needed. A nice big drink.

As she sped from the room, she heard Kai say, "I'll help you."

Knowing that he was going to follow her into the small, private room amplified her confusion. She didn't really want to be alone with him right now, but she couldn't refuse his polite offer in front of her roommates. Crossing her fingers, Jessie hoped April followed them. A third party would help. Maybe. But then she heard April and Harmony begin a low conversation between themselves. They were most likely taking this opportunity to talk about Kai, and just when Jessie could have used their interference.

She leaned over the counter when she got to the kitchen; she wasn't sure what she should be feeling right now, other than conflicted. And guilty.

"Jessie?" Her name on Kai's lips warmed and horrified her. There was so much love and ache behind the syllables. But the feeling he inlaid in the word was wrong. They couldn't be like that, they just couldn't. Jessie twisted around to face him, and she felt tears in her eyes again. "Cousin?" he whispered, his expression sad as he looked her over.

Jessie's tears built to a level she couldn't sustain, and they began to freely slide down her cheeks. Kai immediately walked up to her and brushed them away. "When does it get easier, Kai?" she whispered as she searched his face.

Kai dropped his hand. He stayed close to her, but it was obvious he was being careful not to touch her. "I don't know." Shaking his head, he shrugged. "Someday?"

Jessie hung her head, her forehead just reaching his chest. Kai stepped in and enclosed his arms around her in a warm embrace. Knowing they shouldn't, Jessie slung her arms around his waist and rested her cheek against his body. They both exhaled at the same time, and it felt like a weight was being lifted from Jessie's shoulders. Why did touching him have to bring her such peace?

Kai rubbed her back and placed a tender kiss on her head. She snuggled into his arms, burrowing her head in the space under his jaw. Feeling a warmth and safety that she knew wasn't appropriate made another tear fall from her eye.

Listening to their quiet heartbeats and the girls giggling in the next room, Jessie whispered, "April is going to ask you out after dinner." She pulled her head away from his embrace and looked up at him. Searching his face, Jessie pierced her heart. "I want you to say yes. I want you to go out with her."

Kai's eyes widened, and he shook his head. Jessie's face was blank, emotionless. Her heart was so torn she couldn't even fake a reassuring smile. It had to be this way. They quicker they moved on, the better. Kai opened and closed his mouth; by the confliction in his eyes, it was clear he was trying to find a different solution to their problems…but he wasn't succeeding. It would be so nice, so easy, if they could just shut off the attraction they felt for each other. If she could stop the warmth and affection from growing larger with each and every moment she spent with him. But she couldn't stop it, so maybe April stealing some of his time away from Jessie was exactly what they both needed to sever this connection they had, before it got any deeper.

Because, as nice as it was, the depth of feeling that she had for him was wrong. Wanting his arms to always be around her was wrong. Wanting him to lean down and place his lips against hers was wrong. Wanting him to tell her that he couldn't see April because he was madly in love with her… was wrong.

Kai closed his mouth as he searched her eyes. His face changed as Jessie stared at him. Some decision had been reached while he'd silently debated with himself, and Jessie knew that either way, his answer was going to hurt.

Softly sighing, he slumped in her arms and whispered, "Okay...cousin."

Promise Made, Promise Kept

Kai watched Jessie as discreetly as he could during dinner. She smiled and talked with everyone as if nothing was wrong, but Kai could see the excess moisture in her eyes, the tightness in her jaw. She was torn; she was hurting. He could see the pain, but even if he couldn't, he would have known without a doubt that it was there, because *he* was torn, *he* was hurting. Yet again, they were both feeling the exact same way, and there was nothing either one of them could do about it.

As Jessie gave him a sideways glance before locking her eyes onto her plate, Kai internally sighed and looked over at Jessie's roommate, April. She was definitely beautiful, with long black hair, dark eyes, full lips, a lean body, and an attitude that exuded confidence. But...Kai didn't want to date her. Honestly, he didn't want to date anyone. He just had too much going on right now. Well, no...if he were going to be completely honest, there *was* one girl he would gladly date, if she was a possibility. But, she wasn't.

Kai nodded as he listened to the story April was telling. The flirtatious woman was sitting next to him at the table, across from Harmony and Jessie, and her palm was resting on his knee. Knowing she had the intention of asking him out later, and knowing Jessie wanted him to say yes when she did, Kai was letting her leave her hand there. It felt odd to him, though. Foreign, unwanted.

Picking at his food, Kai tried to make polite conversation with the group. While he did, he wondered if maybe Jessie was right. Maybe, with whatever was building between the two of them, it would be better for both Kai and Jessie if he distracted himself with a little female company. And Jessie liked April, otherwise she wouldn't have asked him to date her. Maybe if Kai was seeing someone Jessie approved of, it would ease the transition. Just admitting that stung. Easing the transition meant making one, and even though he knew it needed to happen, he wasn't ready.

Kai watched Jessie stick a piece of roast into her mouth. Her tongue flashed down to her lip, to swipe away some stray sauce, and a forlorn sigh escaped him. He wished he could feel her lips again, just one more time. At hearing his wistful exhale, Jessie's eyes lifted to meet Kai's. Reluctantly, he shifted his gaze to his plate. He shouldn't think about that. It wasn't helping anything for him to allow his thoughts to keep going down that path.

Popping some roast into his mouth, he smiled. He loved roast, it reminded him of lazy Sunday afternoons at his mom's place. How did Jessie always seem to know just what to do? He never really had to tell her what he liked or what he needed. She just instinctively knew. She was so amazing.

Clearing his throat during a lull in the conversation, Kai looked up at her and said, "This is great, Jessie. Thank you."

Jessie looked up and met his eye; her cheeks turned a slight shade of pink as she absorbed his praise. It was intoxicating. "Thank you," she quietly replied. Glancing at her roommates, she quickly added, "I had help. Harmony made the salad."

The lightly freckled girl grinned. Kai returned the smile but mentally kicked himself. Jessie was trying to keep some space between them by deflecting his compliment. He could try and do the same. "Well, it's wonderful, thank you."

April frowned as she dragged her fork over her plate. "I… offered to help," she muttered, pouting in such an adorable way that Kai had to smile at her.

Wanting to do the right thing, the thing that his cousin had asked him to do, he fortified his needs and desires, reached his hand under the table, and rested his palm over April's. She visibly brightened at the contact, and twisted her hand so she could lace their fingers together. Kai ignored the burning sensation of Jessie watching them and held April's gaze. He knew Jessie couldn't see their hands unless she looked under the table, but he still felt really horrible flirting in front of her. He'd only meant to make brief contact with April, to let her know that he wouldn't reject her invitation later, but she'd latched onto his gesture with a firm grip. It would be rude to pull away now.

Forcing a smile, he politely told her, "I'm sure you helped in other ways."

April giggled as she playfully bumped into his side. Kai heard Jessie sigh, but when he pulled his eyes from the Asian beauty beside him to look over at her, she was studying the remnants of food on her plate. Even though his appetite was completely gone, Kai quietly resumed eating.

After the meal, Harmony whisked the dishes away, and the foursome polished off the second bottle of wine. Relaxing back in his chair, Kai relentlessly watched Jessie. He wished he could talk to her, really make sure she was okay with this, but he didn't see how he could get away from April now. The woman had a firm hold of his hand as she sipped her drink, and she was leaning into his side now, her cheeks flushed from the wine.

Harmony had noticed their hands under the table when she'd taken their plates. With a shake of her head, she'd given Kai a knowing grin, like she wasn't at all surprised that April was getting what she wanted. It had taken a great deal of restraint to not tell her that he was only flirting with April because he'd been asked to. His heart wasn't in it. Thinking of where his heart was really resting made Kai consider calling it a night.

Jessie had the same thought. Standing, she exaggerated a series of yawns and stretches. "Well, I should turn in. You're welcome to stay, Kai, if you..."

Her voice trailed off as her new, taller angle allowed her to see Kai and April's hands laced together. Kai had the strangest desire to rip his fingers away from April. He'd never intended to keep the contact going for so long, and now, if he yanked his hand away after being spotted by Jessie, it would be entirely too obvious why he was withdrawing. Jessie's eyes widened as they lifted to his; she seemed heartbroken and relieved, all at once. Kai wanted to apologize, wanted to tell her that he didn't want this...that he'd rather be holding *her* hand. But he knew he couldn't say that. And Jessie knew it too, so she said nothing about the flirting. Giving him a soft smile, she responded with, "You can stay as long as you like. My home is your home."

Her tone when she said it...well, it was the most loving thing he'd ever heard anyone say to him. Not able to take it anymore, he stood up, finally breaking the contact with April. Making a show of walking over to her in a friendly manner, he grinned as brightly as he could. "Well, again, thank you for dinner." As he stepped in front of Jessie, his arms went around her waist. He hadn't felt like a greeting hug was normal cousin behavior, but surely a goodnight hug wouldn't raise suspicion.

Her arms came up, loosely at first and then exceedingly tight, almost painfully so. Angling his head away from the other two girls at the table, Kai closed his eyes and let the torrent of pain and longing fill him. Inhaling the scent of her, lavender and honey, and everything good and sweet in the world, he whispered, "I'm sorry."

He felt Jessie nod, felt her body lightly shaking as she tried to contain the churning emotions that must be running rampant through her; Kai knew they were in him. Their hug was starting to get inappropriately long, so Kai forced himself to take a step back. "Goodnight, Jessie," he said softly, hoping the ache he felt inside wasn't evident in his voice.

He wanted nothing more than to pull her back into his arms, squeeze her tightly again, and never let her go, but he had to maintain the appearance of distance. He needed to look like he cared for her, without *overly* caring for her. It was an odd, fine, painful line. Slipping his hands into his back pockets, so he wouldn't be tempted to touch her, he smiled and took another step back.

Her eyes were noticeably wet, and she had to blink several times to bring them back to even. With a smile that radiated abundant affection, she nodded. "Goodnight, Kai." Her eyes flicked to April, who was using the opportunity to check her makeup in a mirror next to the dining room table. The sight saddened Kai for some reason; he preferred his cousin's natural look. Her face without makeup was ten times more attractive than any cosmetic could ever hope to accomplish. She was ...perfect.

Jessie's eyes swept back to him. "I hope the rest of your evening goes well." Her smile turned mournful, and Kai had to dig his fingers into his thighs to not hold her again.

She said goodnight to her friends and then walked down the hallway that must have led to her bedroom. Kai heard her door close and he was 100 percent certain that she was crying behind it. The thought killed him. This was too hard...and it hadn't even started yet.

Just as he was about to rush into her room and tell her that he couldn't do this, that he *wouldn't* do this, Harmony stood up and stuck her hand out. "I'm going to bed, too. It was very nice to finally meet you, Kai."

Shoving his torn heart to the back of his mind, he shook her hand. "You too."

Harmony was inspecting him as they shook hands, and suddenly, an odd look crossed her face. "Don't take this the wrong way, but you seem so familiar to me." She shook her head. "Have we met before?"

Kai felt heat rushing to his cheeks, but he made himself laugh as they separated. "Ever been to Hawaii?" he playfully asked. His heart was thudding in his chest while he waited for the puzzle pieces to snap into place, waited for her to remember that she'd seen him at the club…with Jessie.

Luckily, she didn't.

"No." Shaking her head, she disregarded her own memory. "I must be mixing you up with someone else." Yawning, she waved a goodbye to him and then April. There was a playful smirk on her face as she left the room, left him alone with the girl who obviously wanted him.

Taking a deep breath, Kai briefly closed his eyes when he heard April getting up from the table. For a second, he thought to quickly tell her goodnight, saying that he'd call her sometime, but April wasn't going to let him escape that easily. Before he could even turn around, she came up behind him and rested her hand lightly on his back. Even though he didn't want to, his body reacted a little to her tender touch. Just a light flush of warmth. She ran her hand along his side as she stepped around him. "Want to sit with me on the couch?" she asked.

Wondering if he should end this right now, he muttered, "Um, sure, just for a minute. I should really get going soon."

April ran her hand along his arm until she reached his fingers. Grabbing them, she walked him to the couch. She sat down and patted the cushion beside her. She'd fixed her legs in such a way that only a small space remained on the side she'd indicated. Kai would be sitting right next to her, as close as possible. He contained a sigh. This was for Jessie. This was what she wanted.

He sat down and leaned over his legs, resting his elbows on his thighs. It was as far from her as he could get without being too obvious. It didn't work like he'd planned, though; she simply took the movement as an invitation to rest her palm on his back. She rubbed gentle circles into his skin, and Kai hated that his body reacted to that, too. He didn't want to be attracted to this woman, but she was beautiful, and he couldn't help the instinct to want to have a beautiful woman touching him. He just wanted it to be a different beautiful woman.

Feeling more torn now than when he'd started the evening, he nervously ran a hand through his hair as he gave her a semi-smile. April tilted her head as she examined him. "Do I make you nervous?" she asked, her voice low and sensuous.

Kai swallowed. "Yes, actually." For more reasons than she realized.

Laughing, April shifted closer to him, and she was already pretty close. "You don't have anything to worry about, I'm not scary." Her hand ran up his back, over his tattoo. Kai remembered Jessie's hands on his tattoo, and he straightened so April's hand would drop. It did, but now her side was completely pressed against his. Gazing up at him, she ran a hand through his hair. "Do you think I'm pretty?" she asked.

Kai's eyes instinctively swept over her face, flicked down to her lips. "Yes," he whispered, finally feeling honest. That was something he couldn't deny, even to himself. April was very pretty. Different than Jessie, but still, very pretty.

She smiled wider, playing with her bottom lip. Kai stared at the plump skin, a little mesmerized. "Would you like to take me out sometime?"

Kai really hated what he was about to say, but he'd given Jessie his word. "I think I'd like that." He forced himself to smile, and April's eyes locked onto his mouth. She stared at his lips while he stared at hers, and against his will, Kai felt his breath quicken and his heart start to race in anticipation. He didn't want to kiss her, not really, but...

Still smiling, she whispered, "All right then." Her breath was light on his face, intriguing and arousing.

Kai had no idea what he was supposed to do, what Jessie really wanted him to do—fully immerse himself in another woman, or only half-heartedly attempt to move on? April's lips brushed over his while he debated, but she didn't press against them. Instead, she dragged her lips across his cheek and placed a soft kiss by his ear. The tease made his eyes flutter closed. He hated that he liked it, and felt like he was betraying Jessie just by sitting there. But he wasn't. Jessie was family, *only* family.

"Call me," she breathed as she moved away. She rattled off her cell number and Kai found himself eagerly nodding. He almost wanted to pull her back in for a real kiss. Almost.

April stood, a seductive smile fixed on her face. Kai stood with her. He could easily picture April leading him to her bedroom with the heat in her eyes, but instead she grabbed his coat off the couch and led him to the front door. Feeling breathless and confused, Kai walked through it when she opened it for him.

April leaned against the door in such a way that every curve of her trim body was highlighted, begging to be touched. "Call me soon. I'm very impatient." Kai nodded and leaned in. He wasn't sure why. Was he leaning in for a hug, another kiss? Before he could think too much about it, April cupped his cheek and obliged him by pressing those full lips so briefly to his, he wasn't even sure if it had really happened. He gasped when she pulled away.

"It was very nice to meet you, Kai," she whispered as she slowly closed the door.

Feeling dazed and a little dumbfounded, Kai stumbled back to his bike. It was only then that he realized he'd never gotten the chance to show Jessie what else he'd purchased for her. Walking to the back of his bike, he placed a hand on a second helmet that was strapped over the rear seat. He'd picked it up today with the thought that maybe he could take Jessie for a ride sometime, maybe even tonight. But the night had deviated in a way he hadn't expected, and now, instead of doing something nice for his cousin, some small way of repaying her for her kindness, he was about to be put an irreversible gap between them by going out with her roommate.

Kai hung his head as he swung his leg over the bike. It was what Jessie wanted though, what she needed, to break whatever was happening between them. It hurt his heart so much to do it…and that was *exactly* why he had to go through with it. He and Jessie couldn't let this…thing…enter their relationship. They were family. Nothing more.

Starting his bike, Kai looked over at the charming house Jessie lived in. Popping his helmet on, he noticed that one curtain in a window was being held open, and an outline of a body in the dark room was watching him. He knew it was Jessie, and with his expression hidden under the helmet, he let all of his grief show.

Shaking his head, he told her, "I'm sorry, Jessie. I never meant to hurt you tonight, and I don't want to see April. I want to see you, and only you…and that's the problem, isn't it?" Revving the bike, his voice rough under the mask of his helmet, he quietly told her, "I'll do what you asked, but I think it's too late. I think I've already fallen for you."

With those words tumbling through his head and bouncing around his body, bruising him as they beat against him, Kai turned away from Jessie's house and sped into the night.

———————————————————

Jessie watched the red taillight of Kai's bike until it faded into the distance. A tear fell to her cheek as she tried to swallow the rough lump in her throat. The image of him propped on his bike, staring at her watching him from her dark bedroom was forever burned into her brain. He'd held her gaze for ages, and she couldn't really tell anything, but from the tension in his body, she was sure he'd been trying to communicate something to her. Maybe an apology for the way the evening had gone.

Jessie dropped the curtain, letting it swish back down into place. The white eyelets seemed to blink at her as a streetlamp outside flashed through them, and more tears fell down her cheeks. Cruelly, her mind replayed that dreadful dinner, both before and after: her inappropriate flirting, her decision to force him to moving forward, his reluctant agreement…the inevitable first steps toward a new romance.

Both crushed and relieved, Jessie walked over to her bed and sat down. It sure hadn't taken him long to jump on the April-train. But she couldn't be angry with him for that. He was doing exactly what she'd asked him to do. She wanted him to move on, and April was a good choice for him, for now. She would be fun, nothing too serious, no major commitment. April was a good time, simple and uncomplicated, so unlike what they were.

Taking off her shoes, Jessie rubbed her aching feet. She couldn't help but wonder what had happened between April and Kai after she'd disappeared. She didn't want to think about it, but she knew her flirtatious friend well, and she knew that April had most likely been all over him. It was just the way she was—comfortable, confident, and sexy as all get out. Kai would have been helpless against the full force of her charm. Especially since Jessie had made him feel obligated to go along with it. Great.

With a pained exhale, Jessie dropped her head into her hands. It hurt so much; it was unbearable. But she had to get past this. If they could both work past this…desire, then their relationship could be completely normal, natural. April didn't know it, but she was about to help them get through this. But in the meantime, it was going to burn.

With horrific images of April's hands and mouth all over Kai's beautiful body, Jessie undressed for bed. She couldn't stop wondering when their first date was happening. She couldn't stop wondering if it would go well. Then she couldn't stop wondering just how well it would go. She knew from experience that both Kai and April wouldn't be opposed to going all the way, if they felt the right connection. Jessie wasn't sure about Kai, but she was pretty sure April would feel the spark. How could she not? Kai was amazing.

Slipping her pajamas on, Jessie felt like the jagged pieces of her heart were tearing her insides apart. But the scars left behind would heal. And once Kai and April truly started dating, he would be around a lot more, which was good. But their PDA would step up too, which was not good. Jessie wasn't sure if she could handle seeing them holding hands and kissing all the time. As she stepped from her room to the bathroom, she wondered if maybe she should find someone to date, too. Maybe this would be easier, if she wasn't alone, if she had someone to hold hands with and kiss. Maybe the four of them could even double date. God…that was an awful thought.

Jessie came across April as she was exiting the only bathroom in the house. "Oh, hey, Jessie. You okay?"

That last thought made her grimace. She slapped on a tired smile to cover it. "Yeah, of course." She faked a yawn. "Just tired."

April scanned her face. "Oh…are you sure? You look like you've been crying?"

Frustrated, and not wanting to chit-chat with April right now, Jessie wished girls were as oblivious about bloodshot eyes as boys. "I had an itch, scrubbed too hard. Damn wine," she muttered.

April studied her a second longer, then grinned. "Huh, that's funny. My big toe itches when I drink." She giggled as she let Jessie go around her to get into the small room. With April still watching her from the open door, Jessie quietly prepared her toothbrush. She didn't want to talk, but April sure did.

She let out a dreamy sigh. "God, your cousin is gorgeous." She bit her lip as she leaned on the doorframe. "And sweet. He was being so shy with me." Giggling again, she met eyes with Jessie in the mirror. "He told me that I made him nervous. Isn't that cute?"

Feeling sick to her stomach, Jessie nodded, smiled, and then began vigorously brushing her teeth. April sighed again, and when she spoke, her voice was oddly serious. "He seems different than the guys I usually go for. More than just a pretty face." She twirled a lock of hair around her finger as she thought about the man Jessie routinely thought about. "I think I could genuinely like him, you know? Like serious, honest-to-God like him. Kind of scary, huh?"

Jessie carefully rinsed out her mouth. The lingering taste of peppermint from her toothpaste was doing horrible things to her upset stomach. She had *never* anticipated April falling for Kai. April never fell for anyone. But Jessie was certain they would hit it off if they gave it an honest try. Kai was just too... Kai. April falling for him was practically a given. Jesus, why hadn't Jessie considered that outcome before she'd thrown Kai at April? But...maybe...it was for the greater good. It wasn't like she and Kai could hold out for each other. There was nothing that could *ever* happen there. They wouldn't wake up one day and suddenly *not* be family.

April's face shifted to concern as she studied Jessie's reaction. "Are you sure you're okay with me dating him?"

Jessie hesitated. The question was a trap. If Jessie said she wasn't okay with it, she'd damage her friendship with April. If she said she was okay with it...her vision of Kai and April together would happen right in front of her face. Throwing on a smile, Jessie faked nonchalance as best she could. "Of course I'm okay with it, April. You guys could be great together, amazing even. And he's a great guy...you should definitely go for it." God, she was definitely going to be sick now...but this was for the best. For everyone.

April seemed genuinely thrilled by the idea of a lasting relationship with Kai; she even squealed. "Oh, I hope so. I hope he calls soon!" With that, she spun on her heel and skipped to her bedroom. Jessie sighed and closed her eyes. What on earth had she just done? Exactly what she'd had to, that was what.

The next morning, Jessie slept in on purpose. She didn't want to deal with everything that had happened last night. She didn't want to see the excited, elated look on April's face. Just hearing her chipper voice through the walls was bad enough. As she laid in bed, staring at the ceiling, she could hear her cousin's name being mentioned more than once. She could also hear April and Harmony discussing how sweet and charming he was. Then, of course, April shifted to his prowess.

"God, I bet he's a stallion in the bedroom." She giggled, and Harmony laughed with her. Jessie's stomach clenched. He *was* amazing in bed...and she never wanted April to discover that for herself.

Jessie heard Harmony add, "Yeah, he seems like the type who would be very...attentive."

Rubbing her eyes, Jessie wished she could block out the memory of just how much of an attentive lover Kai was. She wished she could plug her ears, too, but almost like she was punishing herself, she kept listening to her girlfriends in the living room.

April was groaning at Harmony's last comment. "God, I know. He's got to be the type who is willing to go that extra distance." She laughed. "Makes sure the woman has a least one good one before he's done." Jessie's hands flew to her stomach as she remembered just how good hers had been... both of them. She tried to not feel queasy at the thought, but she couldn't help the twinge of illness.

Harmony snickered at April's comment. "Well, if you're planning on dating him, I'm sure you'll find out before too long." Jessie groaned, her stomach felt even worse now. Hopefully it stayed down, because she did not want to dash to the bathroom. She never wanted to get out of this bed.

April seemed offended by Harmony's comment. "Bitch, are you saying I'm easy?"

Harmony laughed again. "Hey, I'm only going by your past boyfriends. Have you ever gone past three dates?" Jessie bit her lip; she already knew the answer to that. April was very…descriptive of her *good* dates.

April was silent a second, then laughed. "Okay, yeah, you have a point." She groaned again. "God, he's so hot. Just picturing that man underneath me…good Lord, I need a cool shower now."

Jessie's stomach clenched into a painful knot, but her mind rewound to when she'd had that naked body writhing underneath her. The passionate look on his face, the heated breaths, the thrusting hips, the way he'd used all of his body to make her explode. Thinking about it made a rush of desire surge through Jessie, and her breath quickened at the memory. Damn it.

Harmony shushed April. "Quiet, that's Jessie's cousin you're talking about, and I'm pretty sure she doesn't want to hear about you and Kai having sex." Both girls giggled, and their voices dropped to a level Jessie couldn't hear anymore.

Closing her eyes, Jessie replayed her night with Kai. As wrong as it was, she let herself relive every erotic thing they'd done. She generally shut her thoughts off when they drifted in that direction, but April had shoved the memories at her, and she couldn't hold them back. Her body reacted to her thoughts, and a deep ache throbbed within her core as she remembered the way his body felt when he slipped inside her, when he rubbed against her in all the right places. Sucking on her lip, Jessie's hands drifted under her shirt, to feel the smooth skin of her stomach. She shouldn't think about him this way. And she definitely shouldn't live out the fantasy, shouldn't pretend her hands were his, and shouldn't relieve the ache growing stronger every long second that she thought about his hard, perfect body. It was so wrong. She couldn't let herself go there. Even still, she restlessly stirred in her sheets. She needed something, some sort of release. Her hand ran along her abdomen, slipped under the lacey edge of her underwear. Her legs tensed, her skin pebbled, and her breath grew heavy as her fingers slowly trailed downward, to where the painful need of wanting him was the strongest. She shouldn't do this…but God, she wanted one more time with him, even if it wasn't real.

Her finger hovered above her, a hairs-breadth from satisfying the ache, when the doorbell rang. Icy shock flooded her senses, dousing any fire she'd felt. Disgust filled her as she ripped her hand out of her underwear. She could *not* give in to fantasies about Kai. It was so…

Amid her confusion, she heard April brightly exclaim, "Kai! It's so good to see you again."

Jessie jerked upright in bed like someone had poured ice down her back. Her breath was still embarrassingly fast; her body was slightly shaky from the sudden shift in desire. Kai was here? Again? Looking over at the alarm clock on her nightstand, Jessie saw that she'd let herself sleep in past eleven. What was he doing here? And oh God…was he here for April?

As she listened to April leading Kai into the house, Jessie glanced down at herself; she was a mess and seriously needed to take a shower before Kai saw her. Jessie could hear his deep voice responding to April as he walked into the living room, but she couldn't make out what he was saying. Hearing his voice did odd things to her body, started reigniting the spark the doorbell had so thoroughly quenched. Wishing her heart and her breath would calm down, Jessie got out of bed and cracked open her door.

She could see him from the hallway. He had his back to her and was casually talking with April and Harmony like he'd known them for years, not just a day. Harmony was still seated on a couch, looking up at him with polite interest. April was practically attached to his hip with her hand curled around his arm. Thinking to sneak in a quick shower before Kai noticed her, Jessie began tiptoeing to the bathroom. April laughed at something Kai said and her fingers traveled all the way down his arm, until she was holding his hand. Jessie paused; she couldn't tear her eyes away from the intimate contact.

Almost like he knew she was staring, Kai turned his head and glanced down the hallway. The smile on his face brightened when he saw her, and he instantly released April. Frowning, April followed his gaze to Jessie. Feeling dirty, grimy, and in desperate need of some refreshingly cool water, Jessie awkwardly pointed to the bathroom door. "I'm just gonna... I need..." Cursing her inability to speak, she gushed, "I'll be out in a minute."

Kai was nodding when she flew into the bathroom and slammed the door shut. She bit her lip so hard she almost punctured the skin. Jesus. If he only knew what she'd been thinking about just as he'd been arriving. What she'd almost begun... Actually, she really wasn't sure how he would feel about it. He would probably be just as conflicted as she was.

And probably just as turned on by it, too. It was yet another reason why Kai should date April. They needed to end this attraction. Now.

Even knowing that it was a good thing, Jessie hated the idea of April out there "entertaining" Kai, and she took the fastest shower she'd ever taken in her life. Leaving the water just barely above room temperature, it was also the coldest shower she'd ever taken in her life. The chill helped her regain focus though, and by the time she was scrubbing her hair dry with a towel, all of her inappropriate thoughts about Kai were securely locked away in the farthest corner of her mind, never to be looked at again.

After running her fingers through her damp curls, knowing full well they were going to frizz out when they dried, Jessie dashed across the hallway to her bedroom. She dressed just as quickly as she'd showered. All in all, she'd only taken about fifteen minutes getting ready, but the thought of April mercilessly flirting with Kai for that long left a frenzied feeling in Jessie's stomach. She knew she'd have to firmly deal with that one day, but not today.

As she slipped on some comfortable shoes, she wondered what Kai was doing back here so soon. Surely he would have just called April to make arrangements with her. Cautiously peeking her head out the door, Jessie heard light laughter from the living room. She recognized the sound as both April and Harmony, and she was momentarily elated that Harmony was still here. At least April would keep the PDA to a minimum with her in the room.

Trying to feel a calmness that she really didn't, Jessie lifted her chin and walked out to join the group sitting on the couch. Kai was talking with Harmony, but he twisted to look at Jessie when she entered. Warmth heated Jessie's face, and she couldn't stop her grin at seeing him. Even after all the drama last night, he never failed to bring a smile to her lips. But then April casually placed her hand on his knee, and the warmth evaporated. This was going to be so much harder than she thought. Feeling very proud of herself, Jessie managed to keep a neutral expression on her face.

Kai rose to greet her, and April's hand slipped off him as he stood. With April openly admiring his backside, Kai stepped up to Jessie. "Hey, sorry to barge in on you again... after last night." The smile on his face faltered some before returning. Searching those beautiful blue-green eyes, Jessie was fairly certain that he was forcing himself to be as calm and collected as she was trying to be.

She gave him a reassuring smile. They had to get through the awkwardness if they were ever going to truly be family. "Not a problem. Lord knows I've done it to you several times already." Remembering how her barging in on him usually involved him being shirtless made Jessie laugh and sigh at the same time.

Kai grinned at hearing her humor. Sliding his hands into his back pockets, he gave her a mischievous smile as he nodded his head at the door. "Sorry, I just never got a chance to show you what I picked up for you yesterday."

Intrigued, Jessie looked out the front window. All she saw was Kai's sporty motorcycle. "You didn't have to get me anything, Kai," she said, surprised that he would do something like that for her.

Laughing, he shook his head. "Are you kidding, after everything you've done for me? I owe you...a lot." The way he said those two words drew Jessie's attention back to him. The look in his eyes matched his voice, and Jessie allowed herself to get lost in them for a few seconds, before remembering they weren't alone.

Flicking her eyes behind Kai, she breathed a quick exhale of relief. April was still staring at his backside; she'd completely missed that tender exchange. But shifting her gaze to Harmony, she was met with a pair of curious eyes. Harmony hadn't missed the softness of the moment. Jessie quickly smiled at her friend. Hopefully her casualness would throw Harmony off of whatever track she might have gotten herself on. Harmony smiled back at Jessie, looking none the wiser.

With all of that only taking a second or two, Jessie shifted her attention back to Kai and playfully asked, "Are you giving me your bike?"

Kai seemed caught off-guard by the sudden mood shift. Jessie was faking it for her friends, and hoped he played along. The more casual they were, the better. He broke out into a laugh. "Nice try, but no." Taking a step away from the couch, he glanced back at Harmony and April. April's eyes reluctantly lifted to his face when he spoke. "Mind if I borrow my cousin for a while?" He nodded his head at Jessie.

Harmony smiled and shrugged. "Just bring her back in one piece."

April pouted; she obliviously wanted to be the one being confiscated. "Sure. I guess."

Kai looked back at Jessie. "Want to go out to lunch with me?" The look in his eye spoke volumes. Her friends couldn't see it from their angle, but there was a pleading quality there, like he knew he shouldn't be here, at her house, asking her to drive off with him, but...he couldn't stop himself either.

Jessie sighed softly. She shouldn't say yes. He was supposed to be moving closer to April, not her. Wanting to tell him that she was too busy today, and that he should take April instead, Jessie found herself saying, "Sure, sounds like fun." She just couldn't tell Kai no.

He smiled broadly at her, looking very relieved. Eying the light shirt she was wearing, he glanced out the window. "You may want to dress a little warmer." He shivered under his thick jacket, and Jessie grinned. She hadn't been outside yet, but she was pretty sure it was mid-fifties at least, thankfully dry after the earlier storms, and not nearly as cold as Kai thought it was. "Don't worry. I'll keep the heat up in my truck."

Kai rocked back on his heels and chuckled. "We're not taking your truck."

He winked at her, and Jessie felt her heart surge and butterflies swarm her stomach. Then what he'd said sunk in, and she turned to look outside at his suddenly frail seeming bike. She'd never been on a motorcycle before. Personally, she thought they were death traps. Her eyes widened at the thought of zipping down the road on one, the concrete flying by just a few inches below their toes. When she returned her gaze to Kai, he was clearly amused. "Your bike? But…we'll be cold?"

Kai smiled at her, admittedly, dumb objection. "Which is why you should dress warmer."

Knowing Kai would be even colder than her made Jessie cringe in embarrassment. If he could hack it, she could hack it. But being chilly wasn't really her objection. Seeing her reluctance, April stuck her hand up. "Hey, if she's too scared to ride on a bike, I'll go to lunch with you, Kai."

Jessie tossed April a quick glare. It was more in reaction to her trying to snag Jessie's afternoon with Kai than for calling her scared, but she didn't want April to realize that. Hoping to throw her off, she calmly said, "I'm not scared."

Kai shifted his stance as he watched Jessie; his eyes were amused at her reluctance, but he also looked a little worried, too. Maybe he was wondering if she just didn't want to go, didn't want to spend time alone with him anymore. Not wanting him to ever think that, Jessie smiled. "I'll just layer up, and we can go."

He smiled brilliantly, relieved again. "Great."

Jessie darted to her room to add some more layers and a jacket to her outfit. As she was slipping on the fluffy outwear, she heard Harmony lightly knocking on her open door. "Hey, you got a minute?" she asked.

Even as she slapped a smile on her face, Jessie tensed. Oddly, her very first thought with Harmony entering her room was, *Shit, Kai's alone with April now.* She shook her head to forcefully remove the thought. Kai and April were going to be very alone when they started dating, and she would have to get used to it sooner or later. Trying to relax, Jessie asked, "Sure, what's up?"

Harmony leaned against the door frame. She glanced down the hall to the living room and returned her attention to Jessie. "Everything okay with you?"

Jessie paused in zipping up her jacket. Oh God, had Harmony noticed something? Praying she hadn't, Jessie smiled brighter. "Everything's fine, Harm. Why?" She resisted the urge to cross her fingers as she waited for her friend's answer.

Harmony narrowed her eyes at Jessie and then glanced back at Kai. Sighing, she swung her eyes into the room again.

"Nothing, it's just been weeks since…the breakup…and I like to check in with you every once in a while." She gave Jessie a halfhearted smile, like she felt bad for bringing it up.

Jessie smiled in earnest. "I'm *so* over Jeremy, Harm. No worries there." Walking over to her friend, she placed a hand on her arm. "Thank you though, for being concerned about me."

Harmony rolled her eyes as they started walking back down the hall. "Of course I'm concerned about you. With all your family but Grams gone, it's up to me to bug you about men." She grinned and laughed.

Jessie laughed with her and stopped when she saw April and Kai talking. In a whisper, Jessie unintentionally added, "I'm not alone…Kai's here."

Kai twisted to look at her then, and Jessie beamed at him. He returned her grin, and even with the physical distance between them, Jessie felt the warmth in it. Harmony was silent for a moment then said, "Sure…but…you can't date *Kai*. Maybe you should try and find your Ricardo."

Harmony laughed as she said the fictitious name Jessie had told her, but the comment about Kai struck deep. Her face flushed, Jessie smacked Harmony's arm. Little did Harmony know that Jessie actually *had* found her Ricardo…and Harmony was right, she couldn't date him.

Ignoring the sadness in that fact, and Harmony bellyaching at being smacked, Jessie walked up to Kai. His eyes were curious; he'd seen her hit her friend. "Okay," Jessie sighed dramatically, "I'm ready."

Kai laughed at her put-out expression. "Let's hit the road then." His eyes twinkled playfully. It was astoundingly attractive, and Jessie felt her heart race for more reasons than just the fear of riding a motorcycle.

Ignoring the adrenaline surging, she groaned again. "We're not literally going to hit the road, are we?" Her face scrunched in concern; she actually was nervous about that.

Sighing, Kai lightly grabbed her arm, just above her elbow. Jessie felt the heat of his touch through her padded jacket. "Would I let you down, Jessie?" His eyes searched her face, and Jessie could have sworn he wasn't really talking about dumping her on his bike.

Gazing up at him, she shook her head. "No," she whispered.

He smiled softly, and his hand drifted down her arm. His fingers passed over hers, and Jessie had to stop herself from grabbing his hand. As one, they both looked back at her roommates. "Have a good afternoon, ladies," Kai said politely.

Harmony smiled brightly and told them to have fun. April pursed her lips and gave Kai a seductive smile. Walking right up to him, close enough that Jessie had to take a step back, she cupped Kai's cheek. "See you Saturday night," she said in a breathy voice.

It made Jessie ill that they'd made plans while she'd been getting ready. But what April did next shocked her. In an all too obvious maneuver, she leaned up to his mouth. She was going to kiss him, right in front of Jessie.

Kai's eyes widened as she approached, but he didn't pull away. Jessie wanted to do something, wanted to avert her eyes, but she couldn't stop watching as her friend lightly pressed her lips to his, enclosing them in a soft kiss. Jessie knew that April was forward, but she kind of thought she'd at least hold out until their official first date before feeling comfortable enough to casually kiss him goodbye. Although it was really more of a peck than a full-on kiss. Even still, Kai's eyes half-closed, and he seemed affected by it when she pulled away.

The spell broken, Jessie finally looked away. Needing air, she turned and strode out the front door. She could hear Kai murmur goodbye to her friends, before hurriedly following her out the door. Jessie felt the tears stinging, but she forced them back. He should be with April, they made sense together, and she shouldn't be negatively affected by seeing them kiss. She couldn't kiss Kai, and April could. And Kai deserved to be kissed, deserved to be loved. It was as simple as that.

But still…that didn't mean she liked watching it.

12

A Taste of Heaven

Kai wasn't sure what he was doing, showing up at Jessie's place the day after they'd decided to go their separate ways, but not really. They'd never truly go separate ways, not with what they meant to each other. And not with the fact that they were family. That would never change. Even if the feelings brewing were hard and confusing, they would eventually fade, and the family ties would be all that remained.

As he watched Jessie walking to his bike, he wondered how she really felt about him and April. She couldn't have liked seeing April kiss him. Even if Jessie was only mildly attracted to him, she probably hadn't liked watching it. Kai wished he'd pulled away, but if he had, it would have ruined the perception that he was open to a relationship. He couldn't send April mixed signals before they'd even begun to date. Not when Jessie had asked him to try. And he was trying. For her, he was trying.

Kai smiled when Jessie stopped at the back of his bike, looking unsure what to do next. Regardless of that awkward situation, he was very glad she'd said yes. Kai missed being alone with his cousin, and he wanted to share with her something that was important to him. He wanted them to be closer …even if, in some ways, they had to be farther apart.

Jessie was frowning when she looked back at him. Hoping that she wasn't too upset about the kiss, Kai frowned, too. Her eyes flicked over him, warm, brown and beautiful, and she bit her lip. She opened her mouth to say something, then stopped herself and shook her head. With a quick exhale, she asked, "Where are we going?"

Kai was pretty sure that wasn't what she'd been going to say. He considered bringing up the brief kiss, thought about asking her if she was okay, but really, she either was or she wasn't, and either answer would bother Kai. There was no easy way to get around the pain of this forced space between them, and Jessie didn't seem to want to comment on it, so Kai didn't either. Instead, he stepped up to the back of his bike, unstrapped the second helmet from the seat and handed it to her. "I thought I'd show you where I spend my days."

Jessie smiled as she grabbed the helmet. "Your work? Really?"

It made Kai smile to see the surprise and happiness on her face; visiting his work was clearly something she'd wanted to do. Jessie tore her eyes away from his gaze to stare at the helmet in her hands. She looked like she wasn't sure exactly what she was supposed to do with it. Kai helped her slide it on, his fingers gently brushing against her skin as he fastened the belt under her chin. Once she was wearing it, Kai studied her eyes through the open visor. She was grinning ear to ear until she seemed to remember something he'd told her earlier, then her brow furrowed; it was an adorable expression on her. "Did you buy the helmet for...me? Is this what you got me?"

With a shrug, Kai nodded. "Yeah, I thought you might like riding with me sometimes."

Jessie's brilliant smile returned. "Oh, well, thank you, Kai." She cast an uneasy glance at the bike. "Once this stops terrifying me, I think I'll appreciate that."

Laughing, Kai flipped her visor down. "Just hold on tight. I got you, cousin." He felt perfectly at ease as he casually swung his leg over the bike and settled onto the molded leather. Jessie hesitated and Kai wasn't sure if it was nerves over being on a bike that had her frozen, or nerves over being alone with him. He hoped it was just the bike.

Kai patted the raised section of the seat behind him, where a passenger could easily fit. Jessie's shoulders seemed to slump before she awkwardly climbed on behind him. Kai held the bike as still as he could while she jerked her way into position. Happy that she'd set her fear aside, he twisted around to look at her once she was in place.

Rigid and upright, she sat with her hands clenching her thighs. Kai couldn't see her face through the visor, but he was certain she was worrying her lip. Speaking loud enough so that she could hear him through the helmets, he gave her some last minute instructions, since she'd never been on a bike before.

"Just hold on to me tight." He indicated his waist, so she would know where. Tilting her head, she pursed her lips in a look that clearly said *I'm not an idiot*. Grinning, Kai added, "Lean into the bike with me on corners. You'll want to lean away, but it's easier for me if you don't."

Jessie glanced at the ground, then looked back up at him and nodded. Grabbing her hands, he pulled them around his waist. He felt the rest of her body molding to his back, and paused, savoring the feeling of her clinging to him—the warmth, the heat, the comfort. For a moment, he felt like he was back home. He started the bike, revving it a few times to warm the engine. Jessie's arms cinched around him so tightly, he couldn't inhale. Loosening her grip, Kai yelled over his shoulder, "Relax…have fun. I got you, Jessie."

Then he took off.

For the first several miles, Jessie clung to him like he was her lifeline and she was drowning. He took it easy, swinging wide on the corners so she wouldn't feel like they were going to fall over. But once they got out of the city limits, and Jessie's hold on his waist eased, he opened it up. Kai smiled as he felt the wind whipping past them. It was chilly but not nearly as bad as it had been before, thanks to several new layers of Under Armour.

Kai felt Jessie laugh against his back as she became more and more comfortable with being on a bike. Grinning, he decided to show her just how exhilarating a motorcycle could be. He dipped low into the curves as they began the winding mountain climb, the concrete seemingly rising to just under their knees. He could feel that the bike was perfectly balanced, nowhere near losing control, but for those not used to the sensation, it could be a little frightening. Jessie clenched him tightly again, but she laughed too.

Long before they arrived at Kai's work, Jessie was easily leaning with him, almost anticipating the curves like he did, and her hands had relaxed their death grip on his torso. Actually, as Kai slowly approached the research center, he noticed that her hands had drifted so low on his waist they were resting on top of his jeans more than on his stomach. It did odd, arousing things to have her fingers so near him, but he did nothing to fix her position as he rolled the bike to a stop and shut it off.

Just as he was turning to ask Jessie if she'd had fun, Missy started walking their way. Kai felt Jessie slide off the bike, and, taking off his helmet, he hopped off after her. Once he was beside the bike, Missy stepped directly in front of him, nearly in his face.

"Kai! It is so good to see you on a Sunday! And here I thought my weekend was going to be long and uneventful without seeing your gorgeous self for two straight days. And, I know I've said it before, but goddamn, you're hot on your motorcycle."

As Missy was clearly within hug distance, and looked like she was considering it, Kai held his helmet in front of his body, effectively cutting off the temptation. Shaking his head at his horny coworker, he said, "Talking to you is such a boost to the ego, Missy."

Missy grinned at him; a smudge on her cheek clearly betrayed the fact that she'd actually been working hard in the countryside today. Eager as she could be, she was also very good at her job. "Honey, trust me," she purred, her eyes skimming down the front of him. "Talking to you does way more for me."

Laughing at her, since that was all Kai could do with the situation, he looked back at Jessie. Not having figured out how to remove her helmet, she still had it on, but her hands were on her hips as she stared at Missy.

"Sorry, Jess." Kai slipped his helmet on the handlebar and walked back to her. Tucking his hands up underneath her chin, he loosened the slide. He expected to see an exhilarated smile when he pulled the helmet off, but she was frowning. More specifically, she was frowning at Missy, and there was definite heat in her eyes. Knowing Missy, she probably had her eyes locked onto his ass.

Kai wanted to tell Jessie that his coworker just liked to objectify him, but Missy spoke first. Walking up to Jessie with a look of suspicion on her face, she sullenly said, "You cheating on me, Kai? Who's the girl?" Adjusting her glasses, Missy eyed Jessie the way she would analyze a potential threat to the ecosystem.

Her unreasonable jealousy made him want to groan. Overly flirtatious *and* possessive. Great. "Missy, this is my cousin, Jessie."

Missy's entire demeanor changed. Brightening, she walked right up to Jessie and slipped her arm around her shoulders like they were best friends now or something. "Cousin? That's great!" Pressing into Jessie's side, she gave Kai a seductive glance. "So, cousin, tell me all about Kai. Likes, dislikes, turn offs...turn ons." She raised her eyebrows, and Kai shook his head.

Jessie was too busy gaping at the woman to respond. Removing her from Missy's side, Kai pulled her close to him. "I'm going to give Jessie a tour." Missy nodded, like she thought that was a great idea, and then she started to follow them when Kai stepped forward. Stopping, he looked back at her. "We can go alone, Missy. I wouldn't want to hold up your work." She pouted, and Kai couldn't help but grin. As he grabbed Jessie's hand, leading her to the front doors, he tossed over his shoulder. "See you later, Missy."

Jessie seemed to thaw out from the Missy encounter after Kai showed her the various rooms and labs where he spent his days. Kai wasn't sure if Jessie had found Missy's aggressiveness off-putting, or if she just hadn't liked him being mentally undressed right in front of her; probably a little of both.

After checking out a large portion of the wilderness behind the research center, carefully avoiding the damn beehives, Kai and Jessie reentered the center through the rear of the building. They were both laughing about their little trek through the woods when Kai noticed his boss at the end of the hall. Kai had made sure to keep Jessie away from any sensitive areas, so he didn't think he'd get in trouble for bringing her here, but he wasn't really sure. With as strange as Mason could sometimes be toward him, it could go either way. Kai sort of wished the man wasn't here today. But...he usually was there; he practically lived at the research center.

Straightening his shoulders once he was spotted, Kai grabbed Jessie's hand again; he had to forcefully ignore how nice it felt to have her soft palm resting against his. Walking up to where Mason was paused in a doorway, clipboard in one hand, coffee in the other, Kai gave his boss a small wave.

"Mason, I'm glad you're here." Kai still naturally wanted to call the man 'sir,' but that was one thing Mason still insisted on—informality.

Mason seemed to slump a little at seeing Kai, before bringing his lips up into a smile that was clearly forced. Kai wanted to find out once and for all what the guy's problem with him was, but now wasn't the time. "Kai...I didn't think you were coming in today." By his tone, it was obvious that he was disappointed that Kai had decided to show up. It was almost like Kai was ruining his day, just by being there.

Ignoring the sting of not being wanted, Kai smiled as he shifted his gaze to Jessie. She seemed to be puzzled about something, and was staring at Mason like he looked familiar to her. "I was just showing my cousin, Jessie, around the center."

Mason's eyes widened as he studied Jessie. Extending his hand, he murmured, "Cousin? Well, nice to meet you, Jessie."

Jessie shook his extended hand, but her brows were still furrowed. "Hi..." Narrowing her eyes while they shook hands, Jessie scrutinized Mason's face. "Your eyes...I've never seen someone with a shade so similar to Kai's..."

With those words, it was like Jessie had poured a jug of ice water down Mason's back. He shot up straight, his back rigid and tight, and he practically yanked his hand away from Jessie's. Looking uncomfortable, like she'd just suggested something horrendous, Mason shifted his gaze between them. "It's nice to meet you. I wish I could stay and socialize, but I have too many important things to take care of at the moment." With that, he spun on his heel and darted down the hallway.

Kai was shocked as he watched the tall, gray-haired man flee the area. Kai had certainly noticed the similarity in their eye color, but really, he hadn't thought too much about it. Eyes only came in so many colors, and he was eventually going to find someone with a shade close to his. But Mason had reacted so strangely to the comparison. Did he really dislike Kai so much that he couldn't even stand the thought of sharing a similar trait?

Kai wanted to go find the man and ask him, but Jessie looked a little freaked out by what had just happened. Twisting to face Kai, she muttered, "Did I say something wrong?"

Shaking his head, Kai grabbed her hand again. "No." Looking back to where Mason's lean frame had disappeared, Kai let out a weary sigh. "He just doesn't care much for me, so he probably didn't like being told he sort of looks like me."

Jessie seemed surprised when Kai swung his eyes back to hers. "Oh, how could anyone not like you?" she whispered, her face flushing a light shade of pink.

Seeing her embarrassment made Kai smile. Then the warmth behind her comment made him sigh. "Come on. Let's go get that lunch that I promised you." Still looking flustered, Jessie nodded and they headed back to his bike.

●━━━━━━━━━━━━━━━━━━━●

Jessie discreetly studied Kai as they walked through the hallways. She noted the way his eyes stayed forward and his jaw was clenched tight. Even his warm hand entangled with hers was a little firmer than before. But she wasn't about to complain; touching him felt too nice.

Kai was still upset about running into his boss. The ball of ice in Jessie's stomach hadn't melted one single bit. Had she done something wrong? Offended him in some way? She hoped Kai was right and it wasn't her, but she really didn't see how it could be Kai either. Why would comparing him to Kai would make him act so strangely? Truly, it was a compliment. Kai was extremely attractive. And charming, sweet, funny. How could his boss not like him? Kai was very… likeable.

That fact was solidified when they once again ran into Kai's obviously interested coworker outside. Kai's face changed from annoyed to amused as the wiry woman approached them. The look on his face made Jessie frown. She didn't want to be jealous of anyone, but she didn't like that look being directed at another woman. She still wasn't ready.

Stopping right in front of them, his coworker put her hands directly on his chest. "Oh, no, no, no. You can't leave yet. I'm finally at a stopping point."

Kai discreetly dropped Jessie's hand as he chuckled at the forlorn woman. "Sorry, Missy, I promised my cousin a decent lunch." Jerking his thumb back toward the building, he laughed out, "The only thing left in the break room is Louis's tuna…and I'm not touching that."

Exaggerating a pout, Missy swept her hands down his chest to his jeans. Hooking her fingers into his belt loops, she stepped forward so their chests were touching; he automatically took a step backward. "Maybe a quickie before you go?" She suggestively raised her eyebrows, and Jessie felt her skin start to overheat. Had she seriously just asked him to have sex with her?

Like he was used to it, Kai merely laughed at her again as he removed her hands from his jeans. "Uh, not today, Missy." The woman let out a dramatic sigh as she finally stepped away. "Fine, but I'll have you know, I shaved today… everywhere."

Kai rolled his eyes and shook his head. Smiling down at Jessie, he indicated his bike. "And that's our cue."

Jessie kept her expression blank as a sliver of curiosity and envious anger ripped through her. She wasn't sure if anything was going on between Kai and this woman or not, and even though it shouldn't, it bothered her that she didn't know. Missy didn't seem like his type though. Then again, Jessie didn't really know his type, and he and Missy did share common interests if they worked together. Either way, they were awful friendly with each other. Or at least, Missy was awful friendly with him.

To hide the simmering emotions building under the surface, Jessie slipped her helmet on as quickly as she could. She shouldn't be jealous, she shouldn't be upset, she shouldn't be angry. But when Missy smacked his ass as he walked by, then swooped in to plant a kiss on his cheek, she felt all of those things.

With an amused shake of his head, Kai slipped on his helmet while Missy watched him as eagerly as a lioness stalking her prey. Popping open the visor, he told Missy goodbye. Then he pointed a finger at her and added, "Don't mess with my phone anymore, please. I know it's you."

Missy gave him a sly smile as she rocked back and forth on her heels. "I have no idea what you're talking about, Kai." Then she started humming a song that Jessie could have sworn was "Endless Love."

Still shaking his head, Kai slapped down his visor, and then helped Jessie adjust her helmet. Jessie was still feeling irrational jealousies over things she knew she shouldn't, so she kept her mouth shut as his fingers brushed along her jaw. The intimacy of the tender touch only confused her more. How was she supposed to let him go when he felt so wonderful?

When Kai was finished, he took his seat on the motorcycle and nodded behind himself for her to sit down. With a soft sigh, she did. Jessie loosely held his hips as Kai started the bike. Missy was still watching, practically drooling, as he walked the bike backwards. When they were turned around, Jessie heard him yell back to her, "Hold on," and she instinctively wrapped her arms around his waist as tightly as she could. Then he took off, light rocks spinning under his tires as he zoomed away.

Like being on a roller coaster, Jessie's stomach lifted then settled. She clung to Kai's back so firmly, it was like they were one person. She felt Kai make adjustments with his feet, switching gears maybe. She felt his upper body move as he twisted the handlebars ever so slightly. Keeping her eyes shut, she concentrated on his body movements, and not the fact that they were both way too exposed, should something bad happen.

After several miles, Jessie relaxed, and she again felt the comfort and excitement that she'd felt while driving up here. Getting over the mental block of terror took her a while, but once she did, she found that she enjoyed riding with him. Cracking her eyes open, she watched the colorful trees zipping past. All she could hear was the hum of the bike and the wind rushing through the vents in her helmet, but with the way her body was pressed into his broad back, she imagined that she could hear his heartbeat too, thudding with the beat of the road beneath them.

Smiling at the beauty of the scenery blurring past them, Jessie giggled into Kai's back. She squeezed him in a hug before loosening her grip. As her fingers relaxed against him, they drifted down his stomach. Kai dipped the bike low through the long, curving corners, and Jessie ignored how close their knees got to the pavement. She trusted him; he'd never go so low that their knees touched the ground, and he'd never dump them. Instead of allowing herself to pointlessly worry, she focused on how his thighs moved as he held the bike, how hers shifted as she held him. The muscles in his stomach, hips, and legs did intriguing things with each corner. With her legs pressing against his, her chest flush to his back, her head resting on his shoulder, Jessie felt connected to him in an almost overpowering way. It was erotic and at the same time, it wasn't. It was also exhilarating. As Jessie grew even more comfortable, she began to fully appreciate why Kai loved this. She had no desire to drive a motorcycle of her own, but she'd be a passenger any day. She'd be *his* passenger any day.

What felt like mere minutes later, they were back in the heart of Denver. Kai took them to a small diner that Jessie had been to several times with her friends, and they parked in the back lot. As Kai dropped the kickstand and shut off the bike, Jessie realized that her hands had drifted down to rest on the front of his jeans. She could even feel the basic outline of him. Immediately removing her hands, she felt her face flush red-hot.

Once again glad that the helmet obscured her features, Jessie hopped off the bike. Needing Kai to not touch her for a minute, at least until her embarrassment cooled, she fumbled with the strap under her chin. Determined to remove the helmet on her own, she successfully loosened it as he stepped up to her; his helmet was already resting on the handlebars. Jessie popped it off just as he lifted his hands to help. Kai beamed with pride, and Jessie's emotions evened. She could do this.

The pair enjoyed a leisurely lunch, neither one wanting to hurry their afternoon together. Jessie shared pieces of her life that Kai didn't know about—her dad's recent move to D.C., her mom grudgingly following him there then discovering that she loved it, the numerous amounts of children her brothers had, how she'd decided on her career and where she wanted to go with it, and the details of her romance with Jeremy.

Kai frowned as she explained the details of their failed relationship. "Jeremy sounds like an idiot."

A brilliant smile erupted on Jessie's lips. "Yes, yes he is."

As they ate, Kai talked about things in his life that Jessie didn't know about—his friends back home, being an only child with divorced parents, why he loved his work so much and what he hoped to accomplish with it, the few not very serious relationships that he'd had, most of them ending amicably, unlike her and Jeremy.

After their long lunch, Jessie felt like she'd been around Kai her entire life. He just fit into every section of who she was, and she couldn't imagine not having him around now. As odd as it seemed, since he'd only been in the city a little over a week, it was difficult for her to imagine a time when he *hadn't* been around. Jessie wasn't sure why that was, and she was both comforted and disturbed by the revelation. Especially since she knew their tight bond was about to get a lot looser. Kai had a date with April next Saturday. And then there was Missy. Jessie still wasn't sure just what their relationship entailed. Maybe her bond with him wasn't as tight as she believed. Maybe, like Jeremy, Kai was hiding things from her too.

The thought had her feeling melancholy when Kai eventually dropped her off at her house. Jessie was sullen when she got off her bike and removed her helmet. She tried to hide the sadness, but she was suddenly drowning in doubt about Kai's honesty. And to be honest with herself, she was extremely disappointed that their afternoon was over. She didn't want him to see that though, didn't want him to notice the tears pricking her eyes, so she left her head down and let her hair hide her face.

"Thanks for the ride, Kai. I'll talk to you later."

With that brief goodbye, she spun around so she could make a beeline for the door. She just wanted to hide out in her room, where she was going to spend at least an hour listening to depressing music. But Kai wasn't going to let that happen. He grabbed her elbow as she spun away from him. Stopping, she reluctantly looked back. His expression concerned, he whispered, "Jessie? What's wrong?"

Not sure what she should or shouldn't say, Jessie turned her body to face him. Since the thought of him being dishonest hurt, she decided she wouldn't be dishonest either. Shuffling through her turbulent emotions, she picked a topic that affected her friends as well as her. "That woman you work with... Missy...do you have something going on with her?" She quickly added, "Because April is my friend, and she should know if you're seeing more than one person." Her cheeks heated with embarrassment as she said it. Yes, it was an honest statement, but it really wasn't why she wanted to know.

Kai looked surprised at her conclusion, then he broke into soft laughter. He stopped when Jessie crossed her arms over her chest. Fixing his face, he asked, "Are you serious? Missy?" His voice was as incredulous as his eyes.

Jessie only worried her lip while she waited for a definite answer. Because laughing wasn't a no. Kai's gaze turned adoring as he looked over her face. One of his hands came up to run through a springy curl, and for a second, he seemed torn; Jessie's heart started pounding. "No, I have no interest in Missy." He let out a sad sigh as he played with the strand of hair in his fingers. "Really, I have no interest in anyone..." Hanging his head, he peeked his eyes up at her.

Jessie thudding heart stuttered. With the longing look in his eyes, she could clearly hear the words he wasn't saying—*no one but you*. Butterflies of anticipation swarmed in her stomach as his eyes flashed over her face. Dropping his hand from her hair, he raised his chin. "My only interest right now is concentrating on work, taking care of Gran, and...taking care of you." He whispered the last part.

Jessie felt her heart squeeze. "Me?" Her voice was a whisper too.

He stepped closer to her, so his hips were touching hers. "Yes...you." His hand found hers, and their fingers laced together. "You're always taking care of everyone else, making sure everyone has what they need." His face just inches in front of hers, he breathed, "What do *you* need, Jessie?"

Jessie couldn't speak. He was so close to her, even their chests were touching. His lips parted as his light breath washed over her. Their fingers tightened as his gaze drifted down to her lips. Stepping into his body, Jessie rested her cheek along his. With a shaky exhale, Kai clenched her hand. Jessie closed her eyes, and the blood pounding through her body sounded like a tidal wave in her head.

Knowing she shouldn't let them stand so intimately, Jessie began to pull back. Her cheek slid across his as she retreated, but Kai didn't move; his body was rigid as he clenched her hand. Jessie could feel his hot breath against her lips; it sent a jolt of electricity through her, clouding her mind. Wanting what she knew she couldn't have—and hating herself for wanting it—Jessie gently pressed her lips to his. Kai made a deep noise in his throat that stoked the fire raging within her. Not caring who was looking, not caring who she was and who he was, that genetically and ethically, they shouldn't be together, Jessie let go of her control and gave herself over to her basest desires. She wrapped his bottom lip in hers, and sucked him into her mouth.

He tasted like heaven.

He. Kai. Kai Harper, the gorgeous boy who shared her name. Her cousin. That thought instantly snapped her back to who she was. She jerked away, and that was when she noticed Kai's closed eyes and fast breath. His free hand was slowly reaching up, like he was going to cup her cheek, pull her in for a deeper connection.

"Kai," she whispered, mortified that she'd caved and kissed him.

His eyes sprang open, and remembering where they were and who might be watching, he looked around himself. Stepping back, his breath still unnaturally fast, he ran a hand through his hair. Searching the area, like he was sure someone had just seen that, he quietly told her, "I should go."

Jessie felt horror, disgust, and pain rising within her. She shouldn't touch him like that, especially directly in front of her house where her roommates could see. Her eyes nervously flicked to her front windows. They were completely empty, but Jesus, *had* either of them seen her do that to him? How could she possibly explain that intimate moment?

She swung her eyes back to Kai when she felt him step toward his bike. His head was down, his face looked thoughtful. Jessie hated that she'd completely ruined their nice afternoon with those last few minutes. Knowing she was to blame, she put a hand on his arm. He glanced back at her with confusion clear on his face. Jessie understood; she felt it too.

"I'm sorry," she whispered, staring at their shoes, unable to look him in the eye.

Sighing, Kai's fingers came up to briefly touch her chin before dropping back to his side. "We can't let this..." He paused, and Jessie peeked up at him. Now he was staring at their shoes, unable to look at her either. "I know it's hard, Jessie, but we have to stop...this."

Tears stinging her eyes again, she whispered, "I know... that's why I want you to go out with April. You have a date with her Saturday, right?"

With a sound of weary trepidation, Kai looked up at her. "Yeah..." They stared at each other in silence for a few seconds, then he shook his head. "Jessie...about April. I don't..." He stopped and bit his lip. Jessie felt her heart begin to race again, and she hated herself for it. Closing his beautiful eyes, he smiled sadly before reopening them. "I think I'm going to go over to Gran's. Spend some time with her. Make sure she's getting along all right." He gave her a wry smile. "Give you a break from doing it."

Jessie nodded, her heart relaxing. Grams. Their mutual relative. She was a tough old broad who managed to get around pretty well, but she still needed some personal attention. "Okay...cousin."

Kai gave her a soft laugh and looked away. With a smile on his face, he turned back and said, "Goodbye, cousin."

Jessie swallowed the enormous lump in her throat as she took a step toward her front door. Keeping his eyes locked on hers, he grabbed his helmet, slipped it on, and climbed onto his bike. He revved the engine a couple of times after he started it, and with him still intently watching her, Jessie waved goodbye. Kai nodded in response, then twisted around and sped off. Jessie watched until he completely disappeared, then she closed her eyes and dropped her head.

Goodbye…cousin.

13

The First Date

To say that Kai was confused was an understatement. Here he was, actively planning a date with a vivacious, flirtatious, attractive woman, and all he could think about was his cousin's lips wrapped around his. It was sick. It was twisted. And it was occupying every waking moment he had.

He pictured Jessie's smile when he ate breakfast. He remembered the feeling of having her molded to his back when he drove to work. He imagined the sound of her laughter while he listened to his coworkers. But most of all, he remembered the feeling of her lips against his. He could almost still taste her, still feel the heat.

Someone smacking his shoulder returned Kai to the present. "You still here?" Kai looked up to see Louis frowning at him. The Indiana Jones wannabe was standing in front of him with a hand on his hip, like they were in an old Western and Kai was about to tell him to draw. Considering that the extent of their adventurous day had involved the two of them collecting water samples from a nearby stream, it was a little funny to Kai.

Securing the vials of water into a pack, Kai slung it into the back of a jeep. "Yeah...I'm listening." Knowing that he hadn't really been paying any attention, Kai struggled to remember what they'd been talking about. He instantly remembered with Louis's next statement.

"Good, then take her to Paccione's. You're practically guaranteed a successful mating." Louis shifted his stance and grinned. "In fact, I think that's written right into the menu."

Kai rolled his eyes and shook his head. *Right*. Louis was helping him plan a date with Jessie's roommate. While he appreciated his coworker's enthusiasm, Kai wasn't trying to have a successful mating with April. And going to a fancy restaurant didn't sound like much fun to him. It was just a little too...typical.

Climbing into the rig, Kai shrugged. "I don't know, Louis. That seems a little cliché."

Louis chuckled as he got into the driver's side. Adjusting the numerous gadgets on his belt so he could sit back in the seat, he gave Kai a wry smile. "Clichés are clichés for a reason, Harper. They work. Every species has their version of strutting and feather-preening." His eyes shifted forward as he started the engine. "The human ritual just happens to involve lobster and overpriced wine."

Kai couldn't help but wonder when the outdoorsy, wild-looking man had ever taken a girl to a place where eating the chicken with your hands was frowned upon. As they started back to the center, Kai sighed. He didn't know April well enough to plan a date with her. Picturing what Jessie might have fun doing made him smile. He could easily imagine setting something up for her. Something different, something unique that would make her laugh. Something a little… romantic.

That thought made Kai frown. He shouldn't be planning romantic outings with his cousin. As the incongruous gray buildings came into view, Kai glanced over at Louis. "I was thinking about something outside, a picnic or something. That's romantic, right?"

Kai wasn't entirely sure if Louis knew anything about being romantic. At least, not anything that was original. Louis gave him an appraising look as he parked the jeep behind the buildings. "Take her to Red Rocks."

Kai blinked. Should he know what that meant? Seeing his confusion, Louis explained. "Red Rocks Amphitheater. There's nothing playing this time of year, but you could take her up there and have a picnic on the steps." He cracked open his door, but before he got out, he told Kai, "Most women go nuts for that shit. It works better than piss on a porcupine."

His coworker's choice of bizarre mating practices in the wild was amusing to Kai, but Louis might be on to something. Kai wasn't sure what April was in to, but he could easily picture taking Jessie up there, stretching a blanket out under a clear blue sky. He'd have to layer up to not freeze to death, but then…that could lead to cuddling later.

Kai grimaced as he walked into the building, and reminded himself for the umpteenth time that he wasn't planning an outing with his cousin. No, he was planning a date with April.

He needed to remember that.

As Kai went about solidifying his plans, he spent the majority of his free time at Gran's, making sure she was getting along okay. She rolled her eyes whenever he asked her how she was feeling. At one point, he thought she might pop up and do a jig just to prove she was healthy as a horse. Assuring her that the display wasn't necessary, he did as much as he could without coddling her.

He spoke with April a few times during the week. She called him to confirm their date, then she called him to ask what she should wear. Since he didn't want to ruin the surprise, he only told her to dress warm. Pausing, she'd asked, "Warm? Really?"

There was an odd feeling between them after her question, like she was silently sulking. Maybe she'd been hoping that they'd be going somewhere that required very little clothing. "Is that okay?" he asked.

Her voice all sunshine and cheeriness, she told him, "Yeah, it's fine. We're going to have such a good time!"

Wondering if he was planning a decent enough date, Kai considered running his plans by Jessie. He wasn't sure if he should though. True, they were friends, and he respected her opinion, but he *was* planning a date with another woman. Even though they'd both agreed this was necessary for them to move past what had happened between them, what was still happening between them, Jessie probably didn't want to hear about it. Kai knew he wouldn't want to hear about her dating some other guy. He already hated the tidbits he'd heard about her and her asshole of an ex, Jeremy.

So, whenever he talked to Jessie, he kept the topic off April, and stuck to work or Gran...or her; Kai could listen to Jessie talk about her life for hours. After a two-hour conversation late one night, Kai wondered if that was typical cousin behavior.

Jessie came by his place the next night, looking fresh-faced and flushed when he opened the door. The unexpected visit made him grin, but when he saw what she had in her hands, he smiled even wider. Shaking his head at her thoughtfulness, he motioned for her to come inside.

Beaming, Jessie walked over to the patio set that she was letting Kai use in his kitchen, and placed a couple of thick cushions over the wrought iron chairs. Even though Kai had to admit the furniture was a little hard and uncomfortable, and the padding was a must-needed addition, he put his hands on his hips in mock sternness as she worked them into place. "You need to stop doing nice things for me. I can't keep up, Jessie."

After securing the deep blue fabric to the metal chairs, she stood and admired the small kitchen set for a moment before twisting to face him. "You don't need to, Kai." Tilting her head to the side, she bit her lip. A long, curly lock fell over her shoulder, resting just above her breast. Swallowing, Kai forced his eyes to stay locked on hers. "Besides, I couldn't leave you with butt-numbing furniture."

Jessie laughed after her comment, and her face lit up in a way that made Kai want to let out a lovesick sigh. He didn't though. He only smiled and sat down in his now comfortable chair. Leaning back, he exaggerated a long, happy groan. "Well, my butt and I thank you." Kai laughed; just being in her presence made him feel lighter.

She started to lower herself into the newly padded chair opposite him, but paused halfway down. "Oh," she exclaimed softly, reaching into her pocket. Struggling to contain an imp-ish smile, she pulled out her hand and handed him something. "Here, I got this for you."

Kai watched her warm brown eyes burning with mischievousness as he took the object. Furrowing his brow, he stared at the candy bar in his hands. Then he read the label and started laughing. Glancing up at her, he gave her a crooked smile; her eyes locked onto his lips. "A Bit-O-Honey bar? Because of the bees, right?"

Nodding her head, she started laughing uncontrollably. Kai couldn't contain his smile as he watched her amusement. "Cute," he answered in his most disgruntled voice.

His eyes drifted to her lips as she shrugged and said, "Yeah, I saw them at the gas station when I was filling up on the way over and thought of you."

She stared at him so lovingly, Kai stopped breathing for a second. Mesmerized, he whispered, "Always thinking of me..."

The smile fell from her face. It was instantly replaced by an expression of longing and pain. Kai wanted to reach out for her, wanted to pull her into his arms and hold her. More than anything, he wanted to tell her that they could find a way — that they could be together somehow. Even if it was wrong, even if their family and friends disowned them, surely the bond between them was strong enough to make a lifetime of shame and ridicule worth it?

But his stomach convulsed at the thought of caving, and he looked away from her. As right as it felt sometimes, it also felt horribly wrong. He couldn't entertain those thoughts. Not with her.

Jessie sighed after he broke their intense connection, and Kai glanced back at her. She was worrying her lip as she studied the table; her face was as conflicted as his. Just when he was about to ask her how she was feeling, even though he al-

S. C. Stephens

ready knew she was as torn as he was, she whispered, "Where are you going to take April?"

It was Kai's turn to sigh now, and Jessie looked up at him. Telling her about his date with April would help firm the wall they needed to have between them, so he decided to lay out his plans. Jessie listened, small tears forming in the corners of her eyes. When he was finished, she was silent.

Just as Kai looked away again, she spoke, "It sounds beautiful, Kai. I think she'll love it."

Even though she'd said, "I think she'll love it," Kai clearly heard, "I know *I'd* love it." Returning his eyes to her, he nodded as he swallowed the lump of pain in his throat. Standing, he came around to her side of the table and pulled her into the hug he felt she needed. The hug *he* needed.

Letting go could be so hard.

As the week dwindled, Kai got nervous. He liked April well enough, but really, he wasn't very interested in dating her. Jessie was insistent that he try, though, and his grandmother...well, once she'd found out he had a date, and with Jessie's friend no less, she'd been over the moon. Gran asked him details about April every time he went to check on her.

Looking relieved that he finally had someone, Gran would often switch the conversation to her second favorite topic—Kai's job. She always asked him how he was fitting in there, if he liked it, if he got along with his boss. And she always gave him an odd look when she asked about Mason. With a bright smile, Kai always told her things were great and he was very happy. True, his boss still hadn't warmed to Kai, and he really wasn't sure what he was doing wrong, but he didn't need to worry Gran with his work woes.

She always looked even more relieved after he told her that, like a weight had been lifted from her frail shoulders. When he thought to ask her why one evening, she shifted the conversation again, but this time to Kai's dad. "He misses you so much, dear." Lifting a gray eyebrow, she softly added, "You know, if you ever did become unhappy here, he would surely find a spot for you at the research reserve. You could work with your father every day...and with Leilani, of course." Her lips twisted after mentioning Kai's mother.

Her suggestion surprised Kai. For one, his father hadn't sounded like he missed Kai all that much the last few times they'd talked. The sudden distance between them bothered Kai. He didn't know why it was there. He was hoping it was just that his dad wasn't dealing with the separation as well as his mom. If calling him at all hours of the day and sending him care packages that included things like deodorant and shaving cream was handling it well. But Kai didn't like the edge he'd heard in his dad's voice recently, and he didn't know what to do about it, especially from here. Maybe when he went home for Christmas they could have a sit down, talk things out.

Focusing on his grandmother's second statement, Kai raised an eyebrow. "You want me to go back to Hawaii? Are you trying to get rid of me?"

The old woman gave him a loving smile as she shook her head. Placing a wrinkled hand over his smooth one, she said, "No, dear, I love having you here." She sighed; it was a much sadder sound than the conversation warranted. "I just want you to be happy."

Looking down at the ground, thinking of his cousin, Kai whispered, "I am happy here." Even if being around Jessie was torturous at times, it still filled Kai with a feeling that could only be described as happiness.

That happiness lasted right up to his date night, then it became muddled with uncertainty. As he rode his bike to April's place, he started wondering if Jessie would be there or if she would go out, to avoid the strangeness of him picking up another woman right in front of her. He hoped April wasn't too hands-on if Jessie did happen to be around, but he couldn't ask her not to flirt, and Jessie couldn't ask her not to flirt. Neither one of them had a good reason to tell April to be respectful of Jessie's feelings. There was just no way to bring up what was going on between them without grossing everybody out and embarrassing them both. It was best to stay silent.

Taking his helmet off once he stopped the bike, Kai took a moment to appreciate the clear, beautiful, early afternoon sky. The mountains in the distance created the perfect backdrop for the looming city spread out around him. The bustle of human life reached his ears along with the singsong of birds and the occasional yap of a nearby dog. It wasn't like Hawaii, but Colorado was growing on him. Once he adjusted to the temperature, he thought he could be right at home here.

Smiling at the thought of sharing Jessie's hometown with her, Kai lifted the messenger bag slung across his chest, and laid it on the ground next to his bike. That was one of the downfalls of driving a motorcycle—no trunk space—but he'd managed to finagle everything he needed for a decent meal into the bag, even a bottle of wine.

Letting out a quick exhale, Kai worked on calming his nerves as he walked to the front door. Jessie's truck being in the drive wasn't helping. She *was* here. She would come out to say hello, to be polite to her cousin, and then she'd watch him drive off without her. Kai imagined that was going to hurt, and as he knocked on the door, he wished Jessie had stayed away for this. She shouldn't have to see this.

The door opened wide, and Kai smiled at seeing April standing there. She was very pretty. Given a different set of circumstances, Kai probably would have enjoyed going on a date with her. Having taken his advice, April had layered a couple of long-sleeved T-shirts over a pair of tight, stretchy denims. Her hair was perfectly styled, every strand in its place, and her makeup was meticulous. While she looked amazing, Kai was worried that she wouldn't approve of a helmet potentially ruining the smooth, low ponytail she had her hair in.

"Kai! Hello!" Leaning forward, she gave him a quick kiss on the cheek.

Kai looked down for a second, conflicted. He didn't want to be attracted to April, but he was a man, and her attention was enjoyable. And that made him feel guilty. He felt even guiltier when he looked up and saw Jessie, a few steps behind April, watching them. As April pulled him into the house by his arm, he locked gazes with Jessie. Not able to control it, he stared at her longingly. If he hadn't agreed to this, he would tell April that he really wanted to go out with his cousin tonight, not her. But this was what Jessie wanted, what they both needed.

He watched Jessie swallow and give him a slight nod. "Hi, Kai."

Trying to keep the wistfulness in his face out of his voice, he told her, "Hi, Jessie." By the way Jessie's eyes watered, he wasn't quite sure if he'd succeeded.

Oblivious to the mood in the room, April grabbed a fluffy jacket from the back of the couch. She was attached to his arm in an instant, wrapped, bundled, and ready to go. Kai pulled his attention from Jessie to concentrate on his date. "Ready?" he asked her.

April hugged his arm, pulling herself close into his side. "Yep." Without a second thought, she glanced over at Jessie. "See ya! Don't wait up." She winked after she said it, and Kai closed his eyes to block out the image of Jessie's face paling.

As April tugged him out the door, Kai looked back at Jessie. "Goodbye," he whispered.

Jessie feebly raised her hand in a wave, her already wet eyes looking heavier. It killed Kai to watch April close the door between them. He'd never felt guiltier, but somehow they had to change their relationship. They had to be a family. They had to get rid of the…tension between them.

Once outside, April started digging into her purse, like she was looking for her car keys. Clearing his throat, Kai pointed to his bike. "I thought we'd ride?"

April had seemed to like the idea before, when Kai had picked up Jessie for lunch, so he assumed she'd be thrilled, and she did smile, but one of her hands slinked through the end of her long ponytail, and Kai could tell she wasn't excited about getting her hair messed up. Kai wanted to grimace at the awkward tension he felt building, but he resisted. Walking over to his spare helmet, he helped her put it on. April looked to be containing her reaction as well. Her face was frozen as he carefully slipped the safety device over her once-perfect hairdo. It gave his gut a weird pang to put a present he'd purchased for Jessie over another woman's head. He felt like he was cheating on her, or somehow betraying her. It was a really strange feeling to have on a date.

While the helmet fit Jessie perfectly, it was just a little too small for April; her ponytail was going to be a mess when she pulled it off. He felt bad about that, but as he glanced over at the window and saw Jessie discretely watching them, his thoughts instantly rewound to watching her pull off the helmet; it had been one of the sexiest things he'd ever seen. Her curls had instantly bounced back to life once freed of the contraption, almost as if they'd been taunting the world that they couldn't be squashed so easily.

Kai nodded at Jessie through the window, then popped his helmet on and slung the bag over his shoulder, positioning it in front of his chest so April could hold on to him. As he sat on the bike, still half watching Jessie in the window, he remembered the feel of her body clinging to him. When April slipped on the bike after him, her hands immediately drifted to the front of his jeans; she even slid her fingers through his belt loops. Knowing April wouldn't hear it through their helmets, Kai let himself sigh. There were so many things about this night that he already wished were different.

Like his date.

Giving Jessie one last wistful look, since that couldn't be seen either, he started the bike. Then, he left her. Kai could feel the heat of her gaze as he pulled away from her house, and he let out another sigh. This one came out stuttered, as a moment of intense, painful emotion washed over him. He never imagined when he'd agreed to this just how hard it would be.

Not noticing any of his turmoil, April giggled as she rubbed herself against his back. Her fingers explored his jeans, her thumbs slipping inside his waistband. Kai concentrated on the sensation of her touch, anything to block the emotion that threatening to consume him. Her thumbs slid back and forth over his stomach, and Kai found himself smiling. It did feel nice. Maybe he was being unfair to April, by not giving her a legitimate chance. They would definitely never amount to anything if he always compared her to Jessie, and as he sped away from his cousin, he vowed to not think about her anymore this evening. It was the least he could do for April.

When they arrived at Red Rocks Amphitheater, Kai couldn't stop smiling. It was the most incredible blending of man and nature, and the epitome of everything that he believed in—that people could live in harmony with the world, instead of always trying to conquer it. For a moment, the awe-inspiring view before him took his breath.

Rows and rows of seats were carved into the hillside, directly between the largest, reddest rocks that Kai had ever seen. They proudly jutted out of the ground, commanding attention and respect. The stage was set up at the bottom of the sloping steps, and Kai had to imagine, what with the angles of the rocks and steps, that the acoustics in this place were amazing. He'd love to see a show here.

Standing beside him, April frowned as she pulled out her ponytail and ran her fingers through her hair. Kai could tell she wasn't as impressed by the locale as he was. Maybe she'd just been here several times before.

With a sigh, April indicated the steps. "All the way up there?"

Kai followed her line of sight. She had a point; the steps were quite a ways from the parking area. Taking off his helmet, Kai smiled as he grabbed her hand. "At least we'll be nice and warm when we get there."

April glanced at him and Kai could have sworn she was resisting rolling her eyes. Slapping on a smile instead, she pulled him forward. "Let's go then."

By the time they got to the steps, Kai felt nice and heated, even a little out of breath as the exertion mixed with the high altitude. But he didn't care, the place was amazing. He couldn't get over the beauty of it. The sparse trees, the dusty stone steps, the towering rock monoliths, all of it made him feel about an inch tall.

Kai threw a beaming smile April's way. She was breathing heavier, too, but she didn't look so happy about it. She swatted at a bug flying around her face, then sighed when she examined the dusty stone steps they were going to be sitting on. As Kai noted her unimpressed expression, he couldn't help but think that he was failing miserably at this date.

Suppressing a sigh, he opened his bag and pulled out the thin blanket he'd stuffed inside. It wouldn't do much for padding, but it would help keep the dust off of April's clothes. He laid it out on a wide path between two sets of carved benches. April gave him a polite smile as she sat down on her hip. She shifted a few times to get comfortable, then watched Kai as he sat down and began pulling various objects from his bag.

Not really knowing a whole lot about packing for a picnic, Kai had eagerly listened to Louis's suggestions. Of course, Louis was into far more exotic foods than Kai, and had wanted him to pack caviar, escargot, and foie gras. Kai had decided to pack cold pasta, chicken salad, cheese and crackers, strawberries, and a bottle of red wine instead. It had sounded good to him, and Jessie had nodded in approval at hearing it, but as he studied April's face while pulling out the food, he suddenly got the feeling that she would have preferred the snails.

Keeping a tight smile on her face, she immediately grabbed the bottle of wine. Kai wanted to sigh again, but instead he tried to begin a polite conversation with her.

The date went by slowly for Kai. It wasn't that he was having a bad time or anything, he was having fun, kind of, but April was clearly not an outdoorsy girl and Kai could tell she wasn't having the best evening. She kept her thick coat zipped all the way up and looked a little disappointed that she was covered. Kai remembered her tight, long-sleeved shirts and thought that April was probably more comfortable when she had her body to flirt with. Being bundled up was hampering her seductiveness. She constantly swished away bugs and other minute creatures that Kai didn't even notice, and she picked at the food on her paper plate with her plastic fork. Kai suddenly felt really bad for not going to the cliché restaurant. She obviously would have preferred a high-class meal.

But if she was having a bad time, she never once complained about it. Kai had to give her credit for that. She kept up a nice stream of conversation, most of it about her and the many struggles between her and her parents. Unlike the relationship Kai had with his Mom and Dad, April's parents seemed to continually disapprove of her life and her choices. Kai didn't have much to add to the conversation, since he and his parents had almost everything in common. But for the fact that his parents were no longer married, and outside of work they generally didn't talk much, Kai's family was a pretty harmonious one. Well, it was, before Kai's Dad had gotten so odd. Not cold, but definitely distant, like he was waiting for something.

By the end of the meal, Kai and April were sitting close together on the thin blanket with their legs stretched out in front of them and a plastic glass of wine in hand. April leaned into Kai's side as she laughed at a joke he'd made. He wasn't sure if she was laughing to flirt or laughing because she genuinely thought he was funny. Aside from finding him attractive, Kai was never entirely sure what April thought of him.

After finishing her glass of wine, April had a pleasant rosy glow on her cheeks. Kai was staring at her as the last gulp flowed down his throat. She watched him silently as she grabbed his glass and placed it inside of hers. Oddly enough, she made that simple movement suggestive. Intrigued, Kai watched as she blindly set the glasses on the step above them.

Her gaze suddenly locked onto his lips. Kai could clearly see what she wanted, what she expected, and he wasn't sure if he could go through it. She had kissed him before, briefly, and he'd responded to that, but a part of him didn't want this, and if he leaned down to her lips, if he initiated the contact...

Kai just didn't know if he was capable of that yet.

They stared at each other, their faces tantalizingly close, her warm breath light on his cool skin. He ran his tongue over his bottom lip as he contemplated. April's eyes tracked the movement, and she seemed to approve. Maybe tired of waiting for him, she made her move. Before Kai could even get nervous about kissing her, April's lips were on his. She skipped right past the shy, tentative stage and engulfed him in a deep kiss. Kai didn't want to like it, but she tasted good, smelled good, and felt good, and he couldn't stop himself. His hand cupped her neck and pulled her into him.

April let out an eager moan as their tongues lightly brushed together. Kai's body instantly reacted to the noise, even though he sort of wished it wouldn't. Finally enjoying her evening, April ran her hands through his hair, tilting his head to get a better angle at him. His breath increased as her tongue flicked across his mouth, searching, teasing, tasting.

Leaning backwards, she pulled Kai with her. Against his better judgment, he went willingly. She lay down on the ground, her body half off the blanket, but now that they were connecting on an intimate level, she didn't seem to mind the dust. April groaned as Kai's upper body laid over hers. Their kiss heated as Kai ran his hand down her side to her hip. The lower halves of their bodies were still lying side-by-side, hers flat to the ground. It was a position that would be easy for Kai to take advantage of, if he wanted more from her. But as his mouth moved over hers, he consciously kept his hips away. He wasn't ready. Honestly, he wasn't ready for her hands running up his chest and her tongue probing his mouth, but she wanted him and she was being aggressive about it, and Kai sort of had a weakness for that.

But he wouldn't let it go any farther. And he wouldn't think of Jessie as April's fingers trailed across his T-shirt, where the edge of his tattoo curled over his collar bone. He would not think of his cousin while he made out with her roommate. That would just be…wrong.

14

The Second Date

Jessie felt sick again. She was discreetly holding her stomach under the kitchen table, a fake, forced smile on her face as she listened to April describe her date with Kai. The date itself sounded like it hadn't gone very well. April hadn't liked her hair getting all out of sorts from the helmet. She hadn't enjoyed the long, exertive trek up to Red Rocks; with a half-grin she'd explained that there was only one reason why she'd want to be sweaty with a guy on a date, and it wasn't hiking. And she really hadn't been impressed with the food options. She'd been hoping for lobster in a classy restaurant and hadn't been too thrilled about freezing her butt off, swatting away too many bugs to count, and eating what she considered "camping food." Personally, Jessie thought she was being a little prissy about the whole thing. Maybe it wasn't April's typical date night, but it sounded perfectly romantic to Jessie.

But the part of the night that April had liked, the part that she could not stop talking to Jessie and Harmony about, was the part that was making Jessie nauseous. April and Kai had kissed, and it was much more than just the tiny peck Jessie had witnessed. From the way April told the story, Kai had had her sprawled on the stone steps, moaning and groaning with desire, and had practically shoved his tongue down her throat. She went on and on about how he couldn't plan a date worth a crap, but he definitely made up for it with his mouth.

April couldn't wait to see him again.

Jessie couldn't wait until she was alone in her room again; she had some pent-up tears that needed releasing.

She'd thought watching him leave with April would be the hardest part of all of this. Staring at his bike as it pulled away with April on it had ripped her to shreds. But this? Hearing April describe images that haunted Jessie's dreams? His hands, his breath, his lips? It was too much to bear, and Jessie had no idea what she'd say or do the next time she saw him. She was anxious about their next meeting, nervous and impatient. She wanted to tell him to stop seeing April, wanted to demand that she was the only woman in his life. But she couldn't do that to Kai. What life would that be? For either of them? Not truly having each other, but not having anyone else either…it sounded lonely to Jessie. Lonely and painful. But so was watching him fly away with April. Maybe Jessie should start seeing someone too. She just had no desire to see someone. Anyone but Kai, that was. But she couldn't have Kai, and they both needed to move on.

Interrupting April's hundredth retelling of making out with him, Jessie stood and set her cereal bowl in the sink. Faking nonchalance, she tossed over her shoulder, "I'm glad you guys had an okay time, April. I'm gonna head over to Gram's, see if she needs anything. Catch you guys later."

As she walked past the two of them still giggling at the table, she heard April brightly exclaim, "Have fun! So…how soon do you think I can call Kai?"

Closing her eyes, Jessie didn't answer her roommate. She tried to let it go, but tears stung beneath her eyelids and her stomach roiled. It was right; it was natural. Unlike her and her cousin, Kai and April made sense together.

Her stomach finally felt a little better on the drive over to her grandmother's…until she pulled into her driveway. Jessie sat in the drive with her truck idling, staring over at Kai's bike in the spot right next to her. He was here. If she went inside, she'd have to see him post-date. Would he look different? Would he look like he'd been bitten by the love bug? Would he want to tell her all about it? Jessie had had a hard enough time listening to April, she wasn't sure if she could handle hearing Kai talk about it.

Sighing, she shut the truck off. She wasn't here for Kai. She was here to take care of Grams. Kai was a decent guy. He wouldn't bring up something that would potentially hurt her. Well, he might want to make sure Jessie was okay, but he certainly wouldn't go into specifics like April had. She couldn't hide from him forever anyway. They were family, and family didn't abandon each other. Plus, she'd been sitting in the driveway for a while now; she was pretty certain she'd already been spotted.

Stepping out of the truck, Jessie ran a hand through her curls. Exhaling a long breath, she prepared herself to see the man who occupied so much of her mind…and her heart.

Jessie opened the front door and walked through it like she lived there. Grams insisted that family didn't have to knock. She didn't see Grams and Kai and couldn't hear them, but she knew they were there somewhere. "Hello?" she tentatively asked.

When no one answered her, she realized that they were probably out back, in Gram's greenhouse. She stepped into the sunshine-filled kitchen. The bright yellow walls added to the cheeriness of the room, but didn't help Jessie's mood. Peering out the thin lace curtain over the window, she could see the opaque greenhouse in the back corner of Gram's yard. Inside, she could easily make out two shadowy shapes—a short, frail one and a tall, lean one. Jessie sighed; even Kai's shadow was appealing.

Her stomach started to buzz with nervous energy, and she turned around and considered leaving. If Grams and Kai were tucked away in the greenhouse, then they probably hadn't heard her truck pull in. She could slip out and drive away and they'd be none the wiser. Then Jessie could come back later, when Kai was gone.

Jessie took a step, then paused. She hated the fact that she was fleeing from her cousin. This had been her idea. How did she think it was going to feel when Kai started seeing someone? And not just anyone either, but her roommate, one of her best friends. A best friend who was chatty, and who liked to delve into the TMI zone all too often. And now April's too-much-information involved a man who possessed such warmth, graciousness, and caring, not to mention the most incredible set of tropical eyes, that it made Jessie's heart ache.

"Jessie?"

Turning at the sound of her name, Jessie came face to face with those amazing eyes again. Kai was coming through the back door, his brow furrowed in concern as he watched her. Jessie wasn't sure how long she'd been standing still, debating if she should leave or not. The butterflies in her stomach flew up to her heart and her nerves began to sizzle her skin.

Titling his head, Kai quickly glanced back at where Grams was still poking around in the greenhouse. Softly closing the door, he walked up to Jessie in the middle of the kitchen. "What were you doing?"

Jessie exhaled softly; her breath came out stuttered, and she couldn't quite relax. *Thinking about how to avoid seeing you.* She thought it, but couldn't say it to his face. Hating the tension that she could feel building between them, she gave him an awkward smile; all she could see when she looked at him was April's lips against his. "I was just wondering where the two of you were."

Kai stepped in front of her. Looking down at her tense body, he let out a soft sigh. "April told you, didn't she?" Jessie felt the tears reappearing and looked away. Why did he have to bring it up? Jessie was willing to pretend she was ignorant. A forlorn sound escaped Kai's lips and touching the edge of her jaw, he turned her chin back to him. "Jessie, I'm so sorry. Did she tell you everything?" he whispered, his eyes as remorseful as his voice.

Jessie could only nod. His fingers on her face burned through her body, and she hated it. Hated how much he still electrified her, how much she still wanted to be in his arms. At any given point in the day, Kai's arms were where she wanted to be...and that wasn't helping anything.

After another second of silence, Kai wrapped his arms around her. Jessie closed her eyes; her body was finally getting what it was craving. Her heart and mind weren't as thrilled, however. She couldn't have him like this, and it would only hurt them more in the end to let it continue. Even still, she couldn't make herself pull away.

Into her hair, Kai muttered, "I'm sorry. You shouldn't have to hear about it. I wish I could tell her to not say anything to you, but she wouldn't understand why. I'm so sorry."

At hearing the ache in his voice, Jessie finally pulled away, but just to look up into his eyes. She left his arms wrapped around her and was a little surprised to find that her arms had slipped around his neck; she didn't remember doing that. "You don't need to apologize to me, Kai." She shrugged and looked down. "You didn't do anything wrong."

His head came down to touch hers, their foreheads resting together. Gently rocking against her, he whispered, "I feel like I'm doing something wrong. I feel like I'm...betraying you."

Jessie pulled back to stare at him, surprised that he would feel that strongly about what he was doing. It made her feel even worse. He shouldn't feel guilty about seeing someone, not when the two of them were only family. That was all they could be, and she didn't want him to forever feel guilty for moving on.

She brought a hand to his cheek as he averted his eyes from her. "You're not betraying me, Kai. You're doing what I asked. You're doing the right thing." His eyes hesitantly came back to hers, and his arms around her tightened. Jessie swallowed and said what she didn't really feel. "You should keep pursuing this with April. The two of you could be great together." Stroking his face with her thumb, she added in a whisper, "This thing between you and me...will pass."

Kai closed his eyes and swallowed, like he hadn't wanted to hear that. Jessie felt the same way; she hadn't wanted to say it. She wanted to tell him to never see April again. She wanted to tell him that they could run away, be ostracized from their families and friends, find a way to be together. But even then, the thought of knowingly being with her cousin…it made Jessie ill. She couldn't. As right as it felt, it still made her feel sick.

Kai opened his eyes, but kept his gaze down, studying the inch or so between their bodies. "Still, you shouldn't have to hear about it, and I'm sorry for that."

Hating where her thoughts had been, hating where she could feel them starting to go, Jessie stepped into Kai's embrace, closing every gap between them. Sighing into his ear, she ran a hand through his hair. "It's okay. I like April. I like you. I want you both to be happy." With a shudder, Kai nodded. Idly, Jessie wondered if this was making any of them happy.

After a few long, silent moments, they stepped away from each other. As their fingers disconnected, Jessie felt her heart crack into jagged pieces. Staring at each other, a couple of feet apart now, Kai broke the stillness with a painful question. "What about you? Shouldn't you be happy?"

His eyes searched hers and Jessie answered with a noncommittal shrug; his happiness mattered more to her anyway. With an unsatisfied frown, Kai shook his head. "Maybe you should start seeing someone, too. I mean you shouldn't have to be alone…through this. Maybe if you were dating, it would make it easier…for both of us."

He averted his eyes, but not before Jessie noticed how torn he was over the idea of her being with someone else. Jessie didn't want to think about herself with someone else either. She just couldn't imagine that anyone she might meet soon could even remotely compare to the amazing man before her, but she shouldn't think that, and she definitely couldn't tell Kai that.

She shrugged, even though he couldn't see it, since his eyes were still on the floor. "Who would I go out with, Kai?" He peeked up at her with disbelieving eyes. Maybe he thought she had a little black book tucked away with pages and pages of men who were eagerly waiting for a phone call from her? She let out a soft chuckle at how untrue that was. "You have any roommates I don't know about?"

Smiling, he leaned back on the counter behind him and said, "No...the one perk of having a studio apartment."

Without thinking about what she was saying, Jessie rolled her eyes and muttered, "I suppose I could call up Jeremy." Knowing that the horn dog would probably take her back so long as he got some made her grimace.

"No!" Kai suddenly exclaimed.

Jessie blinked in surprise at his passionate reaction. Face firm and eyes hard, he shook his head. Reaching out, he grabbed her hand, and in a softer voice told her, "No, don't lower yourself for that douche, Jessie. You're too good for him." By his tone, it was painfully clear that Kai thought Jessie was too good for anyone...except, maybe him.

She sighed as he stroked the back of her hand with his thumb. As she felt the awkward tension begin to build again, Kai cracked a small smile and added, "You could always start seeing Harmony?" His grin grew as he interlaced his fingers with hers.

Jessie laughed at his comment, and felt the last of her nerves disappear. A pleasant warmth flowed in behind it as she gazed at him, admired him, and cared for him in the only way their relationship would allow…from a distance. "Cute," she said.

"Oh, Jessica Marie, you're here to check on me, too, I see."

Shock raced up Jessie's spine, and she snapped her head around to watch her elderly grandmother waddle through the back door. Jessie and Kai simultaneously dropped each other's hands and stepped even farther apart. Slapping on a warm smile, even though her heart was pounding, Jessie walked over to help her grandmother into the kitchen. "Morning, Grams. How are you feeling?" she asked, wrapping an arm securely around her.

The old woman snorted as she shifted her gaze from Kai to Jessie. "Besides feeling a little smothered by the two of you worrywarts, I'm perfect."

She narrowed her eyes at the two of them, her wrinkled brow furrowed in concern. "Everything all right here?"

A flare-up of terror raged through her body, and Jessie did her best to swallow it back. Her grandmother could *not* know about them. Free spirited or not, she would surely have a problem with her grandchildren lusting for each other. "Of course, Grams. Kai and I were just…going over his date with April."

Jessie grimaced right after the words left her mouth; Kai gave her a disbelieving look, as well. Why the hell had she just given her grandmother that opening? The sprightly woman jumped all over it too, wanting to hear all about the girl she was positive would one day be Mrs. Kai Harper. The thought instantly soured Jessie's stomach.

Faking a smile, she sighed internally. She couldn't help it if Kai and April were forefront in her mind. And now that Grams only wanted to talk about them, thanks to her, they were forefront in everyone else's mind for the rest of the afternoon.

Later that evening, when Kai and Jessie were saying goodbye to their grandmother, Kai's phone started chirping. Pulling it from his coat pocket, he glanced at the number, silenced it, and then put it back into his pocket. Jessie instantly knew who had just called him.

While he walked with her to her truck, she called him on it. "That was April, wasn't it?"

Sighing, he slowed at the front of her truck. Resting his hand on the hood, he studiously watched his fingers circle a ding in the paint. "Yeah, I didn't want to answer it with you..."

Jessie sighed, too. "It's okay to talk to her in front of me. She was probably calling to set up another date. She's anxious to see you again."

Kai looked startled when he raised his eyes to hers. "Really? I didn't think she had a very good time." He cringed, like he hadn't meant to bring up the date again.

Remembering April at the table going over and over the part she *had* liked, Jessie whispered, "Some of it...appealed to her." Kai looked about to apologize again, but not letting him start, Jessie spoke first, "You're dating her now, and you'll need to talk to her, and if you and I are going to still hang out together, then you should feel free to do it in front of me."

Kai slowly let his breath out as he studied her face. "It feels...disrespectful," he finally said.

The look on his face made Jessie's heart compress, but she pushed the feeling back and forced herself to say the words that needed to be said, no matter how much they hurt. "It's not disrespectful to talk to the woman you're dating. And you and I aren't...anything."

His hand reached up to cup her cheek, and he muttered something under his breath that almost sounded like, "Aren't we?"

Kai drew closer to her, and she drew closer to him. They were within a foot of each other now, and Jessie's heart was leaping from her chest. Her breath was fast and shaky, and she tried to look anywhere but his lips, but she couldn't. They were slightly parted, the breath flowing from them fast and ragged, and the shape of them pulled all of her attention. They were the most inviting pair of lips she'd ever seen.

They were nearly on hers when they suddenly shifted to her cheek. Jessie inhaled a quick breath, relishing the heat and hating it all at the same time. A peck on the cheek wasn't what she really wanted, but it was much more appropriate than where her thoughts had been.

Needing to leave, his lips still lingering near her face, she breathily whispered, "Goodnight, cousin." Then she opened her truck door and left her grandmother's house as quickly as her truck would take her; she hadn't even waited for a response from him.

After that, Kai listened to Jessie's advice and answered all of the phone calls he got from April when they were together. And that was when Jessie started to notice something about her good friend that she hadn't really noticed before. April liked to talk on the phone...a lot.

When Jessie had gone to the store and found an unbelievable buy one, get two free deal on Kai's favorite canned meat, she'd snagged a bunch for him. Later that evening when she'd gone to his place to drop the groceries off, Kai had been on the phone with April when he'd opened the door. He'd given Jessie an apologetic smile and immediately tried to get off the phone with the chatty girl. It had taken him three tries to successfully disengage from the conversation.

When Jessie was at home, watching a little mindless TV, April would, more often than not, be sitting beside her on the couch, laughing on the phone as she talked to Kai. It made Jessie bite her cheek in annoyance to watch her friend twirling a strand of hair, subconsciously flirting with a man who couldn't even see her. But phone calls were all April got from Kai that entire week after their first date.

Since Kai was busy with work and with Grams, they weren't seeing each other again until Saturday night. April wasn't thrilled about their dates being a week apart. She was anxious to speed up their relationship, but Kai was content with the slow pace. And Jessie didn't fail to notice that even though his work did keep him out late during the week on occasion, and even though a lot of his free time was spent with their grandmother, Kai always made time to see Jessie.

They met up at Gram's house to watch a movie with her a couple times. On the second occurrence, Grams had glanced at where they were sitting on the couch, a respectable distance between each other, and asked him, "Kai, dear, shouldn't you spend a little time with your girlfriend, instead of always hanging around a couple of Harper girls?"

Both Kai and Jessie had cringed at her question, but Kai shrugged as he answered her. "April and I are just casual right now, Gran." Looking over at Jessie, he softly added, "Besides, I like spending my free time with Harper girls."

Those words had given Jessie a warm glow that had lasted several days.

In the middle of the week, Kai called Jessie and asked if she wanted to go exploring the city with him. Getting home right around the time she'd gotten off work, he'd met her at the clinic with a huge, adventurous smile on his face. Laughing at his enthusiasm, Jessie hopped on his bike behind him and proceeded to show Kai the numerous beauties her city had to offer.

They drove past Denver Museum of Nature and Science, a beautiful building that Jessie thought Kai would appreciate, even if it was closed. Clearly delighted, he was eager to go back when it was open. She showed him the Botanical Gardens, the Art Museum, and Coors Field. Grinning ear to ear, Kai made her promise to take him to a baseball game in the summer. With joy and laughter, they began making future plans to visit all the places they were driving past, and Jessie found herself starting to look forward to weekends again. At least she would still get a little of his time.

Since it was the last week it would be open for the season, they ended up spending the bulk of the night at Elitch Gardens Theme Park. They played the games and tried out all the different rides. They stayed right up until the place closed, even lingering on the grounds until someone finally escorted them out. They just hadn't wanted the evening to stop.

Jessie woke up exhausted the next day, but she was exhilarated, too. They'd both had an amazing evening. But when she spotted April's glum face at the breakfast table, checking for messages on her phone that weren't there, she felt really guilty, too. Running around the city with Kai, holding hands and laughing, none of that was helping him have a relationship with April.

It made Jessie feel even worse when she considered the fact that their night had almost been a date. It hadn't been, she'd only been showing her cousin around town, but thinking back to the long looks and Kai constantly brushing stray curls out of her face...well, that hadn't been quite so cousinly. And as much as she had enjoyed their time together, that underlying sexual tension was always there. The hunger and passion they'd both struggled to ignore.

April did unknowingly diffuse it at times. She'd call right as their gazes lasted a little too long. She'd text him right as he was beginning to cup Jessie's cheek, and late Friday night, when they'd been sitting on his bed side-by-side, watching an old black and white movie, April had inadvertently stopped them from caving into that tension.

Kai was staring at her, and she was staring at him, the movie in the background playing some melodramatic scene that Jessie wasn't even listening to. She was only hearing her heart thumping in her chest, only feeling her breath passing over her lips. And Kai...she was very aware of him.

They were sitting with their hips touching. They hadn't started out that way, but over the course of the movie they'd slowly inched together. They were leaning against his headboard, and somehow, Kai's arm had snuck around behind Jessie and his thumb was rubbing a circle into her low back. Jessie's knees were propped up, her hands tightly clutching them to her chest. Mainly out of fear. Because she knew if she relaxed her grip on her knees, her hands would drift to Kai's face—that beautiful face staring down at her, watching her as intently as they'd been watching the movie...in the beginning.

Jessie sighed as her eyes flicked between his. She wanted nothing more than to feel his lips press against her...but not on the cheek this time. She wanted them enclosed over hers, tasting, teasing. She wanted it more than she'd ever wanted anything, even though it still made her ill to want it.

Kai sighed too, and by the expression on his face, it was clear he wanted it, too. Jessie knew that she had to get up, knew that it was time to leave him, before the feeling overwhelmed them both. She made a move to stand, but Kai made a move too, and it froze her in place. Kai's move wasn't to get up, but to lean toward her. Jessie's lips parted as she felt him draw nearer. Her already fast heart quickened to a dangerous pace. Kai's breath brushed over her face, light and fast. Then, achingly slow, he bent toward her.

Careful to not let any other part of their bodies move, just their faces touched. A small gasp escaped her as their noses, cheeks, and foreheads brushed against each other. It was more erotic than him flat-out kissing her, and a tingling desire shot through her, igniting her. Kai hissed in a quick breath and exhaled in a low groan; he was feeling the ache too. Digging her fingers into her jeans, to stop herself from grabbing him and shucking off his clothes, she let out a low moan as his cheek lightly ran across hers.

Jessie could feel her control slipping. Her breath was a fast pant as she moved her face to find his lips. Kai let out a ragged exhale as his face adjusted to find hers as well. When his breath was entering her open mouth, mingling with her own, and she was positive that they wouldn't be able to stop this in time, his ear-splitting cell phone ring broke the passion simmering in the air.

Jessie jerked away just as their lips brushed together. They stared at each other with matching expressions of shock and concern, then Kai twisted to find his obnoxious phone. Jessie brought the backs of her hands to her cheeks in an effort to cool her face as Kai grabbed his phone from his nightstand. While he answered the call, Jessie repeatedly ran her hand through her hair. That had been too close, much too close.

"Hello?" Kai's voice was strained and fast, obviously distressed. Swallowing a few times, he closed his eyes and struggled for calm. He pulled away from Jessie, and she did the same. They needed a little space; that was the whole point of Kai being with April.

"No, I'm fine. I'm glad you called, April."

Opening his eyes, Kai gave Jessie a remorseful look. Jessie averted her gaze as fresh guilt added to her turmoil. Needing to walk off the last lingering remnants of desire in her body, she stood up. Kai hugged his knees to his chest as he watched Jessie pace beside the bed.

While watching him listen to the phone as April talked, Jessie finally felt herself come down from that fateful moment; sadness crept in when the lust-fueled high faded. Kai's expression matched hers as he made agreeing noises into the phone. Then he started, and his expression shifted into confusion. "Costume party?" he asked. Jessie's curiosity peaked as Kai frowned. "For Halloween...right. Okay, I'll pick you up at six."

Kai listened for a minute more and then a soft smile graced his lips. "Yeah, me too. Goodnight, April." Disconnecting the call, he tossed his phone on the bed. Staring at it, he ran a hand through his hair. "She, uh, just wanted to let me know about tomorrow." He glanced up at Jessie, his face apologetic again. Then he frowned. "She's taking me to a costume party for Halloween."

Letting out an unhappy huff, he rested his arms across his knees. Jessie smiled softly at seeing his displeasure, then felt guilty that he wasn't looking forward to his date. She wanted him to be with April. She had to keep reminding herself of that. "I hate dressing up," he muttered.

Jessie smiled wider; she hated dressing up, too. Sitting on the very edge of the bed, as far away from him as she could, she shrugged. "I'm sure you'll have fun. What is she making you wear?" It soured Jessie's stomach that she was assuring him he'd have a good time on his date, right after they'd almost kissed. Again.

Kai smirked. "You're going to laugh." Jessie bit her lip to make sure she didn't smile; she only half-succeeded. She was so glad that he was the one being subjected to this and not her. Kai smiled at her attempt to not show her amusement, then frowned. "She's dressing me up as a pirate." With a dramatic groan, he let his head thump against the headboard. "She wants to be a slutty bar wench, and she seems to think I'll look good as Captain Jack." He ruefully shook his head.

Jessie smiled, then frowned. Kai would definitely look good as a pirate, but April... Jessie had seen her dress for Halloween before, and she was going to look unbelievable. She felt her eyes begin to sting as she realized that this time tomorrow night, those lips that had been so tantalizingly close to hers, would most likely be all over April's. She swallowed the bitterness rising in her throat. They should be all over April. They should be as far from her as possible.

Seeing her expression, Kai whispered, "Jessie, I'm sorry about..." He indicated the space beside him, where she'd been sitting. Not having any words, Jessie nodded. Clearing his throat, Kai awkwardly adjusted his position. "Do you want to finish the movie?" His eyes were asking her to say yes *and* no.

Jessie let out a slow exhale. She did want to stay. More than anything she wanted to crawl into his lap and cuddle with him. She wanted his warmth wrapped around her, making her feel safe and cherished, but she also wanted his body all over hers. She wanted them tangled together in intimate ways that they just couldn't be. She wanted him to arouse her. She wanted him inside of her. Then she wanted him to release his lust and desire deep within her. It sickened her how badly she wanted it. Biting her lip, Jessie shook her head. She couldn't stay here any longer.

"I think I should go," she whispered.

Kai nodded, understanding, then his gaze drifted to his hands. Jessie stood and gathered her things. When she was finished, she turned back to him; he was still looking down. She slowly walked over to him, and he lifted his head, studiously watching her approach. At his side, she whispered, "Goodbye, cousin," as she leaned down. She purely intended to kiss his cheek. That was all she'd allow herself. But as his skin drew closer, she couldn't make herself twist to the side like he had earlier. Her lips went straight to his. Kai closed his eyes, not able to turn away either. Her hand came up to caress his cheek as their mouths met—soft, full, wondrous. A perfect kiss. Perfect and awful, because it never should have happened.

Feeling sick, Jessie pulled away and left him on that bed, his eyes still closed.

The following night, Jessie felt anxious. Both because of the soft kiss that never should have taken place between Kai and her the night before, and because April was in the bathroom, putting the finishing touches on her costume. She'd spent a good chunk of the morning getting everything she needed for her outfit and instructing Kai on where to get his. They were going to a club downtown that was having a contest for the best costume, and April was determined to win.

Watching April walk into the living room when she was finished, Jessie thought they might have a good chance at winning. She looked amazing. Sexy and alluring, she had taken the slutty bar wench theme to the extremes. April wasn't the most buxom person, but she seemed to pour out of her laced-up peasant top, the edge of her black bra peeking through. Her long black hair was curled and arranged in such a way that all of it spilled over one of her bare shoulders. The long, tight skirt she wore was slit up both thighs, all the way to the top, and most of her shapely legs were showing. She was wearing fishnet stockings underneath that were strategically ripped in all the right places. Black, thigh-high boots, a wide belt, and gaudy but authentic jewelry completed the outfit.

Grinning, she did a little twirl for Jessie in the middle of the room. Jessie made herself nod in approval when she really wanted to tell her friend to go put some more clothes on. She couldn't tell April that without sounding like her mother though.

The doorbell rang, and Jessie's heart dropped. Kai was here, but not for her. April giggled and bounded to the door. She squealed when she saw Kai standing there. Torn between leaving and staying, Jessie slowly stood up. She watched Kai give April a warm smile and then a soft hug. Over April's shoulder, his eyes found Jessie's, and their gazes locked. Jessie's breath stopped at the wistful passion she saw in his eyes. If April ever saw that expression on him, she'd know that something had happened between Jessie and Kai. His blue-green eyes were sad, remorseful, like he'd rather have Jessie in his arms. It only reaffirmed to Jessie that, even though this was hard, Kai dating someone else was a good thing. He shouldn't want her that way, just as she shouldn't want him.

Kai and April pulled apart, and his gaze refocused on his date. His sadness instantly shifted to a small smile of appreciation for the beautiful girl in front of him. Even though his smile was a contained one, Jessie hated seeing that look directed toward anyone else.

April yanked him through the front door and into the room. She was overjoyed by his outfit. Kai let out a weary groan as she spun him around. Jessie felt sorry for him, but at the same time, she highly approved of his outfit. She was never one to get into the whole dress up thing, but Kai looked incredible as a pirate.

April had him in scruffy, well-worn black trousers, with heavy black boots over the top. A colorful scarf belt matched the ribbon around April's neck, and a white, lacy, bell-sleeved shirt exposed a good portion of his skin, although, not a speck of his tattoo showed. Over his shirt was a black vest topped off with a long, black coat. He had on enough gaudy jewelry to rival April's, but the kicker, and the part that Kai seemed the least happy about, was the ridiculous hat. Wide brimmed with a band around the middle that matched his belt, it absolutely completed the look; it even had a feather.

As April clapped her hands and squealed again, thrilled over her date's appearance, Jessie studied Kai. He didn't look very happy. In fact, he looked miserable. Not noticing, April exclaimed that she just had to touch up her makeup, then they could go. Once she was gone, Jessie walked over to him. Crossing her arms over her chest as a precaution, so she wouldn't be tempted to touch him, she nodded at his outfit. "You look good," she whispered.

He gave her a glum look. "I feel like an idiot." Jessie cracked a smile but didn't say anything. He looked anything but.

As Jessie examined him in his alluring costume, Kai's gaze drifted to the floor. Kicking a nonexistent object with his boot, he muttered, "Hey...um, yesterday..." Biting his lip, he peeked up at her. "I'm sorry."

Jessie wanted to sigh in frustration. Yesterday hadn't been entirely his fault. They'd both given in. Shaking her head, she whispered, "It wasn't just you, Kai." She looked away from him, the memory of his lips on hers was too fresh, too wonderful. And too horrible. "We've got to stop this from happening. We can't...be like that."

He nodded but didn't say anything. Jessie was relieved that he didn't want to delve into their complicated feelings. As she looked him over, she instantly remembered that their kiss would soon be replaced by April's. Even if Kai didn't initiate the act, Jessie was positive April would. Her eyes started to water and blinking, she quickly looked away.

His hand came out to rest on her arm, and Jessie peeked up at him. His unbelievable eyes flicked over her face, worried. "Are you sure you're okay with this?" he whispered.

Jessie watched this man before her, a man about to go off and have an amazing night with one of her best friends. A friend that Jessie knew really liked him. Hating how hard the situation they were in was, hating that she had to share him with another woman, and hating that she didn't want to share him at all, Jessie swallowed and slowly nodded her head. "Yesterday only goes to show that you and I need this buffer between us." Her voice cracked a little on the word buffer.

Her voice cracked on the end of her sentence, and Kai's eyes narrowed at hearing her pain. His hand shifted to her cheek. "Are *we* okay?" he asked, more intently than before. Searching her eyes, he stepped closer to her. "Please tell me we're okay, Jessie. Seeing April isn't worth it to me if we're not okay."

Jessie brought her hand up, resting it over his. Of course they were okay. They were *too* okay, that was the problem. They were perfect for each other. Perfectly matched, perfectly balanced. But they couldn't be anything more than what they were—cousins. Peering up at him, she answered, "You and I are always okay, Kai, no matter what. That's part of being family."

Kai silently studied her; his face was so torn it broke Jessie's heart. Pulling his hand from her cheek, she nodded and forced a smile. He had to do this. He had to leave with April, and he had to try to make a connection with her that would break this thing between the two of them. He had to...or they'd eventually cave into this passion, and then they'd hate themselves.

Letting his fingers fall away from hers, Kai nodded. As Jessie took a step away from him, April skipped back into the room. Opening her purse, she dug inside and pulled out her car keys. Giving Kai an admonishing look, she pointed the keys at him. "We're taking my car this time." She grinned as she glanced at Jessie. "No more helmet hair for this girl."

Kai let out a weary sigh as April grabbed his hand. She waved goodbye to Jessie, then opened the door and yanked Kai through it. Before he completely disappeared, he looked back at Jessie, watching them leave.

"Goodnight," he softly said.

Words not possible, Jessie could only nod. The door closing separated Kai from her vision, but Jessie couldn't move to a window to watch him leave. She couldn't move at all. She just kept staring at the door, waiting for him to come back. Waiting for him to tell her that he couldn't go off with April. Waiting for him to say that he was hopelessly, madly in love with her. But she knew he wouldn't do that, even if he did feel that way. He wouldn't do it because he had told Jessie he was going to try with April. Because neither one of them were going to willingly give into this taboo feeling that was escalating between them.

No, because he deeply cared about Jessie, Kai was going to make himself see another woman. As the sound of April's car starting filled Jessie's ears, she finally found the strength to move. She shuffled off to bed, collapsed onto it, and buried her head under the covers. And even though she tried to block out the image, all she could think about was Kai dancing with April—his hands on her body, his fingers running up her back, and his lips lingering over her mouth.

Her stomach hurt by the time she finally passed out from exhaustion.

15

The Third Date

Jessie smiled at the sight of her grandmother doing a small dance for her. The old woman was flapping her scrawny arms and shuffling her feet in a loose interpretation of the world famous chicken dance. Jessie knew Grams was trying to convince her that she was completely healed, that she didn't need Jessie and Kai dropping in on her all the time. Jessie heard this every time she checked on her, about every other day ever since her grandmother had injured herself four weeks ago.

Jessie giggled as she watched her grams strut her stuff around the living room. She was humming to herself, thoroughly playing up the healthy and vibrant image that she wanted Jessie to believe. Jessie knew she was tough, but she saw the occasional flinches of pain in her jaw when she shimmied her hip the wrong way.

When Grams started shaking her booty, Jessie's light laughter turned uncontrollable. "Oh, all right, you're a healed woman. Got it. Now please stop doing that." Jessie held her

272

stomach as her laughs consumed her. She gave into the feeling, enjoying the lightheartedness for a change. She hadn't been feeling that much lately.

Her personal life for the past few weeks had been hard and confusing, especially last week. Last week had twisted Jessie in ways she couldn't even fully express, and she couldn't talk to anyone about what she was going through. Well, no one but Kai, that was. But since Kai was the focal point of her torment, she couldn't exactly talk to him about her feelings. And talking to him would be fruitless anyway, since they'd both agreed that what Kai was doing was for the best. The worst part was that all of this had been Jessie's stupid idea in the first place. She'd convinced him, time and time again, that he should give April a chance.

Jessie had cried after April and Kai had left for their second date. She hadn't wanted to break down, but lying in bed, imagining them together, the tears had come regardless. April had looked more gorgeous than Jessie had ever seen her, and that was saying a lot. And Jessie knew that Kai noticed April's appeal. What man wouldn't? It hurt to see the attraction, but really, it was all for the better if he was physically interested in April. Lord knows April was sure interested in Kai. Once again, Jessie had heard all about their date the next morning.

While their first date had been sort of a letdown for April, the second date was not. Over breakfast, April let the entire house know just how closely she and Kai had danced together, how his hands had effortlessly slipped over her body, like he already knew her in intimate ways. Between dances, they'd shared quiet conversations over drinks in the back corner, and April just couldn't get over the fact that Kai would let her go on and on without ever interrupting her. Then, right at midnight, they'd won the stupid costume contest. Getting to prance about on the small stage with Kai had been April's favorite part of the evening.

Well, no, that wasn't true. Her *favorite* part of the night had been afterwards, in her car. They'd come back to the house and parked in the driveway. Then April had thrown herself at him, but from her story, it was quite clear he'd eagerly reciprocated. Jessie had had to dig her fingers into her thighs under the table, as she'd listened to April describing Kai's kissing technique; she'd even given herself deep blue bruises on her legs.

It hurt so much. Jessie never would have imagined how hard it was to see and hear him moving forward with someone else. Kai had called her the day after his date, and she'd met him for lunch and a tour of the museum. He never mentioned his night with April when he was with Jessie, but the tension of his evening with another woman was thick in the air. The whole day had felt different. Like, even though April wasn't there, somehow she *was* there. Her spirit was there, hovering between them, and for once, they'd managed to keep a respectful distance.

That killed Jessie, too, but really, it was the whole point of Kai seeing April, to break the connection they had. And even if Kai was only mildly interested in April, he needed to keep seeing her, because it was having an effect on them. A horribly painful effect, but an effect nonetheless.

After their afternoon together, Kai had been busy with work, and a few days had passed without Jessie seeing him. She talked with him often on the phone, Kai checked on her at least once a day. It was almost like he needed the constant reassurance that the two of them were really okay. Jessie also heard about him from April, who took every free moment she had to call him, since she wasn't seeing him either. It annoyed April to no end that their dates were being spaced so far apart, but Kai routinely told her that he didn't have time for another date until the weekend. And last of all, Jessie heard about Kai through Grams, since he stopped by her place on the way home most nights, and Grams told Jessie about every visit.

Coming back to the present, Jessie watched her grandmother settle into her favorite chair. Even if she'd never admit it, she needed to sit down. A sad smile was on Jessie's face as she watched the woman; her earlier laughter now subsided. While she talked to Kai once or twice a day, Jessie was really starting to miss him. She missed the quiet moments they used to share, back when it was just the two of them in the relationship, and she felt horrible that she couldn't let it go. She needed to let it go. She had to share him; she had no other choice. They couldn't be anything more than family. Close family.

"My dear, you look troubled. Something wrong?" Grams gave her a concerned look as she shifted her hip into a comfortable position. Jessie made herself smile and shake her head. Grams didn't buy it. "Boy trouble?" she asked with a raised eyebrow.

Jessie rolled her eyes. Ever since Kai had started dating April, Grams had been relentless. She seemed to think she'd successfully placed one grandchild on the path to happiness, even though Jessie had done the actual placing, and now she was anxious to see Jessie paired off. "No, Grams, and stop trying to set me up." She sighed in exasperation, letting all of her frustrations about Kai and April seep into the sound. "Some guy named Simon called me last night. Said his mother was a friend of yours?"

Her grandmother gave her a wide grin, her wrinkled face was much more youthful in her glee. "Oh, that's Susan's boy. You know, my nurse from the hospital. She said he might call you."

Sighing, Jessie sank down into a chair next to her. "Yeah, well he did…and no, I'm not going out with him."

Grams looked about to protest, but Jessie shot her a warning glare; she was not in the mood to be bugged about dating. Not when she had to endure thoughts of Kai's mouth all over April's. Having to listen to her friend proclaim how "freaking unbelievable" of a kisser he was, made Jessie ill.

Changing her line of questioning, Grams asked, "So, do you and Kai still get to see each other a lot since he started dating that girl?"

Jessie made herself smile, but it felt sad, even to her. Why did Grams always have to bring up Kai? Jessie would rather be bugged about Simon. She shrugged. "Yeah, I guess. I mean, just last weekend we went to the museum…but…I don't know, he's busy getting to know April, and busy with work." She made herself chuckle; it sounded hollow. "I thought I wouldn't lose so much of him if I set him up with my roommate, but…it's different now. There are three of us in the relationship, and it used to just be me and Kai." She didn't mention that was the point of him seeing April.

Jessie's grandmother frowned as she rested her hands on her lap. She adjusted her hip again and Jessie stood up to get her a pillow to put underneath her. Grams smiled, then her face turned serious. "But you still talk often?" Jessie nodded absently as she helped ease the woman's pain. Grams was silent for a long moment, then asked, "Is he happy? With April? With work?"

Jessie paused in helping her get comfortable. She'd emphasized work more than April. Jessie thought back to that awkward moment with his boss and Kai's comment that he didn't think the man liked him. With a frown, Jessie sat back down. "Well, I think he's happy in general. He and April are just starting, so I don't really know about that yet." And she really didn't want to know. Bringing a finger to her lip, she tapped it while she thought. "But work...I don't know. He said something strange once."

Grams leaned forward, her eyes wide. "What did he say?"

The sudden worry in her voice was so intense, it caught Jessie off-guard. Worried about her grandmother falling off her chair, Jessie quickly answered with, "He just said he didn't think his boss liked him, and when I met the man, he did seem odd around Kai. I merely told him his eyes were a similar shade to Kai's, and he practically ran away."

Her grandmother's face paled as she leaned back in her chair and closed her eyes. Concerned over the emotion she saw brewing on the old woman's face, Jessie quietly asked, "Are you okay, Grams?"

Her grandmother looked over at her with aged, tired eyes. "Just feeling that pain now, Jessica Marie." Reaching over, she patted her knee. "Could you get some more pills for me, dear?" Jessie nodded and stood to go get them. Her grandmother grabbed her hand before she walked away. "Don't let Kai get so involved with a woman that he slips away from you. He needs you, Jessica. He needs his family."

Her eyes were intent on Jessie, and swallowing a painful lump, Jessie made herself nod. She wasn't sure that she *could* stay close to Kai though, especially if things between him and April picked up. But Grams was right, he *was* family, and if

Kai ever needed her, she had every intention of being there for him. Grams face was so serious, so troubled, and Jessie had no idea why.

Jessie thought about it all the way home. The look on Gram's face, the tenor of her voice. It was almost like she was anticipating a tragedy in Kai's life. Jessie wondered what could possibly be coming for Kai...right up until she pulled into her driveway and saw his bike on the curb. Then she forgot all about her grandmother's odd statement, and focused on another problem.

It was Saturday, and Kai and April had another date. Their *third* date. And everyone knows what happens on the third date. Well, everyone who knows April, knows what happens on the third date, if not sooner. Jessie knew from listening to April's stories about her dates with Kai that it hadn't happened yet. Much to April's dismay, it hadn't gotten anywhere near happening yet. But April liked Kai, and April liked sex, and she was determined to combine the two things she liked tonight. She'd mentioned that little fact to Jessie this morning. Jessie hadn't been able to eat anything all day long.

Jessie hated it so much. She hated thinking about another woman's hands on his body, a body that had last been touched and caressed by her. She hated that she was about to be erased from his skin. Not that there was actually any physical part of Jessie left on Kai, or vice-versa, but Jessie liked to think that the last person you were with, somehow stayed with you. Their essence stayed a part of you, until it was replaced by someone else. Jessie was fairly certain that Kai hadn't slept with anyone else yet. Not that he would mention that to Jessie. But with how close they were, and how he'd reacted to her comment about his coworker, and how slow he was taking things with April, Jessie just knew there was no one else. Jessie also knew that April would be persistent on this, and Kai was making an effort to move past her. Sex was how guys moved on.

She hated thinking about it…and she couldn't stop. It still filled her with revulsion when she thought of her and Kai's one night together, but it gave her warm feelings, too. Deep feelings that she shouldn't have for her cousin. So as difficult as it was to watch him pursue a romance with April, as hard as it was going to be to listen to April talk about their incredible sex life all the time, Jessie had to endure it. It was the only way for both of them to let go.

Pushing back the pinpricks of tears stinging her eyes, Jessie tore her gaze from Kai's bike and prepared herself to see him again. Butterflies tickled her stomach as she opened her front door. Wrong as it was, seeing him still affected her, even after all these weeks, even after seeing him less and less. Just the fact that the excitement hadn't gone away yet was further proof that they were on the right track. She had to get to a point where the thought of seeing his face didn't make her want to squeal like a school girl.

Walking into her home, Jessie steeled herself to be all right with whatever she might see. Stomach clenched in anticipation, her eyes quickly swept the living room. She let out a soft exhale when she discovered the room empty. Good. She didn't think she could handle stumbling upon them kissing. Thinking the two of them were probably in the kitchen, Jessie turned to go to her bedroom; she didn't want to see the two of them laughing and making small talk before heading out to destinations unknown. She'd seen enough of that recently to last a lifetime.

Moving away from where she thought they were, Jessie ended up facing them. She could only stare in shock as Kai and April stood at the far end of the hallway, in front of Jessie's bedroom door. Her heart started pounding. Oh, God, they were bypassing the date and heading straight for the finish line. Jessie wanted to run, but she couldn't move.

April had him cornered at the end of the hall. She was leaning into Kai, pressing as much of her body against him as she could. Leaning up, she touched her lips to his. He seemed a little uncomfortable with the contact and didn't return the kiss, but he didn't pull away either. Neither one of them seemed to notice Jessie standing at the other end of the hall, watching them.

April smiled, undaunted, and began peppering him with light kisses. Kai relaxed, and his lips began to move with hers. Jessie was horrified yet entranced by their progressing connection. As she stupidly continued staring, she noticed that Kai was tentative, not enjoying it nearly as much as April. Was that because of her?

Just as Jessie thought to leave them alone, her heart heavy, like it was slowly being crushed by a thousand lead weights, Kai pulled away from April. Face intense, like he was contemplating something important, he studied his date. Then, some silent decision reached, his hand wrapped around April's waist, and for the first time that Jessie had ever seen, Kai leaned down to her, initiating the contact. A new kind of horror filled Jessie's gut as she watched Kai's mouth passionately move over her friend's. Betrayal surged through her, forcing her to stomp down the hall. Oddly enough, it was the exact same feeling that had flashed through her when she'd caught Jeremy screwing that other woman.

Red-hot fire burned through every part of her. Seeing them make-out, knowing where it was going to end up… turned out it was more than Jessie could handle. Knowing she was out of line, out of place, and possibly out of her mind, she stormed right up to the pair.

"Hey! You guys mind not doing that right in front of my bedroom?" Jessie wasn't sure which person her question was directed at. Both turned to look at her—April seemed annoyed at the intrusion, Kai looked guilty, like he'd just gotten caught with his hand in the cookie jar. Jessie focused on him. "Are you going to go on your *date*, or are you going to make out in the hall all night?"

Kai opened his mouth, but April was the one who responded first. "We were just getting ready to leave. I thought you were hanging out at your grandmother's house tonight?"

"I changed my mind." Jessie swung her eyes to her friend. She had a suggestive smirk on her face that enraged Jessie, and Jessie couldn't hold back the words that were slowly killing her. "Don't leave on my account, April. All you've talked about since you first saw Kai was getting into his pants. Why bother with the formality of an actual date, when you could just screw him right here on the floor?"

April instantly bristled, while Kai's eyes widened in shock. "Wow, bitchy much? What the hell has you all bent out of shape? What do you care if Kai and I want to get to know each other better? We're both consenting adults."

Jessie knew April was right, and that knowledge pissed her off even more. "God, April, don't be a whore. Have some self-respect," she snapped.

April looked like Jessie had just physically assaulted her. "Seriously? *You* are gonna use that word on me? That's interesting, coming from a girl who just a few weeks ago fucked a total stranger whose name she can't even remember. At least I've gone on a couple of dates with him." She jerked her thumb back at Kai. He closed his eyes, clearly wanting to be anywhere other than here.

Jessie sputtered for a good comeback. All she had was, "At least I wasn't the one walking around with a condom in my pocket that night! You were prowling for action!"

April's eyes narrowed as she stepped into Jessie. "That pervy dude slipped it to me. And I might have had it, but you're the one who used it!" She poked her finger into Jessie's chest. Jessie started a rebuttal, but April was riled up now and beat her to it. "Am I not good enough to screw your cousin? Is that it? You just don't want me near your family?"

Jessie hated this entire conversation, hated that she was fighting with her friend, and hated that April was pointing out Kai's DNA. She didn't want to think about that right now. She didn't want to think about anything other than how to stop April from sleeping with Kai.

Jessie had a scathing comment on her lips, one that would probably end her friendship with April, but just as she opened her mouth to say it, Kai stepped forward and grabbed her elbow. She tried to pull away from him, but his grip was like iron. Turning to April, he said, "Jessie and I need to talk for a minute. We'll be right back."

Her face red and splotchy, April snipped, "Whatever," and crossed her arms over her chest.

Leaving her fuming in the hallway, Kai pushed Jessie through her bedroom door, then walked in and closed it behind them. Jessie's chest was heaving as she watched him slowly turn around to face her. He looked as angry as she felt.

"What the hell are you doing? Do you want her to remember it was me at the club? Do you want her to know about us?"

Knowing she was being jealous and irrational, Jessie sputtered, "What the hell were *you* doing? Were you going to sleep with her? Already?" She knew that sounded ridiculous, since April was right, and she'd slept with him much, much sooner.

Kai glanced behind himself, at the closed door. Jessie could hear April screeching to Harmony in the kitchen, then she heard her boots stomping down the hallway, most likely to complain to Harmony about Jessie. Bringing his sea-green eyes back to Jessie, Kai pointed his thumb over his shoulder. "You think we were about to have sex because we were kissing?"

Jessie stepped forward, closing their distance. Pain, anger, and jealousy clouding her common sense, she spat, "You have your third date tonight. I know what happens on third dates, I know the rule." Jessie pointed at April's bedroom door, right across from hers. "I know what was about to happen in there."

Kai closed his eyes and sighed. He seemed exhausted when he reopened them. Staring at her with wistful eyes, he calmly said, "That's not my rule, Jessie. I had no plans...to do anything."

Jessie stuck her chin out; it was quivering. She wasn't sure why she was picking a fight with him, or why she was picking a fight with April. Neither of them had done anything wrong. "No plans to do anything...but kiss her. I saw you grab her. I saw you lean down to her. I saw *you* kiss *her*." Jessie's eyes began to water as she replayed the event that had finally broken her. She couldn't handle this. Voice wavering, she choked out, "And I already know you don't mind moving fast." Jessie felt her cheeks heat with anger and embarrassment. She shouldn't have said that; it was hypocritical of her.

By the way Kai pursed his lips, it was clear he agreed. Stepping forward, he flung his hands out to the side. In a quiet voice he hissed, "I'm doing what you asked, Jessie. I'm trying to have a relationship with April, to stop this!" He indicated the space between them and Jessie felt her heated cheeks flush. He was right, he was *so* right; she had no room to be angry. None at all. Not finished with his defense, Kai took another step closer. "I can't date April and not kiss her. She's not that type of girl, and you knew that when you set me up with her." Lowering his head, his eyes narrowed as he flicked his gaze between hers. "I'm trying to go slow with her, but April is…aggressive. I have to show her I'm somewhat interested, even if I'm…"

Pulling back, throwing his hands up again. "I'm trying to move forward, Jessie. You said this was okay. I didn't know you were here, and I'm sorry you had to see that, but I'm trying to do what you asked me to do!"

Jessie stepped forward until she was touching him. Just the slight act of their bodies brushing together instantly sent fire through her body. She hated it, and loved it. Shaking her head, her eyes thick with pent-up tears of frustration, she told him, "I know, Kai. I know what I said. I know that I asked you to do something you didn't really want to do. I know that you're doing it for us, so we can be more…like family."

Her voice broke on the word family and she had to swallow the knot in her throat. Kai's pained eyes tracked her movement. Just when he looked about to speak, she interrupted. "But it's too hard. I lied when I said it was okay. It's not. I can't stand the thought of you being with her. I hate hearing

284

about you kissing her. And the thought of you sleeping with her...I can't...I just can't handle it. It makes me sick."

Kai's face softened as he let out a weary exhale. Shaking his head, he ran his hands through his hair. "What do you want from me, Jessie? You're the one who thought placing someone between us would help. Isn't that what you said? We needed a buffer? If April is too close to you, if seeing us together is too hard, then what do we do, Jessie? Who will make this easier? Who should I be with?"

Jessie's hands came up to cup his cheeks, her body moved forward, to firmly compress against his. Against everything inside of her, every single instinct she had, she whispered, "Me. You should be with me. You're supposed to be with me."

Kai rested his forehead on hers, gently shaking it back and forth. "Jess...it's not right. I can't...We can't..." He sighed and didn't say what they were both feeling. Pulling his head away, he stared at her for long, intense moments. Then he brought a hand up to run it through her hair. "We can't, Jessie. We just... can't."

Then his lips crashed down to hers, and the world outside stopped mattering. Her friends in the house no longer existed. The matching blood running through their veins didn't mean anything. All that mattered was his hand slowly running from her hair to her neck. All Jessie could concentrate on was that hand clenching around her, and drawing her in, forcing her lips firmly onto his. In an instant, everything else disappeared.

Twisting them around, Kai slammed her back against her bedroom door. Jessie grunted, then groaned as his lips and his body crushed hers. Her hands drifted down his chest, then around his waist and up his back, under his multiple layers of shirts. Letting the passion they usually pushed back flood into her, she was quickly drenched, throbbing with need. She wanted him. She wanted him so much.

Kai's hips were pushing against into hers, and Jessie could feel his desire for her pressing into her abdomen. She wanted him lower. She wanted him inside of her. Remembering the feel of him, the fullness of him, she wanted him deep in her, thrusting over and over until they both cried out in ecstasy. Jessie's fingers trailed down his back, to the waistband of his jeans. Slipping around to the front, she desperately tried to pop open the button.

An erotic moan left Kai's mouth and the hand on her neck ran up to grab a fistful of her hair. Tilting her head, he drove his tongue inside her. Jessie whimpered with the forcefulness, the uncontainable passion they both felt. She minutely pulled away from the door and he pushed her back into it with a dull thud. Her fingers, finally having unsnapped his button, flattened between them. Jessie let out a soft, frustrated cry. She wanted him so bad, she couldn't take anymore. His hand slipped under her shirt. Pushing aside the fabric of her bra, he cupped her breast. Sucking a quick breath through his teeth, Kai paused to rest his head against hers. A low swear passed his lips as his thumb stroked over her nipple.

Panting, Jessie let out a low groan as she successfully shoved her hand down the front of his open jeans, just barely squeezing in-between their smashed together bodies. She wanted to feel him. She needed to feel him. Just as he let out a noise that made Jessie ache with the need for him to touch her, she grazed the tip of him. His fingers tightened and pinched her nipple, and she cried out again, a little louder than before.

Cursing again, Kai quickly ran his hands down her body and lifted both of her legs around his waist. They staggered forward a step before she slammed back into the door again. Breath heavy, Kai slid his hands down the knit pants she had on, cupping her backside. A stuttered groan left Jessie as she rubbed herself against the hardness in his jeans; his arousal was finally where she needed it most. His lips returning to hers, Kai slipped his fingers inside her underwear. Jessie whimpered into his mouth, then arched her back; she needed him to touch her. Needed it more than anything.

She bucked against him, her back rattling the door, as his finger slowly slid across her wet flesh. Her fingers dug into his shoulders as a bolt of electricity ripped through her body. *Yes ...more.* Pressing her back more firmly against the door, she fought for space between them so she could push his jeans down. She needed more than one finger sliding up and down her sensitive core. She needed all of his marvelous length and width sliding inside of her. His lips attacked hers as his finger running against her picked up pace. She managed to get his jeans partly down his hips, and managed to wrap her hand around the top of him, just as he slipped his finger inside her.

Before she could cry out in ecstasy, the door they were pressed against was knocked on.

"Uh, Jess...you guys okay?" It was Harmony, and she sounded very concerned.

Jessie stopped breathing, stopped moving. Her eyes popped wide open and she stared at Kai; the shock and fear on his face was a mirror of her own. Like a floodgate had been opened, the horror of what they'd been doing crashed down upon her. She immediately yanked her hand out of his pants and slapped it over her mouth. She felt like screaming, she felt like vomiting…she felt disappointed it was over. She'd never been so conflicted in all her life.

Kai also pulled his hand away. Quickly setting her down, he took a step back. His jeans were still open as his gaze flicked from Jessie to the door. The knock sounded again. "Jess?"

Feeling able to breathe, Jessie snapped, "We're fine! Just give us a minute, okay?"

"Jesus. I'm just checking to make sure you guys weren't fighting or anything. There was a lot of banging going on in there. No need to bite my head off." She heard Harmony grumble something else under her breath, then she said, "April would like her date back, by the way," before she walked away.

Jessie crumpled to the floor, her knees no longer able to keep her standing. Tears hazed her eyes as she covered her face with both hands. Barely able to still see Kai over the tips of her fingers and her watery vision, she watched him readjust and re-button his jeans.

When he was finished, he ran a hand down his face; his skin seemed much paler than before. Both of them were silent as their breaths and heartbeats returned to normal. Well, as normal as they could. Jessie felt like hers would never stop frantically racing. Closing her eyes, she rested her head against the door. Had she really just knowingly made out with her cousin? Had she really just shoved her hand down his pants and let him do the same to her? God, had Harmony heard any of that? They hadn't exactly been quiet, what with their panting, groaning, and door banging. Jessie could hear the TV blaring in the living room, but surely they'd heard a little. Harmony had certainly heard enough to need to know if they were okay.

Kai finally broke the silence. "Jessie?" As she glanced up at him, she felt tears sliding down her cheeks. Kai looked torn as he watched her pain. He pointed to the door she was blocking. "I should… I should go…"

A soft sob escaping her, Jessie nodded and tried to stand up. Leaning against the wall next to the door, she bit her lip in an attempt to hold back the confusing tears. Kai silently walked up to the door and put his hand on the knob. Hesitating, he looked over at her. "I'm sorry," he whispered.

Jessie nodded, unstoppable tears dripping off her cheeks. "I'm sorry too."

Kai nodded, and his beautiful blue-green eyes dulled as if the spark behind them had gone out. Looking utterly defeated, he left her alone in her room. Jessie sank back to the floor, and softly sobbed into her knees.

With an aching heart, Kai gently closed the door to Jessie's room. He could hear her crying on the other side of it. He wanted to sink to the ground and join her. He'd just let happen what he'd sworn he would never let happen. He'd made out with his cousin. No, that wasn't just making out. That was a full-on prelude to sex. He knew enough about himself and about Jessie, to know exactly where that would have led, if they'd been left alone.

It made him ill.

Gathering his strength, he struggled to remember what he'd been doing *before* that moment. Had anything happened today before that moment? It was so cataclysmic to him, that it was almost as if the world hadn't begun turning until he and Jessie had finally caved. Souring his stomach even more was the fact that Kai had started it. Jessie might have cupped his face, might have begged him with those beautiful brown eyes to be with her, but he was the one who had slipped. He was the one who hadn't been able to resist the draw of her lips anymore.

Weeks of having another woman's mouth on his had only made his need for Jessie stronger. He hadn't realized it until that split-second he'd debated what to do. Not that he'd really had much choice in the matter. Kai needed Jessie; he couldn't resist her anymore. That was the problem.

Walking in a zombie-like daze to the living room, Kai was shocked at the normality he saw. Harmony was sitting on the couch with a bowl of popcorn on her lap as she watched a movie. April was sitting across from her, a small pout on her lips as she impatiently strummed her fingers against her folded arms.

Kai's world had just been flipped upside down. Why wasn't the rest of the world following suit? Shouldn't the sky be green and cats and dogs have learned to talk in his absence. That was how rocked he felt.

April glanced at him as he woodenly walked into the room. Her frown deepened as she stood up, and Kai suddenly remembered why she wasn't happy. Jessie had gone off on her when she'd walked in on the two of them kissing. Kai let out a soft sigh as his melodramatic thoughts wound down. What was going on with his cousin was intense, painful, and confusing, but what was going on with him and April was just... wrong.

He shouldn't be with someone, just so he *wouldn't* be with someone else. That was how people got hurt. Kai didn't want to hurt anyone, even though he seemed to be really good at it. But continuing to see April would be misleading to her, since his feelings were obviously elsewhere. It would be cruel to let her fall for him, if she was.

April sauntered over to him, her arms locked across her chest like armor. Harmony glanced up, then forcefully redirected her eyes back to the TV. April's lips hadn't shifted from the pout she'd perfected, and Kai's thoughts drifted to kissing her. He'd been trying to feel the heat and passion for April that he felt for Jessie, but no matter how hard he tried, kissing her didn't give him the same flying sensation. He'd even let himself make the first move, just to see if it would help, but he still hadn't felt that spark. It just wasn't there.

Glancing over his shoulder at Jessie's bedroom door, April bit out, "You talk her down off her high horse?"

Kai sadly shook his head. "I'm sorry you got dragged into the middle of that, April, but trust me when I say that all of Jessie's comments were more directed toward me than you."

April looked back at Kai with furrowed brows, like he'd just spoken in another language. Kai supposed he had, since none of that probably made any sense to her. He was going to have to find a way to be honest with April, without actually being honest.

It was clear she was just about to ask him what the hell he was talking about, so Kai grabbed her fingers and walked her to the back door. He needed privacy for this. Knowing what he was going to do made Kai's stomach twist into one giant knot. He had no choice though. Sliding open the door, he walked through it. She shivered and rubbed her arms once she was outside, and Kai stepped back in to grab their coats off the couch. April looked sad as she slipped hers on, like she knew something was up.

Sliding the door shut, so they'd at least have some verbal privacy, Kai noticed Harmony watching them through the glass. When he turned to face April, her eyes were narrow slits as she peered at him intently. Sighing, Kai looked down and mentally traced a long crack in the cement while he composed his thoughts. He didn't want to mess this up.

In his silence, April spoke first. "You want to tell me what's going on, Kai?" Her voice was slightly accusatory, but mainly worried. Kai swallowed. He'd let this go on for far too long. He should have ended things after that disastrous first date. Or never agreed to date her in the first place.

Looking up, he whispered, "This is all my fault. Please don' be mad at Jessie for what she said to you. She was angry at me, not you." He shook his head. "She just didn't express it correctly, but she really was looking out for you." Kai wanted to cringe; he was pushing the envelope of truth in that statement, and he knew it, but in a way, it was true. Jessie's anger had been more for Kai than April.

As April shook her head, confused, Kai said, "She adores you, April. She just doesn't want to see you get hurt." Kai finally smiled. That was completely true.

Still looking like she didn't understand, April shoved her hands in her coat pockets. "That doesn't make any sense. You wouldn't hurt me. You're a good guy."

Kai had to avert his eyes. He hated what he knew that April didn't. A good guy didn't shove his hands down a girl's pants while preparing for a date with a different one. A good guy didn't do *any* of the things he'd done with his cousin. No, Kai felt like anything but a good guy. But maybe he could start atoning, right now. Looking back at April, he whispered, "There's someone else. A girl...from my past."

He had to blink away the emotion stinging his eyes after saying that out loud. April's face went ghostly pale; that was a sentence no woman liked hearing. A wrenching pain ripped through Kai, but ignoring it, he fortified his stomach. He had to do this. "I'm so sorry, April. She and I...we can't be together, and I thought that if I dated you, I could get over her. I thought I could move on." He sighed as thoughts of Jessie filled his brain. "But I can't move on. She's all I think about..."

Sadness swept through him, chilling him to the bone, as the feelings for Jessie that he tried to keep buried deep, bubbled up; each one lashed his heart as it burst open. Kai watched April's eyes begin to shimmer, and he knew she had finally understood what he was saying. So there could be no doubt, he bluntly told her it was over. "I don't see us going anywhere, April, and I think, if we kept seeing each other, I'd just be leading you on." He shrugged and when he spoke again, his voice was ragged with emotion. "My heart is... somewhere else. I'm so sorry."

April was silent for long moments, and her eyes watered to a point that Kai was positive would spill over into tears. Then she inhaled a deep breath, shook her head, and smiled. "I guess I should have known that a guy as great as you, wouldn't be available." She sighed, her shoulders slumping, and indicated where Jessie was in the house with her thumb. Kai tried to block the image of Jessie on the floor, crying. "Is that why she got so weird? Why she didn't want us to sleep together?"

"Yes," he whispered, his voice strained. "She knows... how I feel." *About her*, he added in his head. And she also knew why they couldn't feel that way about each other.

April smiled with one edge of her lip; it was a sad one. "I suppose I should thank you, for telling me about her *before* we slept together. Most men would have waited until afterwards."

Kai gave her an equally sad smile. "I should have said something earlier, and I'm sorry I didn't. I was just hoping to feel...something for you." His smile turned genuine. "I wanted to like you, April, I really did. You're very enticing."

April grinned as she stared at the ground. Shifting her stance, she let out a wistful sigh. "Don't take this the wrong way, but a part of me wishes you'd waited until afterwards." She peeked up at him, a devilish smile on her face.

Kai felt his cheeks heating and bit back a smile. "I think it's better this way. Less confusing." He eyed her for a moment. She was undeniably beautiful, with a sensuous nature that made men weak in the knees, but underneath it all, she had a good heart. He hoped some guy took the time to find it one day. Giving her a serious look, he quietly said, "You don't need to try so hard, you know." She frowned, not following. "To get men to notice you," he explained. "They do. Trust me, they notice you."

April smiled warmly at him. "Whoever this girl is...she's an idiot for not being with you." Kai forced a smile onto his face. No, she wasn't an idiot. She just wasn't an option. But he couldn't tell April that, she wouldn't understand. Not noticing the rigidness of his smile, April sighed and said, "I'm going to miss going out on dates with you."

Kai laughed and gave her a wry smile. "April, you hated the date I took you on."

She laughed. "Yeah, I did." With a thoughtful look on her face, she gave him a once-over. "And you hated the date I took you on, didn't you?"

Kai grinned. "I hate costumes." He playfully raised an eyebrow at her.

Her an amused smile, she admitted, "I hate bugs."

Kai chuckled. "I hate techno music."

"I hate wearing a helmet," she said with a laugh.

"I hate drinks that come with little umbrellas."

"I hate carnations."

Kai laughed, remembering when she'd told him they were her favorite. He shook his head. "I hate being put on display in front of other people, especially when I'm dressed as a pirate."

April tilted her head back in a hearty laugh. Shaking her head, she shrugged. "Well, I refuse to recycle."

Kai laughed with her. "See, April, you and I really are not compatible at all."

She let out a sad sigh. "Yeah, I know." She crooked a playful grin. "You're just hot enough that I was willing to overlook that fact. Plus, I've learned the value of a man who knows how to kiss well, and you…" As her voice trailed off, she closed her eyes and bit her lip.

Kai shook his head as he studied their shoes. Peeking up at her, he asked, "Are we good?"

"Yeah, we're good." She extended a hand out to him. "It was nice getting to know you. Thank you for being a decent guy."

Kai smiled as he shook her hand. "It was my pleasure, April, and I know you're going to make some man very, very happy."

April grinned, then cocked her head. "Just not you."

"Not me, not in that way. But I'd like to think we can still be friends?" He raised an eyebrow at her.

April smiled as she wrapped an arm around his waist. "I can always use another friend, Kai." She grinned as he put his arm over her shoulder, then her expression turned serious. "I hope you get your girl. You deserve to get the girl."

Kai forced the smile to remain on his face as he nodded. It wasn't the fact that he couldn't get the girl that was bothering Kai. No, if things were different, he and Jessie *would* be to-gether, and they would be happy too. Getting her wasn't the problem. It was that he *shouldn't* get her. Dating his cousin wasn't something Kai was willing to do. No matter how much he wanted to.

16

A Clean Break

Kai woke up early the next morning and stared at his
ceiling. He felt like he'd been staring at his ceiling all
night long. It was the last thing he remembered doing—staring at his ceiling while his mind spun with thoughts
and emotions he shouldn't be having, that he wished he could
turn off. Since he was lying in the exact same position he'd
fallen asleep in, Kai wondered if he'd even slept. Maybe he'd
only briefly closed his eyes. If his room wasn't filled with a
gray, pre-dawn light, he might have believed that, but the last
time he'd stared straight above him, he hadn't been able to
make out the texture on the walls in the pitch-black room.
Now his eyes could easily distinguish each pattern in the surface.

He'd been debating what to do last night, after the incident with Jessie. Could they ignore what had happened between them and continue their camaraderie? Could he laugh
and joke with her, and not think about the way she'd moaned
in his ear? Would that sound ever leave him?

Sighing, Kai shifted in his bed. How could they ever trust themselves to be alone again? Not when the memory of that passion, boiling just under the surface, was still there. Always there. Closing his eyes, Kai remembered slamming her back into the door. She ignited a primal part of him. He'd wanted to rip off every piece of her clothing and drive deep inside her. He'd never wanted anyone so intensely. And sickeningly enough, just lying in bed thinking about it, he still wanted it; he could even feel his body responding.

Concentrating on the ceiling, Kai let out a long, slow exhale as he tried to calm himself. He couldn't think about it. He had to stop seeing her that way. Not for the first time, Kai cursed the fact that they'd grown up so far apart from each other. If he and Jessie had known each other as kids, he would only see her as family. But they hadn't. She was a virtual stranger to him, family only because someone had named her as such. He felt connected with her, but not as a relative. No, he felt connected to her...as a man to a woman. And he couldn't. He couldn't knowingly be with her. It was wrong. It was twisted. It was sick.

And yet...

Sighing again, Kai sat up and scrubbed his face. No. If he couldn't stop thinking of her romantically, then there was only one way for them to both get out of this mess. Reluctantly, he turned his gaze to his cell phone. He desperately did not want to have to make the call that he knew without a doubt he *had* to make.

His eyes watered just looking at the time on the screen. Time. He wanted so much more of it with her. But more time would only lead to more chances for them to cave. And they'd already proven to each other, over and over again, that they

298

could, and would, cave to the desire between them. He had to stop the cycle. He had to do the right thing, just like he had with April.

As he picked up the phone, his hand started to shake. In his head, he began scrolling through a list of alternative solutions. There weren't any. Closing his eyes, he pleaded with himself not to do this. He knew he had no choice, though.

Scrolling through his contacts, he looked for Jessie's name. Pressing the button to connect the call, he slowly brought the phone to his ear. His breath increased, and his nerves spiked as he waited for her to pick up.

"Hello?" a groggy voice muttered. It was thick with sleep …or emotion.

"Hey," Kai said. "Did I wake you?"

Bringing his knees up in bed, he slung his free arm around them. He could hear Jessie wrestle around too as she sighed in his ear. "No…I couldn't sleep."

Kai looked down. "Me either."

A few awkward moments of silence passed as Kai worked up the will to say what he had to say. At the same time that he heard Jessie start to say, "About yesterday…" he blurted out, "I broke it off with April." Biting his lip, he wondered why he couldn't just come out and tell her what he'd decided.

Another span of silence passed as Jessie absorbed what he'd said. "Oh. You didn't have to…" Her voice thickened as it trailed off.

Kai sighed. "Yeah, I did." Running a hand through his hair, he wished he could stop his heart from hammering so hard. "I couldn't let her keep thinking that our relationship was going anywhere. And I don't feel for her what I feel for…"

He let his sentence die. Admitting his feelings for Jessie now, wouldn't help with what he had to say later. Clearing his throat, he quickly added, "I never should have let it go on for as long as it did. Stringing her along like that...it wasn't fair to her."

Picking at a loose strand of fabric in the sheets, he waited for Jessie to respond. When she did, her voice was subdued. "Yeah, you're right. I shouldn't have asked you to keep seeing her. I just...I wasn't considering her feelings in all of this, I guess."

She let out such a sad sigh that Kai had the sudden urge to drive over there, run his hand through her hair, cup her cheek, and whisper that everything would be okay, but it wouldn't be. Not after what he was about to do. In a whisper, he started the process. "Jessie...about us..."

Kai's voice cracked and he found he couldn't speak. He swallowed several times to try and remove the blockage, and in the silence, Jessie spoke. "I know, Kai. I know. It was wrong, and I shouldn't have said what I said. I know we can't ...do that, and I'll try harder to not be so jealous or possessive of you. It just hurt so much to see you with April, but I know you're going to be with someone, and I promise I won't—"

Wishing he could just agree with her, Kai cut her off. "We can't see each other anymore, Jessie."

Silence filled the line again. A horrible, aching silence that made Kai's pounding heart sound like a gong, filling the room with an ominous, heavy beat. When she still didn't respond, he whispered, "Jessie?"

He heard her choke, then sputter. In a tightly controlled, warbling voice, she asked, "What do you mean? We can't be alone anymore...or we can't..."

Kai felt his eyes get heavy with building tears. His own voice cracking under the strain, he somehow managed to say, "We can't see each other again. Ever."

Jessie gasped, then muttered, "But...but no...Kai?"

Kai's heart split in half, and he felt the pain of the break slice through every part of him. He didn't think he would ever be the same person again after this. Everything he had been before was gone. Everything was different. Jessie was a highlight in his life. Without her in it...Kai almost didn't see the point. He swallowed, and the tears finally dropped to his cheeks. "I'm so sorry, Jessie. You don't know how much this kills me, but you and I *cannot* be together, and we're heading that way. Can't you feel it?"

He waited for her to acknowledge it. For her to admit to herself that the path they were on was going to end up with them in such a twisted, ethically and morally wrong relationship that it made him feel ill to the core. After a long stillness, she finally whispered, "Yes."

Kai exhaled with relief. At least she understood. "We have to stay apart. We have to go back to when you had your life, and I had my life, and they didn't intertwine."

She exhaled brokenly. "But, Kai...we're family. Family doesn't abandon each other."

Again, Kai wanted to reach out and stroke her, lovingly run a finger down her cheek. "We'll still be family, Jessie. We will always be that, and we won't abandon each other. If you need me, if you absolutely need me...I'm there, no questions asked. But Jessie, we need to let this die, before we can truly be...just cousins."

Kai heard Jessie start to break down. As she started to cry, his tears started falling freely too. "I'm so sorry," he repeated.

Through her broken sobs, he heard her say, "I'm going to miss you, so much. I don't know how I'm going to..." Her voice trailed off as waves of anguish took her over.

Kai clenched the sheets in his hand. He didn't want to hurt her. He didn't want to make her cry. *He* didn't want to cry. He wanted to tell her that he was wrong—that they shouldn't be apart. He wanted to rush to her place, sweep her in his arms, and kiss away her tears. He wanted to lay her down and make her feel the warmth and love between them. He wanted to make love to her. And that was exactly why he had to do this.

"I'm going to miss you too, Jessie. You're so important to me. You're...everything to me."

Biting his cheek, he stopped himself from pouring any more of his heart out to her. It would only hurt them both if they started confessing their feelings for each other now. And while Kai was certain Jessie cared deeply for him, he was 100 percent certain he was in love with her. Breaking it off with April had helped him to see it. He loved Jessie, in all the ways he shouldn't.

Her sobs easing, she timidly asked, "Can we still talk? Can I call you?"

Kai thought of having these heart wrenching phone calls every day; he didn't think he could do it. "Jessie..." he pleaded, not wanting to have to say it. A clean break was best. A clean break healed quicker.

Jessie sniffled. "Right...that probably wouldn't help anything."

Another long silence filled the line, as both their hearts silently broke apart. Feeling the knot of turmoil in his stomach tightening, Kai knew it was time. Time to end the call, to forever end his connection with the only woman he wanted in his life. His voice breaking, he softly told her, "I wish you only happiness, Jessie."

He couldn't imagine his life without her in it.

"Kai..."

Steeling himself, he closed his eyes and pictured her one last time — her smile, her beautiful face framed in dark, curly locks, the sound of her voice when she said his name. She was the one person on this earth that Kai would have liked to experience everything with. He couldn't think of anyone else that he'd rather have on this twisted, rollercoaster of a ride called life.

He ended their relationship with, "You're my best friend, Jessie. I love you." Then he disconnected the call and tossed his phone away from him.

⬤━━━━━━━━━⬤

It was astounding to Jessie how so much could change in her life, while at the same time, nothing changed. She went to work, rubbing out the kinks in Mr. Tinley's lower back. She went to the movies with Harmony and April; still peeved about Jessie's heated comments to her, April always sat as far from Jessie as possible. She checked on her grandmother, who was completely healed and feisty as ever. She even repeatedly shot down Gram's attempts to set her up with "nice" boys.

All of that was routine for Jessie. The only thing that wasn't routine, the only thing that had changed completely for her in the past three weeks, three achingly *long* weeks, was the fact that her cousin had all but vanished. She hadn't seen or heard from him since their last painful conversation on the phone.

She knew he was still around. Grams constantly talked about him, and asked if he was happy. From all Jessie could gather, Kai didn't appear to be doing very well. Grams was convinced that he was miserable because of his work, that his boss was an ass who was bringing him down. On more than one occasion, she told Jessie that Kai should just go home and work with his parents. Grams felt he belonged there, but the thought of him leaving the state made Jessie want to curl into a fetal position.

Even though she and Kai didn't speak, it was comforting to know they were staring at the same starry sky and breathing in the same chilly air. She couldn't stomach the thought of him being so far away that time was actually pushed back four hours.

The idea of him leaving made her feel worse than when she replayed their last horrible conversation—and that made her feel awful. It was quite possibly the worst moment in her life so far. Already on edge from a sleepless night and the memory of crossing a line that shouldn't ever be crossed, Jessie had been a wreck when he'd called her. And hearing him speak the words that had changed their relationship forever had shattered her heart into a thousand pieces: *"We can't see each other again. Ever."*

Jessie was certain those were the worst words ever created in the English language. But then Kai had used words that were even worse. Worse, because they were so wonderful: *"You're so important to me. You're everything to me. You're my best friend."*

And then the kicker, the one that always punched a hole through Jessie's soul whenever she thought about it, both because of what it could mean, and the fact that she wasn't entirely sure what it *did* mean: *"I love you."*

If Kai had said it as a standalone sentence, Jessie would have been positive that he meant he was *in* love with her—man to woman. But he'd lumped it together with, "You're my best friend." To Jessie, that meant that while he was attracted to her, he loved her in a friendly way. It warmed and hurt her, because she loved him that way too. He was her best friend, and she hadn't gotten a chance to tell him.

Jessie couldn't imagine not ever seeing those tropical eyes again. Not ever getting to laugh with him over dinner. Not being able to ever take care of him. They'd only been separated three weeks, but it might as well have been three years. Kai had wanted to go back to a time when their lives hadn't intertwined, but the problem was, their lives already *had* intertwined. Distance wasn't going to remove Kai from being securely wrapped around her heart. It only made her ache in pain, and she knew it was wrong to feel that way.

Forcing herself to go through the motions of life, she showered and dressed for the day. It was just another Saturday. Another Saturday in a long line of Saturdays. Nothing interesting or special about it. No playful smile on a certain boy's mouth to make the day noteworthy. Just another day.

Glumly, Jessie started walking down the hallway to the living room. She tried not to think about the way Kai could perfectly curve his lips into the sexiest smile she'd ever seen. No, she definitely shouldn't be thinking about his mouth.

"No, Kai, don't be ridiculous…"

Jessie paused in the hallway at hearing her cousin's name. She could just see April on the couch with her feet up, chatting on her cell phone. With Kai. Jessie had come across them talking before. While she hated the fact that April got to talk to him when she couldn't, she almost always stopped whatever she was doing to listen to them. Not out of jealousy—Kai and April's relationship had shifted into an easy friendship—but because, if she listened hard enough, Jessie could hear Kai through the phone. She hated feeling so pathetic, that she was actually clamoring to hear the tinny sound of his voice while he talked to someone else, but she couldn't help it. She missed him.

April seemed to sense that Jessie was there and twisted her head to look at her. She gave Jessie an unhappy pout. Things were still awkward between them. Jerking her head around, so she was staring out the slider, April said into the phone, "What was that, Kai? Sorry, Jessie distracted me."

Irrationally, Jessie's heart started beating harder; Kai knew she was there now. Stepping into the living room, she casually turned on the TV, set the volume on low, and sat down close to April. While looking for something to watch, she listened for Kai's voice as hard as she could.

Unfortunately, Jessie couldn't hear what he said in response to April's comment, but April glanced her way. "Yeah, she's fine. Why?"

Jessie's heart squeezed with a powerful ache that hurt so badly, she had to massage the spot with the heel of her hand. Kai was there, just a few feet away from her, and he was asking April how she was doing. It took every scrap of will power Jessie possessed to not rip the phone out of April's hands and beg Kai to come see her. She wanted to hear his voice. She wanted to see his face, but he was right. Their feelings needed to fade before they could be reunited, and that was going to take time. Jessie wished they'd hurry up and vanish so she could be with her cousin again. Her best friend.

Jessie heard Kai give April some response, and April's brows drew together as she continued to study Jessie. Her face brightened, and she smiled. "What do you mean he liked my picture?" She relaxed into the couch as she laughed into the phone, and it was like she was talking to a girlfriend, not the man she'd made out with on more than one occasion. "Really? Is he cute?" She paused, then murmured, "Louis, huh? I've never met a Louis. What's he like?"

Kai was apparently going into detail about this Louis person, because aside from a couple of "yeahs" and "oohs," April was silent. Jessie was pretty sure that Kai worked with a Louis, and wondered if he was talking him up to April just to distract her from the fact that Kai and Jessie hadn't seen each other in a while. Jessie thought that was probably the reason for the redirect. Kai wouldn't want anyone delving too closely into their relationship or lack thereof.

After another couple of minutes, April finally said, "Okay, have fun." She paused, then rolled her eyes. "Okay, I'll tell her. Bye." After ending the call, April started watching the show playing on TV. Curiosity was eating Jessie alive. Kai had obviously meant her there at the end.

Biting her lip, she stared at her friend. She didn't want to seem too eager about a message from her cousin, but she desperately wanted to know what he said. When April finally looked her way, Jessie raised an expectant eyebrow. April sighed. "Kai says hello." She mumbled the message, like just telling Jessie that much was putting her out.

Jessie wanted to sigh in contentment, and daydream about the words coming from Kai's mouth, not April's. She couldn't though. She couldn't look lovesick over her cousin around anyone, least of all April. Jessie managed a nonchalant shrug as she twisted back to the TV. "That was nice of him." Not looking at April, she carefully said, "We've been too busy to talk much lately. How is he?"

Her heart hammered in her chest as she waited for her friend to respond, but instead of answering her, April stood up. "I have a mani-pedi to get to." She indicated the kitchen with her thumb. "Harmony has all the details for next weekend." With that, she strolled to her bedroom.

Jessie was silent as she watched her leave. April was going to stretch out the argument between them for as long as she possibly could. Hopefully things got better soon; Jessie didn't think she could utter, "I'm sorry I was a bitch," one more time. Maybe the trip next weekend would help. Harmony had had the brilliant idea to strengthen their bond with a girl's ski trip. They were all going to Harmony's favorite lodge, deep in the Arapaho National Forest.

With a sigh, Jessie decided to let April sulk for now. She knew she couldn't rush the repair of her friend's hurt feelings, and April had a right to feel slighted; Jessie never should have spoken to her the way she had. Besides being a little too eager with a cute boy she liked, her roommate hadn't done anything wrong. This upcoming trip was probably the best thing for their relationship.

Walking into the kitchen, Jessie found Harmony chowing down on a bowl of cereal. Jessie went through the mechanics of preparing her own bowl while Harmony flicked the edge of the piece of paper she was holding. It looked like a hotel reservation confirmation.

"I got us a double at Mountain Inn Resort." Her pale eyes were sparkling as she said it. Harmony loved skiing. She'd already been up a few times for day trips and was really looking forward to an entire weekend of skiing with just the girls. "This is going to be great, Jessie!"

Jessie smiled at her friend's enthusiasm. "I'm sure it will, Harm." Sitting beside her, Jessie suppressed a sigh. She'd be hours away from Kai. The distance shouldn't really matter, since they weren't speaking anyway, but there it was, just the thought of how much physical space would be between them put an ache in her chest. At least her girlfriends would help fill the space, assuming April stopped being mad at her, of course.

Harmony gave her a concerned look, like she'd heard her internal sigh. With a tilt of her head, she asked, "You all right?"

Jessie let the sigh escape as she dunked the tiny Os floating in her bowl of milk. She wished she could confess everything to Harmony. It would be so nice to finally talk about her confusion with someone, but how do you explain something that awful to a friend? Sure, it wasn't as if she was lusting over a sibling or anything, but still, they were *first* cousins, and what was going on with them was so much worse than idly thinking a relative was cute.

"Just thinking about...stuff," she muttered blandly.

Not about to let that comment go, Harmony put a hand on her arm. "Boy-stuff or April-stuff?"

Jessie wasn't sure how to answer her, so she shrugged. Harmony frowned. "Jeremy didn't call you, did he?"

Harmony leaping to that conclusion, made Jessie's eyebrows shoot up her forehead. She vehemently shook her head. She supposed it wasn't too weird for Harmony to think her troubles stemmed from Jeremy. Jessie had been with him for a while, and really, their break up hadn't happened all that long ago. Jessie just hadn't thought about him in so long that he seemed like someone buried in her ancient past, not someone she'd been considering moving in with less than six months ago.

"No, Jeremy might as well have dropped off the face of the earth for what little I think of him. And I definitely haven't heard from him."

She was grateful for that; Jeremy was a complication she didn't need right now. Harmony studied her as she took a spoonful of cereal. Around her food, she asked, "Is it because of that Simon guy? He called again by the way."

Jessie groaned and dropped her head back. "Goddamn it." Lifting her head, she began violently digging into her cereal. "I told Grams I didn't want to be set up with anyone, then she got one of her newfound friends to get her son to ask me out." Her spoon clinked angrily against her bowl. "And now he won't stop." Jessie had politely turned him down three times already. She was sure he was nice guy and all, but he wasn't what she was looking for at the moment.

Harmony grinned at her irritation. "You could always tell him you've switched sides?"

Jessie laughed, then started choking on some milk she'd been swallowing. Coughing, she smacked Harmony on the shoulder. "Thanks," she finally got out.

When she could breathe again, Jessie frowned into her cereal bowl. She wished she could be honest. Harmony looked

310

about to question her again when they heard April shout, "Catch you later, Harm!" The door banged shut and Jessie shook her head. She'd just been dissed by omission.

Harmony stared into the living room then returned her eyes to Jessie. "Don't let April get under your skin. You know her, this will eventually blow over."

Jessie nodded, then glumly returned to her cereal. Hoping Harmony wouldn't ask her why she had gone off on their roommate in the first place, Jessie asked her about their weekend plans. Smiling bright, Harmony started filling her in on the many perks their lodge provided, and all thoughts of April's annoyance were momentarily forgotten.

After Jessie was done with her breakfast, she ambled around her house for a while. When that did nothing to lift her spirits, she decided to go check on her grandmother. She was sure Grams was fine and didn't need her help with anything, but Jessie did. She needed a distraction, even if the distraction was a painful one; being around her grandmother reminded her of being around Kai.

After having afternoon tea filled with polite conversation, thankfully none of it about Kai, Jessie offered to stay and help her grams make dinner. She just didn't feel like going home and dealing with April's cold shoulder. And, if she were completely honest with herself, she was hoping if she stayed late enough, she might get lucky, and Kai might decide to visit Grams. Although, perhaps that wasn't good luck. As much as she wanted to see his face, hear his voice, she was sure the shock of it would rip open her still-fresh wounds. She might bleed out right in front of her grandmother, and how on earth would she explain that?

Jessie prepped the potatoes and put them in the oven. When they were almost ready, Grams wandered out to her greenhouse to get some fresh herbs to go on top of them. With Grams gone, Jessie's mind started to drift. And as always, it drifted to Kai. Jessie wondered what he was up to today, what he was up to everyday. Not being able to ask him, not being able to check in on him, amplified her heartache. It was in her nature to nurture her loved ones, and when all was said and done, that was what Kai was to her—a loved one.

The kitchen door slamming closed startled Jessie from her melancholy thoughts. Grams had just returned carrying a small bowl and several plastic bags. Slapping on a smile, Jessie made herself seem as relaxed and content as possible. Her grandmother was watching her with pursed lips, so Jessie wasn't sure if she was buying the act or not. "Just a few more minutes on the potatoes, Grams."

Her grandmother's eyes narrowed, and Jessie tensed. She was sure she was going to ask her what was wrong, and Jessie didn't have a good lie prepared. And she didn't like lying to her grandmother either. Hoping to pass her inspection, Jessie kept a small smile plastered on her face; it probably looked as forced as it felt.

Grams examined her for a few more seconds, then smiled and patted her shoulder. "That's good. I got us some chives." She handed the bowl to Jessica, then grabbed a marker and began labeling the small bags.

Jessie wondered why she was marking what they were, since Grams could probably identify the different herbs blindfolded, and then it hit her. Grams was making a care package ...for her grandchild. Before she could stop herself, she asked, "Are those for Kai?"

Her tone came out wistful, and Jessie immediately began studying the chives. She didn't want Grams to see the longing in her face that surely matched her voice. Grams sounded curious when she answered, but not suspicious. "Yes, these are for Kai. I'm determined to turn that boy into a good cook. Every man should know how to make a decent meal for his woman." She sighed and there was a sadness in the sound that hit Jessie a little too close to home. "He might have broken things off with your friend, but eventually he'll find the right girl."

Jessie quickly turned her head away, and was grateful that her thick, curly hair covered her expression. She didn't want to think about Kai finding the "right" girl, didn't want to contemplate him truly moving on. Nodding, Jessie moved to the fridge and began aimlessly looking through it. "I should get you some groceries soon," she muttered into the cool, refrigerated air.

From behind her, she heard her grandmother say, "Don't worry about it, dear. Kai brings me a bundle nearly every time he shows up. As I don't eat that much anyway, I don't think I'll be starving anytime soon."

A soft chuckle escaped Grams, and Jessie was suddenly struck by the image of Kai riding down the road with grocery bags dangling off his arms. Amazed by his never-ending sweetness, Jessie looked back at her grandmother. "Kai brings you food?"

Grams nodded, pride clear in her features. "Constantly, like he's worried my cupboards will run dry in a week." Grams laughed as she rolled her eyes. "If the boy had moved here with something more substantial than a motorcycle, he could save himself some time and bring me a month's supply at a time."

A small laugh escaped Jessie, and her eyes drifted out of focus as she thought of being on the back of Kai's bike with him. "Yeah, he does love that bike…"

Her grandmother sighed. "It probably wouldn't stop him from dropping in all the time anyway. The boy has a heart as big as yours." Jessie's eyes refocused on Grams; she could feel the tiny tears stinging them, and hoped her grandmother didn't notice.

The pressure grew beneath her lids as images of Kai bombarded her. Knowing she wouldn't be able to contain the moisture much longer, Jessie looked away. After a few tears released, Jessie quickly swiped her cheeks dry. Her grandmother placed a gentle hand on her shoulder, and Jessie knew the pretense of being okay was gone. "Are you all right, Jessica?"

No longer trying to hide the fact that she was brushing tears from her skin, Jessie faced Grams with a sad smile on her lips. Her heart thudded as she thought of something acceptable that she could say to explain her overly emotional state. It had to be believable, but it couldn't be anything about Kai. "Of course. It's just…I'm leaving…for a few days…and I'm going to worry so much about you."

Grams smiled as she wrapped her in a tight hug. Jessie felt a little guilty for saying it, but just a little. There was a lot of truth to the statement. Even though she wasn't going to be gone long, Jessie would worry about her grandmother. "Oh, you sweet thing, don't you worry about me. You just go out and have a good time. Enjoy the life you've been given." They pulled apart, and Jessie hastily brushed her cheeks dry again.

She needed to get a hold of herself, but that was easier said than done. The pain of Kai's absence was a physical discomfort, an irreparable hole in her heart.

"Where are you off to?" her grandmother asked with a bright smile.

Thinking about April and how awful this upcoming trip might be did nothing to perk up Jessie's mood. "My roommates and I are going skiing next weekend. Things have been sort of awkward at the house lately, so we're all taking a little mini-vacation."

Her grandmother smiled, like she suddenly understood why Jessie was down. Yes, she supposed her troubles at home could explain her odd tears, but that really wasn't it. Wanting to change subjects, or maybe not talk at all for a little bit, Jessie started preparing the toppings for the potato bar. Grams watched her with thoughtful eyes, then she lifted a finger in the air, like she'd just had a revelation. "You should take Kai skiing with you."

Jessie's heart froze into one solid chunk. She'd love to take Kai with her this weekend. She'd love to teach him to ski during the day, and would love to hang out with him in the lodge at night. She'd love every single second of it, more than she should, and that was the problem. "Um...well..." She didn't know how to tell her grandmother that it wasn't possible, that they'd cut all communication, that they couldn't see each other anymore. Her sadness returned tenfold as she stared at the ground. "It's a girl thing, Grams."

Her grandmother let out a soft sigh, and Jessie peeked up at her. "I know it's a girl's weekend, Jessica, but Kai has never seen that much snow up close, and he's always wanted to learn how to ski." Smiling, she shook her head. "When he was younger, he used to pretend he was slalom racing in the back-yard."

A ghost of a smile drifted across Jessie's face, then she frowned. How could she turn down her grandmother? How could she say yes though? "I don't know...April will be there." She worried her lip, hoping her grandmother accepted that and dropped the matter.

She didn't. "Kai tells me the relationship ended amicably, and they still speak often. Surely April wouldn't mind his presence for just a couple of days?" Jessie opened her mouth to say something, anything, but Grams was done with mild requests. "Please, Jessica? For me? He's been having such a hard time lately. There's a sadness that just won't leave him. I'm worried. He could really use the pick-me-up. He needs you...please take him with you."

Jessie felt her eyes watering again. "He's been down?"

Jessie knew her tone had come out much too hopeful when she saw her grandmother frown. Jessie didn't really want Kai to be distraught, she just wanted to know this was tough for him too. With a shake of her head, Grams sighed. "He's so melancholy lately. This is just what he needs right now." Her lips firmed, and she nodded, like her mind was made up, and no matter what Jessie said, Kai would be going on the trip.

Jessie's heart raced as she started pulling potatoes out of the hot oven. Oh God...she was going to see Kai again, or hear from him, at least. What would he say, what would he do? Would he agree to come? Would they get one last weekend together? And...was that a good thing, or a truly horrible idea? Either way, it was pointless for Jessie to keep objecting. "Fine, Grandma, I'll ask him." Setting the spuds on a plate in front of her, Jessie carefully pulled back the tin foil encasing them. Studying her work, she nonchalantly said, "He'll probably say no though. He's busy with stuff." That would be for the best. He shouldn't go. Too much could go wrong, and even a flawless trip would be devastating.

Peeking up, Jessie watched as a sly smile crossed her grandmother's lips. Jessie knew that look, and her heart sank. Her grandmother wasn't going to let this go. She'd persist until Kai was at the lodge with them. "Nonsense, I won't let him say no." As Jessie felt all the blood rush from her face, leaving her cold and pale, her grandmother's smile widened. "Life is short, Jessica Marie, and you and Kai...you both need to learn to seize opportunities as they arise."

All Jessie could do was nod at her grandmother's advice while dread filled her from head to toe. Dread laced with a razor-sharp edge of hope and excitement. She was going to see Kai again. She didn't want the moment to come, but she couldn't wait either.

17

Skiing

Jessie sat in the backseat of Harmony's SUV, wondering how she'd gotten here. She ceaselessly worked the zipper of her heavy jacket up and down as anxiety ate at her nerves. The sound of country music filled the spacious cabin, making Jessie cringe. Normally she would annoy Harmony until her friend caved and changed the station, but Jessie didn't have it in her to make a peep. Kai was sitting directly beside her.

Glancing over at him from the corner of her eye, she secretly studied him as he stared out the window. He was relentlessly wringing his hands together, and seemed to be feeling as odd and uneasy as she was. Having him right next to her again was pounding her with several conflicting emotions—elation, trepidation, sorrow and regret. Tearing her gaze away, Jessie looked up at the front seat. Harmony was explaining the condition of the slopes. She'd heard from some friends who had just returned that the snow was perfect—fast and deep. Jessie was a good skier and could handle the more advanced slopes, but she'd mainly be on the lower trails this weekend, helping Kai learn the basics. She hadn't seen him for nearly four weeks, and now she would practically be glued to his side. She was as eager for that as she was scared. This was exactly why she hadn't wanted him to come.

She started to look over at him again, but felt his eyes burning into her and stopped. Meeting April's gaze in the rearview mirror, Jessie froze, then slapped on a friendly smile. She didn't want to look sad, forlorn, or lovesick in front of the woman who used to date Kai. April was still annoyed at her though, and quickly averted her gaze to the snowy scenery passing by her window.

Jessie was getting sick and tired of April ignoring her. Yes, she'd been horribly rude, and had basically called her a whore, but honestly, girls said far meaner things over much smaller issues. It wasn't all that long ago that April had told her she was a conniving little cunt for snagging the last pair of 75 percent off boots. Jessie had forgiven her for her comment, why couldn't April forgive her for hers? Of course, there were no kickass boots in April's life to make her feel better.

Smiling at the memory of that long-ago spat, Jessie inadvertently swung her gaze to Kai. He was still looking at her, and their gazes instantly locked. Suddenly, it was like they were the only two people in the car. His eyes, a warm tropical color that clashed so harshly with the chill in the December air, bored into hers, and a shiver ran through Jessie, despite the thick layers of clothes she was wearing.

Kai flicked a quick glance at Harmony and April in the front seat, then leaned toward Jessie. She wanted to hold her breath as he came closer. "I'm sorry about this." His perfect lips twisted into a wry smile. "Gran wouldn't take no for an answer." He looked down then, and his hand shifted to rest in the space between them on the seat. Without consciously thinking of doing it, Jessie moved her hand near his, until the tips of their fingers touched. She was instantly warm.

Kai peeked back up at her at the slight connection. "I thought about telling her I'd go and then staying home, but ..." As his voice trailed off, his eyes focused past Jessie's shoulder, to the white capped trees blurring past them in the distance. A light snowfall was splattering large flakes against the car, and Kai stared at the display with childlike wonder on his face.

Kai hadn't been around snow before moving here. Having played in the white stuff her entire life, being around someone who had never even seen it before now was a little wondrous. Smiling, she filled in the blanks for him. "You've always wanted to ski. I remember."

The memory of how easy it was to be around Kai slammed into Jessie with a force that stole her breath. But that was sort of the problem. It was too easy to be around him. It felt too nice. It warmed her in ways it shouldn't. It gave her thoughts that she shouldn't have about him.

Even now, as the tip of her finger stubbornly started to stroke his, she was reminded of all the reasons they should be apart. But, God, that had been so hard. Being apart was as difficult to her as being together, just for completely different reasons. Around Kai, Jessie was always beating back her feelings for him. Apart for Kai...it was like those feelings were eating right through her, leaving only emptiness and pain in their wake.

Kai nodded at her statement; his eyes looked apologetic for not being able to resist an opportunity to fulfill a childhood dream. He glanced at their fingers on the seat, hers a creamy white, his a deep warm brown. Looping his finger over hers, he locked gazes with her again. The feelings he stirred inside her with just his index finger wrapped around hers, was a thousand times more intense than anything Jeremy had ever given her, and she was well aware of how wrong that was, but she couldn't escape it. That undeniable, horrible attraction.

Jessie made herself pull her hand away when all she really wanted to do was lace their fingers together. She couldn't though, not with April and Harmony in the car. Shaking her head, she tried to clear her thoughts. She shouldn't regardless if her friends were here or not. She shouldn't touch him any more than was absolutely necessary.

Kai let out a soft sigh as he resumed staring out the window. Harmony talked to April while she rested her head back on the seat and closed her eyes, like she was going to take a nap. Aside from Harmony's voice and the annoying country songs playing, the rest of the car ride was made in silence.

A couple of hours later, the foursome pulled into the parking lot of the ski lodge where Harmony had booked their rooms. Kai had luckily found a room in the same lodge, although, not on the same floor. Jessie was happy there would be some distance between them. A little space was good right now.

After stepping out of the car, Jessie watched Kai get out. A huge smile on his face, he closed his eyes and inhaled the crisp air. He laughed as light flakes fell on his face, immediately melting onto his skin. Watching him was mesmerizing. She was so used to snow, so the beauty of it really didn't faze her anymore. It was heartwarming and refreshing to see someone so enchanted by it.

As Jessie stared at Kai with a dopey smile on her face, she heard heated whispers coming from the front of the car. Looking over she saw Harmony and April engrossed in a lively discussion. A sinking feeling in the pit of her stomach told Jessie the discussion was about her.

Harmony had red splotches on her cheeks, and it wasn't from the nip in the air. The flaming spots showed themselves whenever she was angry. April looked just as peeved. Great. They'd only just gotten here and there was already trouble brewing. April suddenly jerked her thumb at Jessie, then pointed over to Kai. The ominous sensation in Jessie's gut hardened into a tight knot of apprehension. What the hell was April up to?

Feeling like she was about to walk into the line of fire, Jessie hesitantly began walking their way. "Everything okay?" she asked, her gaze flicking between April and Harmony. April had her chin up and her arms crossed in a position of defense and defiance. Harmony looked frustrated and trapped, like she was dealing with a crazy person, and she didn't know what to do.

Tossing her hands up in the air, Harmony told Jessie, "She's being completely unreasonable."

April scoffed at her. "I am not. I'm being practical. There are three of us crammed into one tiny room, while Kai has a room all to himself. I'm just saying we should make the rooms even. How is that being unreasonable? And since Jessie is the one who decided to drag him along at the last minute, she should be the one to stay with him. It's only fair," she said with a haughty shrug.

Jessie was so shocked at April's suggestion that it took her a few tries to spit out a response. When she did, it wasn't what

322

she really wanted to say, but it was the first thing that made it past her lips. "I thought you and Kai were still friends? Why are you sore that I brought him along?"

April turned her eyes to Jessie; they were ice-cold, but there was a lingering pain behind the wall of anger. This wasn't about Kai joining them on their girl's weekend, this was about Jessie's unfortunate comment about April acting like a slut. "I'm not mad *he's* here." Returning her eyes to Harmony, April shrugged and said, "It makes sense, Harmony. Why be packed like sardines if we can all be comfortable. And besides, we'll be spending most of our time on the slopes or in the lodge. Does it really matter if we don't all sleep together?"

Harmony bit her lip, and Jessie knew April was convincing her. Jessie felt like the frigid air was freezing her lungs. She couldn't breathe. She couldn't room with Kai, but if Harmony saw April's side of things, how could Jessie argue against it? Because in a way, April was right...if this was any other situation, they would be more comfortable two to a room.

Knowing this was her only chance, Jessie put a hand on Harmony's arm. Her pale eyes were conflicted. "Harm...I want to stay with you guys. I know I messed up girl's weekend by inviting Kai, but my grandmother insisted. It doesn't mean I don't still want to spend as much time with you two as possible though. I want to be in the same room as you guys." *And I can't sleep in the same room with Kai. I just can't.*

Harmony opened her mouth, but April was the one who spoke first. "Look, I didn't want to be a complete and total bitch, but you're not really leaving me a choice. I understand from Kai that you were just trying to protect me...or whatever

...but I call bullshit on that. You basically called me a whore who wasn't good enough for your family. If it was really about protecting me from his past, you could have pulled me aside and told me Kai was hung up on someone else. You didn't, so obviously it had *nothing* to do with sparing my feelings. You just didn't want me with your cousin for some reason."

For a minute, Jessie was too dazed to respond. He'd told her he was hung up on someone else? When she recovered, she immediately shook her head, but April held her hands up. "Save it. I thought I could do this, I thought I could mend us, but seeing you and Kai together just reminds me of that whole night, and I can't do it. If you don't room with him tonight, then I'm going home. I can't sleep in the same room as you. Sleeping in the same house is bad enough."

With that, she turned and stormed toward the lodge. "April!" Jessie yelled, but she ignored her. Kai finally noticed something was going on, and had a concerned expression on his face as he alternated his gaze between Jessie and April.

Jessie let out a frustrated grunt as Harmony put a hand on her shoulder. Her cheeks were still muddled, but she looked calmer. "I'm sorry, Jess. She's just...hurt, I think. She values your opinion, and you were pretty...rough on her." Harmony's brows drew together, like she was wondering why.

Before she could ask, Jessie spat out, "What am I supposed to do, Harm?"

Harmony shook her head; her hair was tucked into a knit cap, but some loose strands brushed her shoulders. "Give her space, and see if Kai will let you crash with him. I really think she'll feel bad for kicking you out of the room, and this whole thing will finally blow over. And besides, you haven't spent time with your cousin in a while, right? Just think of it as a good opportunity to catch up? You can have cocoa, make s'mores, curl up by the fire…it will be just like camp!"

All the color drained from Jessie's face. Curling up with him would be like no camp that Jessie had ever been to. Kai was still looking her way, brows scrunched as he tried to figure out what was going on. Light flakes were collecting in his hair and for a moment, Jessie thought he put every outdoors-wear model to shame. For someone who had never even seen snow, he looked right at home on the mountaintop. Jessie couldn't picture anything good happening if they stayed in the same room together. All night. Alone.

While Jessie tried to understand how this weekend had gone south so quickly, Harmony wrapped her arms around her in a warm hug. "While you're bonding with Kai tonight, I'll work on April. This weekend will be the end of it. I promise."

Jessie sighed and nodded. What other choice did she have but to accept this and hope everything went okay? Besides, maybe this would be the slight revenge that April needed to get over Jessie's hurtful comment. As Harmony pulled away, she casually tossed out, "I've been wanting to ask…why'd you say that to her, anyway?"

It was the question Jessie had been dreading. The one she'd managed to avoid answering for weeks. She still didn't have a good answer for her actions. "I…I don't know. He's family…I just didn't like how she was throwing herself all over him, like he was a toy…or a prize. I thought he deserved better than being treated like a piece of meat." And she was jealous. Very, very jealous. She didn't mention that though. Swallowing the knot in her throat, she shrugged. "I just didn't handle it well, and I have no idea how to apologize to April…"

Harmony gave her a sympathetic look. "I'll talk to her tonight. This will turn out okay, you'll see."

Hoping she was right, Jessie nodded. She pointed at Kai, who still looked confused. "I better go tell him about the new sleeping arrangements." Harmony nodded and Jessie's heart started beating harder. God…she was going to be alone with him all night. *It will be okay. We'll be tired from skiing all day. We'll go right to sleep. That's all that will happen.*

Kai's eyes drifted up her body as she approached, and Jessie instantly had doubts about her mental pep talk. Just that slight visual inspection made her feel exposed. Even with the multiple layers of clothes she was wearing, she felt naked and vulnerable, and a dull ache inside her whispered that she needed more of him, so much more. Kai looked worried, but even that couldn't keep the smile from his face as he took in the winter wonderland around them; the sunlight bouncing off his eyes made them twinkle as much as the ice crystals around their feet.

"Everything okay?" he asked. "That seemed kind of tense."

Jessie sighed. If she'd only handled April differently, none of this would be happening right now. "Yes, no…I don't know." Kai's joy faded as his confusion grew, and she knew she should just spit it out. "April is still hurt about what I said to her. She thought that she could hang out with me this weekend, with all of us girls in the same room, but now… she's saying she'd rather leave than share a room with me."

Jessie sighed as the drama of her life wrapped around her. Studying the ground, she muttered, "Harmony thinks she'll calm down if I leave the two of them alone tonight, and she wants a chance to talk to April, to smooth things out. But in the meantime...I don't have a room. So...can I...?" God, why was this so hard? She should just ask him, and be done with it. Gathering her resolve, her heartbeat thudding in her ear, she whispered, "Can I stay with you tonight?"

Kai's eyes darkened in anger. "April won't stay in the same room with you? Because of what you said to her weeks ago? That's ridiculous! I told her you were just..." He stopped talking and his mouth hung open, like he'd just realized what else she'd said. Looking thrown, he opened and closed his mouth a few times before the words came out. "But...I'm a guy, you're a girl..." As his gaze traveled the length of her body, his face lost a little color. "We can't...they can't ask us to..."

Looking torn, Kai ran a hand through his damp-with-snow hair. Jessie watched the dark pieces lump together into grooves. It was incredibly attractive. She forced her eyes to only look at his chest. "We're cousins, Kai. We're harmless."

Her smile was rueful. They were supposed to be harmless, but somehow things between them had gone horribly wrong. But as far as Harmony and April were concerned, the two of them sharing a room together was no big deal. And it didn't have to be. They could control themselves. Tears stinging her eyes, Jessie looked back up at him. "So...can I stay with you?" She swallowed after she asked. Did she want him to say yes, or no?

Kai closed his eyes, and his jaw tightened, like he was upset. Jessie could understand if he was. This weekend had been going to be hard enough on them without her friends dumping this surprise in their laps, but her friends didn't know what they were really doing. April was asking for space, and Harmony thought Jessie should give it to her. If either one of them knew the truth, they wouldn't have done this; they weren't cruel.

When Kai reopened his eyes, he nodded. "Of course. I said I'd be here if you needed me. I'm not going to turn you away. We'll just keep our distance." He gave her a tentative smile. "We can do this...right?"

Jessie smiled tentatively too. A large flake fell on Kai's cheek and she had to physically restrain herself from brushing it away. Sure, they could do this.

◆———————◆

Four weeks. Kai had made it almost four achingly long weeks without caving, without calling his cousin, or showing up at her work, or dropping by her home in the middle of the night. And that had been difficult. That had taken every ounce of will power he possessed. He'd practically had to mentally abuse himself every day, just so he wouldn't give in to the overwhelming need to see her, to hold her, to touch her. To watch her smile, to hear her laugh. To wrap a long tendril of her hair around his finger. It had been the most difficult three weeks of his life.

Even his coworkers had noticed his mood. Missy had tried, in her own way, to cheer him up. Mainly she'd flashed him. A lot. At this point though, it did make Kai smile. Shaking his head, he'd repeatedly told her, "Thank you, but no thank you." He was pretty sure his continued rejections were doing nothing to dissuade Missy. She was anything but a quitter.

Louis had told Kai that he'd find another potential breeding partner. He was convinced that Kai's quietness had more to do with being dumped by April than anything else. Kai often told him that breaking things off had been a mutual decision. He hadn't been dumped, and he definitely wasn't looking for a "breeding partner." Louis refused to believe him though. Rejecting a beautiful woman went against the laws of nature in Louis's book.

But April wasn't the one holding Kai's heart, and he'd had no problems letting her go. Letting Jessie go though...that tore him apart daily. Even Mason had commented on his attitude. Kai always tried to be as professional as possible with his boss, but he'd been staring off into space more and more frequently, and one afternoon, Mason called him on it.

"Are you happy here at the center, Kai?" The look in Mason's eyes after he'd asked had been almost hopeful, like Kai would have made his day if he'd said no and turned in his notice.

Struggling against the feeling of not being wanted, Kai had raised his chin and calmly replied with, "Yes, very much so, Mason. I'm sorry if I've been distracted lately. It's a... personal matter, but I'll do better to not let it interfere with my work."

A stillness had filled the air, like a moment of calm before a storm. Mason had seemed as if he'd wanted to know more, but then he'd briefly nodded and quickly walked away. Even after all the weeks, Kai had been working there, he had no idea if the man liked him or not.

Kai had been getting through his life since he'd parted ways with Jessie, but in a numb daze that really wasn't living. Jessie's words in her bedroom seared through his soul whenever he had a moment to himself: *You should be with me. You're supposed to be with me.* If Jessie only knew how much he wanted those words to be true. Things would be so easy, if he could just be with her.

But instead he was maintaining his distance—safety through solitude. Then his grandmother had suddenly decided that he needed to go out and have a life experience. She'd told him that he'd always wanted to ski, and he would never get another opportunity to learn how, unless he took this weekend to go up with Jessie. By the way she'd put it, you would think all of the snow was suddenly going to evaporate, and if he didn't jump on the chance now, he was going to miss out on it forever. He had no idea what his grandmother's real motives were behind him going, but she wouldn't let up on him until he'd agreed.

And that was how Kai had found himself traveling miles away from the seclusion of his studio apartment, in painful proximity to the woman he loved. The woman he couldn't have. The woman who distracted his thoughts every waking moment and haunted his dreams every night.

After a few tension-filled hours in the car with Jessie, he'd tried to distract himself by taking in the wondrous setting around him, but even that had paled in comparison to being near her again. Then they'd arrived, and fate had seemingly interceded again, and Jessie had said the words he'd ached to hear, words he was scared to hear. She needed him. He had no choice but to say yes to helping her, not just because he loved her, but because she was family, and family did hard things for each other.

Walking into the spacious entryway of the ski lodge, Kai tried to keep that in mind. He and Jessie were family, and they could share a room without anything happening. Just because he could barely look at her smoky, passionate eyes or curly, wild hair without feeling a tinge of arousal, didn't mean he had to act on it. Kai was an adult, not a hormone crazed teenager. He had complete control of his body, and they could spend the night talking until they fell asleep—him on the floor, her safely on the bed.

Kai took in the space around him as he walked up to the front desk. The hotel was designed to resemble a classic log cabin with large wooden timbers visible under the roof, and a few supporting logs spaced around the open area of the lobby. A large circular fireplace with a cylindrical flue was in the middle of the common room, with chairs and tables spaced around it. It seemed like a very comfortable place to take a break from the chill outside. Several guests were lounging there with warm drinks in their hands while their skis rested on support brackets built along the wooden walls. Hallways branched off from either end of the common room with wide staircases that led to the upper floors. The entire place oozed warmth and comfort.

Smiling at the peaceful setting, Kai gave the elegant woman running the front desk his name. Yes, he and Jessie could be adults about all this. There was no need to stress about something as small and insignificant as sharing a room. And just the thought of spending some quality time with her made him happier than he cared to admit. He'd missed her so much, and now, at the very least, he'd get a chance to talk with his friend again. He'd meant it when he'd called her his best friend. She was. There was no one else he'd rather hang out with. Then again, he'd also meant it when he said he loved her. He did. Deeply.

While the woman checked him into the computer, Jessie walked up to stand beside him. Her beautiful, deep brown eyes swept over the warm, comfortable lobby, and she continually shifted her weight. Kai thought she was probably nervous about their upcoming arrangements. He wanted to assure her that everything was going to be fine, and nothing was going to happen, but he couldn't say that with Harmony and April standing right behind them.

Kai watched as a melted snowflake dropped off a tendril of her hair close to her face, and landed on her fluffy jacket, right over her breast. The water flowed down the quilted design, right over her nipple. A surge of desire slammed into him, and Kai had to look away. What was he saying about being an adult? Right. Well, he'd work on it. And it would be nice if the universe would stop teasing him with erotic raindrops.

The woman at the front desk gave him two room cards and wished him a pleasant stay. Kai thanked her and stepped aside so Harmony and April could check in. Jessie leaned on her skis, her bags in her other hand. Kai held his palm out and she looked up at him. "Let me take your bags," he casually said.

Jessie hesitated a moment, her eyes flicking over his damp hair, then she nodded and handed him one of the bags; her backpack she slung over her shoulder. Wanting to reaffirm to her that this would be fine, Kai gave her a friendly smile. She gave him a cautious smile in return, and Kai found himself staring a little too long into the depths of her eyes. Before he knew it, Harmony was dropping her bags right in front of him, making him jump; he hadn't realized they had finished checking in.

Harmony smiled as she inhaled a deep breath. "It smells like Christmas in here."

Kai had to agree with her. It did. The lodge had a real Christmas tree across from the front desk and the smell of pine was nearly overwhelming. It was comforting though. Tiny sparkling lights were strung along the eaves and around the tree, and Kai could just make out the scent of spiced cider coming from somewhere. It was magical and beautiful, and Kai couldn't wait to spend Christmas here in Colorado. He'd never had a white one before.

Jessie sighed, but she wasn't taking in the decorations, she was staring at April. "April, do you want to sit down and talk? Clear the air? I never meant to—"

April's eyes turned as icy as the weather. "Hurt me? Well, you did. And no, I don't want to talk anymore about it this weekend. I just want to ski and drink. Possibly at the same time." She picked up her bags, hefted her skis onto her shoulder, and started walking toward one of the hallways.

Harmony looked torn as she watched her leave. She gave Jessie a sympathetic smile, then said, "I'll talk to her. See you on the slopes in a bit?"

Lips compressed, Jessie gave her friend a stiff nod. Frustration began bubbling inside Kai. This was his fault, and Jessie was the one being punished. He should try talking to April again, make her understand. He wasn't sure how he could make her see without letting her in on the truth, but he had to try. He hated seeing her angry at Jessie.

Not sure what he was going to do, he took a step to follow April and Harmony. Jessie grabbed his arm. "Don't. Just let Harm handle it. It's okay...truly." She gave him a sad smile, and he wondered if he should really do what she was asking.

Deciding to trust her judgment, he playfully bumped her shoulder. "Want to go check out our room?"

Jessie nodded, and he started leading her in the opposite direction of Harmony and April. His room was the last one on the first floor. They walked in and Kai let out a long whistle. There was an actual fireplace in the room, along with a jetted tub in the corner. The space was decorated as cozily as the rest of the lodge, with large wooden beams along the walls, smaller versions along the ceiling. There were photos of the Rockies along the walls, along with a set of antique skis and poles.

The trip had been sprung on Kai at the last minute, and this room had been the only one available. It was costing him a pretty penny, but Kai was making a decent income now, working for Mason, and he lived pretty simply. He'd had the extra cash and had decided that in a way, Gran was right. Life *was* short, and he'd always wanted to learn how to ski. What better time to start than right now?

Kai set their bags on the king-sized bed as Jessie secured her skis on a rack near the door. Kai didn't have skis; he'd have to rent some before they joined up with April and Harmony. Coming up behind him, Jessie placed her backpack on the bed. "Wow, Kai, this is nice." She glanced over at the adjoining bathroom and then to a table under the window surrounded by plush chairs.

Then her eyes focused on something that Kai had just noticed. There was a rug on the floor in front of the fireplace. It was white, fluffy, and looked like it could have belonged to an animal at some point, although, Kai was fairly certain the lodge had gone with synthetic fur over the real stuff. It screamed—*have sex here*. They both looked away from the rug at the exact same time.

A few hours later, Kai was sharing a hearty laugh with his cousin, and any earlier tension between them was forgotten. While April and Harmony had left to take turns on the more advanced slopes, Jessie had stayed on the "kiddy" slopes with Kai. She was teaching him the basics of skiing, which basically meant she was laughing her ass off.

When he fell for the umpteenth time, landing on his ass that was starting to feel numb, she giggled. She swooped in to help him up, like gliding across the snow was easy. Kai frowned at her, and at the eight year olds who were whizzing past as effortlessly as if they were walking. Nothing like being surpassed by people a fraction of your age.

Sighing as he took Jessie's hand, he let her pull him upright. She continued to laugh as she brushed the snow off his back. Shaking his head at her joy, he adjusted his poles and experimentally slid his feet back and forth. Kai had been so certain he would pick up skiing easily; he'd thought it would be similar to surfing. He was wrong. But still, he was determined to make it down an adult slope this weekend, and that would be easier to do if his cousin didn't find the whole thing so amusing.

Smirking at her, he said, "You just wait until I get you in the ocean. Then I'll be the one laughing my ass off." Grinning at her, he adjusted his goggles.

Jessie gave him a sweet smile, then chucked a fistful of snow at him. She hit him squarely in the face with the loosely packed ball and it exploded into a fluffy white cloud that coated him like baking flour. She bent over in hysterics, then expertly darted away, sliding along the banks fluidly as if she were a bird gliding among the clouds.

Kai shook the snow off him then awkwardly started out after her. He teetered on his skis, feeling like he was either going to fall on his face or his backside, but eventually he caught up with her. Laughing as she glanced behind herself, Jessie bent low over her skis and pushed for speed on the slight hill. Kai's eyes locked onto the perfect ass she was putting on display for him. *Damn.* Grinning, he pushed harder to catch up.

When he was close enough that he could almost reach out and touch that luscious backside, Kai felt himself begin to lose control. The hill had taken a sharp dip and he hadn't been ready for it. Feeling off balance, he racked his brain, trying to remember if it was the V that slowed him down...or if that made him go faster? Was it the other way? Not knowing what to do, Kai resorted to what he would do if he weren't wearing skis—he picked up his feet and tried to walk. Floundering, he lost his balance and fell over again, forwards this time. Jessie had slowed when she'd noticed he was in trouble, and feeling like a jackass, he plowed right into her.

The force of the hit sent them both tumbling into a thick snow-bank along the side of the run. It cushioned their fall and covered them in a powder-fine blanket of white. Gulping icy air, Kai ripped off his goggles. His legs, arms and skis were all tangled up with Jessie's. He was feeling the ache of the impact, so there was no way he hadn't hurt her.

She was lying beneath him, a light layer of snow hiding her beautiful face. She was so completely still that dread began seeping into Kai. Maybe she'd hit her head. Or maybe she'd broken something, and she was in shock. Jesus, was she seriously hurt?

Worried, he yanked his gloves off and cupped her face. The chill of the snow pricked his warm fingers but he ignored the pain as he gently pulled off Jessie's goggles and brushed the powder from her cheeks and mouth. "Jessie?"

Lying perfectly still, she made no response. Kai wasn't sure much he should move her if she did have a head injury. He tried to gently disengage from her body, but they were tangled so badly, he couldn't tell where he ended and she began.

Fear leeched into his voice. "Jessie, talk to me." He leaned into her, trying to feel the warmth of her breath on his cheek. He couldn't feel it; he couldn't feel anything. Starting to panic, his hands brushed over her face and hair. "Jessie…please talk to me. Baby?"

Her eyes snapped open, and she looked up at him with eyes full of wonder. Kai engulfed her in a hug. "Oh, thank God." Pulling back, he anxiously examined her face. "Are you hurt?" After searching her, he searched the snow around her; everything was still fluffy and white—no red, no blood.

Jessie's lips curved into a huge smile as she started to chuckle. Kai paused in his search for injuries. "Were you fucking with me?" he asked, dumbfounded.

She laughed even more at his language. "I'm sorry, I couldn't resist."

Kai twisted his lips into a scowl and did the only reasonable thing he could think of to retaliate. One hand drifted down to the edge of her jacket and lifted it up, while the other grabbed a fistful of pure, icy snow and plopped it onto her stomach. Her eyes went wide, and she sputtered for a second before letting out a blood curdling scream. Kai started laughing as she squirmed beneath him; they were still so entangled she couldn't get away.

Laughing so hard her eyes were watering, Jessie begged him to let her get up. His frozen hand, cold from handling the snow, slid up her shirt. Jessie screamed again, then begged for mercy as she laughed. Kai laughed with her. "You promise to never do that again?" he asked between chuckles.

She tried to push his hands away, but he was so much stronger she actually lost ground and his fingers slid even further up her clothes. "Yes, yes, I promise," she giggled, her words coming out between screams.

Kai leaned over her, stilling her frantic movements. Grinning down on her, still breathing heavy from the exertion and the fear, he said, "Good, because you scared the crap out me."

Her laughter trailed off along with her screams as she locked gazes with him. It was only then that Kai was aware of just *where* his hand was. His fingers had drifted to the place he'd jealously watched the raindrop traverse earlier, only he was much more intimately connected to her than that drop trailing down her padded jacket had ever been. Cupping her breast, he swept his thumb back and forth over the lacy fabric of her bra. His hand suddenly burned with a tingling fire as it switched from icy cold to red hot.

Kai's gaze dropped to her lips as they lightly breathed on each other, just inches apart now. Jessie licked her lips, and Kai could feel her chest under his fingertips rising and falling in a deeper rhythm, almost heaving. Knowing he should yank his hand away and apologize, he slipped a finger into the cup. He closed his eyes as he felt his skin pass over a perfect peak. His growing erection told him he was skirting dangerous waters and needed to retreat, but the light moan escaping Jessie's mouth spurred him on; he wanted to hear more.

Kai could easily imagine the sounds she would make if his lips closed over her nipple. God, it had been so long since his tongue had rolled around it. He pictured the swells of her snow white skin, the soft pink flesh, and he thoroughly hardened as his finger traced a never-ending circle over her quivering flesh.

"There you are. What *are* you guys doing?"

Kai immediately yanked his hand back and opened his eyes. Jerking his head up, he saw Harmony standing over their prone bodies with an expression on her face that was both worried and amused. Every single part of Kai heated in embarrassment, and his arousal faded to oblivion. God, why couldn't he stop those thoughts when it mattered? And, Jesus, had Harmony noticed any of that? He studied the red-head's face, but he couldn't see any signs of disgust. She hadn't noticed just what she'd interrupted.

As Jessie told Harmony they were stuck, Kai tried to move away from her. It was difficult, since their skis were crossed in awkward ways. Looking down at Jessie, Kai mumbled some excuse to Harmony about falling repeatedly. Jessie's cheeks were pale and her breath was sharp. Being caught had scared the crap out of her, too.

Harmony laughed as she reached down to help. "Here, just lie still." She unbuckled Kai's skis from his boots, then Jessie's. As she helped them untangled their legs, she said, "April headed back to the lodge. I thought I'd find you guys, and we could all get dinner together." She smirked as Jessie and Kai quickly became two separate people again. "Good thing I came for you. You two looked like pretzels."

Harmony laughed, but Jessie looked away. Whether she was embarrassed, mortified, grossed out...Kai wasn't sure. All he knew was that he'd screwed up. He sighed as they followed Harmony back to the lodge. Guess he wasn't as much of an adult as he thought.

18

Sleeping Arrangements

Back at the lodge, Jessie handed Kai her skis and asked him if he could put them in their room. Nodding, Kai watched her immediately turn away and dash after Harmony. Not even looking back at Kai, she climbed the stairs to go get ready for dinner in the girl's room. Kai had gone too far with his teasing, and he could tell he'd made Jessie uncomfortable. He couldn't even tell her he was sorry, because really, how many times could he apologize before it just started sounding ridiculously repetitive. Maybe instead of having *Thank you* put on a T-shirt, like he'd jokingly told her once, he should have an apology printed instead.

Rubbing sore, aching muscles, Kai headed to his room with Jessie's skis. They were bright pink, and he received more than a few odd looks as he walked across the lobby with them. Sighing as he slinked into his suite, Kai put away the flamboyant skis and flopped onto his bed. Taking a moment, he blankly stared at his ceiling and let every ounce of his confusion wash over him in waves. First he was fine, then he was hurt, then he was angry, then he was sad. He wasn't sure where his mood was going to settle by the time he met back up with the girls.

Throwing an arm over his eyes, he considered not showing up, but that would seem weird to Harmony and April, and they might even come looking for him. If they did, he could always play it off as being too sore to do anything but soak in his jetted tub...which actually sounded pretty nice. Exhaling in frustration, he sat up. No, he needed to check on Jessie. He needed to make sure his latest mistake wasn't bothering her too badly. The last thing he ever wanted to do again was make her cry. He'd seen enough of her tears.

Changing into a warm, tight sweater and some jeans, he ran his fingers through his drying hair and mentally prepared himself to see his cousin again. After not having seen her for so long during their forced separation, Kai was becoming increasingly uneasy the longer they were apart. He was certain he wouldn't be able to go back to avoiding her after this. He didn't know what that meant for them in the long run, but he needed her too much to push her away.

Hastily leaving his room, he made his way to the lobby where they'd all agreed to meet up. He had to wait forever, but that was to be expected when three girls were getting ready to go out for the evening. Standing near the front doors, Kai passed the time by watching the snow falling outside through the glass. It was so incredibly beautiful, almost unreal.

Lost in the magnificence around him, he almost missed the sound of girls giggling. Slowly turning around, he spotted them a few steps behind him, watching him watch the snow.

Harmony grinned when he finally noticed them. "Island boy, you're so cute."

Kai felt his cheeks heat and wanted to look away, but Jessie was standing right beside Harmony, and once his gaze locked on her, he couldn't turn his head. He inhaled a deep breath and held it. Her curls were loose around her shoulders, brushing over the marvelous cleavage that she was exaggerating with a deeply cut V-neck sweater dress. It clung to every curve, sliding down her hips in an intimate way. And good God, she had on thigh-high boots. Kai wanted to curse at her for looking so good. Maybe he should have had the *Can you dress ugly for me?* talk after all. The brain ruling his lower body vehemently disagreed.

Jessie smiled under his intense scrutiny, but it was eventually April who brought him back to reality. Coming up to him, she teasingly smacked his shoulder. "Snap out of it. I know you've been surrounded by beautiful women before."

She winked at him and Kai rolled his eyes. "Right," he murmured, shaking his head. He needed to stop letting Jessie distract him from this charade they were acting out. This play where they pretended to not be head over heels in love with each other.

Being as gentlemanly as he could, Kai opened the front door for them. Harmony and April played up their gratitude as they sauntered through. Jessie peeked up at him from under her lashes as she passed. "Thank you, Kai," she whispered. He wanted to sigh in a disgustingly happy way at hearing those simple words falling from her lips. It gave him hope that she wasn't too upset with him.

Settling back into Harmony's vehicle, Kai was once again shoved into the back seat with his cousin. While the girls seemed to be getting along better than before, April still didn't want to sit by Jessie. If Harmony's attempt to smooth things out this weekend didn't work, Kai was going to have a little heart to heart with April. She needed to let go of her hurt and forgive Jessie; Kai knew from experience that Jessie's friendship was worth...well, just about anything.

Almost like April knew Kai was thinking about her, she twisted in her seat to look at him. Her long, black hair was pulled up into an intricately twisted up-do. It highlighted her elegant neck, along with the off-the-shoulder sweater she was wearing. April was sure to get some attention tonight. With an amused smirk, she told Kai, "Don't get too disappointed, but the restaurant we're going to doesn't use plastic utensils." She winked at him before turning back around.

Kai had to smile at her obvious reference to their disastrous first date. Shaking his head, he met eyes with her in the mirror. "Cute...Prima Donna."

She laughed as Harmony pulled out of the parking lot. "And don't you forget it!"

Harmony giggled at her friend as she pulled onto the road, and even Jessie softly laughed. She looked over at him and her hand twitched, like she really wanted to touch him. Kai wanted to touch her too, so badly he had to clasp his hands together in his lap.

The dinner wasn't super fancy, but it was nice enough that it took a while. After drinks, appetizers, main courses, and dessert, Kai was feeling a bit run down. Especially when his body started letting him know that he'd used muscles today that had never known hard labor before; he was sore in places that he hadn't even known could become sore.

When Harmony and April struck up a conversation with a couple of guys sitting at the bar, Kai was certain that the evening was nowhere near wrapping up. He really just wanted to crawl into a ball somewhere and sleep, even if it was the floor. Jessie watched him yawn, then she glanced over at April and Harmony. They had their backs to Kai and Jessie. Harmony was twisting a red lock around her finger, while April was letting out a throaty laugh—flirting at its finest. Returning her eyes to Kai, Jessie rested her hand on his thigh under the table. Kai immediately felt alertness seep into him at the contact. Her touch was better than coffee.

"Come on, we can get a taxi back to the lodge." She nodded her head toward the dark of night visible through the large front windows. Kai wanted to object, to tell her that she could stay with her friends and he'd go back alone, but he found himself nodding at her instead. Smiling, Jessie squeezed his thigh once before standing and walking over to her friends. That dress curved perfectly over her backside, framing it in such a splendid way that Kai couldn't look at anything else.

Jessie spoke with Harmony for a minute. They both twisted to look at him. Thankfully, Kai snapped his eyes to their faces just in the nick of time. Giving them a dopey wave, he ordered his suddenly surging heart to calm down. He desperately needed to stop looking at Jessie like that. Harmony nodded, then gave Jessie a quick hug before separating. The guy Harmony was talking to smiled wider at hearing she was staying. His eyes drifted down to her chest, cleverly being emphasized by a teal wrap shirt that knotted right under her breasts, and stayed there.

Jessie slowly walked back to Kai, her eyes drifting over his chest before settling on his face. She smiled that soft smile that he absolutely loved on her, then extended her hand. With a wide grin, he took it. After helping her put on her jacket, he slipped on his own. Then they waved goodbye to the pair of flirty girls and darted outside.

It was lightly snowing and the traffic on the streets was sparse. Not seeing any cabs, they decided to walk for a ways under the snowfall. Kai was cold, but not freezing. Multiple layers were helping with that, but he swore it was Jessie's presence too. He grabbed her hand, not thinking that he might be crossing a line, just wanting to share the warm feeling in his heart with her. Jessie let out a soft sigh as she leaned into his side. With no one to witness it, they walked a few blocks in the snow, looking more like a young couple in love than two cousins walking off a hefty meal.

Finally hailing a cab, they made it back to the lodge, just slightly damp with melted snow. Kai almost wished they'd never found a taxi; he could have walked the entire way back with her, and been just fine with it. Jessie disappeared into the bathroom when they got to the room, saying she wanted to change for bed. She didn't look as uneasy about the idea as she had at first. Maybe she figured they'd gotten the tension out of their system earlier today, with their heated moment on the slopes. Or maybe walking through the snow had just evaporated her fear. Either way, Kai was happy that she only had a smile on her face as she vanished behind the door.

After scrubbing his hair dry with a towel hanging over the back of a chair, Kai threw on some comfortable lounge pants and a light t-shirt. Not wanting them to be chilly, and also because it was a shame not to use it, he turned on the gas fireplace; it instantly erupted into cheery orange-tipped flames. Glancing at the animal rug spread out before the fire, he rolled his eyes and folded it up. Placing it on the chair under the window, he grabbed a couple of pillows off the bed and an extra blanket he found in one of the drawers. When his sleeping place in front of the fire was prepped, he smiled and sat down.

Kai felt a soothing peace flow into him as he watched the flames lick the logs. It was a peace and warmth that he knew stemmed from love. A deep love, deeper than he'd ever felt before. A love he knew he shouldn't feel...but he did. He smiled as he thought of Jessie in the next room. Thought of her examining herself in the mirror as she brushed out her damp locks. Thought of how she might be biting her lip as she thought about him. Feeling mesmerized by the flames and his fantasy, he wondered what she'd choose to sleep in. He pictured her in black lace. Then he sighed and shook his head. No, if he had to choose, he'd want her going to bed with only her perfect skin to keep her warm. Yes, if it were up to him that was what he would pick out for her.

◆————————————————◆

Jessie quietly left the bathroom with her teeth freshly brushed and her face squeaky clean. She felt great, much better than she'd felt earlier. Once the shock of the room arrangements had finally worn off, and once she and Kai had started playing and having fun together, her tension about them sleeping in the same suite together had vanished. She'd missed Kai. Seeing him again...was indescribable. She almost couldn't stand it when they were apart now. Jessie wasn't sure how she'd go back to avoiding him after this. She wasn't sure if she had the strength to resist calling him or going over to his place. Not anymore.

They'd had an amazing afternoon together. Jessie had playfully teased him every time he'd fallen, and he'd stoically taken it and tried again. She just couldn't resist chucking a snowball in his face though, and she really hadn't thought he'd be able to catch her. He'd surprised her by staying on her tail...then crashing right into it. Even then, wrapped up in his body, she hadn't been able to resist playing with him by faking that she was hurt. And then he'd said *that* word. The warmth that had flowed from his mouth when he'd said it, even mixed with concern, was unlike anything she'd ever heard.

Baby. In his worry, he'd called her baby.

Even his retaliation, once he realized she'd been kidding around, was nothing after hearing that word. And then the seriousness had seeped in, igniting them. And he'd touched her...intimately touched her. She'd been silently begging him to do it, and almost like he'd heard her, he'd dipped his finger into her bra and caressed her. It had nearly been too much. She'd almost climaxed with just that tiny stroking. It had been so long...

Then they'd almost been caught and reality had crashed upon her. She couldn't do those things with her cousin. It was wrong, it was twisted, and if Harmony had noticed...she wasn't sure would have happened. Jessie had stuck close to her side after that, wanting to make sure she didn't suspect anything. Luckily, Harmony had been so excited over the fact that she'd finally tackled the advanced slope that she hadn't thought twice about the odd moment she'd stumbled upon between Kai and Jessie.

Feeling better that Harmony was none the wiser, Jessie had dressed as nicely as she could for dinner. She'd borrowed a dress from Harmony. Her friend was notorious for over packing, and had insisted that Jessie wear one of hers instead of going back for her stuff in Kai's room. While still not wanting to sit or stand anywhere near Jessie, April was being far more civilized after a physically demanding afternoon on the mountainside, and Jessie could tell Harmony had wanted to keep the good vibes going. That was fine with Jessie. Harmony had packed her kick-ass boots for her anyway, and while she couldn't wait to see Kai again, she wasn't sure if she should be alone with him right then. His touch had still been lingering through her veins, boiling her blood. And when she saw the look on Kai's face when she walked into the lobby with the girls, she knew the brief time apart had been completely worth it. The way he'd stared at her had made her body flush with heat, and she was instantly happy that she'd chosen Harmony's dress over plain sweater she'd packed for dinner in her bag.

She'd felt a little odd around Kai at first, same as he had seemed to feel around her, but eventually, through quiet conversations and soft smiles, a feeling had bubbled up between them that had blocked out any disgust or awkwardness. By the time the night was fading, and it was obvious he was tired and wanting to leave, Jessie wasn't thinking about their inappropriate moment anymore. All she felt was joy, warmth, and peace as she walked by his side in the snow. Pressing against him, she felt like she belonged, like it was perfectly natural and acceptable. She'd never felt more content in all her life.

That amazing walk home through the lightly falling snowflakes was what made her feel okay about walking out of the bathroom to share the remainder of the evening with the incredible man waiting in the other room. Jessie couldn't think of anywhere else she'd rather be.

Peeking her head around the wall that separated the bathroom from the rest of the suite, Jessie instantly spotted Kai. He was sitting on a few blankets spread out on the floor in front of the fire, like he intended to sleep there. Jessie smiled as she quietly stepped into the room. They hadn't talked specifics about where they would each sleep, but Jessie had assumed, since she was crashing his room, that she would take the floor. Kai hadn't even asked. He'd just given the bed to her. He was generous like that.

Kai didn't react to her presence when she stepped into the room. He only continued to stare into the flames with a soft smile on his face, completely lost in whatever thoughts were occupying his head. With a knot of hope in her heart, Jessie wondered if any of his thoughts were about her.

She silently watched him as he silently watched the flames. The orange glow threw shadows upon his bronze skin, deepening and highlighting the creamy color, making him seem even more exotic and attractive. The firelight danced in his pale eyes, changing the blue-green into a fiery shade that hinted at the passion buried within him. His arms were loosely slung around his knees as he quietly sat there, thinking.

Jessie's heart thumped a painful rhythm inside her chest. He was so perfect…and so unobtainable.

Wanting to share the fire's warmth with him, since she suddenly felt chilled, Jessie walked over to his side. He snapped out of his daydreams when he felt her standing there.

350

Looking up, his eyes locked onto the sleep-shorts she was wearing before drifting to her face. Tucking her hair behind her ears, Jessie gestured to the floor beside him.

Smiling, Kai nodded and moved over so she could sit on the blanket beside him. Jessie carefully sat down and hugged her knees to her chest. She ran her hands over her bare arms; the shirt she was wearing was worn and comfortable, but didn't offer much in the way of protection. Glancing over at Kai studying her, she wondered if her outfit was inappropriate, given their circumstances: the shorts were a little short, the shirt was a little threadbare. When she'd packed her stuff, she'd planned on being in a room with her girlfriends. Comfort had been her only goal.

Twirling a long lock around her finger, Jessie wondered what Kai was thinking. Was he beating himself up about touching her earlier? He wouldn't if Jessie confessed just how badly she'd wanted him to do it, but while that might ease his mind, it wouldn't help their situation, so Jessie didn't mention it.

She stared at the flames and eventually Kai twisted back to stare at them too. Silence permeated the room, but it was a comfortable one. It wrapped around her, warming her more than the heat the fireplace produced. Jessie couldn't keep the smile off her lips.

"What are you thinking about?" Kai finally asked her.

Jessie looked over at him. He'd brought his arms down between his knees and was rubbing his forearm, like he was sore. He was probably sore all over, considering what he'd done today. Grabbing his arm, she took over for him. She *was* the professional, after all.

Jessie grinned as she watched his eyes flutter closed while she worked on his aching muscles. "Nothing really. I was just thinking that this is nice, being here with you."

Kai opened his eyes and looked over at her. "You're not bothered by...?"

He cringed and Jessie knew what he meant—the incident on the slopes. She felt her cheeks heating, but she shook her head. It had been a mild slip-up. One that she'd wanted him to do. The memory of her cousin touching her in that way should bother her, but as her fingers worked up his arm, she felt nothing bad about the encounter. She was only happy that he was back in her life.

Kai smiled at her response, and let out a pleased sigh when she switched to his other arm. "Yeah, this is nice," he murmured, his face relaxed and content.

Jessie scooted closer to him, so she could move up his arms to his shoulders, where he was probably really feeling the strain of this afternoon. Groaning in relief, he leaned into her hands. Sitting up on her knees, she scooted behind him so she could reach his kinks better. Focusing on the tattooed shoulder blade, her trained fingers worked on taming the knots that had formed in his muscles. She smiled when he groaned again, and loved the fact that she had skills that could help him. She also loved hearing that noise escape his lips. When she felt he was more relaxed on that side, she moved to his other shoulder blade. Her body was firmly pressed against his back, much closer than she would be if Kai were just a client. Kai dropped his head forward as she loosened his other side.

Feeling like she'd done all she could with his aching upper body, she dropped down onto her hip beside him. She was closer than she'd intended to be, with her entire side pressed into his. Kai gave her a sleepy, lethargic smile as he gazed at her. "Thank you. I'm so sore." A light chuckle escaped him and he nestled into her body.

Feeling his words heat her down to her very soul, Jessie contentedly rested her head on his shoulder. He let out a sigh that matched her mood as he rested his head on hers. One of his hands found hers and he began rubbing her palm with his thumbs. Jessie sighed; as a masseuse, she very rarely got treated to massages. It was absolute heaven. Cuddling into his side, she slinked her arm over his thigh so her hand was in a better position for a good rub.

As he massaged her palm, he whispered into her hair, "I missed you, Jessie."

Jessie's heart started racing. She pulled away from his shoulder, and he lifted his head so she could move hers. They stared at each other, their bodies flush together, their faces inches apart. Kai's tropical eyes searched hers. "I missed you ...so much."

Jessie swallowed; her throat was suddenly dry. She clenched his fingers with her hand, stopping the massage. Holding him tight, she whispered, "I missed you too, Kai. Every day."

Exhaling, his forehead came down to lightly rest against hers. Shaking his head, he whispered, "It was so hard to be apart from you. Harder than I ever imagined it would be. I wanted to call you all the time. I wanted to see you all the time. It felt like nothing was really happening in my life, since I couldn't share it with you."

Jessie's free hand came up to cup his cheek. "I felt the same way. I hated hearing about you through other people."

He pulled back to look at her; his eyes were sorrowful. "I wanted to hear your voice," she whispered. "I wanted to see your face."

Letting go of her hand, he reached up to touch her hair. As he watched the dark curls twisting around his fingers, Jessie dropped her hand from his cheek and ran it down his back. Pinching the end of a lock between his thumb and forefinger, he murmured, "I think about you. About...being with you." His voice was low and husky, deep with desire.

Jessie's breath hitched. She knew exactly what he was referring to. They shouldn't talk about that, not here, not completely alone with very little chance of anyone interrupting them. *That* conversation would open too many doors that shouldn't ever be opened. Kai peeked up at her face when she didn't respond.

"I think about that night...that night we first met." His eyes drifted over her features as his hand released her hair and touched her face. He ran a finger along her jaw line, then across her lips. "God, I think about it all the time. I can't stop..."

Dropping his hand, he let his voice trail off. His eyes were sad and wistful as he returned his gaze to the fire. Jessie could see the struggle within him, his painful battle of wanting her and not wanting her. It was a war she was all too familiar with. He suddenly looked so lonely, staring into the flames with moist eyes. Jessie ached *for* him and *with* him, and she desperately wanted him to know that he wasn't alone; she was just as deep in this turmoil as he was.

Tentatively, her fingers came up to his cheek. She gently turned his head, making him look her in the eye. "I think about it too. All the time," she whispered.

Kai's soft smile slowly became a frown. "I wish there was a way to go back." He sighed and shook his head. "To go back to that night, when being with you felt..."

He looked down and Jessie smiled sadly. "When all it felt ...was right?"

Returning his eyes to hers, he nodded. "Yeah." There was so much painful honesty in his expression that Jessie almost couldn't stand it. She wished they could go back too...but life didn't work that way. You couldn't un-know things *that* monumental.

Jessie ran her fingers through his hair, now dry after their romantic walk through the snow. Pulling him down, she rested their heads together again. "We can't go back, Kai. We know now."

He slowly shook his head against hers. "What if we just... forgot?" He whispered that so faintly, Jessie barely heard him. Her heart was hammering so hard she almost couldn't hear her own thoughts. Did he mean what she thought he meant? Jessie pulled back to look at him; his eyes were downcast, he wouldn't meet her gaze. To Jessie, that meant yes, he'd meant exactly what she thought he meant.

She cupped his cheek and forced his head up, making him look at her again; the move also brought their mouths closer together. "We can't, Kai."

Even though she was saying they couldn't, with the heat of his breath on her lips, his body tantalizingly close to hers, and no one around to interrupt them, they could. They'd hate themselves afterwards, but with how much feeling was building between them...they definitely could.

Leaning into her, closing nearly every space between them as he rested his cheek against hers, he muttered, "I know." His hand lifted to her shoulder, and began rubbing a circle into the worn fabric. "I just can't stop...remembering." With a sigh, his fingers left her shoulder and slowly started trailing down her chest. Jessie was sure her heart was going to explode it was pounding so hard, and her breath was already heavy with anticipation. She wanted him to touch her again, and she knew how horrible that desire was.

His breath was stuttered, like he was having trouble keeping it even. "I remember the sounds you made." He whispered it, like he didn't want to say it, but couldn't stop himself. His breath brushing over her cheek, tickled her ear, and desire zipped up Jessie's spine.

She sucked in a quick breath at his words, holding back the erotic groan she dared not make. As she closed her eyes, her fingers returned to his hair. Threading them through the soft strands, she grabbed a handful and tightened. Kai hissed in a breath, then spoke again, a little louder. "I remember your body...on top of mine."

Jessie dropped her mouth open; just his words were making her weak. Pulling him closer, she buried her face in his shoulder. His wandering fingers finally came to rest over her nipple, his thumb gently swept across the peak, causing waves of pleasure to ripple through her. When he spoke again, his voice came out broken, choked with passion and confusion. "I remember your face when you came."

Jessie groaned as she squirmed against his body. She could feel the tension coiling within her, begging for release. Just hearing him talk about it was driving her crazy. "Stop," she gasped, her hand in his hair tightening, releasing, then tightening again. "Stop talking about it, Kai." Desire surged through her in pulses, as she struggled to remember that it was not okay to want him. They couldn't just forget who they were, no matter how much they wanted to.

She rubbed her lips against the warm skin of his throat, wishing desperately that she could kiss him. His fingers drifted off the edge of her breast, then fell to her hip. "I remember driving into you," he murmured, his hand clenching her hip. "I remember coming in you...and it's killing me, Jessie."

His hand suddenly shifted. He ran his fingers up her loose shorts, just to the edge of her underwear. The proximity was too much for Jessie. With a low moan, she dropped her head back. He was going to bring her to release and he hadn't even really touched her yet. It was so wrong. It was so right. He groaned as he pressed his lips against her neck. "I don't see you as Jessica Marie. I see you as Jessie, my Jessie, and I want you. God help me, I still want you." His ran his hand up the side of her hip and fisted her underwear.

Pulling back, Jessie grabbed his face with both hands. Bringing her lips so close they were almost touching his, she fiercely whispered, "I want you too. God, so much. What do we do, Kai?"

Feeling restless, unsatisfied, and confused, Jessie wanted him to turn her away *and* lie her down. His breath was heavy as he clenched and unclenched her underwear. She was positive he wanted to rip them apart, but he was stopping himself from doing it. After another painful second, Kai exhaled in frustration and pulled his hand away. "Nothing, Jessie. We do nothing..."

Disappointment flooded through her, overwhelming her reasoning. Do nothing? No. The ache buried deep inside her was too great to ignore. Jessie didn't think she could "do nothing" anymore. It was too late. She needed him too much. She'd missed him too much. She wanted him too much...

Yanking his face back to hers, she made that connection that they both needed, that they'd both longed for. Her lips wrapped around his and groaning, he automatically began moving against her. They explored each other, and just like before, everything faded away but the electrifying sensation of the movement. As his tongue glided along hers, igniting her, nothing else mattered. Not any of the reasons she'd had to push him away, not any of the reasons he'd had to pull away from her. The only thing that mattered now was how much he meant to her and how much his touch enflamed her.

As his hands moved to her waist, frantically pulling her into him, hers trailed down his chest. Stopping at the edge of his shirt, she began lifting the fabric away from his body. Kai broke apart from their kiss when he realized what she was doing. Looking down, he paused only a fraction of a second before helping her remove his light shirt.

Jessie's fingers trailed over his tattoo before drifting down his abdomen. His eyes fluttered at her touch and he leaned in to find her mouth. Between their passionate kisses, Jessie muttered, "I love your tattoo. I love that no one else here has seen it."

Groaning in her mouth, Kai ran his fingers to the edge of her shirt. Achingly slow, he slid the fabric up her stomach. Jessie helped him once he reached her chest, and tossed the worn sleepwear over her shoulder. Reaching for his face, she brought his lips back to her mouth. Now that she had him, she couldn't get enough.

His palm came up to cup her bare breast, his thumb running over her nipple. "I love the way you feel under my fingers," he whispered.

Jessie allowed the erotic moan to escape her. There was no point in holding back now. Tilting her head to the side, she directed his mouth to her neck. Hissing in a quick breath, his lips and tongue stroked a tender spot in the crook near her shoulder. Jessie panted his name as fire shot through her. She tangled her fingers through his hair while he stroked her chest, squeezed her nipple. His lips returned to hers, his breath and movements filled with urgency. Lost in the moment, she drove her tongue through his parted lips.

Panting, he mumbled, "God, I love how you taste."

Knowing he didn't mean her mouth made the pulsing ache grow painful. She needed him so much. Her hands traveled down his chest. "I love the shape of you," she breathed.

An erotic noise escaped his lips and Jessie knew he realized she wasn't talking about his physique. His hand left her breast and grabbed a fistful of her hair. Twisting it, he sighed, "I love your hair."

Kai gently pulled on it and Jessie sucked in a quick breath as bolts of electricity sizzled along her skin. Grabbing his face, she pushed their eager mouths apart so she could stare into his unbelievable blue-green gaze. "I love your eyes," she whispered, her own hooded with desire.

With a sound very similar to a growl, he reattached himself to her lips; the passion in his kiss stole her breath for a few seconds. Groaning he uttered, "God, I love how it feels to be inside you."

Dropping her head back, Jessie pushed her chest against his. Kai's hands slipped down her hair to her back. He pulled her onto his lap, and hovering above him on her knees, she stared down at him. The firelight danced across their bodies as desire danced across their eyes. "I love how it feels when you're inside of me," she whispered, lowering herself onto his lap.

Kai groaned when their hips met. Jessie couldn't believe how ready for her he was, nearly as hard as she was wet. She let that marvelous firmness press against her core, right where she needed it most. The teasing tension building within her was so unbelievable; Jessie couldn't keep herself from groaning in pleasure. All she wanted was release. All she wanted was for him to give it to her. Over and over...

"Do want me?" she muttered, not even aware she was saying it.

With a ragged exhale, he rested his head against her chest, tantalizingly close to her breast. "Oh, God yes. Yes, I do." His hands clenching her hips, he pulled her against him in a steady rhythm. Breathless, he muttered, "I want to be buried in you. I want to be consumed by you..."

"Oh, God...I want that too." She lied back on the blankets, pulling his neck so he would come with her.

As soon as her back was against the floor, Kai lifted her hips and ripped off her shorts. Sitting back on his heels, he dragged his eyes over her naked body. Jessie could feel the heat from his gaze more than she could feel the warmth from the fireplace. As he pushed off his lounge pants, he shook his head at her. "I love how you care for me," he whispered, reverently.

When the last of his clothing was discarded, he lowered himself over her. Holding himself slightly above her, he gave her a soft kiss. Jessie closed her eyes as his words washed over her. Partially reopening them, she ran her hands up his chest to his face. He was so beautiful. "I love the way you see me," she quietly said.

Closing his eyes, he settled himself on top of her. Jessie could feel his hard body pressing against her, and she wanted to care about how disastrously far they were taking this...but she couldn't. She wanted more. Kai ground his hips against her body as her fingers trailed along his ribs. His erection slid against the slickness of her and they both let out unrestrained groans.

Dropping his head to her shoulder, his hips continually pressing his ready body against the folds of her flesh, he whispered, "Stop me, Jessie...please...stop me." His voice was strained, the ache in it palpable.

Tears in her eyes, Jessie shook her head. It was too late, far too late. She didn't have the strength. "Kai...I can't."

He let out a fractured groan as they slid together. One small shift, that was all they needed. Kissing her neck, he muttered into her skin, "God, what you do to me..."

Jessie's hands ran over every inch of his body that she could touch. She knew exactly what he meant by that. The fine line they'd been walking between friends and lovers...they were crossing it, right now. She couldn't even bring herself to think of all the other lines they were crossing. Taboo lines. Lines that would normally be churning her stomach. But there was too much fire in her belly at the moment, and the ache between her legs was entirely too great. More. She needed more.

Jessie adjusted her hips when he rocked against her again, and they both froze when the tip of him slid inside her. "Oh God...you're so warm, so wet, so perfect..." Kai's voice trailed off into incoherent mumbling. Their bodies shook with restraint as they held that position, then Kai shifted his hips and moved to her side.

Jessie whimpered with the loss of him, and her hand drifted down to feel that wonderful length that she'd almost had inside her again. Kai closed his eyes as she wrapped her fingers around him. "God, I wish we could be together..." he murmured.

She leaned over to kiss his chest. "We are. Just touch me, that's enough."

He lifted his head to stare at her, and so much desire swirled in his features that Jessie almost didn't need his touch to climax. Almost. As she began moving her hand against him, he ran his fingers between her thighs. His eyes never leaving her face, he inserted a long digit. Jessie let herself pretend it wasn't his hand entering her, and she was overwhelmed with a burst of sensation. Closing her eyes, she let out a loud moan as she drifted away on the steadily increasing waves of euphoria coursing through her.

She urged his head to her breast with her free hand, and when his mouth finally closed over her nipple, Jessie wanted to scream as the ecstasy burning through her doubled. God, he knew just how to touch her. She tightened her fingers around the warm hardness of him, and her movements became more demanding. She wanted more from him. She wanted to give more *to* him. Kai groaned against her chest, and his searching fingers became more forceful, as well. Jessie cinched her arm around his neck tighter, pulling him into her as she cried out. His mouth sucked harder, his tongue over her nipple frantic.

Jessie buried her face in the crook of his shoulder, her lips touching the black ink reaching up over the blade. Kai shifted his mouth to her other breast as they panted against each other. They were both being swept away on a river of lust, faster and faster. As Jessie worked her hand over his thick length, her palm sliding easily against him with the wetness of her own arousal coating him, and imagined that marvelous manhood thrusting inside her instead of her hand. She moved her hips in time with his finger plunging into her, and he moved his hips in time with the movement of her hand, but they were out of synch with each other as they tumbled toward release.

Kai slipped another finger inside her, and Jessie gasped and gripped his erection tighter. Groaning, he moved harder against her hand. Jessie moved a leg up over his; their hips were positioned in such a way now, that if they pulled their hands away, they would easily connect.

Jessie rested the heel of her hand on her own body. Still holding him tight, she stopped stroking. Kai stilled his hand as well, leaving his fingers inside of her. Pulling back to stare at each other, they kept their hands still and only rocked their hips, like they were making love. Jessie imagined the stiff fingers moving inside her were the thickness she held in her hand; she rocked against his fingers harder. Kai groaned and rocked against her hand harder. They were perfectly in sync now, having sex, without technically having sex. Jessie closed her eyes, and let the fantasy consume her.

As they thrust against each other's body, Jessie felt the buildup quickly coming. Clenching him tight, she leaned in to find his lips. As the apex approached, she started moaning uncontrollably. It was incredible, her imagination was only adding to the sensation. She was so close…almost there. *God, yes…don't stop.*

Speeding up her hips, she hungrily attacked his mouth. Kai groaned as he sped up his movements as well. Still in perfect synch, she felt the beginning of the wave rushing up on her. Dropping her head back, she loudly cried out as it inched ever closer. Her hand automatically tightened on his throbbing mass between her fingers as she prepared for the release. Watching her, Kai panted in her ear, "I want to come with you. I can't...it's not enough..."

Not thinking about anything but sharing the explosion with him, Jessie twisted onto her back. Removing his hand from inside her, she led him right to the spot where she needed him the most. He slipped inside her effortlessly, not even breaking his rhythm, like he'd always been there. His body tensed as she enveloped him. "No, wait, I shouldn't... Oh God ...yes..."

Kai began thrusting in her in earnest, holding nothing back. Jessie, already so very, very close, immediately started to come. Grabbing his hips, she pushed hers up to meet him, prolonging the burst of euphoria in her body. She cried out repeatedly as the waves swept her away.

He dropped his head to her shoulder as he panted in her ear. "I'm so close...God I want to so bad." With a groan, he started to stiffen like he was about to climax, too. He slowed and started shaking his head. "I shouldn't come in you...I should pull out."

Kai started to remove himself from her and Jessie, still carried away on the best high she'd ever had, pulled against his hips, slamming him back inside of her. Being right on the edge, he immediately cried out, "I can't stop...oh God, yes..."

He grunted and groaned as his orgasm overtook him. Jessie felt the warmth spread through her, and at that moment it only amplified her joy; she felt complete. His body rocked against hers for a few long strokes as they both rode out the bliss. After a few residual groans and pants, they both slumped against each other, spent and satisfied.

But after the high completely faded, a darker feeling instantly seeped inside Jessie. She'd just had sex with her cousin …again. But this time they'd known they were related, and they'd done it anyway. Pulling out, Kai rolled over and stared at the ceiling. His breathing was still fast, but other than that, he was completely silent.

Jessie didn't know what to say, what to do, or how to feel. She stared at the ceiling with him, as small tears fell from the corner of her eyes. Why did the best, most intense connection she'd ever had with anyone, have to be with him? Why couldn't she stop having feelings for him? Things would be so much easier, if she wasn't in love with him.

She closed her eyes after finally admitting that to herself. She was in love him, and not just in the familial way. Needing to process this new information alone, she slowly stood up. Kai sat up on his elbows as she moved away from him. "Where are you going?" he quietly asked.

Wiping the tears off her face, she shook her head. "I just need to go for a walk…get some air."

He nodded and looked away. His face mirrored all of the horror, remorse, and conflict that hers did, and Jessie wondered if he loved her too. For his sake, she hoped he didn't. As quickly as she could, she grabbed some clothes that she could wear in the main lobby. Sitting up now, Kai kept his eyes on the floor. He either wasn't able to look at her anymore, or he was giving her privacy.

Once she was cleaned up and dressed, Jessie went to their door. Pausing, she glanced back at him still on the floor in front of the fire, completely naked and completely beautiful. Knowing she wasn't returning until the morning, she whispered, "Goodnight, Kai."

He finally looked at her, and Jessie was surprised to see tears on his cheeks. "Goodnight, Jessie." His voice was scratchy, like he was barely containing the emotion warring within him. And she could clearly see the emotion now. He did love her...and it was killing him. It was killing them both.

Closing the door, blocking out the devastating grief on his face, Jessie wondered who it was that had said all the world needed was love? Apparently that person had never been in a situation like hers before. An absence of love was what Jessie needed.

19

Time to Say Goodbye

Kai ran his hands down his face, and was surprised to find his cheeks damp. Had that really just happened? Had he really just made love to his cousin, or had he fallen asleep in front of the fire, and all of that had just been some horrible, yet wonderful dream? If his spent body wasn't telling him that he'd—once again—had the best orgasm of his life, he probably could have convinced himself it was just a fantasy, but he wasn't so demented that he could delude himself in that way.

It hadn't been a dream. He really had been thrusting into Jessie. He'd listened to her cry out in ecstasy, felt her body clench around him as she came. And he'd released inside of her. Right now, she was carrying a part of him within her. The thought made his stomach feel like it had just been sliced open.

Standing, Kai glanced down at his limp, fulfilled body. At least one of them was happy about this. Shaking his head, he closed his eyes and debated having another heart to heart with his seemingly independent male parts. He'd already told that stubborn piece of equipment that it couldn't have her. Of all the times to rebel…this was the worst.

Running a hand through his hair, Kai stared into the fire. No, he couldn't separate his body into warring factions like that. The truth was…he'd wanted her, heart and soul, head to toe. He loved her so much he wanted that to happen every night. He wanted to hold her afterwards, kiss her, fall asleep in her arms. Warm, safe…content. He wanted to go slowly with her, take his time making love to her. He wanted to drape her across that damn clichéd animal rug and explore every perfect inch of her.

But it was wrong to feel that way, wrong to want those things. It went against everything he was comfortable with. It filled him with self-loathing. Why couldn't he be stronger? Why couldn't he turn away from her? Why couldn't he shut off his feelings whenever she was near him? He knew he needed to do that somehow, and he also knew that if he really couldn't…then he couldn't stay near her anymore.

Sighing, he shuffled to the bathroom. Kai needed to shower. Having the lingering scent of her on his body was too much to bear. Even still, as he turned on the water, he took a deep inhale, savoring her fragrance on his skin. As much as he wanted to get rid of every trace of her, he also wanted to keep it with him forever.

Annoyed at his body's constant emotional tug of war, Kai glanced at himself in the mirror. He could just see the edge of his tattoo curling around his collar bone. Jessie loved his tattoo, loved that it was something only she knew about. Even something he'd done as a teenager, as a rite of passage with his friends, now reminded him of her. Would anything not remind him of her now? Kai ran his fingers over the black ink as he remembered his past and contemplated his future. He didn't know what to do. For the first time in his life, Kai had no idea what direction to go. Stay? Leave? Ignore her again? Continue their friendship? Somehow.

Seeing the hot steam escaping the open shower door, Kai figured he could start with that. Stepping into it, he sighed in relief. The scalding water pummeling him helped ease the tension in his aching muscles; being surrounded by his favorite substance helped ease his spinning mind. Right at that moment, Kai wished he were back home. He could listen to the surf for hours, could paddle out into the water early in the morning when no one else was around, and could work through his problems with only Mother Nature as his companion. Of course, when he was back at home, his biggest problem had been deciding which twin he should ask to prom. God, how he wished he could return to the easy questions.

Kai emerged from the shower clean if not refreshed, but now that his body smelled like the lodge's generic body wash, he missed the lingering trace of Jessie on his skin. Missed it a lot. Wrapping himself in a towel, he hesitated at the bathroom door. Should he really walk into the room like this, if she *was* back from her walk? And where did she go, anyway? Kai hoped she hadn't gone walking around outside. Bad things could happen to pretty girls who wandered in the middle of the night.

Worry spurring his actions, he rushed into the main part of the suite only to find it empty. He looked around for any sign that Jessie had come back, but everything was exactly how they'd left it. Even their discarded pajamas were still strewn beside the fireplace. Setting his mouth into a hard line, he shut off the stupid, overly romantic firelight. He'd rather be cold than be reminded of what had happened. Picking up their clothes, he shoved them into open bags. Then he folded up the blanket and put it away. Kai couldn't sleep on it now, not when the image of Jessie's pale skin draped across it was burned into his brain.

Without bothering the pretense of getting any sleep tonight, Kai changed into casual clothes. Sitting on the edge of the bed, he played with his hands while he waited for Jessie to come back. He wasn't sure what he would say to her. He was sorry? It seemed like such a tiny word now, one that had lost all its meaning, since they'd used it so much. Plus, she'd technically kissed him first. But then again, he'd stoked her to a boiling point with his damn evocative talk, and even after she'd asked him to stop…

Jesus. None of that should have happened. He should have moved away from her, said goodnight, and let that be the end of it. He should have ignored the warmth and love in the room and they should have gone their separate ways. That was how the evening was supposed to play out. Not like this, with both of them disgusted, and hating themselves for caving into temptation.

Kai sighed as he slumped over his knees. He really didn't like to think of Jessie all alone out there, struggling through this emotional tidal wave on her own. Was she sobbing now? She'd been lightly crying in the room. And damn it, hadn't he thought earlier in the evening that he never wanted to make her cry again? How quickly he'd ruined that.

Standing up, Kai started pacing. Maybe Jessie had gone to Harmony and April's room. Maybe she'd finally confessed to them that she had horrible feelings for her cousin. Maybe she'd told her friends she was in love with him. And he knew now that she was. She hadn't said it, but he'd seen the look in her eyes as she'd said goodnight. She was in love with him, in the same sick, twisted way that he was in love with her. Kai wished she wasn't. It would be so much easier for her if her problem was only that she was attracted to him.

But they were in love. Deeply in love.

Kai watched the clock as he ceaselessly roamed the room, wondering when she'd come back. He wished he knew exactly where she was. Even though his stomach felt like it had been turned inside out, he still needed to know she was okay. The window showed a dark sky outside, with movement in the inky black that suggested it was still snowing. Kai wouldn't get through the night if he didn't know if Jessie was out there or not. He needed to know she was safe.

As Kai strolled out to the lobby, he wondered where to go first. The lights were low since most of the guests were sleeping. It was pretty late, but the bars were still open, so Harmony and April might not even be back yet. Walking up to the glass front doors, Kai tried to peer out to the parking lot, to see if he could spot Harmony's car. It was dark though, and the thick snowflakes obscured his vision. While he couldn't differentiate between the colors of the cars in the dull orange parking lot lights, all of them looking varying shades of gray, Harmony's had a wheel cover on the back and dark, bug deflector on the front. None of the vehicles he saw matched.

Sighing, he turned back to the lobby. If the girls weren't back yet, maybe Jessie had somehow managed to get the front desk to give her a key, and had snuck into the room, waiting for them to come back. He had to know, and that meant, he needed into Harmony and April's room. Determined to be the suave, sexy, flirtatious man who could get any woman do to anything he wanted them to do—which was going to be stretch for Kai—he started walking up to the front desk. He didn't expect the girl who had checked him in earlier to still be there, but he was hoping her replacement would cave into a set of sea-green eyes. Eyes that Jessie loved.

Shaking that thought out of his head, he stepped up to the desk. It was empty, but a small placard proclaimed that the person on duty would be back in fifteen minutes. Kai sighed. They were probably using the restroom or grabbing a bite to eat and would be back soon, but he really didn't want to wait. He needed to be doing something constructive. Not wanting to stand there, looking forlorn and dejected, he decided to wait in the common room.

Looking around the room full of empty chairs and tables, all surrounding a low-burning circular fireplace, filled Kai with a melancholy loneliness. Turning away from yet another fireplace, he looked around for the most comfortable chair in the place, so he could rest his aching body. He found it immediately and smiled when he did. The plush, padded chair looked like you'd sink into it so far, you'd have to be helped back out. Comfortably nestled into the chair was the woman Kai had been hoping to find. She was sound asleep, and her long, curly locks flowed over the arm of the chair as she used it as her makeshift pillow. Sighing and shaking his head, Kai fondly gazed down at his exhausted cousin. Her face was pale, her lips slightly parted as she released shallow breaths. Her cheeks were red and splotchy, like she'd fallen asleep crying. Kai hated that she had.

Kneeling before her, he brushed a strand of hair across her cheek behind her ear. She twitched at his touch, but didn't wake up. "I'm so sorry, Jessie, for everything," he whispered. Leaning over, he softly kissed her cheek. "I love you so much," he said in her ear, knowing she wouldn't hear it.

Jessie stirred and made a noise but didn't say anything and didn't open her eyes. Kai's eyes drifted down her body, then he scooped her into his arms. He couldn't leave her out here alone all night. It wasn't safe, and Jessie meant everything to him. He couldn't abandon her. Family didn't abandon family.

Careful to not wake her, he lifted her up. She grumbled something under her breath and ran her arms around his neck, but she still seemed asleep. Pausing, Kai took a second to enjoy the feeling of her body in his arms, but that feeling was the source of *all* their problems. With a heavy sigh, Kai walked her back to their room.

He fumbled with the room key in his pocket, but eventually he got the door open and staggered inside. Kai was getting tired now, too, since she was safe and secure, and he no longer had to worry about her. Gently closing the door with this toe, he walked her to the bed. He laid her down, then removed her shoes and adjusted the covers around her. Jessie sighed in contentment, stretching before turning away from him and curling into a ball. Kai listened to her low, even breaths, happy that, for once, he could take care of her.

His hand trailed down her back for a second before he yanked it away. He couldn't shut off his feelings for her. He couldn't stop how much he loved her. And now that he'd had her, freely and soberly, he knew he would always want her.

Swallowing a painful lump, he took a step away from her. There was no future for them. At all.

Mind made up, Kai grabbed the pen and the pad of paper sitting on the desk and wrote Jessie a note. He didn't want her to worry when she woke up and found he was gone; he knew how awful it was to not know if the person you loved was all right. After finishing his note, Kai quietly gathered up all of his things. Once he was finished packing, he glanced back at Jessie's sleeping body.

Knowing what he had to do, and knowing it would break both of them, made a tear roll down his cheek. "I'll always love you, Jessie. Always."

More tears followed the first, and he quickly opened the door and walked through it before his resolve completely left him. Walking to the front desk, he was relieved to see that the night person was back. She blinked sleepily, then opened her eyes wide when she saw a guest who was obviously checking out.

"Hello, sir...is there a problem?" Tilting her head, she seemed a little nervous about the prospect of having a disgruntled customer on her shift.

Swallowing back the bile of regret in his throat, Kai shook his head. "Um, no...I just..." He handed her the room key and his credit card. "An emergency popped up back home and I need to leave." The woman smiled politely, but it was obvious she was relieved that she wasn't going to be yelled at. Nodding, she took his information and started pressing buttons on the computer. While she worked, Kai pointed back down the hallway. "My cousin is still using the room tonight, so...don't kick her out or anything."

The woman gave him a comforting smile. "No problem, sir, you've paid through checkout tomorrow, so she can use the room until eleven."

Kai nodded, wondering what Jessie would think when she woke up back in their room with Kai and all his stuff gone. Hopefully the note he'd left properly explained things. He wished he could explain in person, but it was better this way. For both of them. Sighing, Kai pointed at the phone on the front desk. "Do you think you could call me a cab? I need to get back to Denver."

The woman paused while reaching for the phone. "Are you sure? Denver is a couple of hours away. That's going to be an expensive cab ride."

Kai glanced back at the hallway where his cousin—the love of his life—lie sleeping. Feeling like joy would never touch him again, he twisted back to the curious girl at the counter. "Yeah...I'm sure."

—————————⬤————————————⬤—————————

Jessie's eyes flew open. Her heart raced as foreboding flooded through her. Looking around, she tried to recall where she was. She didn't remember falling asleep, but she was sure she hadn't been lying down anywhere, and as her arms curled tighter around her legs, all she knew with certainty was that she was lying down.

Her hand stretched out to touch the heavy quilt on top of her and reason started to filling in the blanks of her memory. She was in one of the lodge's rooms. But whose room was it? Dread washed over her in waves. Had a stranger carried her back to their suite...for who knows what? The rational side of her brain immediately told her that was ridiculous. Women who were absconded weren't tucked into rooms in the same hotel where they were staying. No, if something nefarious had happened to Jessie, she would have woken up in the back of a van, gagged and tied.

Relieved that at the very least she was safe, she slowly sat up. In the early morning light of dawn, she could clearly see that she was back in her own room. Logically, that could only mean one thing: Kai had found her, picked her up, and gently put her to bed. She'd been so out of it, physically and emotionally drained, that she hadn't even noticed her cousin's loving attention.

Her cousin.

Her heart squeezing in pain, she looked around the room for him. They should talk about what happened. They should talk about what they were going to do next. Jessie was so torn on the matter, she felt like two different people. Half of her wanted to tell Kai that it was one of the greatest nights of her life. She wanted to beg him to forget everyone else, to forget all the taboos, and let the love between them grow unrestrained. The other half of her wanted to spend a good hour in the bathroom, scrubbing every inch of him off her. No matter how much they cared for each other, there was something intrinsically sick and wrong about what they'd done. The "ick" factor was too strong to ignore...or forget.

She'd made love to her cousin.

Jessie had spent a good chunk of last night crying—horrified over what they'd done, but mostly, aching. She wanted him, she needed him, she loved him...and he was just out of reach. Unobtainable. It was like a railroad spike had been wedged right in the middle of her heart. She couldn't pull it out, and she couldn't leave it in there. How the hell did they move on now?

As she finally noted the emptiness of the room, her uneasiness returned. Where was he? The space in front of the fireplace was empty, and the bag that had been tossed beside the table under the window was gone. Its absence alarmed Jessie the most. Had he left the lodge? Would he really take off without saying goodbye, without talking to her about what had happened?

Jessie shot up off the bed. Lamely, she searched every nook and cranny of the room hoping to find him, and hoping that if she couldn't, it was only because he was out getting some coffee, and any second he'd walk back through the door. But all of his things were gone, and there was no trace of him left in the room. Even still, Jessie clung to the hope that he had just changed rooms, and he was still here in the lodge somewhere. Then she found his note.

She'd almost overlooked the pad of paper sitting alone ominously on the desk. But then she'd noticed the swirling handwriting splashed across the page, and stopped dead in her tracks. Letters left behind for people to find were seldom filled with good things. Jessie's heart thudded in her chest as she tentatively approached the pad of paper. Scared of what it might say, she slowly began reading it.

My dearest Jessie,

I know it's too little, too late, but I'm so sorry about last night. That shouldn't have happened, and I promise you, it won't ever happen again. I'm making sure of it this time. I decided to go home. I just couldn't stay, and I'm so sorry for that. I wish you only the best, cousin. I'm going to miss you so much.

Love always,

Kai

So many things about the letter brought Jessie to the edge of panic. He couldn't stay? He decided to go home? He was making sure last night never happened again? He was going to miss her? It all sounded so much more serious than him just going back to Denver. It sounded...permanent. Like he was truly leaving, like he was heading back home...to Hawaii. The thought of him giving up everything he'd built and worked for her, because of...her...it killed Jessie. It wasn't right. He shouldn't have to leave. They should be able to make this work...somehow.

Jessie tried calling him, to reason with him, to beg him to stay if she had to, but his phone went straight to voicemail. She opened her mouth to leave a message, but the words wouldn't form. She needed to speak to *him*, not a machine. Knowing she couldn't stay in this lodge a second longer, Jessie gathered up all of her stuff. She just couldn't hang out while Kai was making plans to leave the state. And she knew, without a shadow of a doubt, that that was what he was doing. That was his solution to make sure they never crossed that line again.

Once Jessie had her skis and her bags, she strolled down the hall at a fast pace. When she passed the front desk, she paused. Would they know anything about Kai leaving? Even just knowing how long ago he'd left would help. *How much of a head-start did he have?* If the window was small enough, Jessie was positive she could catch him. At the front desk, an energetic man was chatting with a tired woman. She seemed exhausted, like she'd been up all night, but she still giggled at something the man said and playfully put a hand on his shoulder; the guy seemed clueless that the girl was flirting with him.

Deciding that they could at least tell her if he'd settled the room bill or not, Jessie walked up to the cozy pair. The man instantly snapped to attention, giving Jessie a glorious smile. The tired woman took a little longer to shift into professional mode.

"Good morning, Miss," the man said. "Are you checking out?" He eyed her bags and skis, appraising what needs she might have of him.

Jessie had no idea what her needs were…other than information. "I was hoping you could tell me when a guest checked out last night."

The man frowned at her in the most polite way a person could frown. "I'm sorry, Ma'am, but that information is confidential. Company policy." He gave her an apologetic smile. The woman beside him discretely ran her eyes down his body.

Jessie sighed in annoyance. "Well, it was my cousin and… there was a…problem and he had to leave suddenly…and…" Jessie had no idea what to tell him that could possibly circumvent the lodge's privacy policy. Frustrated tears sprang to her eyes, and she knew she was seconds away from a meltdown.

The woman perked up, raising an eyebrow. "That was your cousin?" She eyed Jessie appraisingly, like she didn't see the resemblance, but then she shrugged. "You don't have to worry about the room, if that's your concern. He settled the bill when he turned in his key. You can use the space until checkout at eleven, just hand in your key before you go." She gave Jessie a wide smile, like she was sure that information had just solved all her problems.

Jessie leaned toward the woman as much as she could. "You were here last night when he left?"

As if to emphasize how long ago that was, the woman yawned as she nodded. "Yeah, he said he had an emergency and needed to leave, but he wanted to make sure you could stay. I called him a cab."

Jessie's eyes widened. "A cab? To Denver? When?" She couldn't even comprehend how much that had cost him. Had he really needed away from her so badly?

The woman tilted her head, thinking. "It was just after my break so maybe...1:30?"

Jessie looked away as her tears came dangerously close to falling. Outside, the front door was being lit by the warm rays of the early morning sun. The entire glass masterpiece gleamed orange. It reminded Jessie of the firelight last night. It also reminded Jessie that Kai had had plenty of time to get home and start making arrangements...to leave.

The man beside the woman scoffed and Jessie returned her attention to him. "There's no way a cab drove him home," he said to his coworker.

Jessie scrunched her brows. "What do you mean?"

Throwing on his professional face, he looked over at Jessie. "Denver is too far. Unless he was carrying a thick stash of cash, no cab driver would have driven him that distance." He shrugged. "They'd lose too many other fares if they did. The buses around here only drive within the county, so the cab probably took him to the shuttle pickup in Frisco. That goes to downtown Denver daily."

Jessie smiled. Maybe he was maybe still there then. "Do you have a schedule of the pickup times?" Nodding, the man rummaged through his papers until he found one. Eager for some sort of information on her cousin's whereabouts, Jessie snatched it from him. Relief hit her when she saw that the earliest departure time to Denver was 6:30am, with an arrival time a little after 8:00am. If he truly hadn't been able to catch a cab home last night, then he'd only just left a little while ago. She hated that he'd spent the night in a grimy transfer station, but she loved the fact that he wasn't on his way to an airport right now.

Jessie returned the brochure to the man, thanked them both for their help, then gathered her things so she could go wake up her friends. As she walked away, she heard the woman seductively murmur, "I didn't know about that shuttle." Then she heard him reply in a low voice, "These are the things you have to know working here." By the flirty tone, Jessie reconsidered how oblivious he was to the fact that his coworker wanted him. They probably didn't have the obstacles in their lives like she and Kai had; she hoped they went for it.

When Jessie got to Harmony and April's room, she started pounding on the door. She was painfully aware that it was really early in the morning, and annoyed guests around her were going to call the front desk and complain about the noise, but Jessie had an abundance of nervous energy rushing through her and she couldn't calm down enough to causally knock. She had to get to Kai—fast. She couldn't let him leave town like this.

As she pounded on the door, she heard muffled cursing and what sounded like someone falling to the ground. Muttered oaths to kick someone's ass filtered through the door, and Jessie suddenly remembered that her friends had been out late last night, flirting with boys. They might even have company in the room with them, and that might complicate things. But it didn't matter. If the boys were there, they'd have to get up and get out. Jessie needed her friends.

Blinking in the much-brighter hallway light, Harmony appeared in the crack of the door. Her hair was wild and messy, making the redhead look like she'd been electrocuted recently. Rubbing the sleep from her eyes, she gazed at Jessie like she was sure she was hallucinating. "Jessie? What the...?" Letting her voice trail of, she threw the door wide open; she looked completely awake now as she studied Jessie's face. "What's wrong? What happened?"

That was when Jessie realized that the tears she'd been holding in had started gushing down her cheeks. She brushed them away in irritation. She couldn't lose it right now; time was ticking away from her faster and faster. Jessie took a deep breath to steady her voice. "I'm sorry, I know it's early, but I need a huge favor." Before she even finished speaking, Harmony was nodding and motioning her inside.

April grunted on her bed and sat up on her elbows. At seeing Jessie, she glanced at the clock on the nightstand, then back to Harmony closing the door. "Jesus, Jessie? What the hell? Is there a fire or something?" Sitting up, she flicked her eyes around the room, like she was searching for the flames. Under normal circumstances, that might have made Jessie laugh, but not today. Nothing about today was normal.

Jessie set down her stuff and sat on the edge of Harmony's bed. Harmony sat beside her and rubbed her back. Noting that there weren't any visiting boys in the room, Jessie exhaled a shaky breath. "It's Kai...he left last night." Her eyes shifted over to Harmony. "I'm sorry, I know you really wanted to spend all afternoon here, but I need to go home..." Her voice trailed off, guilt stealing it.

Biting her lip, Harmony looked over at their skis by the door. Jessie knew what she was blindly asking her friend to do was hard for her. This was Harmony's favorite thing, and this weekend was supposed to be about the three of them enjoying it together. Now Jessie was asking her to forfeit their last few hours here to go chase after a boy. Even to Jessie, it sounded unfair.

At hearing Jessie's pronouncement, April sat up and scooted to the edge of the bed, closer to Jessie. "Kai? He left? Is he okay?" While she and Kai might not have worked out in the romantic sense, she liked him, and the concern apparent on her tired face was genuine.

Jessie felt another tear slide down her cheek as she shrugged. She really didn't know if he was okay or not. The last she'd seen of him, he'd been staring after her, looking to be on the verge of the same epic breakdown she'd had. Jessie had to imagine that wherever he was right now, he was anything but okay. "I'm not sure. He left while I was sleeping."

Harmony's eyes slid back to Jessie. "He didn't say why he was taking off? He didn't wake you up and say goodbye?" Her brows narrowed as she tried to reason out why he would do that. "Did you guys have a fight or something?"

Jessie opened and closed her mouth a couple of times. She had no idea how to answer her. She couldn't tell them what had happened. They'd be horrified. She couldn't mention the note. They'd want to read it, and it was too...intense...for cousins. Feeling her cheeks heat as she thought about what to say, she suddenly remembered what the woman downstairs had said. "The person at the front desk told me he'd mentioned an emergency...or something." She looked between her friends. "I just, I don't know what that means, and I need..." Swallowing a knot in her throat, she murmured, "I really need to see him."

Harmony nodded as she patted Jessie on the back. "Of course. We'll go home, make sure he's okay." She looked over at April as she got off her bed and came over to sit on Jessie's other side. Returning her eyes to Jessie, Harmony asked, "Can we eat first? Maybe do a run or two?"

Feeling even worse, Jessie shook her head. "I know I'm spoiling the weekend, but I'd really like to leave as soon as possible. He's only a half hour or so ahead of us, and he has to get a taxi to his place from wherever the shuttle drops off at. We could get there at the same time...if we left now." Her voice shaky, she looked between her friends. "I just really want to make sure he's okay." And that he wasn't making arrangements for a flight back home.

Harmony gave her an encouraging smile. "Hey, it's okay. He would have woken you up if it had been anything really serious. Maybe it was just a work thing?" She shrugged after her attempt to lighten Jessie's worry, and if Jessie hadn't known the truth about Kai's dilemma, she might have been relieved by Harmon's suggestion. As it was, she could only nod as Harmony got to work shoving things into her bag.

April slung an arm around Jessie's shoulders, and Jessie leaned into her, grateful. It was the first time in a long time that April had been anything other than snarky with her. "She's right, you know. Kai would have told you if it were a family emergency." She shrugged in an adorable way. "I mean, that would affect both of you, right? He'd want you to know." She smiled like what she'd just said was a positive thing. Jessie wanted to cry again.

Seeing the despair on her face, April squeezed her tighter. "Hey, I'm sorry about throwing a fit over the rooms. Threatening to leave...giving you no other choice but to stay with him. That was kind of petty. I was just...hurt, I guess." She leaned her head on Jessie's shoulder while Jessie sniffled. "Harmony and I talked a lot last night, and she's right...I was being bitchy about the whole thing." Glancing up at Jessie, she gave her a small smile. "It's not like I haven't called you worse." April winked at her and Jessie managed a small laugh.

With a sad sigh, Jessie thought of everything that had happened between her and April recently, and all of it was because Jessie had tried to place April between herself and Kai. Truly a bad idea. All she had done was added jealousy into the relationship with her cousin, and strained the relationship with her friend. And the worst part was, she couldn't explain any of that to April. "I am so sorry I went off on you." Blushing, she added, "I know it's a poor excuse, but it really was more about him than you."

April put her hand over Jessie's and squeezed. "Yeah, the girl in his past that he can't let go of. I know, he told me." Jessie felt a tightness around her heart. That girl was her, but April didn't know that. April's face brightened as she sat up straighter on the bed. "Hey, maybe that's it! Maybe it's the girl? Maybe she realized what an idiot she was being, called him, and begged him to come back. Maybe he fled in the middle of the night to run to her." She let out a romantic sigh and shook her head. "I bet by tonight, he's on a plane back to Hawaii, where she'll be waiting for him at the airport. Then they'll kiss, an orchestra will play, and everyone will live happily ever after."

Jessie closed her eyes. April had just unknowingly played out her greatest fantasy, but it wasn't reality. No, in the real situation, Kai wasn't running to Hawaii to get the girl, he was running to Hawaii to get *away* from the girl. Away from her. He could very well be on a plane by tonight, heading home... alone. No orchestra would be waiting for him and there would be no happily ever after with the woman he loved. Not in this fairy tale.

Harmony paused in packing her bag to smirk at April. "Well, aren't you the closet romantic?" Grabbing a pair of pants, she chucked them at April. "Now pack up, I'm not doing it *for* you...again." Harmony pursed her lips while April stuck out her tongue.

What felt like an eternity later, the girls were all piled in Harmony's car, ready to leave their getaway spot. Harmony let out a sad sigh as she cast longing glances at the lodge in her rearview mirror. Jessie felt guilt resurface, but she just couldn't sit around and try to have fun for a few hours while Kai slipped farther and farther away. She didn't blame him for planning on leaving, for going back home. She just couldn't stomach the thought of him leaving her without saying goodbye.

And besides, Jessie could make it up to Harmony with another trip in a couple of weekends. If there was one thing that was easy to do in Colorado, it was ski in the wintertime. Maybe she'd treat her friends to the best room in the lodge, as a way to thank them. That was, if she ever felt like doing anything fun again.

Sighing, as she hoped for the millionth time that they were gaining on him, Jessie felt April beside her pat her knee. "Hey, relax. I'm sure he's fine." Jessie gave her a half smile, not really in the mood to chitchat about Kai. April brightened as an idea struck her. Digging through her jacket, April pulled out her cell phone. "Did you try calling him?"

Jessie slowly nodded. "Yeah…it went straight to voice mail. Maybe the battery died?" Or maybe he shut the phone off? She didn't mention that possibility though.

April tried him anyway, but she got the same result as Jessie. Jessie bit her lip to keep the tears at bay. She hated the idea that Kai might have intentionally shut the phone off — intentionally shut her out. That was a whole new level of torture. April frowned as she put her phone away. Then, with a small smile on her face, she said, "Want to hear about the guys from the bar last night? It might take your mind off things?"

Jessie smiled softly, and April bit her lip. "Mine was a tight end for Oregon State…and yeah, he had a very tight end." She giggled while Harmony shook her head.

Jessie managed a tiny laugh. "Sure, tell me all about him." Anything to stop worrying about Kai.

Settling in, Jessie listened to her friends talk about all the fun, innocent flirting they'd done last night. Jessie tried not to let it happen, but words and sounds of her own night with Kai filtered through her head while they spoke, breathing in her ear, whispering how he needed her, how much he thought about her, her own sounds as he finally entered her. Telling her that he couldn't stop, the erotic noise he made when he came…

It was a devastatingly long drive home with all of that in her head, and by the time Denver rolled into view, Jessie's stomach was knotted so tight, she wasn't sure if it would ever relax. Jessie told Harmony how to get to Kai's place. When she pulled up to the apartment building, Harmony stared at it with an odd expression on her face. Too anxious about Kai to care why Harmony looked perplexed, Jessie opened her door.

"Isn't this where Ricardo lives?" Harmony's voice froze Jessie in place, with one foot on the sidewalk and one still inside. Oh God, she'd forgotten all about the fact that her roommates had been here before.

April scrunched her nose at Harmony while Jessie's heart started thudding in her chest. "Ricardo?" April asked, confused. Then her eyes widened and she looked over at Jessie. "Oh, the Latin lover one night stand. We picked you up here that night?"

Jessie shook her head and shrugged. Drunken memory loss seemed like her best option. "I really have no idea. I doubt it was the same place." Stumbling out of the vehicle, she prayed her friends didn't start putting the pieces together now; she had enough turmoil going on inside.

Harmony leaned over the seat. "No, it was definitely this place. I remember the design on the door." She let out an undignified snort. "Oh my God, how funny that Kai lives in the same building." She grinned impishly at Jessie. "Do you think he knows Ricardo? Maybe they've run into each other in the hallway."

April laughed at that and started humming, "It's a Small World After All." Eager to end the conversation, Jessie quickly said, "Can you guys take my stuff home?" Still humming, April nodded. Jessie paused a moment to appreciate the friends who had done so much to help her, and not just this morning either. She really was blessed. Giving them each a warm smile, she shook her head. "Thank you, guys so much for doing this. You both really mean a lot to me, I hope you know that."

April tilted her head, then leaned out the door and pushed Jessie farther away. "Don't get all mushy on me, I feel guilty enough." She gave Jessie a quick wink, closed the door, then rolled down the window and blew her a kiss. "We love you too."

Harmony agreed with her sentiment, then added, "Let us know if Kai is okay. He's family, so, we love him too."

Jessie nodded and waved as Harmony pulled away. She had no idea what she'd tell them about Kai. She didn't want to have to manufacture an emergency, but she couldn't tell them the real problem. Jessie was stuck in her lie and she really, really hated that feeling.

Walking through the door of Kai's apartment building, her loud heart started pounding even harder, and her palms grew slick with sweat. Jessie didn't know if they'd beaten him back here or not. Maybe he'd gotten home much earlier than she realized, and he'd already gone to the airport. Maybe he was already on a plane…leaving her. Woodenly, she shuffled to his door. She stood in front of it, listening for sounds. Something, anything. It was completely quiet though. Holding her breath, she raised a hand and knocked.

No one answered her. She tried again, louder, but still nothing. Feeling desperate, she wrestled with the doorknob, but it was locked. Her rational voice began screaming at her that Kai wasn't in there so making more noise wouldn't help anything, but her heart didn't want to accept the possibility that she'd missed him. Not able to give up, she struck the door with the side of her hand. "Kai!"

"Jessie?"

The sound had come from down the hallway, and Jessie immediately turned toward it. Kai was standing in front of the elevator, staring at her like he was seeing a vision that couldn't be real. Jessie let out a long, cleansing exhale. He was still here. She wasn't too late. Emotionally exhausted, she sagged against his door as he slowly approached her. He was still carrying his bags from the trip, so he hadn't even been home yet; she *had* beaten him. His face was worn, his eyes heavy with weariness. It seemed that he hadn't slept at all.

Amazement was in his eyes as he stepped in front of her. "How...? What are you doing here?"

Straightening, Jessie took a step toward him. "You left? You just...left?"

Kai looked away, his shoulders slumping. "I had to, Jessie. I couldn't stay. Not after..." His gaze on the floor, he pointed at his door. "Let's go inside." He dangled the keys in his hand and Jessie stepped aside so he could unlock his place. His body brushed against hers as he opened the door and stepped through, but he still kept his eyes from her.

Her heart hurting, her stomach churning, and fear permeating every cell, Jessie tentatively followed him into his apartment. *The* apartment. The place where this whole mess had started.

Kai set his bags down in the kitchen and leaned back against the counter with his hands carefully tucked behind him. Still not looking at her, he stared at the floor. As she closed the door behind her, she wanted to cry again. He couldn't even look at her. Jessie stayed with her back against the door, forcefully ignoring the memory of her back being shoved against that door. Things were so different now than that night, back when he'd only been the elusive "Ricardo" that her friends loved to tease her about.

Her voice warbling, she finally broke the silence in the room. "Kai...?"

She couldn't say any more than that, but it was enough to make Kai finally look at her. His eyes were wet. "I needed to get away from you, Jessie, because staring at you in that bed ...all I wanted to do...was join you."

Jessie closed her eyes; the words washing over her were as soothing as his hands had been earlier. He hadn't fled in disgust. He'd fled from desire, from love. Opening her eyes, Jessie wondered if that was any better. His pained eyes confirmed that he didn't think it was. He shook his head. "I can't let myself cave into these feelings I have for you. It's wrong, Jessie." Kai shrugged, his expression tired and hopeless.

Jessie begged the water in her eyes not to fall; she didn't want to cry again. "I know," she told him. He nodded and looked down again, and once again the room swam with quiet tension. "Are you leaving?" Jessie whispered into the stillness. One tear disobeyed her. Traveling down her cheek, it dripped to the floor with a heavy splash.

Kai glanced at her glistening cheek before returning his gaze to her eyes. He seemed torn, like he wanted to sweep her into his arms, but also wanted to keep his distance. Swallowing, he looked between her and the door she was leaning against. "Is that why you rushed here? You thought I'd come home, get my stuff, and head back to Hawaii...today?"

Closing her eyes, Jessie nodded. She felt him take a step toward her, heard his shoes move across the linoleum. "Jessie, I would never leave here without...saying goodbye first."

When she opened her eyes, he was standing a few steps in front of her, his arms loose at his sides. Jessie couldn't help but note that he hadn't said he wouldn't leave. "But you are, aren't you? You're leaving Denver?"

He looked down again, and Jessie saw a tear fall from his eyes to land on his jeans. Jessie's stomach wrenched. "Not today..." he whispered.

She took a step toward him. "Kai..."

His hand came out to stop her from getting any closer. "I can't be around you, Jessie. I thought it would get easier...but it's only gotten worse." He looked up at her, telltale tracks on his cheeks. "The more I get to know you, the more I want you. You're perfect for me. Take away the fact that we're family, and you're *perfect* for me." He shook his head. "And I think that's what really kills me. You're everything I could have asked for...and I can't have you."

Kai lips compressed as he struggled to not lose control, to not breakdown. Jessie nodded. "I know. You're all I've ever wanted."

Shaking his head, he closed his eyes and ran a hand through his hair. The hand trembled, along with his voice. "I thought that we could get through this...attraction together, but it's gone so far beyond that now, I don't think it's even possible to work through it."

Jessie stepped forward. Standing a foot away, she reached out and swiped her thumb under his tired eyes, drying the tear marks. He let out a soft exhale as he leaned into her touch. "What are you saying, Kai?"

His eyes slowly opened, and a new tear ran over Jessie's thumb. "We need...space, Jessie." Reaching up, he grabbed her hand and pulled it away from his skin. His words mixed with his action in an ominous way that caught Jessie's breath. As his tropical eyes searched hers, he whispered, "We tried just being family, we tried placing another person between us, and we even tried not seeing each other." He shook his head as Jessie felt her own tears freely falling down her skin. His sad eyes watched them as he continued. "And all that did…all that lead to was the two of us…"

Stopping, he bit his lip. Jessie flushed as thoughts of their last encounter ran through her mind again. His eyes flicked over her face. "Even now, I want to hold you, I want to kiss you, and I want to tell you that I…I…" He stopped again and sighed. "And I can't. I shouldn't. Because this is wrong."

He released her hand still in his, and took a step away from her. "If we stay in the same city…if we stay around each other at all, it's going to happen again. Our lives are too connected. With Gran, with your friends…the world is too small." Kai averted his eyes, like he couldn't bear to look at her directly while he was breaking her heart. "I can't do this. I can't hurt my family like that. I can't let you hurt *our* family like that. As much as I want you, as much as I need you, this is wrong, Jessie. It's twisted and sick and…" he looked back at her, his eyes hurt, tired, and apologetic, "…and I can't stop thinking about you. So…for now…I need to go home."

Jessie felt her chest constrict. She couldn't breathe. Somehow, she managed to croak out, "Will you come back?"

Another tear fell from his eye as he shrugged. "I don't know."

She nodded, feeling dizzy. Not knowing how she'd survive the pain just starting to eat a hole through her stomach, she muttered, "If not today, when will you leave?"

393

Kai sighed, and his hand started to reach out to her before dropping back to his side. "I need to let work know that I've had a change of heart. I thought I'd give them two weeks, starting tomorrow..."

Jessie found herself stepping back, running into the door. She was grateful for its hard, unforgiving shape; it was the only thing keeping her upright. Two weeks? That was all the time she had left with the love of her life?

Her hands lifted to her cheeks as she struggled with the simple act of standing and breathing. Who knew that things she'd been doing since infancy, could suddenly become so hard? But the pain she felt was so much worse than any other pain a boy had given her. It made the crushing blow of discovering Jeremy's betrayal seem like a pleasant experience in comparison. And it was ten times worse, because she knew he was right. She couldn't be angry with Kai, because he was doing the right thing. If he stayed in Denver, even if they tried to never see each other, life would find a way to cross their paths, and they would cave again. They loved each other too much to resist the pull. She was positive of that now, and so was Kai. That was why he was breaking his own heart to put himself as far away from her as possible, and Jessie knew that she had to let him leave. They shouldn't be together. They couldn't be together. Even still, she had no idea how to be apart from him either.

As she felt herself starting to sink to the floor, Kai's arms were suddenly around her. He gave her strength, helping her stand, and she clutched at him, never wanting to let him go. Her arms cinched tightly around his neck, and his arms wrapped completely around her ribs. She finally felt whole...

and it sickened her. Weeping into his shoulder, she managed to get out, "Can I be there…at the airport, when you leave?"

Kai pulled back to look at her, his fingers coming up to brush her tears away. Nodding, he rested his head against hers. "Yeah…I'd like that." He sighed as he shook his head. "No, I *need* that."

She exhaled a stuttered breath and unintentionally brushed her lips against his. "We shouldn't see each other until then," she whispered.

Kai choked back a sob as his lips brushed against hers. "I know," he murmured.

Jessie allowed a tender kiss between them. It was short, but held far more emotion than any other kiss she'd received in her lifetime. Immediately after their lips parted ways, she whispered, "I'll miss you, Kai."

He let out a broken exhale. "I'll miss you too, Jessie."

They reluctantly pulled apart from each other, neither one wanting to let go, but both knowing they had to. Kai cupped her cheek when they were a foot apart, searching her face like he was memorizing it. Then he kissed her forehead. Jessie closed her eyes as he murmured into her skin, "Goodbye, cousin."

He stepped away from her so she could open the door. With her hand clenching the doorknob so hard she knew she'd be bruised in the morning, Jessie spent long seconds gazing at him — his exotic beauty — the stunning eyes, the deep skin, the intricate swirls of his hidden tattoo. And all of his physical attractiveness overshadowed by the goodness in his heart — it seared her. Jessie didn't think she'd ever love anyone else the way that she loved him. Her voice calmer than it had been since she'd entered this fateful apartment, she told him, "I love you, Kai."

His lips curled into a small, sad smile. "I love you too... Jessica Marie."

20

Truth Hurts

Kai woke up Monday morning feeling a ripping pain in his stomach that he hadn't felt since he'd first discovered the truth about Jessie. He knew what he had to do, and he knew it was the right thing to do, but that didn't make his decision any easier. If anything, it was harder. Because a part of him wanted to ignore what was right. A part of him wanted to race to the woman he loved, a woman who loved him back. They'd finally admitted it to each other, and instead of the declaration being a heartwarming moment that brought two people together, it was driving them apart. Thousands of miles apart.

Sitting up on his bed, Kai stared at the river rock photograph that Jessie had given to him. She was so caring, so wonderful. He couldn't imagine his life without her in it. But he had to go. It was time to return to the home he'd left behind. Life had been so simple when he'd boarded the plane to come out here. Thinking about how different the return flight was going to be filled Kai with dread. It was going to be so hard to leave, especially with Jessie there, seeing him off.

Kai sniffed and stared at his sheets. That might be the last time they see each other. Ever. He couldn't truly comprehend it, and tried to think of ways around the finality of that ending. Maybe they could try not seeing each other again. Maybe, if Kai cut off all ties with April and Harmony, he'd lessen his chances of running into Jessie. But Gran…there was no way around that one. Their mutual grandmother was big on family togetherness. Although, even she wouldn't approve of the level of togetherness Kai and Jessie had. But she'd make staying here and remaining separate from Jessie impossible. Eventually she would force them together, just like she had this past weekend.

Kai could already see at least a half-dozen times where they would have to be together—Christmas, Gran's birthday, Kai's birthday, Jessie's birthday, Easter, Grandpa and Gran's anniversary, one she still celebrated every year, even after his death. Sighing, he got out of bed and trudged to the bathroom. He'd somehow managed to fake an illness that had gotten him out of Thanksgiving dinner a while ago, but Kai couldn't do that every time there was a family event. Not without raising some serious red flags. No, there was just no way they could remain here together and not see each other.

Turning on the shower, Kai recommitted himself to leaving. It was the only way to stop them from loving each other the way they wanted to—man to woman, boyfriend to girlfriend…husband to wife. Kai scrubbed his face to erase that thought from his brain. *That* was most definitely not an option.

Kai and Jessie weren't anything but family. Kai had even made that distinction when he'd professed his feelings for her. As he ran his hand under the warm water, he wondered if Jessie had caught the significance of what he'd said. He'd called her by her full name, a name that only family called her. Because even though he might not think of her that way, there was no denying who she was. In his head, she might be Jessie, the warm, caring girl he'd met at a club one night, but in reality, she was Jessica Marie, his first cousin, by blood. And while he might be able to fool himself into believing their relationship was okay one day, the blood didn't lie, and there was no getting around the fact that they were family.

No, being together…wasn't an option.

Kai undressed and stepped into the shower. The familiar peace of the running water melted into him, although it wasn't as soothing as it once was. Kai was fairly certain nothing would completely soothe him anymore. And now…now he had some decisions to make. Namely, who he should talk to first.

Lathering his hair and body with the shampoo Jessie had picked up for him, Kai debated calling his parents. He imagined hearing his father's reaction to Kai telling him he was giving up and returning home. Recalling his father's distance lately, his thoughts turned dark. He'd been so odd with Kai, sometimes cold, sometimes detached; Kai had no clue what he would say about him quitting. He was sure he'd be deeply disappointed, though, especially since Kai couldn't give him a solid reason for packing up and leaving town. As much as Kai wanted to tell his dad what was going on, he wasn't sure if he could handle hearing his father's condemnation right now.

Rinsing his hair clean, Kai considered calling his mother first. She would probably have the opposite reaction. Seeing as how he was still receiving bi-weekly care packages from her, including everything from local foods from home that he couldn't get here, to new underwear, he imagined that she would be overjoyed to have him back. But she worked with Kai's father. She would tell him Kai was coming home, and that led Kai right back to scenario number one, and he'd really rather wait a few days to have that talk. Things were hard enough at the moment.

Hating how childish all of that sounded, Kai shut the water off and stepped out of the shower. Honestly, he was an adult. He shouldn't be nervous to talk to his parents. Kai considered talking to his grandmother and decided he would drop by after work today and tell her. She probably wouldn't be thrilled with the news, but she would be understanding and supportive. She'd repeatedly told him that he should go home if he wasn't happy working at the center. While that wasn't Kai's reason for leaving, he would let her think it was. It was easier that way. And he had a feeling that, if he asked her not to, she wouldn't tell his father he was coming home. For a while anyway.

That would give Kai time to figure out what he was going to say to the man who'd done him such a huge favor by getting him such a coveted job. Kai knew his parents' connections within the scientific community had gone a long way in helping him skip a few steps, and he didn't want to take that for granted. A part of him felt like turning away from the dream job he'd been given was like slapping his dad's generosity in the face. Kai wasn't prepared to do that to him just yet.

Walking back to his room, Kai got dressed in his multiple layers of clothing, followed by his teal work shirt. Truly, the very first conversation he needed to have today was with the boss who didn't like him, anyway. Surely Mason would be ecstatic. He probably wouldn't think about him again once he stepped out of the center's doors for the last time.

Once Kai was outside his studio apartment, he locked the door. He instantly envisioned Jessie pounding her fist on it yesterday, desperate to talk to him. He'd fled from her, taking a taxi to a dismal transfer station where he'd waited on a hard park bench with a bum and a couple of drunk college kids. He'd been exhausted, but his mind had been spinning so furiously, sleep had completely evaded him. He'd flip-flopped between returning to Jessie or staying on that hard, cold bench. Eventually, and with an enormous amount of will power on his part, he'd stayed where he was, and the shuttle had finally come and picked him up.

And then when he'd finally gotten to his apartment... she'd been there. It was like magic, like he hadn't left her at all. Kai couldn't even imagine how she'd gotten there so fast. And at first, he hadn't been sure why she'd rushed over. He'd left that note for her just so she wouldn't worry. She could have rested at the lodge with her friends, and they could have talked in the evening when she got home. But she'd been terrified he was leaving, that he'd run away without another word, without closure.

He was a little surprised that she thought he was capable of doing that. And maybe that was the smarter thing to do. Maybe it would be easier for both of them if he just... disappeared. But he couldn't imagine leaving the state forever without one final goodbye with her. Regardless of how painful that moment was going to be, he needed it.

As he sped through the city, Kai began preparing all of the speeches he would have to tell people. It was the beginning of what would eventually be goodbye. His studded tires thudded along the dry road, thankfully still clear of snow and ice. It hadn't snowed in the city yet, but farther up the mountains, where his work was based, a thin layer typically blanketed the forest.

Kai had spun out on the slick stuff a few times before he'd invested in snow tires. Louis told him almost every day that a bike was not going to cut it come February, and he'd made him a pretty generous offer on an old truck that he'd converted to burn bio-diesel. Before the ski trip, Kai had been considering buying it, especially on days when the icy wind picked up. When the chill cut straight through all of his protective layers, the thought of driving in an enclosed cabin sounded nicer and nicer. But now…Kai didn't need to worry about it anymore.

Pulling into the parking area, Kai shivered as he shut off his bike. He hadn't taken two steps away from his Honda, his helmet in hand since he wasn't a big fan of riding with a frozen skull, when Missy stepped up to him. Wearing an oversized parka with fur around the trim, she looked like she'd just been exploring the arctic.

"Morning, Kai." She smiled as she slowly eyed the length of him. When her gaze returned to her face, she frowned. Grabbing a section of his insulated riding pants, a little closer to the crotch than he was comfortable with, she said, "These do nothing for you. I can't wait until the weather warms up." Her lips twisted into a smile as she wriggled her eyebrows.

Kai removed her hand and started walking toward the building. He didn't care how he looked, so long as he was warm. "Good morning to you too, Missy." Kai didn't mention to her that he wouldn't be here when the weather warmed up. He intended to tell his coworkers, but his boss should come first. Besides, he wasn't sure what Missy would do once she found out he was leaving.

She huffed as she squeezed through the door with him. Once they popped through the other side, she poked a finger into his shoulder. "By the way, I'm very happy you're not seeing that August person anymore."

Kai cracked a smile as he waved at a group of people starting their morning routines. Continuing on to the storage room, where he could change out of his riding gear, he told her, "You mean April?"

She blew out a quick puff of air. "Whatever the month was, I'm just glad it's over. She was never right for you." Looking up at him, Missy batted her lashes beneath her black-rimmed glasses. Kai was all too aware just who she thought was perfect for him.

Shaking his head, Kai opened the door to the storage room. As he could have predicted, Missy darted in behind him. Once they were alone in the room, she backed against the door and seductively began to unzip her jacket. Kai really hoped that was all she took off in here. Twisting away from her, he set down his helmet and started unzipping his heavy coat.

From behind him, he heard the sounds of her undressing; her low voice floating over the top of it. "She has to be mental, if she let someone like you go."

Kai ignored her comment, like he always did, and slid his riding pants down his hips. He had them mid-thigh when she let out an approving whistle. Twisting around, he smirked at her. Luckily, she had only removed her winter coat, and was fully dressed. Now that she had his attention again, she gave him a seductive smile. "If I had you, you'd never get my claws out of you." Growling, she mimed a cat clawing the air.

Kai unzipped the ends of his pants and slid them over his shoes. Laying them on a shelf near his jacket, he straightened to look at her. "Well, Missy, it's a good thing you never had me then." He raised a corner of his lip. "And I'm pretty sure I've already mentioned this, but it was a mutual decision to stop seeing each other. We're even still friends."

Missy rolled her eyes as she grabbed her gadget belt off a shelf. "Too bad for her, yay for me," she muttered. Kai sighed. Grabbing his own belt, he moved around her to leave the room. She surprisingly let him, an innocent smile on her freckled face as she adjusted her outfit. Then just as he stepped through the door, she cupped his ass; he heard her laughter as the door closed between them.

Frowning at the door, Kai put on his belt. One thing he wouldn't miss around here was his too frisky coworker. Turning, Kai started heading toward Mason's office. He still wasn't sure what he was going to say to the man, but he supposed it really didn't matter what he said. Whether he was telling him he was leaving, or telling him he was staying forever, Mason would probably react in the same odd, awkward way.

Deep in that thought as he walked down the hall to his boss's office, Kai didn't notice Louis approaching him. He didn't notice until Louis bumped his shoulder. Startled, Kai looked up at the scruffy man; his beard was even thicker than when Kai had first met him.

"Hey, so...Kai." Louis looked up and down the hall, like he was about to tell him something so vastly important, no one else could be around to hear it. Seeing that they were alone, he leaned into Kai's side. "I've been meaning to talk to you..." He let a dramatic pause fill the air that was almost uncomfortably long. Just when Kai was about to ask him what he wanted, he got on with his request. "I'm going to ask out your ex, but I don't want to break the guy-code, so I'm checking with you first. That okay with you?"

For a second, Kai had no idea what he was talking about. Then it struck him, and he smiled. "April? Really?" Kai glanced down at the adventurer-hero-wannabe. He tried to picture him on a date with April. He couldn't.

Louis's face was dead serious as they walked down the quiet hall. "Yeah, and I know that dating a friend's ex is an off-limits kind of thing, especially since the two of us are tight and all, so I just wanted to make sure I wasn't infringing on another Alpha male's territory."

Kai smiled at the reference and looked away. He hadn't realized Louis thought so much of their relationship. It warmed him, then it saddened him. He'd be leaving Indiana Junior behind soon. Louis took his silence for uncertainty. "Look, I don't want to mess us up or anything. Guys have to stick together. Say the word and I'll keep away from April, because your friendship means more to me than a nice ass." Leaning in, he asked Kai, "*Does* she have a nice ass?"

Kai laughed and clapped him on the back. Remembering some of the outfits he'd seen April wear, Kai nodded. "Oh yeah, it's pretty nice." Kai patted him again before dropping his hand. "I don't care if you date her, Louis. Truly, it doesn't bother me."

The pair slowed as they approached Mason's office. Excited, Louis grabbed Kai's shoulders and hopped up and down, like Kai had just told him that they were going to Disneyland or something. Kai hoped he could pull his enthusiasm back a notch or two for April. Although, she probably wouldn't mind the attention. Putting his hands on the man's shoulders to calm him down, he looked him squarely in the eye. "If she says yes..." Louis scoffed at that, like April saying no wasn't even a possibility. Kai bit back a smile at the man's confidence. "If she says yes, take her to that nice place you mentioned, and order that snail thing. And Louis..."

Louis raised his shoulders under Kai's hands and shook his head. "What?"

Dropping his hands, Kai smacked his shoulder. "She's a friend of mine, treat her like a lady."

Louis straightened his stance and rested a hand on the tranquilizer gun at his hip. "I am the epitome of a gentleman on a date, Kai." He raised an eyebrow at him and leaned in. "Why do you think I'm so successful at the mating ritual?" Kai grinned as Louis patted his back and started walking away. "Don't wish me luck, because I won't need it!" He called over his shoulder.

Standing in front of Mason's door, Kai watched the strange man saunter down the hallway. Definitely an eclectic group of scientists they had here. Laughing as Louis scratched an itch in the shaggy head of hair that probably hadn't seen a speck of shampoo in quite some time, Kai tossed out, "Oh, you might want to shower, too!"

Not turning to look back at him, Louis raised a finger in the air. "The female species loves the scent of machismo, Harper. Remember that, the next time you snag a date with a hottie." Twisting to finally look at Kai, he smirked as he paused at the corner of the hall. "Then maybe she won't dump your sorry ass." Winking, he added, "Hey, if you get lonely, you could always hook up with Missy again."

Then he darted around the corner and disappeared. Kai softly laughed to himself. He'd actually miss Louis, and his odd, sometimes correct advice. Imagining Louis and April together made him shake his head. Regardless of his confidence, he silently wished Louis luck. He was going to need it.

Kai's momentary lightheartedness crashed back to bitter reality as he twisted around to face Mason's door. Once he opened it, he would begin the process of leaving Jessie. He was horrified *and* anxious to get that ball rolling. Closing his eyes and exhaling a slow, controlled breath, he knocked on the door.

Almost immediately, a worn voice replied with, "Enter."

Kai stepped into the room, softly closing the door behind him. His heart started thudding in his chest as he spotted Mason, sitting at his desk cluttered with journals and notes. Even though things between Kai and Mason had been strained at times, Kai enjoyed working here with him. He wasn't eager to tell him he was leaving, and he had no real reason to offer Mason except that he'd changed his mind. It seemed like a shallow excuse to Kai. Empty. But it was better than the truth.

Mason silently studied Kai as he approached his desk. There was an odd expression on his face, like he was calculating and debating. Did Mason know what Kai was about to say? He didn't think so, but the idea that he might know made Kai even more nervous as he sat in a chair across from him.

Tension filled the room, making Kai's palms sweat. God, why was this so hard? Mason was a stranger who didn't like him. Of all the conversations Kai was going to have in the next couple weeks, this one should be the easiest. Running his hands over his slacks, Kai cleared his throat. *Might as well get this over with.* "Um…Mason, I need to talk to you about some-thing…and it's sort of hard to talk about. I'm not really sure where to begin…"

Mason's reaction to Kai's words surprised him so much, that he couldn't continue his thoughts. He crumpled in his chair and let out a sigh that was both weary and relieved. His chin quivered with emotion, and his eyes started to shine with building tears. The nerves inside Kai started to morph into dread. What the hell was wrong with his boss? As Kai debated what to say, he was struck with an odd desire to run.

Suddenly, Mason's expression turned hard. "He told you, didn't he?" He shook his head at Kai, his voice both incredu-lous and agitated. "I can't believe he actually told you. After everything he did to get you out here with me, so *I* could tell you…he told you anyway. He said he would give me until the end of the year. I can't believe he was so impatient, that he couldn't give me just a few more weeks with you. He had to know how hard this has been for me. Not that he would care if I was suffering." He sighed. "Maybe I deserve to suffer after what I did to him…"

Kai felt like someone had just lifted the floor and shook it so hard his head was rattling. He'd never been so confused in all his life. He'd also never been so concerned. Something was going on here that he didn't know about. Something that involved him...and Mason.

Kai opened and closed his mouth a few times, but he didn't know what to ask. Suddenly looking exhausted, Mason rubbed his face as he sighed. "I told Leilani this wouldn't work, that she and Nate should sit down and tell you together, but she begged me...said you'd take it better if it came from me, that maybe you wouldn't hate her if I softened the blow for her. Ridiculous. But somehow she convinced me, and I agreed to take you in, so I could tell you...so I could get to know you." His face hardened as he shook his head. "But then Nate decides that your relationship with him is getting worse, and he needs this...monkey off his back so he can repair the damage *he's* caused by being too scared to talk to you." With a scoff, he looked up at the ceiling. "And then he goes and tells you anyway...right as I'm working up the nerve to do it. I shouldn't be surprised. He always was impatient."

Anger raced up Kai's spine. Nothing Mason said was making any sense. What the hell did his parents have to do with...anything? "What the hell are you talking about? What would my mom and dad want *you* to tell me? What could possibly be so awful, that they couldn't talk to me about it first?"

As Kai fumed, he watched all of the blood drain from Mason's face. He grew so pale that Kai was a little worried he'd pass out. Under his breath, he heard Mason mutter, "Oh God ...you don't know." Then Mason's expression completely changed. Clearing his throat, he steepled his fingers and calmly asked, "I'm sorry, what did you want to talk to me about, Kai?"

Kai wasn't an idiot, and he wasn't about to be deterred by such a lame attempt at diversion. Like any well-trained researcher, he was going to follow the evidence until he got his answer. What the hell was going on here? "What does my dad want me to know, that you're supposed to tell me?"

All the rigidness left Mason, and he seemed to melt into his chair. His face was the picture of defeat. And remorse. "I am so sorry that you have to find out this way, Kai. I truly am. I need you to know that."

Not sure how much more of this Kai could take, he grit his jaw and spat, "Find out what?"

Closing his eyes, Mason let out a long sigh. "Just over twenty-three years ago, your mother and I fell madly in love. Much to my later regret, we...carried out an illicit affair behind Nate's back." As Mason opened his eyes, Kai's heart started racing, and he suddenly didn't want to hear anymore. Mason wasn't about to stop now though. "While we were together, Leilani became pregnant." His hands splayed out to indicate Kai. "*You* are the result of our union," he whispered.

Kai shot up out of his chair. No. That was not true. He was not saying that Kai was...that Mason was...no.

While Kai shook his head in disbelief, Mason stood at his desk. Slowly walking around it, he quietly said, "I am your biological father, Kai. That is what Nate wanted you to know."

The world started shifting, spinning on its axis in a different direction. Lights darkened, and all Kai knew for sure was that he needed to get out of here before everything imploded. He started backing up, away from Mason, this complete stranger...who was nothing to him. Nothing! "No...you're demented." He pointed a shaking finger at Mason. "Nate Harper is my father!"

Mason took small steps toward him, palms beseeching. "Not by blood, Kai." Kai backed up until he hit the door; he was still shaking his head. Mason sighed. "I know this is hard to accept. I only recently found out myself. But it's true, Kai. Genetically, I *am* your father."

Pressing flat against the door, feeling like it was the only thing holding him up, Kai whispered, "No...there's been some mistake..."

With a sad smile on his face, Mason put a hand on Kai's shoulder. Kai flinched away from his touch, and Mason dropped his fingers. "I thought so too at first, Kai. But Nate had you tested when you were younger." Mason shook his head. "I'm sorry, but you're not his. And to the best of my knowledge, that leaves only me."

Kai opened his mouth to protest, then he shut it. Arguing without proof on either side was pointless. And what he'd just said, struck a chord and opened a painful memory. His gaze drifted to the floor. "When I was younger..." When he looked back up to Mason, moisture was heavy in his eyes. "Is that why my parents got divorced? He found out the truth?"

Mason paused, then nodded. "Yes. He couldn't forgive her for what she'd...for what *we* had done. But know that her love for you never faltered, Kai. And...if it makes any of this easier for you...you were conceived with a great depth of love, on both sides." His hand once again reached out for Kai, but dropped before connecting.

Kai let his head rest against the door behind him. He was shaking. He couldn't stop the reaction. Everything he'd known, everything he'd believed...was a lie. Quiet filled the room, and when Mason spoke again, his voice was thick with emotion.

"I didn't want to tell you this, Kai. Honestly, at first, I didn't even want to be bothered with it." Kai's gaze snapped to Mason's, and he shrugged. "I've spent the bulk of my life alone. I know nothing about kids, and I have no clue how to be a father. My work is my life...and I like it that way." He smiled warmly at Kai, and Kai could again see tears brewing in the older man's eyes. "But meeting you, working with you. Seeing your passion and integrity...I have grown to deeply respect and admire you, Kai, and I would be proud to call you son." His voice broke after he squeezed that out.

Kai blinked, and a tear almost escaped his eye. He couldn't believe what he was hearing. Up was down, down was up. "But you hate me," he whispered.

Now Mason blinked. He took a step toward Kai, but again stopped himself from touching him. "Oh, no, I never hated you, Kai." He shrugged. "You were just...thrust on me, and I didn't know how to deal with the...situation." Looking down at the floor, he sighed. "I had a hard time dealing with what I had been asked to do. I knew it would change you, hurt you, and regardless of what I've done in my past...I'm not a cruel man." Mason returned his gaze to Kai. The regret in his eyes was clear. "I was torn, but I never blamed you or hated you. Ever. I'm sorry if I made you feel that way. It was not my intention." Smiling he added, "You're an incredible asset here. Improbable as it sounds, I hope you stay."

Kai couldn't even ponder the possibility of staying. He couldn't ponder much of anything at the moment. His entire world was wisp and smoke, intangible. "I don't believe this ..." His hands came up to run through his hair, then an idea struck him. He pushed away from the door. "Did you see the test results?"

Mason blinked in surprise, then shook his head. "No... but, I don't really need to."

Kai narrowed his eyes. Why would a man of science not need proof? "Why?"

Mason gave him a wry smile, as he pointed to Kai's eyes. "Let's just say that I see a lot of similarities."

Kai shook his head, he couldn't accept that limited connection. "Because of our eye color? That's not good enough." Stammering a bit, he looked around the room, searching for something to make his world solid again. "I need proof. I need a test."

Mason's smile turned prideful. It was an expression Kai wasn't used to seeing on him. "Always the scientist. Yet another way we are alike." Before Kai could comment, Mason shrugged. "We have the machines here. I could test us now, Kai, if that would ease your mind."

Nodding, he moved away from the door so he could open it. Proof and facts he could deal with. Something physical, something real. "Nothing right now is going to ease my mind," he said as he yanked open the door. "But it will end the doubt." Without meeting Mason's eyes, he stormed through the door.

From behind him, he heard Mason sigh and say, "Yes it will, son. But are you ready for that?" And that was one question Kai already knew the answer to. No. He wasn't ready at all.

21

I Need You

Jessie was exhausted as she drove home for her lunch break. She was glad her next appointment had cancelled, and she didn't have to go back to work for a while. There was something about the ambiance in her massage room—the soft flickering candlelight, the quiet soothing music—that reminded her of Kai. She already missed him, and he wasn't even gone yet. But they weren't seeing each other until their goodbye, so it was almost like he'd left already.

Jessie couldn't even bring herself to think about what their last moment together would be like. She knew it was going to be awful, one of those cheesy, godforsaken movie moments where the woman blubbers uncontrollably while the man stoically walks away, never to be seen again. It was a scene that always made Jessie groan whenever she saw it, and now it was about to be her life. And she was positive that she would be just as much of a wreck as the fictional woman in the movie.

Just driving down the road with her hands safely at ten and two, her vision started to haze with unshed tears. She couldn't seem to go much longer than an hour before the urge to cry started creeping up on her. Jessie blinked repeatedly to clear her sight. She had to be stronger than this, or else she'd never make it through the next couple of weeks.

Of course, it didn't help that she hadn't slept more than a few hours since racing home to see Kai. After their heart-wrenching conversation, Jessie had walked to a nearby café. She'd felt numb as she'd settled into a secluded corner, but then the tears had come, and she'd laid her head on the table and sobbed.

They'd finally said I love you, and it had been awful. Wonderfully awful. Being able to express their feelings had only made the situation that much crueler. It probably would have been better for both of them, if they'd never said it. Because now she knew. She'd wondered if he felt that way about her, and now there was no doubt. He loved her. She loved him. But that didn't diminish the chasm between them. It was inescapable, as Kai had smoothly pointed out while professing his devotion.

I love you too...Jessica Marie.

Jessica Marie, the full name that only her family ever used with her. He'd made it crystal clear in that one sentence that while he loved her, ached for her, he wouldn't be with her any more than she would be with him. And now he was leaving, and Jessie couldn't sleep.

Jessie vaguely remembered a concerned elderly couple at the restaurant. Noticing her bloodshot eyes and distraught appearance, they'd kindly given her a ride home. Feeling empty inside, Jessie had thanked them for their graciousness.

She'd thanked fate when she discovered that her roommates were still asleep; she didn't want to answer their questions. She'd spent the rest of the afternoon staring at her ceiling while her mind spun.

Eventually Harmony had popped in and asked her how things had gone with Kai. Amazingly enough, Jessie had been able to shrug...and lie. She hated herself for doing it, but she told Harmony that a childhood friend of Kai's had been seriously injured, and his prognosis didn't look good. Harmony had been appropriately shocked. The story allowed her to be melancholy around her roommates without too many raised eyebrows. It also created a convincing reason for Kai to return home. Jessie had told her friends that Kai was making arrangements to go back and spend some time with his friend ...and then she said he wasn't sure if he would return. Harmony had hugged her after she'd admitted that; Jessie hadn't been able to stop the tears.

Sighing at how dramatic her life had become lately, Jessie glumly pulled onto her street. She planned on spending her entire extended lunch break blankly staring at the TV. She didn't even care what was on; she just wanted to not think for a while.

But when she approached her house, all thoughts of doing anything left her. Her heart started to race as she neared her driveway. Jessie couldn't believe what she was seeing, and briefly considered the possibility that in her exhaustion, she'd fallen asleep at the wheel and was having a vivid dream. That scenario seemed far more plausible than what she was looking at.

Resting in the driveway, where April usually parked her Jetta, was Kai's vibrant motorcycle.

Jessie didn't see him anywhere near the bike as she pulled into her driveway. What was he doing here? And in the middle of the day? They were supposed to be avoiding each other for the next two weeks. Him being here made absolutely no sense.

Unbuckling herself, Jessie tossed open her door and called out his name. Willing her heart to stop rattling against her ribcage, she glanced at the bike, then the front door, then the empty street. She did all of that in a rapid succession. Where the heck was he? And why was he here? She started walking toward the back of the house; her breath made a cloud of fog in front of her face as she panted. "Kai?" she yelled again.

"Jessie…"

Her name being uttered by a low voice returned her attention to the front of the house. Striding to the front door, she still didn't see him anywhere. But then he lifted his head. He'd been sitting on the edge of the first step, farther from the door and lower to the ground than she'd been looking. An overgrown bush was creeping toward the house there, and between the leaves and his low, stone-still position, Jessie's anxious eyes had passed right over him.

As he peeked up to her, Jessie's heart flew up her throat; she darted to his side as quickly as she could. Pushing aside some bushes, she knelt directly in front of him. He stared at her blankly, his expression devoid of emotion. He was still dressed in his work clothes, so he'd probably gone in today, but for some reason he didn't have a jacket on, and he was shivering uncontrollably in the frigid December air.

Jessie rubbed her hands up and down the long-sleeved shirt he was wearing under his polo. Kai had started acclimating to the climate, but even Jessie would be freezing in the outfit he had on. "Kai...what are you doing out here?"

He just continued staring at her, his jaw chattering as he shook. His lips were pale and his face was worn, like he'd just witnessed a horrible accident that he couldn't stop seeing in his mind. Jaw trembling, he finally shifted his gaze to her and spoke. "I'm s-s-s-sorry. I know...I'm not...supposed to be here." His eyes filled with tears, and Jessie's heart compressed at seeing the raw pain in them. "I just didn't know where else ...to go," he stammered, so cold he could hardly speak.

She brought her warm hands to his face and cupped his cheeks; they felt like ice packs. Glancing at his body, she noticed his wet, dirty slacks. Peeking at his bike, she noted the lack of a helmet. Turning back to him, she scooted closer and encouraged him to lean against her. His entire body was shaking as badly as his jaw. Running her hands around his shoulders, she said, "Where's your coat...your helmet? Did you ride here like this?" She pulled back to look at him. "What's wrong, Kai?"

His eyes searched her face. "Everything...is a lie."

Not understanding, Jessie shook her head, then tucked her arms under his shoulders in an attempt to get him to stand up. "Come on, let's get you inside. You're frozen." Kai awkwardly stood and Jessie supported him while she opened the door. They stumbled through it together; Kai still seemed too dazed to do anything on his own. Compassion and apprehension shot through Jessie in waves. Something bad had happed to him. He was obviously in shock.

Feeling the warmth of her house on her chilly cheeks, Jessie helped Kai to the couch. With both of her roommates at work, the home was quiet, filled only with the sound of Kai's chattering teeth. Jessie wrapped some blankets around him, and once he was draped in fleece, she sat down and massaged his hands to get the blood flowing again. The change in temperature made him sniffle, but after a few long, silent minutes, his shaking eased and stopped.

When he was calmer, he started speaking. "It was a match. It was actually a match." His brows bunched together as he said it, like he couldn't believe whatever he was talking about. "He was telling the truth," he whispered.

Knowing she couldn't help him if she was clueless, Jessie grabbed his chin and gently pulled his gaze her way. "What was a match?" she asked carefully, not wanting to send him into another bout of panic, since he seemed calmer. Still immensely bothered by whatever truth he'd learned, but calmer.

Kai shook his head. The set of his mouth matched the disbelief in his eyes. "He's my father. I'm his son."

That information didn't help to clear up the confusion any. His father? Had he talked to Uncle Nate today? Jessie couldn't imagine what Kai's father could have possibly said to make him react like this though. Unless…Kai had told him the truth about why he was going home. Jessie wasn't sure why Kai would do that, but it was the only thing she could think of that would explain his current emotional state. Feeling the chill from Kai's skin all the way to her bones, she dropped her fingers from his face. "Does your dad know, Kai? Did you tell him?"

Kai's gaze shifted to stare through Jessie, like she wasn't even there. "He's known for so long. How could he lie to me, for all this time? And mom…she had to know, or at least suspect, from the very beginning. Why didn't she tell me? Why didn't either one of them tell me?" His voice trailed off as his eyes watered.

Confused, Jessie began rubbing his back in a warming circle. Sadness and revulsion began bubbling within her. She didn't quite understand all of what Kai was saying, but ultimately, he'd said yes. His family knew their horrible secret. It wouldn't be long now before more family members knew about them. Maybe Jessie's parents would be next. Her eyes filled with tears as she thought about them knowing what she'd done. What would they say? What would they do? What could she and Kai do now?

Sighing, Jessie rested her head on his shoulder. Wishing they didn't have to talk about it, she whispered, "What happens now, Kai?"

Kai shook his head so hard that he jostled Jessie from his shoulder. She peeked up at him in concern. His lips were still tinged with a slight blueness, and he was still staring off with that dazed expression, like his world had just been turned upside down. While Jessie was certainly upset, she was puzzled over the severity of his reaction. And his odd comments. Many of them just didn't make any sense. Like, "it was a match." Jessie still had no clue what that meant.

Kai's voice was hollow as he answered her. "I don't know. What do I say to them now? What do I say to my...to *him*?"

Jessie scrunched her brows. She was obviously missing a vital piece of this conversation. Sweeping tiny slices of hair from his forehead, she whispered, "I think I'm confused. What on earth are you talking about, Kai?"

He locked eyes with her then, like he suddenly realized she was still there. Then he freed his arms so he could engulf her in a hug; he squeezed her so tightly her breath was shortened. "I'm sorry I'm here, Jessie. I just needed to get out of there, and I didn't know where else to go. I thought about driving to your work once I realized you weren't here, but after I sat down on your step, I couldn't make myself get back up again."

Jessie took a deep, steadying breath when he pulled back to study her. More like himself than he had been since she'd found him, he quietly said, "I'm sorry, but I can't do this on my own. I need you."

Jessie instantly drew him back into her embrace. Concern overriding her curiosity, she fervently nodded. "Of course. I'm here for you whenever you need me, Kai, no matter what else is going on." Finally relaxing in her arms, Kai nodded against her shoulder. "Can you tell me what happened?" Jessie asked after a silent minute.

Kai moved away from her and sighed. Swallowing a harsh lump, he closed his tropical eyes. Reopening them slowly, he quietly said, "I just found out that Nate Harper...isn't my father."

It was about the last thing in the world that Jessie had expected to hear him say. She couldn't even really comprehend the words he'd just spoken. It made no sense. Of course Uncle Nate was his father. Who else could be his dad? "What?" she asked, reaching for his hand.

Kai shook his head as their fingers intertwined. "I'm not his son...and he knew. All this time...ever since I was a small boy...he's known I wasn't his." Leaning back against the couch, he looked over at her; his eyes looked older than she'd ever seen them.

"What do you mean? Of course he's your dad...right?" Jessie still couldn't wrap her head around what he was saying.

By Kai's expression, he was having trouble as well. "No. I saw the test...we can't be a match." Exhaling a slow breath, he ran a hand down his face. "He can't be my father...because someone else is. I matched with him perfectly...all the markers were there. There's no denying the genetics."

All Jessie understood was that Kai had seen proof, proof he wasn't Uncle Nate's child. Curiosity drove her to ask who was. "Who is your father then?"

Kai laid his head back on the couch with a sigh. "Mason Thomas is my father." Looking exhausted by the admission, he closed his eyes.

Jessie was floored. "Your boss, Mason?"

Kai opened his eyes and twisted his head to look at her. Wearily, he nodded. "I went into his office this morning to give him my notice...and he told me he'd had an affair with my mother, and I was the end result." He shook his head as he searched Jessie's face. "I didn't believe him. I made him prove it...and he did. He compared our DNA. You can't fight science..."

"Oh God...Kai." Jessie leaned over to wrap her arms around his blanketed body. She couldn't imagine finding out that her entire childhood was a lie. She couldn't imagine someone telling her that her father was genetically a stranger. Kai sniffled as she held him. "I'm so sorry. That's...that's awful." Pulling back, she stroked his cheek. His eyes were moist as he watched her.

"The worst part...the absolute worst part...is they all knew." He shrugged. "My parents have known since I was young. My mom somehow knew since I was born. And they all lied to me. They all let me believe..." His eyes brightened with rage, and he turned his head from her.

Jessie calmly returned his gaze to her. Soothingly rubbing her thumb against his skin, she told him, "You were a child, Kai. They probably didn't want to upset you like that at such a young age."

Kai dropped his gaze. "It doesn't feel any easier now." He peeked back up at her. "And they sent me to...to my real father, so he could tell me." He shook his head, and a tear finally dropped to his cheek, around her fingers. "After all this time, they still couldn't do it." Bringing his hand out from under the blankets, he pointed across the room to the mountain range he'd left behind this morning. "They sent me to a stranger and let him rip my life apart." He dropped his hand, defeated. "Why would they do that?"

Jessie dried his cheek and pulled him into a hug. "I don't know, Kai. It couldn't have been an easy decision for them. And it's probably been tearing them up, waiting to hear if you ...knew."

Kai pulled back from her suddenly, his eyes wide with understanding. "That's why." His gaze drifted over her shoulder as his mind made some mental connection. "That's why my mom always asks about work, always asks if I like my boss. She's been waiting to hear if he..." Kai sighed and closed his eyes. "And my dad...no wonder he's been so distant lately. They were both waiting for me to...to suddenly hate them or something." Opening his eyes, he shook his head. "Their entire reason for arranging for me to be out here was a lie. How am I supposed to feel about that?"

Jessie ran her fingers down his shoulder to grab his hand again; it was finally warm. "Angry. Hurt. Confused." She shook her head. "Whatever you're feeling right now is just what you should be feeling, and it's okay to feel it." Kai stared at her a moment, then nodded. Jessie sighed as she gazed at their joined fingers. "Do you think...Grams...knows?"

She peeked up at him when she heard his weary exhale. "Yeah...I think she does. She stopped coming around when my parents got divorced. I didn't think much about it until I was older, and then I just figured she didn't like someone hurting her son..." Hanging his head, he shrugged. "But that wasn't entirely it. She hates my mom because she knows about the affair. Because she knows about me."

Jessie lowered her head to look up at his face. "You can't know that. Divorces happen for all sorts of reasons, Kai. She didn't necessarily know. Your dad might not have told her."

Kai's features smoothed to blankness and his voice lost all emotion. "She asks if I'm happy at work almost every time I see her. Why would she do that...if she wasn't waiting for me to be suddenly unhappy?"

Jessie looked away, thinking. He was right. Grams always seemed like she was waiting for Kai to have a breakdown. In fact, she was always telling Jessie that she needed to stay close to Kai, that he needed the two of them. Jessie had just assumed that she'd meant in the grand scheme of things, they needed each other, but she hadn't. She'd specifically meant that once Kai found out the truth about his father, he would need their support.

Compassion for Kai flooded through her. Everyone he was closest to had kept this from him. She slowly nodded. "You're right...she knows, she's always known."

Kai's face crumpled into a worn, heartbroken expression that tugged on Jessie's soul; she hated seeing him in pain. Closing his eyes, he leaned into her side. "I'm so glad I have you, Jessie. I don't know what I'd do without you."

Jessie's eyes started to brim with tears. Not able to stand his grief anymore, she pulled him in for another hug. Kai buried his head into her shoulder as he held her tight. Gently rocking him, Jessie warmed and comforted him the best she could. She wasn't really sure how to help him though. How do you help someone who just found out that the person they believed was a family member their entire life...wasn't family at all?

A sudden realization struck Jessie to her core. *He*...wasn't family. Not to Jessie. Genetically speaking, Kai was as much of a stranger to Jessie as Jeremy had been. Every muscle tensed as stiff as stone, as she finally comprehended what Kai's news meant for the two of them.

Confused by the rigidness in her body, Kai pulled back to stare at her. "Jessie?" he whispered, searching her eyes for some clue of what was wrong.

Jessie didn't know what to feel. She'd wanted him for so long, but he had always been out of reach. Taboo. But now... while they would still seem like cousins to most, they weren't. That changed a lot. That changed *everything*.

"We're not related, Kai," she murmured, her voice as dazed as his had been earlier.

Kai studied her for a moment before his mouth fell open in understanding. He'd been so preoccupied with trying to come to terms with the reality of his parentage that he hadn't had a chance to think about their situation, and what his true lineage did for them. His eyes flicked across her face. "We're ...not related," he repeated.

They both stared at each in silence, processing. Jessie's heart began to race as Kai's eyes pierced through every inch of her. Her breath increased as they watched each other, frozen, unable to move. Being in love with each other had been so wrong for so long that it was a little hard to move past that feeling.

But...they did.

At the same time that Kai leaned toward her, she leaned toward him. Their mouths met, and they exhaled in relief as they were finally able to connect without feeling the bitter bite of guilt and revulsion. They kissed softly, letting just their lips explore the other's. It was simple and honest and pure, and it nearly split Jessie's heart wide open. She'd wanted this for so long, wanted him for so long...and it was finally okay to have him.

Kai strung his fingers through her hair, not deepening the kiss in any way, just savoring the curled strands that he loved. They sat on the couch side-by-side and moved their mouths together as innocently and sweetly as if it was their first kiss... with anyone. Jessie reveled in his soft lips, the way his hand brushing through her hair would sometimes run down her cheek. She couldn't remember the last time she had been with a boy and just enjoyed the simple act of kissing.

But they weren't teenagers anymore, and they'd been denying themselves this moment for a really long time now. After a long eternity of tenderly feeling each other, Jessie pressed harder against his lips and finally flicked her tongue against the tip of his. Kai's chest rumbled with approval and he tilted his mouth so he could caress his tongue along the length of hers.

Jessie ran her hands up his chest and around the back of his neck to his hair. Her fingers threaded through the dark strands, grazing his scalp in the process, as their mouths began to move with more urgency, more passion. Kai ignited her body with every movement of his lips, exhale of his breath, and touch of his tongue. She wanted to expand on this feeling blossoming inside her, wanted to know what it would be like to connect with him intimately, without the horror they'd been fighting through. Now that he was essentially a stranger again, in the genetic sense, she wanted to express how much she loved him physically. She wanted to give him *every* part of her.

As her fingers tightened in his hair, his hands moved to rest on her neck. His thumbs stroked along her jaw, while their mouths moved in perfect sync—exploring, tasting, indulging. Taking a chance, Jessie decided to be the forward one. She was going to ask for what she wanted, now that she could do it with a clear conscience.

Breaking away from his searching mouth, she pulled back to gaze at him with lust-filled eyes. His eyes—those beautiful ocean orbs that had captivated her from the very first glance—stared straight back at her, unafraid, unregretful, and burning with desire. Jessie absorbed the passion emanating from him, then breathily said his name. "Kai?"

He kissed her softly before pulling back to stare at her again. "Yes?"

She smiled briefly, wondering if his thoughts were in line with hers. "Will you do something for me?"

Shaking his head, Kai leaned in for a long, deep kiss. "Anything," he whispered. His breath tickled her skin, but that one single word amplified the ache deep within her.

Jessie gently pushed him away from her; she wanted him to see her face when she spoke her heart. Her gaze drifted between his eyes while he waited for her to speak with a soft smile on his lips. When she finally did, a similar smile was on hers. "Make love to me?"

———————————●————————————————————————●———————————

Make love to me.

The words echoed through Kai's head in waves as he lost himself in the beautiful depths of Jessie's eyes. In moments of weakness, moments of loneliness, he'd fantasized about her say that to him. But he never thought it would happen. There had always been too much in their way before, too many barriers that even the immense love between them couldn't overcome. And then, on possibly the worst day of Kai's life, all of the walls had been broken down for them.

So many horrible and painful things had been running through his mind this morning that the one bright spot in all of this ugliness hadn't been immediately apparent. Jessie had had to point it out. By losing the genetic tie to the man he knew as his father, he'd also lost the genetic tie to Jessie. They were free, nothing more than...step-cousins. And not even that, since his parents were no longer married. They were ex step-cousins. And he could live with that.

Kai could scarcely believe that the woman he'd wanted for months, the woman he'd quite possibly been waiting for his entire life, was now available to him...with no guilt, no disgust, no regret. The joy in his heart made all of the earlier ache evaporate. The sting of betrayal was still there, but he shoved it deep down. He'd deal with that pain later. Right now, he wanted to feel something...incredible. Something life-altering. Kai wanted to show Jessie how much he loved her, how deeply entrenched she was in his heart.

Kai opened his mouth to answer her, but a knot of emotion closed off his throat. Swallowing, he tried again. "I'd make love to you every day, if you'd have me."

As she gave him a love-filled smile, her eyes began to water. "I'll have you," she whispered, softly laughing on the end. The heat in the low sound radiated throughout every part of him, melting the residual chill in his body. He finally felt warm again.

Hating to be apart from her, Kai's mouth returned to Jessie's. Their lips never parting, he shrugged the unneeded blanket off his body. Wrapping his arms around her waist, he encouraged Jessie to stand with him. Walking backwards, he led her to the hallway, to her bedroom. The memory of their previous slipup heated his blood, but unlike before, the flashes of desire were welcome; he couldn't wait to touch her soft skin again.

Jessie's arms slipped around his neck as she shuffled forward, following his steps. It was difficult to walk backwards, especially in a house that he didn't have memorized. It was even more challenging with a gorgeous woman sliding her tongue along the roof of his mouth. Kai couldn't help but close his eyes and groan. He also smacked right into an end table. Laughing as they broke apart, Kai involuntarily sat down on the edge of the table. Jessie took the opportunity to straddle his thighs and press her chest into his face.

Crooking a grin, Kai leaned down to kiss a soft mound through her jacket. Jessie bit her lip then ripped off her jacket. Kai's mouth started to widen, but then he froze mid-smile. Not satisfied with just her jacket, Jessie also stripped off the

tight sweater she was wearing. Desire shot right like a light-
ning bolt as he stared at the bounty on display for him. And…
dear God…she was wearing black lace. He was instantly hard
as she dug her hands through his hair and forced his lips to
the swell of snow-white skin above her bra cup. Damn, he
loved it when she was aggressive.

Cupping her backside as he tasted the sweet flavor of her
flesh, he pulled her hips into his. She let out an erotic groan
when she pressed against his readiness. Kai loved that he
couldn't hide how much he wanted her, loved that she knew
just how much he ached for her. And he really loved the moan
she made when she lowered her hips to his and ground
against his erection. Kai felt his body throb and had to remind
himself to be patient. Taking her on the end table in the living
room was probably not what she had in mind. Although, with
the desperate way she rubbed against him, the location might
not matter much at this point.

Grunting, Kai stood with her. No, he was going to do
something that he had been wanting to do for a while now.
He was going to take his time. Kai resumed their trek to the
bedroom, only now Jessie was the one walking backwards.
Jessie had a lot less trouble traversing her home blind, and
didn't bump into anything. As the shuffled along, Kai's hands
traveled down her neck, to her chest, to her jeans. He started
unfastening them, and with Jessie's help, halfway down the
hall they were halfway down her hips. Jessie shimmied them
all the way off while simultaneously kicking off her shoes. By
the time they were at her bedroom, she was free of the denim,
and all she was wearing…was black lace.

Kai stopped and stared at the beautiful woman before him
once they were both inside the door. Smiling, he reached be-

hind himself and pulled the door shut. With just their breaths filling up the space in the quiet room, they reunited.

Kai's wandering fingers slid over the bare areas of her body, highlighted in that wondrous lace. Jessie's hands slipped under his shirts, lifting them up. Kai helped her stretch the multiple pieces of fabric over his head. Jessie's breath quickened as he was slowly exposed. Lips parted, she lightly trailed her fingers up his skin. Every time her fingernail grazed him, it sent electricity shooting through him. Her lips lowered to his chest and Kai closed his eyes as her tongue swirled around his nipple. His body twitched as the throbbing ache grew painful. He needed her. So much.

Breathing heavier, Kai shucked off his shoes, then worked on his pants. He was having trouble concentrating, especially when Jessie playfully nipped his skin. He fumbled with his pants as he hissed in a breath, and eventually Jessie helped him. Always helping him.

She helped him push down his slacks and Kai kicked them away. Jessie automatically slipped her fingers into his boxer-briefs and gently pulled them off too. Sinking to her knees, she lifted each foot in turn, removing the last piece of Kai's clothing. Still on her knees, she gazed up at his face. Kai's breath caught at the captivating look in her eye. He'd never had anyone look at him like that before. There was so much love, adoration, and friendship there, that it stirred his soul. But underneath that well of love, there was a passion smoldering in her eyes that ignited his body to a breaking point. He felt on fire. He needed her.

Bending down to her, he gently pulled her back up his body. Her fingers ran up his chest as their lips melded together. Kai made short work of the scant scraps of clothing still left on her, and once her body was as bare as his was, he led her to the bed.

Jessie sat down on the edge, then seductively crawled into the middle of the mattress and waited for him. Kai smiled down at her, loving how free and comfortable they were with each other. There was nothing that he couldn't imagine telling her, nothing he couldn't imagine doing with her. And now that he was allowed to think the thoughts that he'd held back for so long, he found there were quite a few things he wanted to do with her.

But there would be time for that. If it were up to him, there would be a lifetime of exploring, a lifetime of learning different ways to touch each other. They had endless nights to be together now. Or he hoped so, anyway.

Running his hands up her thighs, making her squirm, he kissed her knee. "I love your legs." He smiled wider. "And I really love it when you wear those boots that go all the way up them."

Laughing, she tilted her head as she smiled down at him. Kai ran his fingers along the outside of her hips. Pausing to place a kiss along the edge of her hip-bone, he muttered, "I love how you sway your hips when you walk, when you're feeling sexy." Peeking up at her, he gave her a crooked grin. "You should always feel sexy."

Noting that her breath was faster, he ran his hands over the curves of her hips, and his mouth over the softness of her belly. His body was screaming at him to plunge inside her already, but he wasn't listening to that part of himself yet. He'd wanted her for too long...he wanted this to last. He ran his tongue up her stomach to her belly button, dipping inside for a quick second. "I love when your shirt lifts just enough for me to see this. I love seeing your skin, it drives me crazy."

Jessie shifted her body under him. Reaching down, she grabbed his shoulders and tried to pull him up to her. "Oh God, Kai, *you're* driving me crazy."

Chuckling, Kai resisted her impatience. He would have to be patient enough for the both of them...for now. Keeping his lower body well away from her, he grazed his fingers over her ribs. She sucked in a breath, laughing a little when he tickled her. Smiling, Kai kissed one rib and then another, working his way up her chest. Her breath grew even heavier the farther up he traveled, and her fingers abandoned his shoulder to tighten in his hair. Kai exhaled as a chill washed through him.

"I love the heart hiding under here," he said, kissing the underside of her breast. "I love how you care about people." He ran his tongue between her full breasts. "I love the way you care about me." He kissed above her breast, over the wonderful heart he loved and adored, and wanted near him, always.

Jessie squirmed, moaning as he teased her. Raising her hips to find him, she pulled down on his hair, trying to alter the position of his mouth. "Kai...please..."

Grinning, he closed his mouth over her nipple. Tilting his head, he watched as she gasped and dropped her head back. Letting out an erotic groan that made him quiver, her hands traveled to his hips. Tugging, she tried in vain to get him to connect with her; his knee propped between her legs easily kept him just out of reach though.

Letting go of her nipple, he moved his mouth to her exposed neck, and lightly ran his tongue up the salty curve. Once he reached her jaw, he laid a soft kiss there. "I love the sound of your voice. Even over the phone, you affect me." He ran his mouth over to her ear, grazing her skin along the way. Jessie shivered but he knew she wasn't cold. Into her ear, he breathed, "I dream about hearing you climax. Nothing... compares to that sound. Just thinking about it makes me hard."

Jessie whimpered as she wriggled beneath him, restless, her hips desperate for attention. "Kai, quit teasing...touch me." Kai sucked on her ear lobe for a moment, loving the words that traveled right down his throbbing body. He wondered how wet she was for him...pictured it in his mind. Just the image of it almost made him lose control. Pulling back his focus, he quickly found her mouth.

He let the desire and passion he'd been stoking consume him. Their kisses turned frantic and needy, and he felt himself getting lost in her. "Jessie..." Stopping them, he looked down on her. He had one more thing he wanted to say. The most important thing. "I love you...so much."

Jessie's dark eyes were overflowing with emotion. "I love you too, Kai."

With those words, he readjusted, and lowered his entire body over hers. Jessie gasped in his mouth when his erection slid against her. Kai groaned when her desire coated him. They were both so ready to be together, guilt and remorse free ...finally. Jessie's legs wrapped around him as her hips rocked him into place. As Kai felt the tip of himself press against her entrance, he heard her groan, "I want you buried in me, I want to be consumed by you."

His words echoed back to him—by her—had to be one of the most erotic things a girl had ever said to him. "God, that's hot, Jessie." He barely got the breathy words out before he could no longer contain the need to be inside her. Adjusting his position, he pushed into her warm, wet body, as far as he could go.

Dropping his head to her neck, he paused a moment to pant into her skin. Oh…God. She felt so good wrapped around him; it was like finally coming home. Jessie moaned in his ear. Her legs clenched him tight, and her hands on his hips held him still, held them together. "Kai…you feel…you're…so perfect."

He lifted his head to look at her face. Her eyes were closed in bliss as she enjoyed the sensation of him filling her. Kai started to ache with the need to move, and slowly rocked his hips back. Dropping her mouth open, Jessie exhaled in a quick pant. The erotic look on her face was almost more than Kai could bear. Biting his lip, he almost pulled all the way out of her, then he plunged in again. The cry she let out was pure ecstasy, and Kai reveled in the fact that *he* had made her feel that.

Kai maintained long, smooth strokes, nearly pulling out before plunging back in. He felt the tingling sensation along the entire length of himself; it was exquisite bliss. Jessie apparently felt the same way. Her groans and pleas for more had him hovering near the brink. He fought through the pleasure, wanting to savor the moment for as long as he could, wanting to give Jessie as much joy as he could.

Moaning in his ear, she clenched his tattooed shoulder blade. Her fingers lightly scratched the skin, and the jolts of electricity it gave Kai made a satisfied noise escape his throat. At hearing him, she dug her nails into his flesh, intense, but careful to not hurt him. Hissing in a quick breath, Kai grasped her hip and dropped his head into the crook of her neck again. *God yes, more.*

Jessie's legs wrapped around him tighter, pulling him deeper inside her. Kai pressed his lips against the heat of her skin, the slight taste of sweat on his tongue. Jessie tilted her hips to meet his, in perfect unison with him pushing down to meet hers. Their pace naturally began to increase as they both felt the rapture building into something...uncontainable. Pure pleasure ran all the way through Kai's body, making his legs shake as he sped toward the edge.

Panting and groaning underneath him, Jessie grabbed a fistful of his hair and held him to her. Muttering her name, Kai ran his lips along her jaw to her mouth. Jessie's back arched with every centimeter he got closer, and when he found her lips, she drove her tongue inside him.

The need surging through his body as he thrust deep inside her, faster and faster, built to a point that made him cringe. He was so close. He hoped she was close, too. He wasn't sure he could hold out much longer. Then he heard her bite back a whimper of frustration, and he pulled back to look at her. Eyes closed, her expression was a mixture of elation and concentration. It almost seemed like she was willing herself to not come. Was she really holding off, so they could release together?

Lifting himself up, so he could stare down at her, he murmured her name. She opened her eyes, and he cupped her cheek. His movements slowed as he took in the look of barely controlled passion on her face. Groaning, he whispered, "Don't hold back...let go."

She squirmed as he slowed even more. "Let go..." The ache of restraint nearly killing him, he added, "I'm right there with you, Jessie, let go..."

Then he dropped his hand to the mattress and thrust harshly into her. "Oh, God...Kai..." was all she got out before she started verbally letting him know that she was indeed letting go.

Kai dropped his chest to hers. Driving into her with abandon, his body stiffened and the building tension grew so profound that he couldn't speak anymore, only groan. Jessie let out a long, satisfying cry as her walls tightened around the length of him. The ecstasy in her voice rang through his head, barreling him over the edge.

His stomach clenched, his body jerked, and he felt the tension building to an apex. Knowing that she liked hearing it, he sucked in a quick breath and, just as he started releasing, he groaned into her ear that he was coming. Her body tightened harder around him as the warmth rushed from him to her. As he cried out with the perfect, intense burst of rapture exploding from him, he felt her grab his face to make him look at her. They locked gazes, and the sounds of their mutual satisfaction filled the quiet room as they watched each other experience a moment that neither one of them thought they'd ever get to have together again.

22

Happiness

Jessie let out a content sigh as Kai slid over to her side, and wrapped his arms and legs around her like he never wanted to let go. Her body tingled with the aftereffects of outstanding sex, and Jessie thought she'd never been so completely satisfied in all her life. Running her hands ran around his back, she pulled him even closer, and with a soft exhale, he buried his head in her neck. Making some sort of content grumbling noise deep in his chest, Jessie thought he was probably just as satisfied as she was. Feeling her wildly beating heart begin to slow, she tenderly kissed his head.

"We just made love," he murmured into her skin.

Jessie laughed, and Kai adjusted his position to look at her; the peace on his face matched hers. "I know," she said with a smile as their heads rested side-by-side on the pillow.

His grin was wide as he brushed away a curl resting over Jessie's cheek. "And I don't feel ill."

Relief and happiness flowed through Jessie like a steady river. "Me either," she said, gently pressing her lips to his.

Kai was smiling as their lips separated. "And you're not running away."

Thinking of the times before this that they'd had sex made Jessie giggle — an amazing testament to just how much things had changed. She'd rushed out the door to meet up with Harmony and April after the first time, and then she'd rushed out the door to be alone after the second time. She *had* run away from him after both instances, just for completely different reasons. Kissing him a few times as they snuggled close together, she vowed to never run away from him again. "Hmmm..." she murmured into the warmth of his lips, "is this what I was missing?"

A laugh rumbled Kai's chest. "I can be quite cuddly, if you give me a chance."

They languidly kissed, and the euphoria of lovemaking slowly started mixing with the heavy emotion of the past few days, making Jessie long for slumber. As she closed her eyes, Kai whispered between their lips, "A part of me is inside you again."

Grinning against his mouth, she murmured, "I know."

He kissed her jaw, then her cheek. "And you're sure that doesn't bother you, even a little?"

Jessie pulled back to look over his face. He didn't seem bothered by the idea, only curious about how she felt. Brushing the backs of her fingers over his cheek, she shook her head. "No, not at all. You're not family, not by blood anyway, and I'm...completely okay with this." She smiled. "And you still being with me...it makes me feel closer to you."

Kai grinned and Jessie covered her face with her hand. "God, I sound like a lovesick idiot, don't I?"

He gently removed the fingers covering her eyes. "No... you sound..." he laughed, "just like me actually. I was just thinking almost the exact same thing." He shrugged. "Just... that I feel closer to you."

Fighting back a tired yawn, Jessie smiled, and continued kissing him. "Well, I love that a piece of you is inside of me." With a sultry laugh, she added, "I could use all of you inside me."

Kai rumbled an approval and shifted his body to lean over the top of hers. Their gentle kissing switched to a connection full of passion and promise, and Jessie felt her body start to reawaken. It amazed her that being with Kai could do that to her; no other guy she'd been with had been able to arouse her so soon after sex. Kai might just be the kind of guy she could make love to all day. She'd heard women talk about days like that, but she'd never encountered any guy she'd *want* to do that with. Until now.

His hands ran down her sides as their breathing picked up pace. "All right...just give me a minute or two," he muttered against her lips.

Seeing this playful side of him made her laugh, and he laughed with her, locking gazes. Sighing, she ran a hand down his cheek. "I am so happy right now," she whispered.

Kai smiled wider before his beautiful face turned serious. "I am too. I didn't think it was possible...to feel this happy."

Jessie frowned as she stroked his cheek. "Are you?"

Sliding over to her side again, he frowned at her question. "Of course I am. Why wouldn't I be?" His smile was peaceful as he stroked her ribs.

Jessie sighed and shook her head. "I know things between us are...better," they both crooked a grin at her choice of words, "but…I didn't just find out that the man who'd raised me wasn't my real father. I didn't just find out that my entire childhood was a lie." She cupped his cheek and studied his eyes. "Are you okay, Kai?"

With a sad sigh, he lowered his gaze to the sheets. "I don't know. I just…can't think about that yet." When he looked back up at her, a love beyond comprehension was in his tropical eyes. "One life-changing event at a time."

Jessie grinned as she ran her arms around his body. "Life-changing?"

Pulling her tight in their side-by-side position, he nodded. "You've change everything for me, Jessie. I really don't know what I'd do without you."

Jessie let out a happy sigh; a yawn of exhaustion accidentally slipped out right behind it. Kai smiled then yawned himself. Jessie ran her thumb across the weariness she could see under his eyes. "You're tired," she whispered.

He nodded. "It's been a long day. A long week. A long autumn."

Jessie nodded, then softly kissed him. Yes, it definitely had been. Closing her eyes, she murmured that she needed to call work and let them know she wouldn't be coming back. Kai handed her the phone from the nightstand, then adjusted the bedspread so it covered their naked bodies. Jessie yawned as she dialed, relaxing into his warm skin under the warm quilt. The combination was a natural sedative, and she could barely keep her eyes open. Upon hearing the receptionist pick up, Jessie began lying her ass off. Letting all of the tiredness seeping into her body seep into her voice, she told the woman that she'd thrown up after lunch and was staying home. The receptionist didn't want to get sick, so she heartily agreed with Jessie's decision, and told her she'd take care of her clients.

After she hung up the phone, Kai laughed. "Such a liar," he muttered.

Now that she was free for the afternoon, the exhaustion she'd been fighting completely took over. Tucking her arms in-between them, she sighed in contentment as Kai's warm body enveloped hers. "I couldn't really tell her the truth now, could I?"

He let out a tired laugh, then kissed her head and exhaled in a long, happy way. As a peaceful silence filled her bedroom, Jessie felt her head drift in and out of sleep. Hearing Kai's breath start to slow down, she wondered if he was already there. Then his low voice broke the quiet. "Can I stay?"

Jessie wasn't sure if he meant here in her bedroom or here in Denver. Regardless, her answer was the same. Sleepily kissing the edge of his tattoo, she muttered, "I think the better question is, can you ever leave?"

Kai squeezed her and sighed. "I can handle that. I love you."

She mumbled something that loosely resembled, "I love you too," then sleep swept her away.

Jessie could have slept all day. She was so warm and content in Kai's arms. In fact, it was quite possible that she had been sleeping all day. She didn't care; her dreams were all of Kai, of what their life could be now that they could be together.

She was deep in a dream of watching him emerge from the ocean — the waves pounding behind him, the water dripping from his body, a seductive smile on his face as he ran his fingers through his dark hair, the low slung board shorts

442

clinging to the shape of him, outlining what was only hers now—when a loud voice in the real world seeped into her subconscious. "Hey, Jess, you can't bitch about us leaving stuff everywhere and then... Oh, hey, sorry, I didn't know you had comp...and...oh my God."

The alarmed voice intruding on her fabulous dream of a dripping wet Kai rudely jerked her to awareness. For a minute, Jessie wasn't sure where she was, what was going on, or why the voice sounded so disgusted. Then ice-cold realization flashed through her body and her eyes shot open as wide as they could go. In all the euphoria of finally letting go with Kai, Jessie had sort of forgotten that she had roommates who knew him, and knew he was her family. Or they thought he was, at least. April and Harmony didn't know what Jessie and Kai knew.

As Jessie's eyes locked onto Harmony's pale face, her body went rigid. Kai, lying beside her now, shifted his position as he woke up. He sat up on his elbow as he tried to push away the fatigue and figure out what was happening. Blinking sleepily, he looked up at Harmony; the redhead's mouth was practically on the floor as she gaped between the two of them.

Kai startled and glanced down at Jessie, a horrified expression on his face. They'd both been so tired that they'd slept until evening and hadn't heard her roommate come home. They hadn't had time to dress, and Kai's bare chest, combined with Jessie's bare shoulders as she held the covers in place, made what they had done all too obvious, even to the most clueless person. And Harmony wasn't some dimwit who would have needed it spelled out anyway. Just the two of them being asleep in a bed together would have been enough proof; adults just weren't found together like that for innocent reasons.

The bang of the front door closing signaled the arrival of her second roommate. April's voice drifted back to them. "Kai parked in my spot, is he here? And what's up with Jessie's clothes everywhere?" Snapping out of her daze, Harmony fled from the room.

That got Jessie moving too. "Shit, Harmony, wait!" She scrambled out of bed, finding the first pieces of clothing she could — her underwear and Kai's bundle of T-shirts. Throwing them on, Jessie dashed out of the room to talk to her grossed-out friend.

Rushing into the living room, Jessie saw a sickly pale Harmony shaking her head and lifting her hand at April, like April had asked her what was wrong but she just couldn't speak. Not sure what to say first, Jessie slowly walked up to her. "It's not what you think, Harm."

Harmony took a step back with her nose wrinkled. "Really? Because I think it's exactly what I thought."

April alternated her gaze between the two of them. "What are we thinking?" Her dark eyes flicked down to Jessie's odd outfit. "Hey, you get lucky today, Jessie?" Then her gaze locked onto the name of the center where Kai worked, embroidered on the front of the polo. "Hey, isn't that where...?" Her voice trailed off as her attention was diverted by something behind Jessie.

Jessie wanted to close her eyes and disappear, but instead she twisted to look at what — or who — had stolen April's attention. Kai was walking down the hallway, dressed only in his slacks, since Jessie had stupidly put on all of his shirts. Given the fact that he'd just left Jessie's bedroom, given the fact that Jessie was wearing the other half of his outfit, and given the fact that most of Jessie's clothes were strewn about the living room and hallway, April should have immediately understood what was happening. Oddly enough though, the first thing she commented on as Kai stepped up to Jessie's side was his tattoo. Biting her lip, she murmured, "Nice tat, island boy."

With an annoyed grunt, Harmony smacked her shoulder. "April, God, concentrate."

Taking a deep breath, Jessie reached down and laced her hand together with Kai's. That maneuver seemed to finally snap the pieces into place for April. In rapid succession, she pointed at their hands, their semi-dressed bodies, Jessie's shirt piled on the floor by the end table, Jessie's bedroom, and then back at them. Her mouth dropped as wide open as Harmony's had. "Holy shit! Were you two fucking?"

"No! God, April." Even though technically April was right, what they'd done couldn't possibly be classified as crudely or simply as she'd put it. Not in Jessie's head anyway. Fucking implied a lack of feeling. And between her and Kai, that was never lacking.

April looked lost. "Well, why does it look like you were, and why are you two...doing that." She waggled her finger at their laced together hands.

Jessie sighed as Harmony raised an expectant eyebrow at her. Jessie was about to say something when Kai spoke up. "We're in love."

April scoffed. "Well, duh, you're family. Of course you love each other."

Kai raised his hand and shook his head, but Harmony beat him to his explanation. "That's not what he said, April." The incredulity on her face was evident, so was the disgust.

April started to turn toward Harmony, but then she stopped and stared at Jessie. "Oh... You're...*in* love." April gasped in surprise, then her eyes softened. Shifting to Kai, she asked, "She's the girl from your past, isn't she? The one you couldn't get over. The one you couldn't be with."

Kai nodded as he looked over at Jessie. Squeezing his hand, Jessie gave him a small, sad smile in return. Being forced apart had hurt them both so much. Harmony closed her eyes and raised her hands, like she was trying to ward off the vision of their tender connection. "Okay, you're in love, fabulous. But I really don't want to hear the details of this freaky incest thing you've got going on here. If you'll excuse me, I have...somewhere else to be."

Harmony started leaving, and Jessie dropped Kai's hand to grab her arm. Jessie thought April would be the one most upset, but she was simply staring at Kai with speculative eyes. "Wait, Harm, it's not like that. We're not family."

Harmony paused and both girls shifted their eyes to Jessie. Harmony looked like Jessie had just told her she was really a man or something. "What? You said he was your cousin? I'm so confused..."

Looking back at Kai, his half-naked body distractingly alluring, even in the middle of this awkwardness, she murmured, "We thought he was. He just..."

She let her voice trail off and like he knew Jessie didn't want to spill his secrets without permission, Kai filled in the blanks. "It turns out my mom wasn't entirely faithful to my dad, and the man I thought was my father my whole life...

Jessie's uncle..." His eyes flicked to Jessie, then back to Harmony. "Well, it turns out he isn't my father. My biological father lives here in Denver. I've been working for him this whole time and didn't even know it."

Harmony seemed completely floored as she looked between Jessie and Kai. Jessie was torn between giving Kai a supportive hug and keeping a firm grip on Harmony, so she wouldn't take off on her. "You're not related?" Harmony asked slowly.

She turned back to Jessie far enough that Jessie finally felt like she wasn't going to bolt, and she dropped her arm. Smiling, Jessie shook her head and returned to Kai's side; they simultaneously slipped their arms around the other's waist. "No, we're not related."

Harmony compressed her lips as she took in their affection. She still seemed to be having a little trouble absorbing this new reality, but she didn't voice any more objections. Shaking her head, April suddenly said, "He's Ricardo...isn't he?"

Jessie closed her eyes and hung her head. She'd really been hoping none of them would piece together that this wasn't the first time she and Kai had had sex. Sure, technically this entire time they hadn't been related, but she and Kai hadn't known that...and they'd done things anyway. A little surprised April had figured it out so quickly, Jessie lifted her eyes to her beautiful friend. "Yeah, he is."

As Harmony's eyes grew comically large, Kai leaned down to Jessie and whispered, "Why is she calling me Ricardo?"

Ignoring him for a second, Jessie concentrated on her shocked friends. Well, Harmony seemed shocked. April still just seemed contemplative. Jessie wondered what else the astute woman was putting together. Face full of disbelief, Harmony pointed a finger at Kai. "*He* was your one night stand? I thought you said you just found out you weren't related?"

Jessie heard Kai mutter, "Oh...right."

He seemed about to answer Harmony, but surprisingly, it was April who spoke up first. Twisting to Harmony, she said, "They didn't know." Harmony shook her head, still not understanding, and April glanced back at Jessie. "I'm right, aren't I? You'd never met before. You probably hadn't seen a picture of each other in a bazillion years." With a grimace, she shook her head. "And we got you really, really drunk."

Jessie nodded, relieved that she didn't have to say it. She glanced up at Kai. "I didn't know he was in town yet. He didn't recognize my nickname. A million little things went wrong, and we didn't catch on to who we were...until later."

Harmony's expression finally softened. "Wow. That had to have been a shock. To find out you'd just slept with your cousin?" Her face morphed into mild disgust and she crossed her arms over her chest, but even still, Jessie thought she looked a little less bothered by it all.

Kai let out a long, weary exhale. "You have no idea." Shaking his head, he smiled at Jessie.

Jessie squeezed his waist before returning her attention to her friends. "Once we found out, we obviously tried to stay away." She shook her head. "But we'd never met before. He didn't feel like family to me, and I didn't feel like family to him. We were just...hopelessly attracted to each other." Jessie flushed and looked away. Kai chuckled as he squeezed her hip.

April tapped her finger against her lip, thinking. "Is that why you went out with me?" She pointed to Jessie as she spoke to Kai. "So you wouldn't have feelings for her?"

Kai nodded, his eyes deeply regretful. "Yes. I'm so sorry, April. It was really stupid on my part to involve you like that." Looking back at Jessie, his eyes turned sad. "I was really hoping that being with you…would stop me from falling in love with her." He smiled as Jessie stroked his back. "It didn't. I fell anyway."

Harmony shook her head. "That's why you left the lodge. There was no emergency…was there?"

Kai looked down while Jessie looked away. No, no emergency, just feelings they couldn't control. "No," Kai whispered. "No emergency…but I still had to leave."

Tears pricked Jessie's eyes at the memory of waking up and finding him gone. She didn't ever want to feel that way again. "We caved. We…slept together…"

Her cheeks burned with embarrassment after admitting that to her friends, and the tears she'd been fighting fell down her cheeks. Kai brushed them away, his eyes sad as well. Harmony laid a hand on Jessie's arm and Jessie turned to look at her. Harmony's eyes were surprisingly moist as she watched her friend's pain.

Feeling encouraged, Jessie expanded on her torment. "We both felt like we'd done something so wrong…so horrible. But we loved each other so much, we knew it would happen again if Kai stayed in Denver…" Her voice trailed off, and she couldn't finish. She was so grateful that that future wasn't happening.

Resting his head on her hair as he pulled her in for a hug, Kai finished the part she couldn't. "I made plans to head back to Hawaii, to distance us with space, since nothing else was working. I found out who I really was today, when I met with my…biological father, when I turned in my notice." His voice thickened with emotion. "I couldn't deal with the truth. I came here, to see Jessie. She helped me through it, and when we realized…"

Her eyes teary, her face wistful, April clasped her hands together. "When you realized that you *could* be together, because you weren't really cousins, you finally got to express the love that's been building between you."

The entire room quieted as everybody stared at April. Finally, Harmony laughed and slung an arm around her shoulders. "God, you really *are* a closet romantic." Jessie felt her residual sadness roll off of her as she laughed along with Kai. April sighed and shrugged.

Wiping her cheeks dry, Jessie looked between her roommates. "So…are you guys going to be okay with this? With Kai and I dating?" She felt like crossing her fingers. If her friends understood, if they accepted the two of them, then maybe she could get her family to accept them, too.

Harmony sighed and looked over at April. April shrugged and glanced back at Jessie. "I got drunk at a party once and French kissed my cousin. It happens."

A muffled chortle escaped from Harmony, and all eyes turned to her. Her cheeks turned rosy as she shrugged. "I lusted after this guy at a family reunion once, thinking he was a friend of my second cousin. We were halfway through 'show and tell' when I finally figured out that he was an *actual* cousin."

A light laughter filled the room as Harmony shrugged again. "Obviously our experiences weren't as severe as yours, but..." she sighed and stepped forward to give Jessie a hug, "I guess I get it. You didn't know. You tried to stop once you did." Pulling back, she looked between Kai and Jessie. "But love is a hard thing to shut off."

Harmony's grin turned mischievous as she patted Kai's shoulder. "I'm really glad you aren't actually related though, because listening to the two of you having sex would have seriously grossed me out." She grinned. "Sorry. I can only be so understanding."

Jessie flushed as April laughed. "God, Harmony, we wouldn't have..." With a sigh, she let that one go.

After a few more questions about what had really been going on for the past couple of months, April and Harmony finally let Jessie and Kai go back to her bedroom. Jessie felt light and airy as she closed the door and leaned against it. Her roommates knowing and accepting, had been more cathartic than she'd thought it would be. Releasing all the pent up lies she'd been telling had lifted a mammoth weight from her shoulders. She finally felt like she could breathe again.

Smiling, Kai sat on the edge of her bed. "Do you feel better?"

With a grin as wide as her heart, she nodded. "Yeah, so much better. You?"

He nodded in turn. "Yeah...it feels good to let April know the real reason why I couldn't be with her." He leaned back on his hands, opening his chest in a delightful way. "She just wasn't you." The edge of his lip curved up in a sexy half-smile.

Jessie gave him her sexiest smile in return. She felt so relieved that the truth was finally out, that she wanted another round of their earlier bliss; she even felt her body begin to tingle at just the idea of Kai being inside her again. Jessie was immensely grateful that her friends had come to terms with the idea of them having sex under their mutual roof; she had a feeling there would be a *lot* of sex in her near future.

His crooked grin stayed on his face as he looked her over. "And what are you thinking about?" he asked softly.

She pushed away from the door. "I was just thinking that you should get dressed."

Not expecting those words from her, Kai frowned. Smiling even wider, Jessie walked over to him, swaying her hips in the way she knew turned him on. Sliding her hands up her ribs, she hooked his shirts on her fingers and pulled them up her body. By the time she was directly in front of him, she was only wearing her favorite pair of black lace underwear. "I believe these are yours," she whispered, as she tossed his shirts onto his shoulder.

Straightening on the bed, Kai's eyes immediately locked onto her breasts, conveniently positioned directly in front of his face. One of his hands reached out and gently cupped her backside, under the seductive fabric. The other slid up her back, pulling her toward him. Jessie's eyes traveled the length of his body before settling on the bulge in his slacks. It was achingly apparent that he was ready to reconnect with her, too.

As the forgotten shirts slipped off his shoulder, Kai's lips closed over a nipple. His tongue flicked the peak, and Jessie closed her eyes and let a groan escape her. It only felt completely right between them now. *He* felt right, and after everything they'd been through, she wasn't bothered in the slightest if everyone within earshot knew it.

Kai smiled as he trailed his fingers down Jessie's bare back. She trembled, smiling into her pillow as she lay on her stomach next to him. Already having spent all day in her bed, Kai felt like he could spend an eternity here and be completely happy.

Sitting up on an elbow, his recently spent body perfectly relaxed, he shook his head as he drew a circle into her pale skin. "Is it wrong...?"

He let that trail off, and Jessie opened her eyes to peek up at him. "Is what wrong?" Her voice was lazy, relaxed. Her last orgasm had been a good one, for both of them.

He smiled wider. "That I actually feel a little happy about Nate Harper not being my real father now." Sighing, he shook his head. "I wouldn't have been able to do what we just did with a clear conscience if he was." Kai laughed as he replayed the multiple things he'd done to her that were very...uncousinly.

Laughing with him, Jessie flipped over onto her back. She did nothing to hide her wonderful breasts from him and grinning, Kai leaned down to suck on one. She trailed her fingers through his hair as she exhaled a slow breath. "Yeah...me too. I liked a few of those things."

Cocking an eyebrow, he peeked up at her. "A few?" Her moans had suggested otherwise.

She laughed deep in her throat, then pulled his head up to her lips. "Okay, maybe everything. God bless you for knowing exactly what to do with that tongue." As if to emphasize her point, she flicked her tongue into his mouth. Kai closed his eyes, remembering the taste of her. He couldn't quite recall anything that had ever tasted better.

Sighing, he pulled away from her. Her chocolate brown eyes flicked over his face, concerned. As happy as Kai was, he knew there were still hard conversations they had to have. They should talk to their grandmother. Well, Jessie's grand-mother. He should probably have another talk with his boss… his real father; he'd sort of dashed out of there the second after he'd laid eyes on the irrefutable proof. And Kai definitely needed to talk with his parents, a conversation he wasn't look-ing forward to. Jessie should talk with her parents too, if they were going to continue with this relationship. And he wanted to. He was almost looking forward to getting all of the hard conversations with family members out of the way, because at the end of them, if all went well, he would still have Jessie. It would be just the two of them, alone in a bed together, loving each other physically and emotionally.

Running a finger through her hair, watching a long strand wrap around his finger, he smiled and shrugged. "I know Nate Harper isn't really my father." Kai paused; those words still felt weird to him. Swallowing roughly, he continued, "But regardless, I love him." He tore his eyes from her dark hair to find her studying him with a small smile on her lips. He smiled. "He loved me as a son, even when he knew I wasn't his. That's pretty incredible if you think about it."

Jessie nodded, running a few fingers down his cheek. "Uncle Nate is a good man."

Kai could easily see the resemblance to the man who had raised him in the woman beside him. There was comfort in that fact now. "Yeah, he is." He shook his head. "I'm not really sure what Mason is like, and maybe he's a good man too, but I think I got pretty lucky with the father who raised me."

Kai felt a peaceful calm flowing over him as he said it. True, he didn't like what his parents had done, what they'd kept hidden from him, how they'd lied, how they'd chosen to tell him the truth. But he had to respect all of the support, wisdom, and unconditional love that he'd been given by the man he'd known as father.

Jessie let out a happy sigh. "And he did a really good job raising you. You're a good man, Kai. You're a great man," she whispered.

Pride and love filled him at her words. He wanted to be a good man for her. He wanted to be everything for her. He knew that every day he would strive to be the man that she saw when she looked at him. "You amaze me...how you see me."

She shrugged. "I only see what's really there."

He shook his head, a little dazed, and she pulled him down for a long kiss that left him breathless. After a moment, she pulled away; she was a little breathless too. "What are you going to say to your parents when you talk to them again?" she asked.

Kai looked away. "I don't know. I'm not really sure what to say. I mean, I love them, but I still have questions over things that they did. I'm still not happy that they lied to me. I'm not happy that my mom had an affair." He paused, think-ing about his parent's relationship. "How could she betray her husband like that?"

Jessie sat up in bed, still not covering herself. Trying not to be too distracted over that fact, Kai sat up with her. "Maybe your mom found herself in love with someone she wasn't supposed to be in love with." Her eyes darted down his body. "Maybe she tried to do the right thing, when she got in too deep." She peeked back up at his face. "She couldn't have known you weren't Uncle Nate's, not in the beginning." Kai frowned and she quickly added, "I'm not excusing what she did, I'm just saying…she got herself in a bad situation, and she made a hard choice to stay with her husband, to raise you as a family."

Kai nodded and looked down. He understood being in a hard situation. He also understood falling in love with someone he wasn't supposed to fall in love with. And the awful fact was, if his mother hadn't done what she'd done, he wouldn't be able to be with the woman *he* loved right now. In a weird way, his own romantic happiness was born from his mother's infidelity. He supposed he couldn't really condemn her for that. Too much.

Shaking his head, he looked up at Jessie. "Why didn't they just tell me when Dad found out? They got divorced when I was thirteen. Why keep up the pretense for so long?"

Jessie lovingly stroked his hand resting on her knee. She shrugged. "That's exactly why, Kai. You were thirteen. Your parents were going through a divorce. Uncle Nate obviously loves you…he didn't want to break you."

Kai sighed and laced their fingers together. "Why now then? Why after all this time…"

Jessie leaned into him, so her breast was touching his arm. Even though their conversation had turned serious, Kai smiled at the contact. She sighed and kissed the edge of his tattoo. "I don't know. Maybe they finally felt you were old enough? Maybe it's been eating away at them all this time, and they just needed you to know the truth."

Kai nodded at her guess. He knew she didn't have any firm answers, but he liked having someone to share his concerns with. "Why send me here? Why couldn't they tell me themselves?"

Jessie gave him a wry smile, like she knew he was aware that she didn't know anything for sure, and it amused her that he still asked. She answered though. "They had to be terrified. You and your parents are close, right?"

He nodded and looked down. "Yeah. I mean, I talk to my mom nearly every day, and my dad, before I left we were tight." Kai sighed forlornly, returning his gaze to the comfort of her body. "I wish one of them had told me. Or both of them, together."

She shrugged. It made her chest move in an intriguing way that made Kai smile again. "I don't know what their real reasons were, but if it were me, I'd be terrified of losing you." He looked up at her face and she bit her lip as she searched his eyes. "Maybe they thought it would be better if it didn't come directly from them?"

He leaned in to kiss her, then sighed against her lips. "Better for whom?"

She kissed him softly a few times, sucking on his lip. "I'm sorry they did that to you, Kai."

Kai was already beginning to forget the conversation they were having. He unlocked their hands and cupped the breast that had been teasing him. Rolling the weight in his fingers, he rubbed his thumb over the peak. He heard her inhale a sharp breath.

"Kai..." she whispered, desire clear in her voice. "What are you going to do now?"

A list of all the things he could do—to her—was shuffling through his head, but he was pretty sure that wasn't what she'd meant. His hand slipped down her chest anyway, ducking under the covers and aiming for the sweet spot that he hoped was completely saturated for him. His fingers were delightfully rewarded with a hot wetness as he slid them between her folds. She arched her back and moaned his name as his lips traveled up to her ear.

"My plans haven't changed. I'm still going to go home, Jessie."

She looked over at him, her breath fast as her body writhed under his fingers sliding against her. "What?" she managed to get out, her eyes rolling back in her head. "But…"

Hiding a grin, Kai encouraged her to lie back on the sheets. She did so, but a frown was firmly on her face as she struggled to contain her rising passion. His searching fingers twisted to probe inside her, plunging deep while his thumb circled the sensitive spot on the outside. He'd discovered early on that she really liked that. She gasped and clutched his shoulders, her frown forgotten.

Almost jealous of his hand, he rubbed his hard member against her thigh. In her ear, he panted, "I need to talk to them face to face. I just can't do it over the phone." She moaned, moving her hips in a determined rhythm with his hand. Dropping his head to her shoulder, Kai groaned into her skin, "I was hoping you would go with me, help me through this, like you always help me."

She moaned yes, and he felt his stomach clench like he was going to release all over her, just from the sound of her voice. Pushing his fingers deeper into her, he frantically kissed her neck. "God, I don't want to be apart, Jessie. Now that we're together, I don't want to ever be apart. Come with me. Please, say you'll come with me."

Clutching his head to her, she arched her back as she clenched around his fingers. "Yes, I'll come...yes, God, yes, I'll come." She expressed her desire to go with him several more times and Kai smiled into her skin.

He wasn't sure if she was actually agreeing to come home with him, or if she was even aware of what he'd been asking her, but he didn't mind. Kai loved satisfying her, and would do it over and over again if he could. Besides, he was certain she would say yes when he asked her again during a less ... provocative time. He was positive there was no way she would ever turn down a trip to paradise.

Jessie moaned his name over and over as she came down off of her high. Kai pictured her glorious, writhing body, scantily covered by the tiny pieces of a bikini, an outfit she'd once told him she rocked. He pictured her smiling at him in the ocean, imagined the sun beating against her skin, the wind billowing in her hair, and the water splashing up her thighs. He grinned as he watched the ecstasy on her face. The small smile on her open mouth as her breath started to recede, her eyes closed as she relished the pleasure he'd just given her. She was so beautiful, and she was all his. And Kai suddenly couldn't wait to go home.

23

Father and Son

The early morning sky was a clear, perfect shade of blue near the horizon. As it lifted from the earth, the blue shifted to lavender and then a rosy shade of pale pink. It was almost like the world was blushing as it looked over the two young lovers lying beneath it. Jessie smiled as she stared out her bedroom window. Kai rustled beside her, but he was still deep in sleep. Jessie knew from experience that unless she woke him up, he'd sleep a bit longer. He'd been a fixture in her bed for the past couple of days, and she was getting to know his patterns. And if she really needed him awake for any reason, she knew the best way to get him there. Kai really liked being woken up with her lips securely wrapped around him.

She'd practiced that the other night, when she'd woken up early in the morning with an ache that needed to be satisfied. Jessie blamed it on the erotic dream she'd been having, but truly, she thought it was more likely the novelty of being able to freely have the man she never thought she'd get. Well, that and Kai was the most unbelievable lover she'd ever had. That didn't hurt either.

Not able to face his real father again yet, Kai had taken some time off work. Not wanting to waste any time together, Jessie had followed suit, feigning her sudden illness for a little while longer. Her roommates were also keeping their distance, both of them staying away from the house after they got off work, only venturing home late in the evening, when they probably figured the two love birds were done for a while. Jessie felt a little guilty about that...but not really. She and Kai had endured some pretty hard times. They were reveling in the fact that as far as *their* relationship was concerned, the hard times were over.

With a content sigh, Jessie reached a hand out to touch the tattoo on his back. Twirling her fingers to mimic the swirls, she thought about the hard times yet to come. Kai needed to deal with his real father, needed to speak with his parents, and they both needed to talk with their grandmother. It seemed a little unfair that most of the emotional moments coming up were Kai's, not hers. If she could, she would take his pain for him, spare him from feeling it. But life didn't work that way, so all she could do was be there for him. And she intended to. She'd be there every step of the way.

Smiling, Jessie thought of Kai asking her to go to Hawaii with him. Once he'd asked her again during a quiet time, and she'd really understood what he was saying, a flutter of excitement had tickled her stomach. True, it was going to be a hard trip for Kai, and Jessie planned on supporting him in every way that she could, but putting the emotional hardships aside for a moment, she was finally going to paradise. She couldn't wait.

But first things first, they needed to talk to Grams. At the bare minimum, they needed to let her know that they were aware of Kai's true parentage. They also wanted to confess to Grams that they were in love and that they were together. They figured that out of all of the family members directly involved with this, she would be the easiest one to tell.

Yawning, Jessie quietly slipped out of bed and put on some warm lounge pants and a loose, long-sleeved t-shirt. She didn't bother with real clothes, or underwear, since she was pretty sure when Kai woke up she'd be undressing again, but it was chilly in her home and the comfort was nice.

Smiling at the sight of Kai's slumbering body as she made her way to the door, Jessie noted the pile of his things sitting on a chair next to her dresser. He'd gone to his apartment a couple of times, to pick up things he needed. Used to small spaces, he'd carved out a nice little corner for himself in her room. Jessie loved it.

She was grinning as she opened the door. She'd have to do some laundry for him soon, to save him from making another trip to his place. She didn't mind though. Jessie loved doing things for him, and laundry was a pretty simple way to show her affection. Besides, she wanted him to stay as long as possible. Clean clothes were a good incentive.

Nearly skipping down the hallway, she noticed the kitchen light was on. Knowing that not everyone had put everything on hold for an amazing rock-your-world love fest, Jessie figured it was Harmony, prepping for her day.

Laughing, she surprised her friend by slinging her arms around her shoulders. Harmony spilled some of the coffee she was pouring into her cup. "Oh, Jesus, Jessie. It's way too early for you to scare me like that."

The redhead twisted to look at her, and Jessie knew exactly what she would see — a woman grinning like an idiot from ear to ear. She couldn't help it. For the first time it what felt like forever, she was finally happy. Perfectly and contently happy.

Harmony smiled softly and shook her head. She was all done up for work as a paralegal in a local law firm, and her hair was swept into an orderly bun at the nape of her neck. "I don't think I've ever seen you...glow like that." Stepping back, she took a quick sip of her coffee. "I'm glad he makes you so happy. You deserve it, after that last creep."

Leaning back against the counter, Jessie's head swam with pleasant thoughts of the gorgeous boy asleep in her bed; she could barely even recall what that the "creep's" name had been. "Yeah, he makes me very happy."

Chuckling, Harmony took another sip of coffee. It was clear she was amused by her head-over-heels friend. Raising a pale eyebrow she said, "Are you two ever going to rejoin the real world, or am I going to feel like I'm back at my college dorm for eternity." She laughed again as she lightly shook her head.

Jessie wanted to be embarrassed about her and Kai's eagerness, but she was just too damn happy. Smiling, she shrugged. "Sorry. We're just making up for lost time."

With a smile, Harmony patted her shoulder. "I know. I guess we can put up with it for a little while longer." Walking past Jessie to the living room, she put on her stern face. "But just a little while, Jessie."

Her friend was smiling warmly as she turned away, so Jessie was pretty sure she was teasing...or mostly teasing. She probably *was* a little tired of the erotic noises continually drifting out of Jessie's bedroom. Staying where she was against the counter, Jessie sighed and smiled to herself. She knew she was being overindulgent with her crazy-in-love feelings, but she didn't care. She *was* crazy in love, and she wanted to relish in it for as long as she could.

Glancing over at the pot of coffee on the counter, she thought about pouring herself a cup when she swore she heard a noise at the front door. She switched her gaze to the clock on the microwave, sure she was hearing things. It was hardly a decent hour for someone to visit.

Furrowing her brow, Jessie walked into the living room where she could hear Harmony talking with someone. When she saw who it was, shock nearly froze her in place. She'd only seen the man once before, but Jessie would never forget those eyes, not when she was staring into their duplicate on such a frequent basis.

Mason Thomas, the reason Kai was alive, was standing in her doorway, looking like he'd rather be anywhere else.

Harmony twisted from the older man at the door to Jessie when she heard her approach. "Uh, Jess, this guy says he needs to talk to Kai?"

Harmony stepped back from the door when Jessie stepped up to it. "Mason? What are you doing here?" She glanced down the hallway at where Kai was still obliviously sleeping, then turned back to his reluctant father.

Mason swallowed uneasily as he rubbed his hands together in the frigid outdoor air. "I'm sorry for the intrusion, especially this early in the morning, but I was wondering…is Kai here?" His tropical eyes had a pleading quality to them that Jessie found confusing. Kai had never thought the man liked him, but he seemed…worried.

Jessie shrugged. "Yeah, he's sleeping." She tilted her head to indicate where he was. Mason briefly closed his eyes, relief visibly washing through him. Even more confused now, Jessie blurted out, "How did you find...him?"

Mason's eyes opened and he looked past Jessie, to the point where his long lost child was. "It took a bit of investigating." His eyes returned to hers. "I spoke with his mother earlier this morning." Grimacing, he shrugged. "I explained to her that Kai had found out the truth a few days ago, and I hadn't seen or heard from him since. Once she got past her panic attack, she mentioned his grandmother."

Jessie felt a sinking feeling in the pit of her stomach. "Did you talk to Grams?"

Mason's eyes narrowed. "Right...you're the cousin. Well technically you're not, but you do share the same woman Kai has always believed was his grandmother." Jessie could only nod; she really didn't want to go into the family dynamics with this man. He shrugged. "I needed to find him, to make sure he was...okay. I called her, she mentioned you, so I figured Kai was hiding here."

Jessie ran her fingers down her face. Great, her grandmother knew Kai was aware of the truth. Kai's mother also knew. Jessie knew they couldn't hide in their newfound utopia forever, but she'd hoped to at least ride out the week. Sighing, she stepped aside and welcomed him in.

Harmony gave Jessie a swift hug and wished her well before popping out the door for work. Jessie had Mason sit on the couch and told him she'd wake up Kai. If he was at all curious about their relationship, he didn't show it. He only seemed to be concerned and uneasy. As he sat with his hands over his knees, his feet ceaselessly bouncing up and down, it was clear that he was completely out of his comfort zone. But he was here anyway, here to speak to Kai...his son...and that said a lot about the man.

Leaving him alone and nervous on her couch, Jessie ran into April as she emerged from her bedroom. Yawning and rubbing her eyes, she pointed down the hallway. "Someone here?" she asked.

Jessie nodded and whispered, "Kai's dad."

April's eyes widened. "Oh..." She moved to sneak a peek at him, but Jessie grabbed her elbow. "He's nervous. Don't spy on him, okay?"

She frowned and then sighed. "Yeah, all right. I have to get ready for work anyway." She sighed again as she disappeared into her room, and Jessie could have sworn she murmured something about missing all the good drama.

Shaking her head at her friend, Jessie opened her bedroom door. Kai stirred and twisted his head to peek up at her. Stretching, he murmured, "Good morning." He yawned right after he said it, the satisfied smile he'd had on his face the last few days still firmly in place. Softly closing the door behind her, Jessie wished she didn't have to say what she was about to say; it would certainly remove that beautiful smile. Seeing the reluctance on her face, Kai cautiously asked, "What's wrong?"

As he sat up on the bed, she sat down. Jessie could see the goose bumps on his arms and she rubbed his skin, warming him where she could. Still smiling, he patiently waited for her to answer.

Sighing, she nodded her head at the door. "Your dad is here."

Kai's expression twisted to confusion. "My dad is here from…" His sentence trailed off as his eyes blazed with understanding. "Mason? Mason is here?"

Jessie nodded as Kai flung back the covers and stood up. Her eyes drifted down his bare body before she reprimanded herself and made her gaze stay focused on his face; now wasn't the time. Kai seemed shocked as he looked for clothes. Understandable, Jessie was a little shocked that Mason was here too. Stepping into his underwear, Kai asked, "Did he say what he wanted?" He found some jeans and pulled them on while Jessie shook her head.

"No, just that he wants to see you." She lowered her voice. "I think he was worried about you."

Kai paused in putting on his shirt. "Worried?" He finished slipping the material on and smoothed it over his fabulous frame. "Why would he be worried about…me?"

Jessie gave him a wry smile. "Kai, regardless of *when* he found out about you, you're his blood. He's naturally going to be concerned about your wellbeing, especially since he's gotten the chance to know you recently." She shrugged. "I'm sure when he didn't hear from you for a few days…he panicked."

Kai closed his eyes for a minute and shook his head. "My phone died at the lodge…I never charged it again." He sighed. "My mom must be freaking out too, since she hasn't been able to get a hold of me either."

Jessie cleared her throat, and Kai immediately snapped his eyes open. "What?" he asked, his voice flat.

Jessie looked down at her bed, their bed, and picked at a loose piece of string coming off the blanket. "Well, your dad didn't know how to find you. He probably thought you went back home…so he…"

Hearing Kai sigh, she looked up at him. "He called my mom, didn't he?"

Jessie nodded. "And Grams."

Kai's mouth dropped open, then he ran his hands down his face and groaned. Peeking at her between his fingers, he muttered, "I guess the honeymoon is over, isn't it?"

The summation of their few days of bliss made her smile. But he was right. Their uninterrupted time together was over. Sighing, she stood up and laced her hands around his neck. "Back to the real world, babe."

He slipped his arms around her waist. "At least you're still a part of that real world."

She gave him a tender kiss. "I'm not going anywhere you're not." They pulled apart, and Jessie bit her lip. "Let's go see what your dad has to say." Kai slumped, then nodded. Grabbing her hand, Kai pulled Jessie from the room. His face seemed loose and relaxed, but Jessie felt the tension in his fingers; he was nervous.

Mason looked up from examining a spot on the floor once they were at the end of the hallway. A small smile ghosted across his lips as he stood up. He seemed nervous, too, but also relieved that Kai was still here, still around. Stepping toward the pair as they approached the couch, he extended a hand to Kai.

"Kai, I'm glad I found you."

Kai glanced at the hand being offered to him, but he didn't drop Jessie's hand to take it. Furrowing his brow, he examined the man who had rocked his world. "What are you doing here, Mason?"

The obvious distance between them made Mason sigh as he shoved his hand into his pocket. His aged face—a bit wearier than Jessie remembered from the first time she'd met him—relaxed into neutrality. "You ran out on me. I haven't seen or heard from you for days..."

Kai hung his head, then peeked up at him. "Are you here to fire me then?"

Shock ran through Jessie as she flicked her gaze between Kai and Mason. She hadn't considered that Kai might get in trouble for ditching work. Sure, he'd had a really good reason to not return, but a job was still a job, and certain responsibilities were still expected from the employees, regardless of their personal problems. It was why she'd had to call in with a fake illness every day.

The same shock Jessie felt passed through Mason's face, disturbing his attempt at detachment. Sputtering, he stepped up to Kai and reached out for him before stopping himself and putting his hand back in his pocket. "No, of course not, Kai. The job is yours, for as long as you want it. I understand why you fled." Exhaustion seemed to overtake him, and all trace of indifference vanished. "I just wanted to make sure you were okay...son."

His gaze softened as he stared at Kai, and Jessie couldn't help but note the obvious similarities between father and son. Besides the eyes, there was something about the angle of the jaw, the slope of the nose, the basic bone structure. Kai's coloring and ethnicity helped to mask a lot of the connection, but once you knew the lineage, there were just too many markers to ignore the truth. This man *was* Kai's father.

Still having trouble accepting it, Kai stiffened; his hand loosely held hers and suddenly clenched it painfully tight. "Don't call me that," he bit out.

469

Mason looked away from him, but nodded. Jessie placed her other hand over Kai's clenched fist and tried to ease the tension she felt there with soothing circles. Jessie understood Kai's anger and confusion, but none of this was really Mason's fault. From what Kai had told her, Mason had just recently found out about him.

Kai's death grip on her hand loosened as Mason returned his eyes to him. "I'm not trying to replace the father who raised you, Kai. That was never my intention."

"Then what are you doing here?" he asked in a tight voice.

Mason bunched his brows in disbelief. "Is it so hard for you to believe that I care about you?"

Kai looked over at Jessie. She slung her arm around his stomach, holding him tight as she rested her head on his arm. Glancing back at Mason, he shrugged. "I'm not sure what to think or feel right now. You'll have to excuse me if I'm a little ...uncertain how to act around you."

Mason nodded, but his eyes were locked on Kai and Jessie's embrace. Flicking his green-blue gaze between the two of them, he lifted an eyebrow. "Are you two together? As in, a couple?" His tone seemed nothing more than curious, a man of science studying an interesting phenomena of nature in front of him, but Jessie felt herself flush with heat.

Kai pulled her tightly against him. "What we are isn't really relevant."

Mason's eyes snapped up to his face. "Oh, I know. I didn't mean to pry. It's perfectly fine if you are together. There are no inherent genetic dangers in a sexual relationship between the two of you. I was just...curious." He smiled apologetically, like out of everyone in the room, Kai should understand curiosity.

The blunt way he talked made Jessie's cheeks feel like they were on fire, but Kai seemed amused. He even smiled a little. Maybe seeing an invitation in his mirth, Mason pointed to the couch. "Do you mind if we sit, Kai. I'd love to have a conversation with you." He smiled widely for the first time. "I'd love to get to know you, if you'd let me?"

Kai inhaled a slow breath. On the exhale, he slowly nodded. "All right, I can handle…talking."

Jessie wondered if she should leave them alone, but Kai led her to the couch; clearly he wanted her to stay. Jessie sat beside him, still holding his hand in support. Mason sat on the smaller couch, looking nervous, but happy too. He seemed to have been genuine in his desire to get to know Kai.

Rubbing his hands on his slacks, Mason cleared his throat and gave Kai an apologetic smile. "You'll forgive me if I don't know how to act around you either." He laughed lightly as he shook his head. "It's not every day that you find out you have a twenty-three year old son."

Kai laughed at his remark, then smiled over at Jessie. "Yeah, I suppose that could be a shock."

Hearing Mason let out a weary exhale, they both redirected their attention to him. "I suppose I should start at the beginning. Your beginning anyway." He indicated Kai on the couch, then smiled sadly. "Leilani Harper was the most beautiful, exotic, vibrant woman I had ever seen. I couldn't help but fall madly in love with her…"

His expression alternating between reflection, remorse, and lingering love, Mason began describing the series of events and bad choices that led to Kai's creation. Kai seemed

uncomfortable hearing such intimate, and not always flatter-
ing, details about his mother. But by the end of Mason's tale,
he'd scooted to the edge of the couch, listening raptly.

Mason had a way of painting their relationship that made
it easy to see why they'd fallen so deeply for each other, even
though it was wrong for them to do so. Jessie couldn't help
but steal glances at Kai throughout Mason's confession. While
she and Kai couldn't be together for entirely different reasons,
the heartache they'd all shared was the same. Jessie found
herself sympathizing with Kai's mother. She couldn't imagine
being torn between two lovers like that, and then having to
leave one behind for the sake of the child, a child who could
have been fathered by either one of them. That was hard to
picture, but she could easily understand being in love with
someone who was forbidden.

When Mason was finished, Kai hung his head and nodded. He seemed to better understand the turmoil his mother
had gone through. As Jessie rubbed his back, she hoped that
when Kai saw her again, he wasn't too hard on her. Her
choices hadn't been the best, but her decision to stay with Uncle Nate had in large part been for Kai's benefit. Either way,
her decision must have been hard.

April emerged from her room to leave for work. Having
heard parts of Mason's tale, she gave Kai a swift hug and a
light kiss on the cheek. Jessie was a little surprised as she
watched the affectionate moment between them that she no
longer felt any jealousy over their contact. Maybe that was because April and Kai's relationship had shifted into an easy
friendship, or maybe it was because Jessie was now bonded
with Kai so firmly that she had no question where his heart
was; he showed her every chance he got. Or maybe, it was just

because she'd gotten to *know* Kai over the last few months, and she was certain he'd never stray. That just wasn't who he was. He was loyal and trustworthy, loving and honest. He was devoted to his family, and there for anyone who needed a hand. Inside and out, Kai was just a good person. And besides being the man who occupied her bed and her heart, he was also her best friend. Her soulmate. As Jessie waved goodbye to April, she was certain that, unlike his mother, Kai would never find himself in a position where he had to choose between two lovers. Jessie was absolutely certain that Kai's heart was hers...and only hers.

Jessie stood to make the father and son cups of coffee when the conversation shifted to lighter topics. Mason seemed genuinely curious about Kai, about who he was and what he enjoyed, and he endlessly expressed his regret over seeming standoffish to him upon his arrival. The whole situation had completely thrown Mason off, and he wasn't someone who liked to be off-track. He'd been struggling with the task that had been given to him from day one.

After giving the pair their coffee, Jessie kissed Kai's forehead and gave him some privacy so he could truly get to know his father. Hearing Kai laugh while he described the numerous bee stings he'd hidden from Mason on his first day at work made her smile. Slipping into her room, Jessie crawled onto her bed. With the scent of Kai still on her pillows, she listened to his deep voice as it drifted throughout her home.

It filled Jessie with a surprising amount of warmth that he was making an attempt to bond with Mason. Maybe that was because if Kai bonded with Mason, it would only reaffirm that Uncle Nate wasn't his real dad, reaffirm that it truly was okay for them to be together. Jessie knew in her heart that being with Kai was the absolute right path for her, and she knew they were strangers, in that sense, but still, having him develop a close tie to someone who didn't share a branch on the Harper family tree was a good thing.

Smiling, Jessie closed her eyes and let the image of Kai's sea-green gaze sweep her away into slumber.

24
Life's Little Surprises

K ai smiled as he shook hands with Mason. That had gone better than he'd ever thought it would. Now that Mason wasn't sick with dread over having a conversation with Kai that he didn't want to have, he was easier to be around—open, curious, and eager to form a lasting bond with Kai. Kai wasn't sure if he was ready to include him in family functions yet, but he definitely felt more comfortable about returning to work.

"I never thought I'd say this, but thank you for coming here and talking to me," Kai said as he walked Mason to the front door.

Mason let out a noise that was half amusement, half disbelief. "It was something I never imagined myself doing it…but I'm glad I did. You're an amazing young man, Kai, and I'm happy that you're giving me a chance to get to know you. It begs the question though…will you be staying with us?"

While Kai was a bit flustered by a person he'd always assumed hated him suddenly calling him amazing, the thought of what his future held now made him smile. "Yes, I'm going to stay here...in Denver." His gaze drifted to Jessie's bedroom, where the girl of his dreams was waiting for him. When he returned his eyes to Mason's, there was happiness and curiosity on the man's face, but no disgust. He knew about Kai and Jessie, and he didn't care. Kai hoped it went as easily with the rest of their family. "This is home now, and so is the center. I'd be honored to keep working with you and the team."

Even though Kai was fairly certain Mason wouldn't turn him down, nerves still flashed up his spine. He really hadn't wanted to give up his job. He loved the work, and he'd never really wanted to leave. Mason's expression instantly proclaimed his answer, even before he said it. Smiling brightly, he nodded, "Good. You would have been impossible to replace."

The warmth of Mason's praise swept over Kai. He wasn't at a point where he needed to impress the man as a son, but as an employee, it was extremely gratifying to have his hard work acknowledged. Kai immediately relaxed. He still had Jessie; he still had his job. It almost seemed too good to be true. He wasn't about to complain though. Suddenly remembering what he needed to do made Kai cringe. "I hope you don't mind, but I need a little more time off. I need to see my parents." The thought of having those conversations filled him with dread again.

The expression on Mason's face turned sympathetic. "Yes, I suppose you do. Go easy on your mother, Kai. She had her reasons for keeping you in the dark." Mason suddenly seemed thoughtful, like he was surprised he would say something so forgiving about Kai's mother. Kai figured that Mason still had deep feelings for Leilani, no matter what had happened between them.

476

Hoping he could be as accepting as Mason was, Kai nodded. The least he could do was try and understand his mother. A feeling flickered over Mason's face, and before Kai knew what was happening, the man was wrapping his arms around him in a tight hug. The unexpected contact made Kai's muscles tense, but he forced himself to relax and loosely return the gesture. When Mason pulled away, it was clear he was embarrassed over the show of affection. "Well, yes, take all the time you need,' he said, clearing his throat. "Getting tickets on such short notice can be pricey. I'll make arrangements."

Kai knew that, and he was floored that Mason would make such an offer. "You don't have to...but thank you. Very much." Mason smiled and turned to open the door. As he did, Kai added, "I'll call you when I get there. So you know I arrived safely. So you won't...worry."

Mason looked back at him, clearly touched. Seeming too emotional to say anything, he merely nodded at Kai before walking away. Feeling an odd sort of uncomfortable happiness, Kai gave Mason one last wave before shutting the door.

As Kai walked down the hallway to Jessie's room, he thought about his impromptu sit-down with Mason...his father. It had gone much differently than he'd ever pictured something like that would. Not that he'd ever truly given much thought to having a conversation like that before a few days ago.

During Kai's twenty-three years on this earth, it had never entered his head that the man who'd raised him, wasn't related to him. But why would he ever think that? As a child, he was told a fact and he'd clung to it as truth, as any child would. His parents were his parents. His family was his family. It was the foundation every life was based upon. And having that yanked away…Kai almost felt like one of those people on daytime TV, the ones who find out late in life that they were adopted, that the family they'd assumed was their blood, wasn't.

As Kai opened the door to Jessie's bedroom, a brief moment of sadness washed over him. He almost wished that was the case for him. As he stepped through the door, he thought about Mason describing Kai's mother, the look on his face when he'd defended her. He'd obviously deeply loved her. Probably still did. And then there was the man who'd raised Kai. The heartbreaking divorce that had split their family in half had obviously shattered him as well as Mason. Even Kai's mother — torn between two loves, only to lose them both — had suffered. No. All in all, if Kai's family secret had just been that he was adopted, it would have been a lot less painful, for a lot more people.

Kai's creation had cleaved a path of destruction through so many lives. Kai paused as he shut Jessie's door behind him. He wasn't sure how to feel about that. Guilt, grief, sympathy …indifference? It was enough to send a person spiraling into a vicious cycle of self-pity. But staring at Jessie asleep on the bed, clutching Kai's pillow to her chest like she was holding onto him, Kai smiled…and let it go. Whatever torment his existence had created wasn't his fault. He hadn't asked to be born, hadn't requested the drama surrounding his birth, and couldn't have possibly altered the way he was conceived. Nobody could. And besides, any changes to his parents' troubled past would have resulted in a different child being born into the world, not Kai. Anything being modified anywhere, would have led to a future where Kai wasn't in this bedroom, listening to his soulmate lightly breathe through barely parted lips. And at this moment in time, Kai loved where he was. He didn't want anything to change.

Kai smiled softly as he climbed into the bed behind her. Wrapping his arms tightly around her, he buried his head into her shoulder. Inhaling the calming scent of her, the loose strands of her curls tickling his cheeks, he laced his fingers through hers. She stirred under his touch, snuggling her back into his chest, like she wished they were even closer.

"Hey," she said sleepily. "Did your dad leave?"

Exhaling a soft breath, Kai kissed her ear. "Mason left, yes."

Jessie stretched the sleep out of her body and twisted to look at him. "And how are you doing?"

Kai propped himself up on his elbow and looked down on her. Warm, compassionate eyes were staring back up at him, just a hint of desire in the dark depths. Shaking his head at her never-ending concern and love, he shifted her until she was on her back. "I'm fine."

She ran her fingers along his shoulder, unconsciously tracing the curve of his tattoo under his shirt. "Are you sure?"

Kai leaned down for a long, slow kiss, only answering her when he was satisfied. "Yes, I'm sure. I'm fine." Kai sighed as he brushed a stray strand of hair off her cheek. "We should go see Gran though. She's probably worried about me."

Jessie nodded as her arms laced around his neck, pulling him back to her lips. "Yeah, okay…in a minute," she muttered between their mouths.

Kai laughed, but deepened their kiss, angling his head to feel more of her mouth on his. Between the softness of her lips and the teasing flicks of her tongue, Kai began to wonder if he would ever get used to making love to her. He didn't think so.

The fire she ignited in him, even with just a simple swish of her hips when she walked past him, was beyond anything he'd ever felt before. Every time with her felt like the first time. He wasn't sure if that was because the love he felt for her was so intense, or if it was because he'd been so sure he'd never truly get to have her. As he lost himself to her soft moans and pleas for more, his hands running over the wondrous curves of her body, he decided that was one mystery that he could be content with never knowing the answer to.

When they finally dragged themselves out of bed and out the front door, Kai blinked in the bright daylight. Laughing to himself, he thought maybe they'd been sequestered in Jessie's relatively dark bedroom for too long. As he turned to watch Jessie shade her eyes from the sun, he thought she might agree.

Smiling, Jessie grabbed his hand and walked with him to her truck. As she started it, butterflies flared to life in Kai's belly. Speaking with his newfound father was one thing, he'd only just met the man, but speaking with his grandmother, the woman who had loved him his entire life, even though she'd had no biological reason to care for him, was making Kai anxious. He wiped his palms on his jeans. For once, he was incredibly warm.

Without a word, Jessie placed her hand over his; it was cool, she was calm. Kai clenched it back, grateful for the strength her presence gave him. She gave him an encouraging nod, and he nodded back. Neither one of them needed to verbalize the moment.

Kai wondered what he would say to the woman he'd known his entire life to be his grandmother. He was nothing to her, really, just her son's ex-wife's bastard baby. He could definitely see why Gran did not like his mom now. Regardless of the torturous situation Kai's mother had found herself in, ultimately she'd hurt Nate. As a mother, that level of betrayal was probably unforgivable to Gran.

Kai was absorbed in these thoughts as Jessie made her way through the frozen streets of Denver. He was only distracted when the squeals of sirens and the flashing of swirling lights broke his concentration. Jessie pulled over so a fire truck and police car could race past her from behind; the speed of the vehicles made her truck shake. Jessie looked over at Kai as the emergency vehicles sped by. Her face was drawn in concern for whatever poor soul needed assistance on this chilly day.

Kai glanced at her, then shifted his attention to the rescue vehicles. As Jessie merged with traffic, he watched the mammoth fire engine pull onto a familiar street. "Jessie," he whispered, ice flooding his veins.

He heard her gasp, but he couldn't pull his gaze from the disappearing end of the police car to look at her. As Jessie's truck surged ahead though, he knew that she had pieced it together just as quickly as he had. The poor soul needing assistance today lived on their grandmother's street. Their grandmother was old and frail, even if she pretended not to be. She'd already suffered a painful fracture just a few months ago. What if she'd fallen again? What if she was really hurt? What if, what if, what if...?

Jessie's truck slid as she took the right angle to Gran's street way too fast. Kai grabbed the handle above the door, but didn't say anything about her fishtailing around the corner. His throat was locked up with fear anyway. He didn't know how he could forgive himself if Gran had been lying in her home, hurt, while he'd been busy with Jessie.

As Jessie slid to a stop as close to Gran's house as she could get, Kai saw that nearly the entire neighborhood had come out to watch the spectacle. His heart racing, Kai couldn't see much of what was going on with the rescue crew. The fire truck that had breezed past them was stopped on the road, partially blocking traffic as it rested beside the parked cars. The police car had parked sideways, helping to keep back the flood of curious bystanders. As Kai and Jessie raced through the crowd on the sidewalk, trying to understand what was going on, the whine of an ambulance siren cut through the air.

Dread filling him, Kai watched the ambulance lights as they flashed in a repeated circular pattern. The vehicle slowed as it approached Gran's house; all the people and vehicles on the road was impeding its progress. Kai wanted to shout at the mob to move, to give the medics space, but at that moment, the ambulance siren went dead, the lights shut off.

Kai shoved his way through the crowd. Something about the ambulance halting its urgent wail signaled doom to Kai. If they were no longer in a hurry to save the person inside...then it was only because...they were too late.

Pushing his way through the mob created a stir that didn't go unnoticed. By the time he got to the squad car, the people around him were irritated. Kai was sputtering something about letting him pass. All he could think about was getting to Gran, and it was only when a uniformed police officer grabbed his shoulders that he focused his attention on something else.

Holding him tight, the officer informed Kai that he needed to wait on this side of the squad car. Shaking his head at the man, Kai urgently said, "Please let me go…that's my grandmother's house. I need to make sure she's okay."

The cop looked him over, then past Kai to Jessie, who had caught up to him and grabbed his hand. She was no longer calm, her palm as clammy as his own, but Kai held her as if she were the only real thing left in the world. Nodding at the both of them, his face serious but solemn, the police officer indicated that they could pass.

As he rushed forward, Kai's heart pounded so hard he thought he might need a medic soon. Frantic, he looked around for the silver haired woman who had never given up on him. "Kai…" He heard Jessie's panicked voice beside him as she searched the chaotic area, but all Kai could focus on was finding the hurt person who was causing this circus of confusion.

Ignoring a pair of firemen who seemed to be looking around as well, maybe hoping an inferno would blaze to life somewhere, Kai shifted his attention to the late arriving medics. Pulling Jessie's hand, he started striding toward one who was talking with what looked like the head fireman. Kai started breathing heavily as he approached the pair. He couldn't imagine Gran gone. When had he seen her last? Had he told her he loved her?

Kai stepped up to the men, and overheard a conversation that confirmed his greatest fear. "Elderly woman. Dead on arrival. Nothing we could do for her. We've started interviewing some of the neighbors, but it seems that she had a heart attack."

Kai put a hand over his mouth, feeling like his stomach was going to surge through it. Jessie started to sob. Tears stinging his own eyes, Kai forced his voice to break free from his throat. "I'm sorry, did you say...?"

He felt the tears spill down his cheeks, and did nothing to wipe them away. She was gone? He felt his heart deadening as the men looked him over, and then he noticed something behind them that made his entire world start spinning. Another fireman and the other medic were wheeling a stretcher out of Gran's front door. The EMT was sadly shaking his head and zipping up a bag over the body. It was a black bag.

Kai's voice choked up completely as the stretcher was wheeled right past him. Jessie's sobbing increased, but Kai could only gape in stunned disbelief. She can't be dead. They had too much to tell her. He had too many questions. He wanted to know why she'd hidden the truth, why she hadn't told him who he was the minute he'd arrived here. He wanted to tell her about his feelings for Jessie.

He wanted... *He* needed...

Disgust at his own selfishness filled him. The world had just lost an amazing woman. Jessie had just lost her last relative in the city. His father, the man who'd raised him, had just lost his mother. And Millie Harper, the woman so filled with life and vitality that it was hard to picture her any other way, would never get to see another sunrise, would never get to play matchmaker for another grandchild, and would never get to see the tomatoes she'd just planted in her greenhouse come to fruition.

And they'd said heart attack. Was that because of him? Did he do this? Did he cause her so much stress and worry that her aged heart couldn't handle it? Was all of this...his fault? God, why the hell hadn't he called her?

Jessie twisted in his arms to cry against his chest, and Kai wrapped his arms around her, clutching her tight. This couldn't be happening. How did he go from so incredibly happy to so incredibly sad in just a couple of hours? The men offered their condolences for the loss they saw before them, and a warm hand rested on Kai's shoulder. The hand patted him consolingly as a familiar voice said, "Sad, isn't it?"

Kai and Jessie broke apart at the same time and snapped their gazes to the person who had spoken. Kai felt all of the blood drain from his face as he looked over what could only be a ghost. Millie Harper stood before Kai, favoring her tender hip as she sadly stared at the ambulance doors banging closed. Sighing as she shook her head, she calmly looked back at him and said, "She came over for tea, then boom...dead." Her gray brows bunched together as her wrinkled lips pursed. Her eyes, warm and very much alive, flicked back to the ambulance beginning to drive away. "Gosh...I hope it wasn't the tea..."

Kai and Jessie slackened their embrace from around the other as Kai's gaze darted between the woman he'd sworn was dead, to the ambulance obviously holding someone else. Focusing on his grandmother, he took in the handmade Christmas sweater, the khaki slacks, the slippers on her feet, and the slight dirt under her nails from endless plant pampering. He'd been so sure she was gone that seeing her alive almost didn't seem real.

Smiling warmly, she stepped forward and embraced him. "Oh Kai, I'm so glad you are okay. I was so worried about you." Her gaze turned sympathetic as she examined him. He could still only gape at her. He wasn't even able to return her hug.

Jessie found her voice first. "Grams? We thought..." She grabbed her grandmother, knocking the woman back a step.

Confused, the older Harper stroked her granddaughter's back. "Jessica, dear, what is the...?" Her voice trailed off as her eyes followed the leaving ambulance. "Oh, did you two think...?"

Kai's eyes overflowed with tears as he nodded. "We thought you...had a heart attack." Kai stepped into her, enclosing his arms around her and Jessie.

His grandmother, by nurture if not nature, shushed them both and patted their backs. "Oh, no, sweethearts, that wasn't me. My ticker is just fine." Kai and Jessie pulled back to take her in, still surprised that she was a living, breathing person and not an apparition. Smiling softly, she brushed dry one child's cheek, then the other. Cocking an eyebrow, she said, "It will take much more than a leisurely cup of tea to end this old girl. I plan on going out in a blaze of glory...sky diving or something."

Kai shook his head and inadvertently chuckled at her; the release felt wonderful. Thank God she was okay. Grudgingly letting go of her, so they didn't accidently crush her to death, Kai asked, "Who was that then?"

Gran sighed as she looked across her lawn, to the neighbor who had helped Kai on his first visit to his grandmother's house. "Betty...my neighbor." Shaking her head, she returned her eyes to Kai. "She was centuries old, and really didn't take very good care of herself. But she was sweet, in a nosey sort of way."

She paused a moment as she reflected over the loss that had taken place in her home, then her expression brightened. "While I'll miss that old broad, I can't help but think that her home was a rental, and will probably need a new tenant now." She gave him an endearing smile. "You could move out of your tiny little apartment. You could be my neighbor...if you're staying, that is." She raised her eyebrows inquisitively, waiting for his answer.

Kai had to laugh that she'd found a silver lining in all of this. But then he sighed, as he looked over the hope on his grandmother's face. She was praying he would stay here, even knowing what he knew now. And he planned to, but not in the way she was imagining. His home was with Jessie, and his grandmother needed to know that, but his relief that she was alive evaporated his earlier nerves about sitting down and talking with her. He could get through this, because she was okay, and she was still going to be okay after he told her everything that was in his heart. They all would be.

Rubbing her shoulder, he told her, "Well, about that, Gran..." He glanced over at Jessie, then grabbed her hand. "Jessie and I have some things we should talk to you about. How about we go inside?"

When the trio walked back into the house, Kai easily spotted the evidence of today's tragic events—an overturned chair in the kitchen, a shattered teacup on the floor. Gran sighed as she looked around. "She invited herself over for tea. I knew your father was speaking with you, Kai, since he called me this morning, so I welcomed the distraction. Plus, I liked Betty. She was a sweet old gal. I tried to help her when she collapsed, but there was nothing I could do."

She sighed again, her face forlorn, and Kai patted her shoulder. "You did your best, Gran."

Releasing Jessie's hand, he got to work cleaning up the mess. Gran shouldn't have to keep looking at the reminder.

Jessie moved to help him, and Gran shook her head. "I can handle that. You two don't need to."

Her face sparkling with relief and love, Jessie smiled at the older woman. "We know you can, Grams, but we want to help. So please don't be difficult and let us."

Gran threw her hands up in the air, but there was a prideful smile on her face. While Kai and Jessie cleaned up the mess, she explained again everything that happened with her neighbor. As badly as he felt for Betty, Kai was still awed and amazed that Gran was fine; he'd been so sure that had been her on the stretcher.

After the kitchen was returned to normal, Gran lifted an eyebrow at Kai. "Ready for that talk now? I'm sure there is a lot you want to say to me."

Grabbing Jessie's hand again, for support and comfort, Kai nodded. Yes, there were several things he wanted to say. They moved to the living room, where everyone would be more comfortable. Kai and Jessie sat close together on the couch, while Gran took a seat in her favorite chair. Kai and Jessie were still holding hands, but Gran didn't seem bothered by the affection. If anything, she seemed pleased that they were closer than ever after the bombshell Kai had just received; hopefully she'd still feel that way after she learned just how close they really were.

Kai stroked the back of Jessie's hand while he tried to think of a good way to open the conversation. His grandmother watched the movement with furrowed brows, but then her expression shifted to concern. "Kai, dear, are you all right? What you learned about your life, couldn't have been easy for you. It's been difficult...for everyone involved."

Kai had to agree with her assessment. This sham, this lie …it had stressed his relationship with his father, caused him to doubt his mother, and made him think for a long time that Mason hated him. He glanced at Jessie before answering his grandmother. She was the only bright spot to come out of it, and it was bright enough to shove the dark spots so far into the background, they didn't hurt him nearly as much as they should. Returning his eyes to Gran, he calmly said, "Honestly, I'm fine, Gran." He frowned as he considered that she wasn't really his grandmother. "Do I still call you Grandma?"

Reaching over, she swatted his knee just as she'd swatted his bottom when he was a toddler. "Of course you do. Who fathered you doesn't change the fact that we're family." Her aged eyes shifted from Kai to Jessie. "We are *all* still family."

Jessie bit her lip, and she and Kai locked gazes. Kai knew just what she was thinking, since he was thinking it too. They had to tell her, and she'd just given them an opening. When they both looked back at her, Gran was clearly stumped over their silent conversation. Kai cleared his throat. "Um…Gran." He worried his lip for a moment, unsure how to proceed. How did he explain that he was in love with the woman he'd been told was his cousin? "I…well, we…" He indicated Jessie with his free hand while simultaneously lifting their joined fingers. "We've decided…not to be family."

Gran bunched her brows, deeply confused. Then her expression turned fiery. "Now listen here, Kai Harper, you can't just decide something like that. You *are* family, regardless of what your blood says, and I won't allow the two of you to think otherwise. You don't abandon family, and you can't choose to not be connected anymore. It doesn't work that way."

Kai grinned and a nervous laugh escaped him. "Well, no, we're still going to be connected, Gran. Deeply connected... just not in a family sort of way."

Still not understanding, Gran shook her head. Kai was about to try and explain further, when Jessie laughed and looped her arms around his body. Snuggling into his side, she said, "What he's trying to say is that we're dating. We're boyfriend and girlfriend." She turned to him and smiled so brightly, Kai felt it all the way to his toes. "We're in love with each other."

Kai peeked at his grandmother, to see her reaction. Many things fluttered across her face. Understanding, compassion, clarity, and curiosity. "Oh...I see," she whispered. She seemed paler than before, and definitely shocked. She hadn't seen that coming. Kai hoped the news didn't send the ambulance back here.

While she looked like she was struggling with something more profound to say, Kai's eyes narrowed in concern. "Are you...okay?"

He searched her for any sign of heart trouble, and she immediately snorted in irritation. "Well, of course I'm fine with it. Love is always a good thing." She pointedly raised an eyebrow. "The world could use more of it." Shaking her head, she added, "I will need a minute to adjust to the idea though. But...Kai isn't blood family, so...I guess, I'll get there. Eventually."

Feeling more relieved than he ever thought possible, Kai leaned over and placed a hand on her knee. "Thank you, for understanding. Your support means the world to us."

His grandmother was silent as she studied Kai and Jessie. She seemed to be gauging their happiness, and deciding what she could really be okay with. Kai tensed while he waited for her to change her mind, but then her expression softened and she patted his hand. "I always knew the two of you were good for each other…I just never imagined that you'd be good together in that way. But you are a perfect match, even I can't deny that, and I'm thrilled to see you both so happy."

Her absolute acceptance dissolved the lingering tension in his body. But his grandmother's smile shifted into concern as Kai removed his hand and leaned back on the couch. "Do you understand, Kai?" When it was clear he wasn't following her, she added, "Do you understand why I couldn't tell you about your real father? Why I never wanted you to know?"

The smile fell off Kai's face as his grandmother unknowingly battered his heart with a sledgehammer. "No, I don't. Why would you hide the truth from me?"

She sighed as she adjusted her sore hip. "I suppose I was trying to protect you. In my head, Nate will always be your father. I didn't see the point of you knowing, since the truth would only bring you pain." Her lips twisted into a wry smile as she watched Jessie watching Kai. "I certainly never saw what a benefit the truth could be to you."

Kai let out a soft laugh as he glanced at Jessie. "I suppose I can understand that. I just wish the news had come from someone I knew." With a sigh, he hung his head. "I think that would have been an easier way to hear it."

Leaning forward, Gran grabbed his cool hand with both of hers. When he peeked up at her, she pressed her lips into a firm line and matter-of-factly stated, "I will never keep anything from you again. I promise."

Kai nodded then sank down in front of her chair and wrapped his arms around her body. Warmth enveloped him as he tightly held the woman who would always be family to him. Regardless of blood, fate had given her to him, and he wouldn't let her go without a fight. And who knows, maybe someday he and Jessie would get married, and she would be true family again. It was a possible future that filled him with hope.

Like she was reading his mind, his grandmother murmured into his ear, "You'll always be family to me, Kai. I love you."

As he squeezed her back just as tight, he responded with, "Blood or not, I love you too."

When he pulled away from her, she was sniffling but happy. She studied him with clear relief on her face, like she was glad he was handling the news so well. He was probably taking it much better than she'd ever imagined. While Kai knew there would be good days and bad days, he also knew he would make it through. Even though his parents had cracked his foundation...had fallen from the slim pedestals he'd put them on...he had his grandmother's unconditional love, and he had Jessie's, and there was an enormous amount of strength in their support.

As Kai sat back on his heels, Gran's watery eyes shifted to Jessie on the couch. "Thank you, Jessica, for being there for him. I'm positive that your...love...is what got him through this." Jessie placed her hand on Kai's shoulder, and when he peeked up at her, there were tears in her eyes. They were happy tears though. Yes, she was definitely the reason he was still able to smile right now.

While Kai absorbed every feature on the face he loved, he heard his grandmother chuckle and say, "Well, since I seem to be such a frail, near-death woman to the both of you, how about you stay and make sure I eat something." Kai looked back at her; she was smirking. "You wouldn't want me to die of malnutrition, would you?"

Kai kept his face as serious as possible as he nodded, then he broke into a soft laugh. Gran laughed with him. With a shake of her head, she watched Kai stand up, then help Jessie to her feet. "I suppose I'll have to stop trying to set you both up with people?" she said.

Raising one corner of her lip, Jessie sullenly replied with, "Please do. I don't need any more Simons calling me twenty-four seven."

Wait, what? Kai looked back at Jessie with a small frown on his face. "Who's Simon?"

Jessie and Gran shared a look of secret knowledge, before Jessie smiled coyly at Kai. "No one important, sweetheart."

Kai's frown deepened until Jessie leaned forward and gave him a light kiss. Then he let it go. Didn't matter anyway. Kai knew without a doubt where Jessie's heart was. Gran sighed as she watched them, and Kai looked back at her. "I don't know how I missed the signs," she murmured, her face full of wonder. "Just goes to show you, no matter how old you get, life can still surprise you."

As Jessie stepped into his arms, Kai had to agree with his grandmother's comment. Yes, life could be very surprising at times. And as he was sure his grandmother would agree, that was what made waking up every day worth it.

25

Aloha

K ai stretched back in his padded seat and sipped the remainder of his champagne. The roar of engine noise was faint to his ears as he reclined as far as the seat would go. Kai had never flown first class before, but as the meticulously put together woman walking down the aisle stopped, took his glass, and asked him and Jessie if they needed a refill on their drinks, he thought he might never fly any other way again.

Smiling, he shook his head at the stewardess. "All right, let me know if you do need anything." Her voice was bubbly and bright as she fluffed his pillow before stepping off to help another passenger.

Kai's eyes drifted to the windows. All he could see out of the tiny ovals were swatches of wispy, white clouds, but he knew that below the cloudbank they were quickly approaching his hometown, his home island.

Jessie squirmed in excitement, her eyes glued to the window immediately to her right. Kai smiled at her enthusiasm.

She was just as eager to see the ocean as he'd been anxious to see the snow. It was something that was remarkably odd to both of them, since he'd lived all his life near the water and she'd lived all of hers near the mountains. Kai loved that he could give this experience to her, even if landing back home was coating his stomach with a black tar of dread.

He wasn't worried about his parents accepting his relationship with Jessie. After Gran had given them her blessing, his stress on the matter had eased considerably. Besides, after what his parents had done to him, and to each other, they really didn't have any room to talk on the subject of love. So far as Kai was concerned, they didn't have a say on who he dated, even if that person had always been seen as a family member. His father would have an especially hard time with that, since he was Jessie's legitimate uncle. There was no getting around it though.

But Kai had come to terms with that situation. What was weighing down his stomach, sizzling his nerves, was the thought of confronting his mother and father on the lie that had permeated so much of his childhood. Rationally, he understood the reasons why he'd been kept in the dark, but his heart was screaming and protesting, yelling at the top of its loud, thumping voice that he had been betrayed. Betrayed by the very people who were supposed to be his rock.

He hated that his body was in such disagreement. That wasn't his style. He saw facts and made a logical conclusion based on those facts. That was how he worked his job. That was how he tried to live his life. If he had come across this situation in the wild, say, a gorilla female had duped a strong male into accepting her child as his own, Kai would have been awed by the miraculous ingenuity and perseverance of mother nature. But when the subjects in question were human... when they were *him*...the detachment of science flew right out the window, leaving only emotion and pain.

As Kai's clammy fingers tightened on the leather seat, he marveled over the fact that Mason had purchased these tickets for him. When Kai had returned to Jessie's placed after their visit with their grandmother, there had been a message on her machine from Mason, leaving the details of the flight.

Not only had he arranged for them to leave the very next day, but he'd booked them first class. And it made Kai smile that they were round-trip tickets. It made him surprisingly happy that his birth father wanted him to stick around. He'd been so sure the man hadn't liked him that it was still shocking to know that Mason might actually *love* him. It blew Kai's mind. He wasn't sure if he loved the man in return yet, he was still practically a stranger to Kai, but he was willing to give him a chance. He was willing to get to know him. It seemed like the least Kai could do after all this.

Kai exhaled a slow, steady breath as the cloud cover broke and the dark blue depth of the Pacific Ocean erupted into view. He knew that before too long those near-black waters would shift to a bluish-greenish color that sort of matched his eyes. Then he'd be back home. Mason had also told him in his message that he'd spoken with Kai's mother again. She was meeting them at the airport.

Jessie squealed and grabbed his hand, squeezing it. His stress relieving exhale turned into a light laugh. She was so excited about arriving that it took away a great deal of his tension. When her face turned back to his, her wide, chocolate eyes were glowing in their delight. She giggled and grinned, but her smile faltered as she looked over his face. "Hey, you okay?"

Kai forced the smile to return to his face but her frown only deepened; clearly she saw right through it. Knowing he couldn't keep his emotions from her, he sighed; she knew him far too well. Shaking his head, he shrugged. "I'm just...a little nervous about this."

Her hand squeezed his tight as she leaned over and placed a light kiss on his lips. "I know." Pulling back, she gave him those smoky eyes that quickened his heart. "I'm here for you." Smiling, Kai moved in for another kiss. He was glad to hear it. He had a feeling he would be leaning on her a lot this trip.

Reveling in the light, languid sensation of kissing her, Kai glanced out the window over her shoulder. Seeing something he knew would interest her, he pulled apart from her mouth. "Hey," he whispered, nodding toward the window. Her eyes were burning like she no longer cared about any view that wasn't him, and she leaned in to find his lips again. Laughing, Kai kissed her then muttered, "Jess, you're missing it."

"No, I'm not," she mumbled in a low voice.

Kai laughed again, then forcibly turned her head away from him. Resting his chin on her shoulder, he looked out the window with her. Out of the corner of his eye he watched her mouth fall open as she gasped. "God, Kai...how could you ever leave this place?"

They were still a ways away, but the closest island in the string of islands that collectively made up the state of Hawaii, was quickly growing larger and larger in the glass window-pane. The innate beauty of his home made a peaceful smile grace Kai's lips. Green was the first thing he noticed. It was green in a way that most places weren't anymore, green with the lush life of jungle vegetation. Fog ringed the taller mountain peaks, mere hills compared to the mountains of Colorado, and the blue-green water endlessly lapped against the white-sand beaches. It really was, as Jessie was constantly telling him, paradise, and Kai sighed in contentment. He might be coming home to a bittersweet reunion, but he was still coming home, and a part of him had really missed it here.

Jessie's face was glued to the window as they finally started their descent. She giggled as she watched the emerald island growing and expanding, until the only thing visible in the window was the lushness of life. As the more urban areas drew near, she finally turned back to him. "We're here!"

Kai nodded as he felt the plane begin to slow down. Yes, they were here and his parents were waiting for them. Smiling at Jessie, Kai clenched her hand as the plane lowered to the ground, lightly bumped against the pavement of the runway, and then forcefully screeched to a stop. He was immensely happy that she had decided to go on this little trip with him. As much as she'd wanted to, she hadn't been sure if work would let her go, especially since she'd called in sick so many times already this week. But the last phone call she'd made had ended with them telling her that another masseuse would cover her clients and it was no problem if she wanted to take the rest of the week off. Kai had her until Monday...and he was really happy about that.

The plane disembarked, Kai's section exiting first, and Kai clenched her hand even harder. He'd never in his life imagined that seeing his parents would cause him so much stress. But he supposed that was part of the problem—they weren't both his parents, and they'd hidden that fact from him. His dad was a genetic stranger and his mom…well, she sort of felt like a stranger after all he'd learned about her.

A beautiful Hawaiian girl greeted them as they exited the plane. She gave them the standard "aloha" greeting and draped a couple of leis over their necks. Jessie thanked her as she fingered her flowers. Her smile was so bright, her delight so clear that Kai momentarily forgot his discomfort. He thanked the greeter with a quick, "Mahalo," before pulling Jessie toward baggage claim.

He wanted to whisper in her ear that she'd just been lei'd in public, but as they approached baggage claim, his eyes locked onto a pair of people that he'd known very well for most of his life. He instinctually straightened as he met gazes with first his father, then his mother. They'd surprisingly come together; they generally avoided being at the same place if they weren't at work, and Kai knew exactly why they did that now.

Jessie stopped when she felt his stance change and twisted to look at what had his attention. "What is it, Kai? Are your parents here?"

Kai wasn't sure how to answer that simple question anymore. Knowing what she meant though, he only said, "Yeah."

His feet felt encased in cement, but he made himself trudge over to the people who had shaped his formative years. Stopping well before them, he gave them each a polite nod. It surprised him some that he managed to move at all; his entire body felt like one rigid, immobile piece. "Mother… Nate." Kai noted the chill in his voice. He wished it wasn't there, but he couldn't do anything to alter it, either. These people had sent him thousands of miles away, so that someone else could tell him that his childhood had been a lie. They would have to excuse him if he felt a little bitter about it.

His mother began to cry once she heard his tone. Kai's eyes drifted to the dark-haired woman, her deep skin color an identical match to his own. The sight of her cheeks wet with tears cracked Kai's resolve, dulled the hard edge of his anger. Regardless of what they had done to him, Kai didn't want to hurt them. They were family.

Nate Harper, the man Kai had always known as his father, cleared his throat. Kai reluctantly swung his gaze to his. There was so much of Jessie in the color of Nate's eyes that a lump formed in Kai's throat. He watched those deep brown eyes water and felt his own sting in response. He'd loved this man so much, his entire life. Their bond had been unbreakable, but now…it felt worn, frail.

The aged face staring back at him was so familiar it was calming. Seeing Nate reminded Kai of everything he'd wanted to be when he grew up—strong like his dad, smart like his dad, adventuresome and funny like his dad. While Kai's hair was pitch-black like his mother's, and his skin was just as deeply tanned as hers, when young Kai had envisioned himself as a man, he'd always imagined himself with sandy hair and pale skin. He'd always seen himself as a spitting image of Nate Harper. Was all of that simply because he'd believed they shared the same DNA, or was it because they'd shared an immense, impenetrable love for one another? Kai firmly believed it was based on love.

As his father struggled with words, Kai cleared the knot that was choking off his voice. "Dad?" he whispered.

Kai had never seen his father cry before—truly cry—not until today. Tears streaming down his face, he stepped up to

Kai and engulfed him in a tight embrace. Kai's own tears were unstoppable then, and he hugged him back just as fiercely. Love. DNA. Family. Between a parent and a child, genetics wasn't what fueled the bond. While Nate might not technically be his father...he was love, and love made him family.

"I'm so sorry, Kai. I'm so sorry I didn't tell you myself. I'm so very sorry, son."

That was repeated over and over into Kai's ear, until Kai heard himself responding with, "It's okay, Dad. It's all right, I forgive you."

Finally pulling back from his father, both of them wiping their eyes, Kai looked over at his mother. "I forgive both of you." He shook his head at her and shrugged.

How could he hate someone for loving him so much, that they'd do anything to keep him from feeling pain? That was all his mother had ever done for him; tried to shelter him from the sharp sting of the truth. As the tiny woman attacked him, sobbing apologies into his shoulder, Kai found that he couldn't even hate them for sending him to Mason. True, hearing it from them would have been better, would have been easier, but the outcome would have been the same.

Plus, Kai had had a lot of practice recently at understanding regret. After everything that had happened between him and Jessie, when they'd both believed they were blood-related, he'd regretted several things that he'd done. So he understood that his parents were beating themselves up every chance they got over the way they'd chosen to break the news to him, and he wouldn't add to their grief by torturing them about their decision. But he did intend to sit down and talk with them about it. Much like with Mason and his grandmother, Kai wanted to understand. He wanted to know them, as people, not as the infallible parents he'd believed them to be. He knew they'd both made mistakes with him, and with each other, and he wanted to sit down and discuss it with them. But first, he wanted to introduce them to his girlfriend.

Peeling his mother off of him, he moved over to where Jessie had stepped back so she could watch the exchange from a respectful distance. She was drying her cheeks and Kai warmly shook his head at her. She shrugged and sniffled; that emotional display had gotten to her. He loved that it had. Jessie had such a good heart, and he wanted to show it to his parents. He wanted them to be okay with who she was. And after everything that they'd done to him, really, accepting her as the love of his life was the least they could do.

Exhaling a slow breath, he grabbed both of her hands and then slung his arm around her waist. That intimate move got the attention of both of his parents, and they started examining Jessie with curious eyes. Kai watched Jessie flush as he pulled her closer to his parents, and felt her squeeze his waist tighter when she was right in front of them. Looking down on her, Kai quietly said, "Mom, Dad, this is my best friend, the love of my life, my girlfriend…Jessica Marie Harper."

Even though the busy airport was bustling with holiday travelers, Kai could have heard a pin drop at that moment. Looking over at his parents, he almost laughed at the near-identical, stunned expression on each of them. They each knew her name, same as he had known that name. His mother appeared shocked and dismayed at the revelation, and his father had paled considerably. Since Nate and Jessie actually *were* blood related, it had to be startling for him to see Kai with his arm around his niece.

Kai and Jessie gave them another quiet moment to absorb the news, then Jessie stuck her hand out. "It's nice to meet you, Leilani." Kai's mother loosely took the hand offered and shook it. After that, Jessie waved her fingers at Kai's still-open-mouthed dad. "Hi, Uncle Nate, it's nice to finally meet you."

That phrase seemed to snap everyone out of their astonishment, and both parents twisted to Kai. "You can't date her," his mother and father said almost simultaneously.

Kai smiled as he let them voice their concerns for a few minutes. When they both seemed flushed but finished, he merely said, "We're not related. We *can* date, and we're going to." He smiled down at Jessie as she rubbed soft circles into his back. "I love her, and I'm not spending another day without her." Glancing at his parents, he raised an eyebrow. "Is that going to be a problem between us?"

They both shut their mouths and offered no further objections. There was nothing they could say to change his mind anyway, and perhaps they realized that. Since neither parent was saying anything else condemning on the subject, Kai looked at Jessie. "Come on, I want to show you *my* hometown."

She eagerly nodded, biting her lip, then she leaned up and kissed him. Kai thought he heard his father sigh, but he ignored him. He ignored everything but the warm woman under his lips. That was enough. She was enough.

Kai and Jessie were alone in a car with the man Kai had believed was his father his entire life. Jessie watched her uncle as they drove along in complete silence. She hadn't ever met the man before, but the resemblance to her was there in the color of his eyes and the shape of his face. Jessie squeezed Kai's hand as they sat together in the back seat. Before he'd known the truth about his background, Kai had probably had a hard time looking at Jessie without seeing shades of his father in her countenance.

Kai squeezed her hand but didn't look at her. His eyes were locked onto his father's back. Both men looked speculative. With Leilani following in the car behind, the small group eventually made it to one of the two homes Kai had been raised in. As Kai took in the familiar modest dwelling, the corners of his lips curved up. Jessie supposed a part of him was happy to be back here, even if it was sort of painful.

Her uncle's house was in a pretty secluded area, with green life abundant all the way around it. The flat, black-roofed home had a barn behind it, and Jessie remembered Kai telling her about how he used to go horseback riding with his dad. At least Kai had very good memories with her uncle. Hopefully they outnumbered the bad ones.

When Jessie stepped out of the car, the humid air immediately made her feel moist with dew. Kai stepped out after her, looking perfectly at ease in the environment. Walking around the car to her, he extended his hand. Jessie grabbed it and stepped close to his side. Uncle Nate took in their closeness, but didn't comment on it. Jessie was glad he was choosing not to say anything, and hoped he was starting to accept the two of them as a couple; she really didn't want to create tension in her family by loving Kai.

Leilani pulled up to the house a few seconds later and also glanced at Jessie and Kai. Her only response was a smile though, as she helped Kai and Jessie get their bags from the back of the car. Uncle Nate moved to help them as well, and between the four of them, they had their things situated in Kai's old bedroom pretty quickly.

Jessie noticed that Kai's parents kept their distance from each other. It was clear that any love between them had died the moment Uncle Nate had discovered the truth. It saddened her that they'd each had to experience such pain and loss, but even still, she was happy about the situation. It was the only reason she and Kai could be together.

Leilani stayed for a quiet, peaceful supper, then reluctantly said her goodbyes for the evening. As she hugged Kai for the fifth time, her face shifted into sadness. She seemed certain that if she left Kai alone with his father, Kai would feel differently about her the next time he saw her. Knowing Kai like she did, Jessie was pretty sure that wouldn't happen. He would make up his own mind about his mother.

Jessie yawned as she said her goodbyes to Leilani. When the door shut behind her, Kai squeezed Jessie's waist. "Why don't you go to bed. I'll...be there in a minute."

Knowing that Kai was probably just as jet-lagged as her, since he'd finally adjusted to her time zone, she looked past him to her uncle. Nate had his head down; he was obviously waiting to talk to his son in private. Switching her attention back to Kai, Jessie held him close. "I'm here when you need me." He smiled and nodded, then gave her a goodnight kiss.

Hoping the conversation between the two men went well, Jessie shuffled off to Kai's childhood room to get ready for bed. After changing and brushing her teeth, she climbed onto his small mattress and looked at all the signs of young Kai's life around the room. While it wasn't a child's room anymore, there was plenty of evidence that it had been once — old stickers on the dressers, army men shoved in a gap between the window frame, a poster of a bikini clad girl on the wall. Smiling at the image of Kai as a boy, Jessie closed her eyes and let the exhaustion flow through her. As she started fading into sleep, she heard low voices coming through the wall. Realizing that Kai and his dad must be right outside the bedroom window, Jessie fought through the fatigue to listen to their conversation.

Kai's voice broke through the stillness of the night. "Dad, why didn't you just tell me? I mean, I can understand not wanting to let me know when I was young...but I haven't been young for a while now." He paused for a second and Jessie shifted to face the direction of the open window. "Why keep me in the dark? Why send me to Mason?"

Uncle Nate let out a long, beleaguered sigh. "I tried to tell you, Kai. You have no idea how many times I stared at you and tried to tell you." He sighed again and paused long seconds before continuing. "But every time, the anger, the betrayal...it all resurfaced, and I...I just couldn't make the words come out."

Feeling sympathy for her uncle sweep over her, Jessie sat up. None of this could have been easy on him, and he'd been dealing with it for so long. He must have been a wreck. He must have been desperate for it to end, and at the same time, terrified. Nate continued in a soft voice, and Jessie pressed her head to the wall to hear him better. "After years of that, of not being able to talk to you like I wanted to talk to you...it ate at me. I needed you to know, but I still couldn't tell you."

He paused again, and Jessie tried to picture having a conversation like this with her own father. She couldn't. "I figured, since I physically couldn't get the words out around you, and Leilani absolutely refused to tell you...maybe he... maybe Mason could finally do something right...and maybe he could tell you." Her uncle sighed heavily again. "Once I had that thought, it consumed me, and then I *needed* him to be the one to tell you. In my mind, there were no other options."

Jessie looked down at the black and white sheets of Kai's bed, torn for the both of them. For all of them really. Kai exhaled, not speaking for long moments. "I wish *you* had somehow found a way to tell me, Dad. It hurt so much to have a stranger do it." Jessie closed her eyes, remembering how she'd found Kai. She'd never seen someone so shaken up.

Her uncle didn't respond to that right away. "I'm so sorry, son. I was wrong. I promise you I will never deceive you like that again." Jessie smiled as she settled against Kai's pillows. Maybe they would all come out of this stronger. As she closed her eyes, Uncle Nate spoke again. "I'm so...I'm so grateful you still call me Dad." There was so much relief in his voice; it made Jessie smile.

Kai laughed a little, and the sound lightened the heavy mood Jessie could feel pouring in from the outside. "Of course I'll still call you Dad. It's who you are, blood or not."

Jessie heard the men shuffling, and imagined they were hugging. "I love you, Kai."

"I love you too, Dad." Jessie started falling asleep with a smile on her face and tears on her cheeks, happy that even though the blood bond had been broken between them, the bond of love hadn't been.

After that candid conversation, things between Kai and his father were less tense. Their relationship evened out, once the sting of deception and lack of communication started dulling. They often sat on the lanai after dinner, talking late into the night while Jessie crawled into Kai's childhood bed. Before she fell asleep at night, she'd be comforted by the sounds of their reconnection. Through the walls she would listen to her uncle repeat his guilt and grief at not having had the strength to tell Kai himself. And for his part, Kai was pretty sympathetic to the man's feelings. When Jessie asked him about it, Kai told her that it wasn't his dad's fault that he hadn't been the one to create him, and he couldn't imagine having to tell a child something that hard.

And after that first day, Kai's parents were silent about her and Kai's relationship. Jessie had to believe that it was extremely awkward for them though, especially for her uncle. It was difficult for him to see beyond the fact that Kai was his son and Jessie was his niece; the cousin connection was just too strong to ignore. Jessie understood. Even for her, it was weird to call Kai's dad, Uncle. A part of her wanted to drop the familial term and just call him Nate, but it was too ingrained in her. It seemed to be ingrained in Nate, too, since he always called her Jessica Marie, and only Jessie's family ever did that.

But he didn't ever say anything negative about her and Kai being together, not even when he walked in on a pretty intense make-out session they'd been having on his couch. Instead of freaking out over the display, he'd only mumbled several apologies and hastily fled the room. Jessie tried to keep the PDA to a minimum after the incident. She didn't want to make Kai's family — her family — uncomfortable, especially in their own homes.

On their final day in Hawaii, Kai took Jessie to a private beach that he loved, to do something with her that Jessie had been hoping they'd be able to do this trip. Something she'd been dying to do ever since arriving here. Something she, in all honesty, had been waiting her entire life to do.

Sitting on a surfboard, Jessie floated peacefully in the relative calm of the Pacific Ocean. Being just behind the breakers, she stared in awe at the tumultuous waves crashing onto the comparatively hard beach. She had no idea how people did this. She'd been attempting to successfully ride one of those waves all morning. So far, she'd swallowed about a quarter of the ocean, but hadn't even successfully popped up onto the board.

A wave of water splashing across her face tore her attention from the pounding surf. The sun beat on her bare skin as the muggy air kept her warm, despite the slight chill of the deep water. Brushing aside the droplets, Jessie looked over to see Kai laughing at her. He'd spent part of the morning trying to teach her the basics on land, but Jessie hadn't wanted to be shown up, since Kai had mostly succeeded at skiing. She'd insisted that they head out into the water, and practice surfing for real.

Kai laughed even harder at the look of annoyance on her face. The water droplets gleamed in his slicked back hair and for a moment, Jessie couldn't recall seeing anything more natural than Kai in the water. Shaking his head, he teased her with, "Not as easy as it looks, is it Mountain Girl?"

Jessie attempted to douse him with a tidal wave of water, and nearly fell off her floating board in the process. Kai tilted his head toward the sand. "Come on, one more try then we'll go in."

Jessie sighed, but nodded. She could try one more time. Kai chuckled, then started paddling away. Smiling as she watched his muscles expanding and contracting under that fabulous skin, his dark as night tattoo matching his black board shorts, Jessie slowly started paddling after him. Kai's shouted some last minute instructions to her, then scanned the break for the wave he wanted. Seeing it, he took off. Jessie watched him effortlessly hop up onto his board and ride the wave toward the shore. He held his position perfectly, his body gloriously tight as he used every blessed muscle to steady himself, until the momentum of the wave dropped off and he slipped into the water.

Wondering if she'd ever be able to do that, Jessie searched …for something. Shrugging, since she really had no idea what to look for, she paddled toward the endlessly cresting water. Balancing on her hands, she mentally prepared to jump both feet up. This was the part that usually had her tumbling into the water. Holding her breath, Jessie went for it. Surprise and shock hit her as she managed to get both feet onto the board at the same time. She nearly fell off in her excitement, but managed to hold it together long enough to slip over what turned out to be a very gentle wave. Mimicking Kai's body and position, she made minor adjustments to keep the board steady. She was expecting it to feel like skiing, but it really didn't. The only thing the two had in common was the rush. That was the same.

She dived off the board at the end, when she finally felt herself starting to fall, then grabbed her board and swam back to the shore. Kai was watching her, whistling as he stood on the beach with one hand on his hip, the other on his board.

Jessie giggled as she ran up to him, excited that she'd actually done it. His eyes flicked down her bikini and she felt a different sort of excitement rush through her. Throwing an arm around his waist, she leaned up for his lips. He congratulated her between kisses, and his hand wrapped around her waist drifted down to cup her backside.

Dropping her board onto the soft sand near their feet, she slung her arms around his neck. He dropped his board too, angling it back so it didn't hit hers. Both hands now free, he grabbed her ass so firmly she squeaked. A pleased noise rumbled low in his chest. "You were right."

Feeling like they should be somewhere much more private, so it would be completely okay for those miraculous fingers to slip inside her bikini, she murmured, "What was I right about?"

Chuckling between their lips, he said, "The bikini. You do rock it."

Breaking apart from him, Jessie shook her head in amusement. Gazing at the eyes that were more astounding than the waters she'd just crawled out of, she felt a pressure in her chest that bordered on the edge of pain. Love beyond reason. That was what she felt for him. She was sure, more sure than she had ever been in her life, that the man in her arms was going to be her husband one day. She didn't quite know how that would happen, since in the eyes of the law they were technically still cousins, but even if it was only a symbolic marriage, she knew Kai was the one she wanted beside her forever.

He grinned crookedly in a way that quickened Jessie's heart. "We're heading home tomorrow. Are you ready to leave all of this behind?" He indicated the magnificence of the island paradise around them.

Her gaze never leaving him, she firmly said, "I'm going wherever you're going, whether that's staying here on the beach, going back home to the snow...or just making out in the back of your mom's car."

Grinning wider, he leaned back in to kiss her. "Well, being wet will make you cold...so let's get you dry first." He cocked an eyebrow at her. "Then we can make out."

With a laugh, she nodded, then they began collecting their stuff. As they drove back to Kai's strange sounding hometown, Jessie took a moment to appreciate the bounty of life on display for her. She wasn't sure when she would be back, but she felt pretty confident that her future with Kai would include a few more trips this way. He would at least want to see his folks once a year. Jessie had a feeling that she would be insisting on it. Smiling at the beauty of the waterfalls tucked behind the emerald green vegetation bursting with tropical flowers so vivid they seemed unreal, Jessie hoped their next visit wasn't too far in the future.

While they had spent the nights here with Kai's father, during the day, Jessie and Kai had spent most of their time with his mother. Kai's relationship with her was different than before, or so Leilani had confessed to her one afternoon, while Kai had been playing in the surf nearby.

Listening to Kai's mother express her grief over the constant lies and deceptions she'd had to tell him—that she'd had to tell both of Kai's fathers—Jessie couldn't stop the compassion she felt for the woman. Yes, she had hurt and betrayed three good men, and what she had been a part of with Kai's fathers was horrible, but Leilani had gotten in so deeply over her head that she hadn't been able to see another way out except to lie. Repeatedly.

As Kai drove his mother's car back to her place near the beach, Jessie wondered if Kai and Leilani would ever have that tight bond again. She hoped so. Even though her own parents had moved away a while ago, Jessie understood the importance of tightknit parent-child bonds. There was nothing quite like knowing that no matter what, no matter who she became or what she did in her life, someone had her back, someone loved her unconditionally. She wanted Kai and his mother to have that again.

As they drove up the gravel driveway, the feminine version of Kai stepped from her porch with a smile and a wave. Her long, dark hair billowed away from her face in the breeze as she gingerly approached the stopping car. Kai sighed as he parked the car, and Jessie twisted to look at him. "She loves you, you know."

Kai tore his eyes from his mother to look over at Jessie. Smiling, he nodded. "Yeah, I know. Sometimes I don't feel like I know much, but that, I do know."

He leaned over and gave Jessie a light kiss. Even with all the time they'd had together, even knowing that they could openly be together now, it still quickened Jessie's heart when he touched her. She had to force herself to not grab a thick section of his hair and forcibly pull him back to her mouth. That wouldn't be appropriate, not with his tiny mother opening the car door.

"Aloha, Jessie," she warmly said.

Jessie returned her greeting. "Aloha, Leilani." While Jessie's uncle had some reservations about Kai and Jessie being together, Kai's mother didn't appear to. Once the initial shock had worn off, she'd accepted Jessie with open arms, even periodically giving them space to...connect. Jessie had a sneaking suspicion that she was going out of her way to be accommodating because she'd do anything to win back Kai's devotion. Jessie didn't blame her, so she wasn't about to call the woman out for it.

After Kai stepped out of the car, he gave his mother a brief hug. Wrapping her arms securely around his waist, she gazed up at him with hope clear in her eyes; she so wanted Kai to forgive her. "Mason tells me that your flight back is early in the morning tomorrow. I'll drive you to the airport, sweetheart."

Kai seemed taken aback by that. "You talked with Mason?"

Leilani flushed and turned her head away from Kai. Jessie could tell she felt guilty for even bringing him up. She could also tell that she still had feelings for the man. It was pretty evident by the way she said his name; it reminded Jessie of the way she often said Kai's name. "Um, yes. We...keep in touch." She looked back at him, and in her sparkling eyes, Jessie could see the residual love she had for the man who'd given her such an amazing son. "He's been worried about you. He calls in nightly to check on you."

Kai looked away, toward the beach. Jessie had been with Kai when he'd called Mason to tell him they'd landed safely. It had surprised Jessie that he'd done that, and amazed her that he would be so considerate to a man he barely knew. Of course, a lot of things about Kai amazed Jessie. And a lot of

514

things about Mason seemed to amaze Kai. Shaking his head as he watched the surf, he muttered, "I'm surprised he does that."

Leilani rested her head on his shoulder. Kai reflexively hugged her tighter against him. "Of course he does, Kai. He loves you. You're his son...even if he just found out about you."

Kai closed his eyes, and his head drooped. Jessie saw the weariness in his features, and knew it wasn't from their rigorous morning on the waves. All of this turmoil was getting to him. Jessie couldn't wait to take him back home, settle him into her bed, and massage away all of the kinks in his body, if not his heart. His heart...she would work on over time.

Opening his eyes, Kai started walking with her toward the house. He had a childhood bedroom here too, and it marveled Jessie how similar his room was to hers at her parents' old place. They'd even shared the same interest in music, both having Beatles posters on their walls.

Sighing, Kai rested his head on his mother's as they unconsciously shifted their walk toward the water. "Why didn't you tell me, Mom? Before I went over there? Why did you tell dad you absolutely didn't want me to know? Don't I have the right to know who my father is?"

Leilani paused in her step, removing her head from his embrace to look up at him. "I'm so sorry, Kai." She shrugged. "Yes, it's true...I never wanted you to know the truth. I didn't see how you could not hate me, if you knew what I'd done." Her eyes watered as she searched his face. "And you...are the most important thing I have. I couldn't risk losing you."

With another weary sigh, Kai squeezed her tightly. "You're not going to lose me, Mom. I love you...regardless of your past."

Leilani couldn't stop the tears and hastily brushed them from her cheeks. "Well, Nate insisted that you know the truth, and then he insisted that I contact Mason, and get you a job there with him." She sighed and looked away, toward the beach, just like Kai had. It seemed to have a calming effect on both of them. "I've been a wreck every single day, wondering when I would get the call. Wondering when you would hate me. Wondering what day Nate would finally get his revenge on me for betraying him." She sighed, the sound both tired and remorseful.

Kai twisted her to look at him. "Dad doesn't want revenge on you. He didn't want to hurt you, he just wanted..." He paused, and his eyes drifted back to Jessie. "He just didn't want to keep living a lie. He wanted the truth released, so he could be free." Smiling, he returned his eyes to Leilani. "So we could all be free."

Knowing Kai meant their relationship just as much as he meant his parents' relationship made tears spring to Jessie's eyes. They'd been living a lie by trying to deny the feelings between them. They'd attempted to label it as familial love, when it had been so far beyond that. The truth had released them from that lie, just as surely as it had released Kai's parents. Uncle Nate was right...knowing the truth mattered.

Kai and his mother spent a good chunk of that afternoon opening up to each other. Much to Jessie's surprise, Kai even told her the truth about how they'd first hooked up. He thankfully didn't mention the one night stand, but he confessed that their attraction had started while they'd thought they were

516

cousins. Sitting on the golden sand with Kai and his mother, Jessie twisted to look at Leilani sitting on the other side of her son. Leilani gave him a warm, compassionate smile, like she understood being in a hard place, and Jessie supposed that she did.

"That must have been very difficult," she said, her hand resting on Kai's knee. "For both of you."

Kai nodded as he looked at her, then he shifted his gaze to Jessie, sitting so close beside him their hips touched. She couldn't help the lack of space between them; she just needed his body to be touching hers. Leaning down to kiss her head, Kai murmured, "Yeah, it was..." Looking back at Leilani, he slung his arm around her shoulders. "But we're good now, Mom. Really good, and even though all of this has been really hard to deal with...I'm okay." He looked back at Jessie, his eyes putting the ocean to shame with their beauty. "I'm great ...because of Jessie."

Jessie felt her entire body heat with pride and love at his words. In and out of the bedroom, the things he said always had such a strong effect on her. She hoped that never faded.

Leilani's wistful sigh pulled both of their attentions back to her. Her expression happy but reluctant, she shook her head. "You're going to stay in Denver, aren't you? Permanently."

Kai sighed, too. "I'll visit as often as I can...and you can always call me." He grinned and added, "Even at four in the morning."

Leilani laughed too, then slung her arms around his neck. "I love you, Kai. I'm very proud of the man you've become."

Kai hugged her back, just as tightly. "I love you too, Mom." When they pulled away from each other, he gave her a crooked smile. "At least that part of my life didn't change... you're still my mother." Leilani smiled brilliantly, her eyes misting. Kai watched her reaction for a second then pulled farther away from her. "You *are* really my mom, right?" He barely got the question out before he started laughing.

Leilani smacked his shoulder before hugging him tight again. "Yes, I'm your mother!" All three of them enjoyed a moment of levity, then Leilani smiled and rested her head on Kai's shoulder. "I'll miss you."

Exhaling softly, Kai rested his head against hers. "I'll miss you too." Chuckling, he raised his head. "But look on the bright side." He flicked a quick glance at Jessie before swinging his eyes back to his mother. "Maybe you'll get grandkids soon."

Jessie's eyes grew so large they hurt, and Leilani squealed and reached across her son to embrace her. Jessie glared at him as she hugged his mother, but Kai only laughed at her expression. Great. Now that he'd thrown the door wide open, the baby talk was going to start pouring through it. Jessie sighed inwardly as she patted the eager woman's back. She was positive a pair of handmade booties were in her near future.

A Future Together

The plane ride away from Hawaii was a completely different experience for Kai than the plane ride there had been. He was completely relaxed by Jessie's side as they reclined in their first class seats. He still felt a lingering ripple of bittersweet happiness after having said goodbye to his parents at the airport. He'd eventually come to terms with what both of them had done to him. And truly, they had hurt themselves as much as they'd hurt him. Maybe more. His mother especially.

At the gate, she'd squeezed Jessie so tightly that Kai had clearly seen the strain on his girlfriend's face. "It was so nice to meet you, Jessie. Take care of my son."

Jessie had flicked her eyes to Kai, a soft smile on her lips. "I will."

Before Kai could even return Jessie's warm smile, his mother had engulfed him in a vice-like hug. "I'll call you every chance I get," she'd told him. Then she'd patted his arm and added, "Now hurry up and get to work on that grand-baby."

Remembering the look of excitement on his mother's face as she'd contemplated a baby in Kai and Jessie's future made Kai grin and shake his head. His mother had certainly made her fair share of mistakes, but in her heart she was a good person, and he loved her, so he'd had no choice but to make peace with her, because he was his reason for being.

She'd finally stopped asking for forgiveness, but he could see the regret in her eyes whenever she looked at him, whenever she looked at Nate. She deeply regretted hurting two men that she genuinely cared for. Kai was positive that he didn't ever want to go through what she had gone through. He didn't ever want his heart torn between two people. Yet another reason he was grateful he could be with Jessie. She fulfilled every part of him, satisfied every desire, want and need. Not being completely faithful to her was unfathomable. Just the thought of it made him nauseous. She had his heart, every single corner of it, and he was positive the feeling was equally reciprocated.

His mother's last words to him had been warm and sweet, like the mom he knew her to be. "I love you so much, Kai. I'll miss you every day. And who knows, maybe I'll fly over and visit. I wouldn't mind seeing Denver."

The small smile on her face had seemed nostalgic and hopeful, and Kai was certain a visit from her would also include a visit to Kai's biological father. Kai was okay with that. His mother had been alone a long time. Mason too, actually. Despite the havoc they'd caused, the two deserved their shot at happiness.

As the perky flight attendant refilled his orange juice, Kai's thoughts shifted to his father. Leaving Nate had felt much like when he'd arrived in Hawaii. It had been just as intense, but for different reasons this time. Back then, Kai had been hurt and confused, but love had ultimately led him to forgiveness. Parting with him had been emotional.

Once his mother had backed off a respectful distance, his father had stepped forward. Smiling softly at Kai, he'd told him, "I'll miss you, son." Swallowing a lump in his throat, he'd added in a choked voice, "I know you'll do great things at the center with Mason. After all, you're a Harper...in spirit at least."

Feeling an almost desperate need to let him know that he would always be his son, Kai had thrown his arms around his father, cinching him tight. "I *am* your son. I'll always be your son...always."

He'd kept repeating it to him over and over. Kai wasn't sure why at the time, and wished he'd been able to stop, since he'd managed to bring his father to tears, but he thought he finally understood. Kai hadn't been assuring his father, he'd been trying to assure himself.

A piece of Kai, a dark piece that he didn't like to look at, was afraid that the man who'd raised him...would abandon him now. Kai's logical brain immediately discounted the idea. After all, if that were really going to happen, it would have happened when Kai was a teenager. If Nate Harper was going to turn his back on him, like he had his marriage, he would have done it years ago, when Kai was young. But logic doesn't always win, and the fear was still there...a lingering worry bubbling to the surface.

Kai supposed that no matter how old a person got the fear of being abandoned, of being rejected by those who were loved the most, was always tucked away in some tragic corner of the soul, where all childhood fears reside. Most people spent every day ignoring those fears, discounting them as readily as they discounted the Boogie Man and the monster under the bed. But when they slipped out, when they found a chink in the armor of who a person was, like a noxious weed, they took hold.

Kai swallowed his drink and rolled his eyes at his own dramatic inner monologue. He glanced over at Jessie to see her eyes were closed; her face was relaxed. She looked a little tired, but that was to be expected after all the ups and downs they'd had recently. Clutching her hand, he was relieved to know that things would probably mellow out from here. Jessie didn't open her eyes, but she smiled when she felt his skin against hers. She loved being close to him, same as he loved being close to her.

Glancing down her body, his eyes rested on her flat stomach. Intrigued by the idea he'd haphazardly tossed out to his mother, he imagined her stomach full of life. His life, his child. While the thought had once appalled him, it warmed him now. Kai had always pictured himself having children in the future, he'd just never been sure who he would have them with. He was sure now. While he'd mainly been joking with his mother, it was something he wanted, something he wanted with Jessie. Maybe not right away, but someday.

Bringing her left hand to his lips, he also imagined placing a ring on her finger. He wanted that too. Now that the option was open to him, it was really all he could think about. They still needed to break the news to her parents, since they were still under the impression that Kai was a cousin, but after everything that Kai had been through lately, he felt sure they could do it.

Jessie looked over at him as his lips rubbed back and forth over the finger he so wanted to encircle. Her dark eyes swept over his features. "What are you thinking about?" she asked.

His gaze lingered on those luscious lips for a second before he answered. Biting back a smile, he shook his head. "I was just thinking that it's legal for first cousins to get married in Hawaii."

Her eyes widened, and she grinned. "I see…that's interesting that you know that."

She raised an eyebrow at him and Kai laughed. "I had a good reason to look it up."

Jessie laughed then sighed contently. "You see us getting married one day?" she asked, her fingers coming up to stroke his cheek.

Closing his eyes, Kai leaned into her touch. "Yes," he said, reopening them "Don't you?"

Color stained her cheeks a beautiful shade of pink as she nodded. "Yeah…someday."

Smiling, he rested his head against hers. "I know legally we're probably still cousins. If we want to get married without all the…complications, there are probably a ton of hoops we'll have to go through. I don't know what they might be, and we might need legal help to prove we're not related. But maybe it's as easy as having my birth certificate changed to show that Nate Harper isn't biologically my father?" Kai shook his head, making their noses brush together. "I kind of hate the thought of doing that, but I would gladly go through with it to freely be your husband. Regardless of the obstacles, I want that future with you. I want you to be my wife."

He pulled back to look at her, and her eyes were wet with tears. Moving her hand from his face, he clenched it tight. "I love you, Jessie...always."

She smiled as the tears dripped down her cheeks. "I love you, too."

They leaned in for a series of light, soft kisses that made Kai feel a little dizzy. When they withdrew, Jessie raised an eyebrow at him. "Most of our extended family will still think we're related."

Kai shrugged, not caring anymore. "Let them. We know the truth. Besides, it's just the multitude of aunts, uncles, and cousins that we never see anyway. We only ever hear about them in Gran's Christmas letter." Kissing her softly, he smiled. "Our close family will know the truth. And they'll accept us because they love us."

"We'll need to stop referring to ourselves as cousins around other people then. This might freak them out." She leaned over and gave him a soft kiss as she ran a hand through his hair.

Kai laughed, deep in his throat. "It will be our inside joke." Jessie giggled and laughing with her, Kai returned himself to where he most wanted to be in this world...her lips.

Once they were back in the city Kai was nearly as fond of as the one he'd left behind, he again felt fueled with direction and purpose. He knew where his life was going again, and that was a comfort that he drew a tremendous amount of strength from. He would remain here in Denver, working with Mason, learning from the man who academically inspired him. He would help Jessie take care of Gran, making sure she stayed strong, healthy, and independent for as long as she could. And he and Jessie…they would share every aspect of their lives with each other, and he would be the best boyfriend, lover, and friend Jessie could ever dream of having. Kai would make her forget that any other man had ever existed before him.

Smiling as they exited the airport, Kai finally felt like his future wasn't going to be filled with pain and longing. He was going to have everything he'd ever wanted, with the girl he'd always dreamt of having.

Immersed in those cheery thoughts as they climbed into Jessie's truck, Kai started with surprise when his phone rang. He'd charged it before leaving for his impromptu trip home, but no one had called him in days. As an overdramatic, sappy song started pouring out of his speakers, he groaned and cursed his coworker.

Jessie, clearly recognizing the song, laughed as she started her vehicle. "*Wind Beneath My Wings*…really?"

Grimacing at her comment as he glanced at the caller ID, he shook his head. "Missy. I seriously don't know how she keeps getting a hold of my phone." Jessie let out a hearty laugh as Kai smiled at the screen. Bringing the phone to his ear, he answered the call with, "Mom, we just left you. Do you really miss me already?"

As Jessie pulled away from the parking lot, he heard his mother's laughter. "I miss you all the time, Kai. I just wanted to make sure you landed okay."

Smiling over at Jessie, Kai grinned. "We're fine, Mom. Perfectly fine."

Hanging up after a brief conversation with her, Kai gazed at Jessie the entire time she drove them home. *Home.* Being with her truly felt like being home now. Not the paradise he'd left behind, and definitely not the tiny studio apartment he'd been staying in. Wherever *she* was, was home.

She glanced at him as he watched her. "You know, I've been thinking..."

"Yeah," he murmured, reaching out a finger to brush a strand of hair behind her ear. She closed her eyes briefly before snapping them open. Good thing too, since she *was* driving.

Swallowing, she flicked her eyes at him and shrugged. "Well, Grams did mention that her neighbor's house was free, and I was thinking, maybe..." She let her thought trail off as she studied the road. Kai watched her bite her lip, and there was almost a nervous look on her face.

Kai straightened. Was she really considering Gran's offer of Kai moving next door, in her recently deceased neighbor's place? He furrowed his brow. Yes, a house would give him more space, but in relation to Jessie, it was more of a lateral move than anything. It wouldn't bring them any closer together. It was a little farther actually, since he wouldn't drive past Jessie's place on his way home from work anymore.

Noticing his expression, Jessie smiled and he relaxed. In a near whisper, she shrugged and said, "Do you think Harmony and April would mind if I told them I was moving out? Because...maybe you and I can move next door to Grams. We'd be able to take better care of her, and we'd have a place to ourselves...if you wanted...to live with me, that is." Her hand sneaked over to grasp his, and Kai's heart quickened. She wasn't asking him to move away, she was asking him to move in, to start their life together.

526

While she cast him anxious glances, Kai laughed lightly and laced their fingers together. "I think that sounds like a great idea, Jessie."

She broke out into a breathtaking smile, and Kai leaned over to kiss her cheek. Then he nuzzled her neck, making her giggle and squirm. Living *with* her? Now that was a move Kai could whole-heartedly support. She was his home, anyway.

―――――――――――――――――――

Pulling up to her house, Jessie was flooded with euphoric bliss. Kai had asked her to marry him on the plane. Not in so many words, but that had been the gist of it. He wanted a life with her. He wanted his future to always have her in it. Jessie couldn't believe how much just knowing where his head was at, knowing where he envisioned them going, made her feel safe and content. It was like, all of a sudden, she didn't have to worry about where she would be later in life, or who she would be with. She knew, with absolute certainty that she would be with Kai.

Glancing over at him as she shut off the engine, she was positive he felt the same safety and contentment. He'd asked her to marry him, and she'd said yes. Everything else was details. They'd even begun the first one. They were going to move in together. They were well on their way to starting a life together.

Grinning at each other, they grabbed their luggage and made their way to Jessie's house...for now. Harmony met them in the entryway and engulfed Jessie in a huge hug. Jessie was exhausted from the emotional week and all the traveling and transitioning. She really just wanted to crash on her bed for a few hours, but she dropped her bags and held her friend tight. She'd be leaving her soon, after all.

"I'm so glad you're back. I missed you guys!" Harmony disengaged from Jessie, then attacked Kai. With a laugh, he hugged her back just as tightly as Jessie had. It warmed her that Kai was so fond of her friends.

"We missed you too, Harm," she tiredly replied.

Her freckled friend finally released Kai. Slipping her hands into her back pockets, Harmony watched Kai pick up Jessie's bag and start to take it back to Jessie's room. Smiling at his thoughtfulness, Jessie watched him leave too. Once he was out of sight, Harmony shifted her attention back to Jessie. "Hey, I hope you don't mind, but I sort of did something while you were...busy this week."

Not knowing what she was possibly referring to, Jessie cocked an eyebrow and waited for details. Harmony sighed and shifted her weight. Biting her lip, she shrugged and said, "Since you and Kai are pretty much a couple now...I snagged your date."

Jessie blinked. Her date? Other than Kai, Jessie hadn't been on anything that resembled a date in a very long time. "Uh...what are you talking about?"

Harmony giggled, and a warm smile escaped her. "Well, I guess you never really dated him. But he called for you all the time trying to get one with you."

Still confused, Jessie shook her head. "Who are you...?" Suddenly remembering her grandmother's attempt to set her up with her nurse's son, Jessie's jaw dropped to the floor. "Oh my God! Do you mean Simon?"

Harmony cheeks flushed with color. "Yeah...I hope you don't mind."

She really didn't. Shaking her head, Jessie wondered how in the heck that had come about. Maybe seeing the question in her expression, Harmony gave her a shy smile. "You wouldn't ever talk to him or call him back, so I just started talking to him for you." She shrugged. "I don't know, he was just really sweet on the phone and the more he called for you, the more we started talking."

Jessie felt embarrassment and remorse heating her cheeks. She knew Simon had called her a couple times, and she felt bad that she hadn't just admitted to him outright that she wasn't interested. At the time though, Jessie had been a little ...preoccupied.

Harmony glanced back at the hallway as the object of Jessie's preoccupation returned. Kai grinned at seeing both of the girls watching him. Shrugging again, Harmony twisted back to Jessie. "The last time he called, he called to talk to me." Her smile turned bright. "We had our first date last night...and it was great. He's smart and funny and so nice, and he loves to ski as much as I do...and you're not mad, are you?" She said all of that really fast, and her expression turned anxious, like she was sure she'd just done something really wrong.

Shaking her head, Jessie laughed and hugged her again. Kai came up to them and cocked a curious eyebrow. Jessie ignored him for a second and answered her friend. "Of course I'm not mad." Giving Kai a pointed look over Harmony's shoulder, she added, "I was never interested in dating Simon anyway."

Kai smiled as he looked down at the floor. Harmony pulled back and squeezed her friend's arms. "Good, because I really like him."

As Harmony started giggling and going on about how great Simon was, April stepped into the room from the kitchen. Jessie waved at her and April's face went ghostly pale. Quicker than Jessie would have thought possible, April ducked back into the kitchen. Jessie exchanged looks with Harmony then Kai. Both of them seemed puzzled and an odd tension began to build in Jessie's belly. What the hell was that about? Maybe April had decided she couldn't handle the strangeness of Jessie and Kai's relationship. Maybe she couldn't even stand to be around them now.

Feeling like her legs were suddenly made of lead, Jessie trudged to the kitchen. Kai and Harmony followed her. April was dressed to the nines and chugging back a glass of wine. She looked like she was about to head out for the evening, either on a date or searching for one.

After swallowing the last bit in her glass, she let out a nervous giggle and quickly spat out, "Oh, you're back, great. I can't wait to hear about your trip, but I have a date tonight with that guy from your work, Kai. Louis. Remember, I asked about him once? Well, yeah, he called, and he's taking me to that four-star downtown, so I gotta go. Anything I should know about him, Kai? He's not a psycho or anything, right? Well, I guess I can handle a little bit of craziness for Lobster Thermidor. Oh, look at the time...I should go. We're meeting there, and I don't want to be late on my first date with him..."

All of that was spat out rapid-fire in one breath. Jessie blinked several times as she absorbed the multitude of information. No one in the room answered any of April's various questions as everyone gawked. Clearly, April was a nervous, babbling mess. Thinking maybe she was just anxious about her date, although, Jessie had never seen her anxious for a date in her life, she asked, "You okay, April?"

Her gorgeous friend closed her eyes and slumped against the counter; she suddenly looked exhausted. Peeking one eye open, she wrinkled her nose. "Don't kill me."

Sighing, Jessie crossed her arms over her chest. This wasn't going to be good. Kai looked over at Jessie then back to April. "Hate you for what?" he asked.

April inhaled a deep breath and let it out slowly. Then she flung her hands out to her sides, and she started babbling again. "Okay, see the thing is, I thought since the two of you had come out of the closet, or whatever, everyone knew about it. Especially since you were going to talk to Kai's parents in Hawaii. I just sort of assumed that it was common knowledge that you two are bumping uglies now."

"April!" Jessie exclaimed, trying to steer her friend back on track. "What happened?"

She sighed, her shoulders slumping in defeat. "Your dad called."

The hair on the back of Jessie's neck started to rise. She definitely didn't like where this was going. "And?" Jessie felt Kai slip an arm around her waist, and it was only then that she realized her posture was rigid. Dropping her arms from her chest, she tried to relax.

April sighed, yet again. "He asked for you, and I told him you were on your way back from Hawaii. Then, he was naturally curious about what you were doing in Hawaii, and I didn't think much about it, because *again*, I thought it was common knowledge, so...I told him you and your boyfriend were visiting his parents there."

She shrugged and Jessie swallowed. Well, that was okay ...she could work with those facts. Nodding, she muttered, "All right, if that's all he knows, then it's not that big of a deal really."

April shot down that slim hope with her next comment. "I might have also gone on to mention that Kai was your boyfriend, and that his parents included your uncle..."

"You didn't!" Jessie felt herself tightening back up. Her dad was currently under the impression that she was dating her cousin...shit. "Damn it, April, all you had to do was tell him that I'd call him when I got home!"

April cringed then stuck her chin out. "I'm sorry, but your dad is like this super scary FBI investigator dude. He cornered me! I had to talk!" She shrugged apologetically. "I tried to explain Kai's situation, but your mom flipped out and grabbed the phone and we sort of got disconnected." She pointed to the handset on the counter. "It just happened like twenty minutes ago, so I'm sure you could call back..."

Groaning, Jessie brought her hands to her face. Great, both her parents thought she was sleeping with her cousin. "April..."

"I'm sorry! Your dad intimidates the hell out of me! And you know, you could have told them about all this *before* you left for your little vacation." Jessie peeked through her fingers to see April scowling at her.

Jessie sighed then let a soft laugh escape her. "It's fine, April. Really, I needed to talk to him anyway. This just...sped up the process."

April's irritated expression evened out into a smile, while Kai let out a heavy breath. "I forgot your dad was FBI." Looking down at Jessie, he cringed. "He's going to shoot me, isn't he?"

Jessie chuckled at Kai and shook her head. April took that moment of distraction to mutter apologies again and dart out of the room, pulling a laughing Harmony with her. Jessie sighed again. "I guess I should call him back." She closed her eyes. "This is going to be such an awkward phone call."

Kai laughed. "You're telling me."

He gave her a wry smile, and Jessie tried to hold onto the light feeling that she got by being near him. Trying to squish the butterflies stirring nervous holes in her belly, she gave him a crooked grin. "Ready to be introduced to my family?"

Kai smiled. "I was born ready."

Jessie couldn't stop the laugh that escaped her, but she managed to frown, too. "That's not funny, Kai."

Grinning, he slipped his arms around her waist. "It kind of is...now."

She placed her arms over his and leaned up to give him a light kiss. "I love you," she murmured.

Kai nodded, smiling warmly at her, and Jessie prepared herself for a tough phone call with a long, slow exhale. Releasing Kai, she slowly walked over to the phone. She could almost hear the executioner's drums beating in her head, banging out a hollow, ominous rhythm. Wrapping her hand around the receiver, she inhaled for ten long counts.

Kai grabbed her free hand and gave her a supportive nod. Jessie squeezed it back as determination filled her. She could do this. She could turn her family around. She was positive that once they realized Kai was no more related to her than her ex-douchebag Jeremy had been, they'd accept him. And then, once they got to know Kai, she was positive they'd love him, too. He was just so different from every other guy Jessie had ever been with. So wonderful, so caring, and so kind. There was no way they wouldn't get past his last name and eventually come to terms with him and Jessie being together.

As she punched in their phone number, peace flowed through her. And really, even if they couldn't, even if they somehow rejected him forever, it didn't matter anymore. Jessie knew the truth, and she knew her heart. Kai wasn't related to her. Kai loved her, and she loved Kai. They were going to be together for a long, long time…possibly forever. They were going to get married one day. They were going to have children one day. And those children would be beautiful and perfect and genetically safe, because she and Kai were genetically different.

It was as simple as that.

As Jessie heard the long rings finally silence as the phone was picked up, she felt completely relaxed. She knew her parents would always love her, even if they didn't approve of her relationship, and either way, all of this would end up okay, so long as she and Kai got to be together. Clutching Kai's hand tighter as her dad's gruff, "Hello," sounded in her ear, she brightly said, "Hi, Dad. I heard that you called, and I wanted to clear up some things."

Her dad immediately started barking questions at her, but Jessie didn't answer them. Instead, she waited for him to finish, then she waited a little longer. Once his end of the line went silent and stayed silent, Jessie looked up into Kai's amazing ocean-like eyes. "If you are willing to listen now, I would like to tell you all about someone who means the world to me.

I want to tell you about a man who you think you know…but you don't. I want to tell you about the man who I *do* know. Dad…I want to tell you about Kai Harper, my…"

She searched for a word that would adequately describe Kai's importance to her. Boyfriend? The word was too paltry, too simple and insignificant. As her and Kai's gazes remained locked, Jessie thought about what he meant to her, what they meant to each other. He'd found her at her lowest point, after being broken and betrayed by someone she'd thought she loved. Kai had picked her up, helped her put her feet back on the ground, and had made her feel appreciated, respected… and loved. And when his world had crumbled around him, Jessie had been the one to hold him up, to help him through the pain of discovering who he really was. They were each other's rocks, each other's support, each other's best friends, and each other's lovers. And Jessie could only sum up her feelings for him one way. "He's my…everything."

The End

Acknowledgements

This book would not be possible without the help of my beta readers—Sam, Lori, Becky, Kyla, and Nicky. Your input means the world to me!

A huge thank you to Sarah at Okay Creations, Madison and Chelsea at Madison Seidler Editing Services, and Julie at JT Formatting. Thank you for your patience with my ever-changing schedule! And thank you to my agent, Kristyn Keene of ICM Partners, and everyone at my publishing house, Forever Romance, for helping me get this book out into the world.

Last but not least, thank you to the fans! Your passion fuels mine.

About the Author

S.C. Stephens as a *New York Times* and *USA Today* bestselling author who enjoys spending every free moment she has creating stories that are packed with emotion and heavy on romance.

Her debut novel, Thoughtless, an angst-filled love triangle charged with insurmountable passion and the unforgettable Kellan Kyle, took the literary world by storm. Amazed and surprised by the response to the release of Thoughtless in 2009, more stories were quick to follow. Stephens has been writing nonstop ever since.

In addition to writing, Stephens enjoys spending lazy afternoons in the sun reading fabulous novels, loading up her iPod with writer's block reducing music, heading out to the movies, and spending quality time with her friends and family. She currently resides in the beautiful Pacific Northwest with her two equally beautiful children.

Connect with S.C. Stephens

Email:
ThoughtlessRomantic@gmail.com

Facebook:
https://www.facebook.com/SCStephensAuthor

Twitter:
https://twitter.com/SC_Stephens

Website:
authorscstephens.com

Also by S.C. Stephens

Thoughtless
Thoughtful
Effortless
Reckless
Untamed
Collision Course
Conversion
Bloodlines
'Til Death
Furious Rush

CPSIA information can be obtained
at www.ICGtesting.com
Printed in the USA
FSOW03n2010180516
20617FS